No. 1

Antony J Stowers

First published in Great Britain in 2020 by No. 1 Books
This paperback edition published in 2021 by

No. 1 Books
36 Carlton Road, Long Eaton
NG10 3LF, UK

Copyright © 2021 Antony J Stowers

The moral right of Antony J Stowers to be identified as the author of this work has been asserted in accordance with the Copyright, Designs and Patents Act, 1988.

All rights reserved. No part of this publication may be reproduced, stored in a retrieval system or transmitted in any form or by any means electronic, mechanical, audio, visual or otherwise, without prior permission in writing from the copyright author.

ISBN: 978-1-5262-0822-4

This book is produced entirely in the UK, is available to order from book shops in the UK, and via UK-based Internet book retailers for purchase in the UK. This book is a fictional story based on the true events of the birth of the railways in the North East of England 1810 – 1825. Fact and fiction are blended through real-life personalities, known historical events and ordinary people whose lives were impacted by this revolutionary technology.

Printed and bound in Great Britain by CPI Books, Croydon
110 Beddington Lane, Croydon UK CR0 4YY.

For more information on books and plays by Antony J Stowers
www.tonystowers.com

Why and How

On 27th September 1825, a rudimentary steam-powered locomotive pulled coal wagons and hundreds of passengers 26 miles from a remote coal pit called Witton to a hamlet named Shildon and then on to the port of Stockton-on-Tees via Darlington, a wool-trading town of 2,000 residents in the north east of England. The history books say what happened that day changed the world. I set out to find why.

I wrote this book for three main reasons. The first was that the history, I felt, was 'flat' with almost all the available literature on the events leading up to *the* event comprising mostly passive, third-person narratives, outdated journalistic techniques, top-heavy technical facts and descriptive passages from amateur writers, civil servants and scribes of the ages of varying degrees of education and grammar. The second was that the opening took place a distant 200 years ago and before the invention of photography, so it seemed to me our story would be reliant on the trust between the reader and the author as, apart from the odd still images, it lacked material or auxiliary support from other art forms. A final reason was to understand more *why* that day changed the world. Indeed, in one way, the long and winding road that took George Stephenson some ten to fifteen years to finally get to the end of, also took this book almost as long to research, to write and to accurately capturing the details without losing the excitement and mastering the precision vital to creating an artwork that would stand up to scrutiny under expert eyes and do so over time. Nobody had ever done it. I was in virgin territory, nothing to compare it too, a unique one-off: describing the S&D story as it might have happened in almost real-time – years, months, weeks, days, hours, minutes and seconds all accounted for.

I started with the 19th April 1821 and spread out in all directions, into the future and into the past, adding real or fictional events as I went along, and even returned to that first date entry some years later to tighten and revise it, as more details emerged from the archives and history books. I was trying to keep it up to date. Thanks to the Facebook group Friends of the S&D Railway, huge amounts of unknown, obscure or missing details have emerged from under the dust-covered archives since I started writing ten years ago and this has caused two previous book revisions as more has come to light.

The problem with this project wasn't what to put in but what to leave out, to avoid the fiction becoming swamped by the non-fiction. I'd never please everyone so I set out to only please myself in the end but the devil of course is in the detail and those who look closely or know a little about the subject will see that some places and people herein are fictitious and some aren't.

There'll never be a definitive telling of the true story on which this book is based because so many were involved in it as engineers, surveyors, investors, politicians, soldiers, navvies, miners, etcetera and ordinary people and a hundred trades and professions, each with their individual and highly subjective accounts. So researchers and historians can cross-check certain details in a dozen ways and from a hundred angles and viewpoints but nobody will arrive at a single version by which all players line up 100% accurately and it is because of this universal anomaly you now have this unique book in your hand.

AJS, November 2021.

Special thanks to:

Friends of the Stockton to Darlington Railway Group, Beamish Open-air Museum; Tony Fox, Historical Association Durham, Killhope Mining Museum; Timothy Hackworth Museum; NRM Shildon; the Francis Frith Collection; Darlington North Road Railway Museum; Preston Park Museum, Stockton-on-Tees; Darlington Reference Library; *A Treatise on Railroads* by Nicholas Wood; NRM York; *Northern Echo Railway Centenary Supplement*; *A Social and Economic History of Industrial Britain* by John Robottom; *The Life and Times of George and Robert Stephenson* by Samuel Smiles; *The Diaries of Edward Pease*, Robert Roper of Haggerleases; Peter Hayward, North of England Newspapers; Barry Lamb in Darlington; the A1 Steam Locomotive Trust; *Lost English* by Chris Roberts; *An Utterly Impartial History of Britain* by John O'Farrell; *The Year 1000* by Robert Lacey; Barclays Bank Archives; Brusselton Incline Group; and Stockton Borough Council and Libraries. The works of Thomas Hardy and DH Lawrence came in useful for cross-checking details of everyday life in rural and mining communities.

Thanks also to Sylvia Suddes, developmental editor at foolproof-proofreading.com, for her invaluable assistance and contributions to this project. I see her subtle flecks of genius everywhere, our words interlaced.

This book is dedicated to the memory of Anthony 'Zeb' White, my English Language teacher at Secondary school, who died in 1978. He was a one-off as a teacher who inspired us to believe in ourselves and strive for originality no matter what our background. A bit like George Stephenson, they simply don't make men like him anymore. As Stephenson borrowed freely from his contemporaries' efforts to enhance his own production, so I 'borrowed' from other sources to enhance mine.

Main research sources:

www.wikipedia.org

www.railcentre.co.uk

www.spartacus.schoolnet.co.uk, www.priceminister.com

www.historyhome.co.uk

www.britannica.com,

www.darlingtonandstocktontimes.co.uk

www.aboutbritain.com

www.gracesguide.co.uk

www.railbrit.co.uk

www.thisisstockton.co.uk, www.thisisdarlington.co.uk

www.engineering-timelines.co.uk, www.guardian.co.uk

www.haggerleases.co.uk, www.regencyengland.com

'The locomotive is not the invention of one man, but of a nation of

mechanical engineers.'

Robert Stephenson 1803–1859

CONTENTS

Foreword by Tony Fox - Page 7

Map – Page 9

1810 – Page 11

1811 – Page 13

1812 – Page 19

1814 – Page 28

1815 – Page 36

1816 – Page 55

1818 – Page 66

1819 – Page 80

1820 – Page 97

1821 – Page 105

1822 – Page 118

1823 – Page 140

1824 – Page 147

1825 – Page 165

Tuesday 27th September 1825 – 292

Foreword by Tony Fox

It has been some time since I last considered using historical fiction in the classroom, but I have been inspired anew. About a year ago I came across Tony Stowers' 'No. 1' as we were both considering assisting in the 2025 Stockton and Darlington Railway commemorations.

I have a specific interest in the development of transport on Teesside which is the focus of his novel and the spark that ignited me was: *'There can be no doubt that when a novel is well-researched and well-written, as this book is, it can capture the essence and spirit of the time.'* - Harvey Watson's review of *The Welsh Linnet*, by A J Lyndon, in *Battlefield* (Vol. 22, Spring 2018). A frequent problem I have found is that students struggle to get a feel for the period - they can relate facts about it, but these don't help them *relate* to the period, to get the flavour of the time and this leads to misunderstanding and misconceptions. As Harvey says, Historical Fiction can help to *'capture the essence and spirit of the time.'* This is something I think is a positive – in 'No. 1' the reader gets a fantastic feel for the period, both geographically as well as aesthetically. A further strength is the research, it is clearly very well researched; by way of example, one can examine the detail he goes into on Isaac Pease's illness, or the description of the Stockton dockside at the end of the novel. Without a doubt it is also well written; there are some passages which I re-read just to appreciate the construction of the prose and it is also clearly from someone who knows the regions of the North East of England thoroughly; little anecdotes remind you how distinct the regions within the North East were, and to some extent still are, especially the pit villages to the North of Shildon. The minute-by-minute description of Locomotion Number One's journey from Brusselton Bank to Stockton's quayside, which is the culmination of the novel, is outstanding; this part might just be the finest piece of historical fiction I have read.

The focus of 'No.1' is firmly on the attitudes, values and experiences of the people of the North East in the post Napoleonic War period, but more than this it is viewed from multiple perspectives. The challenge an author usually faces when dealing with multiple characters is superficiality, the characters can lack depth and become stereotypes. In 'No.1' the primary character, Lewis, meets a myriad of them, some well-known, some fictional and some less well-known. The well-known characters, Stephenson, Hackworth and Pease for example, are superbly fleshed out; the actions, speech and descriptions are highly credible, enriching my understanding of these men. They are far from being the stereotypes we see in most literature but it's not just the main and famous characters that have a deep richness. Tony's narrative style focuses on the individuality of the people and we get the firm impression that he is writing about human beings, people who have thoughts, desires, weaknesses and fears. His characters have a range of constantly altering emotions which influence their immediate actions.

I think the quality of 'No.1' lies in the depth of characterization and the detailed contextual narrative; where leaps of imagination and poetic license are firmly anchored to the historical detail, without undermining the quality and flow of the narrative. Reading 'No.1', I have learnt a great deal, but more than that, I have found it an enjoyable experience, I read the novel for pleasure, and was left a little empty when I reached the end. I re-read passages looking to use quotes and found myself back inside the story. It invigorated me to research aspects I'd hardly considered before and changed my views on the significance of a few individuals.

Tony Fox, Historical Association, Durham, September 2018

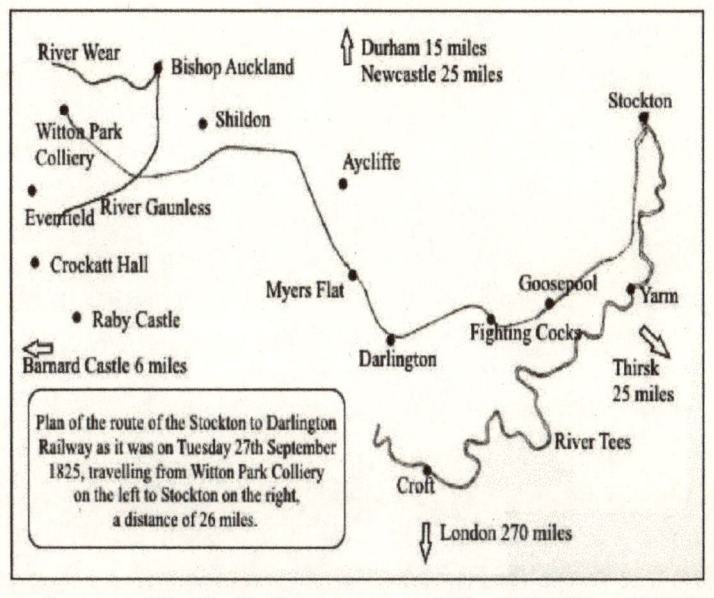

Plan of the route of the Stockton to Darlington Railway as it was on Tuesday 27th September 1825, travelling from Witton Park Colliery on the left to Stockton on the right, a distance of 26 miles.

* * *

The original official name of the first engine that pulled the first train for the Stockton and Darlington Railway Company on the 27th September 1825 was 'Active' but, more visibly noted for its formal hand-written entry in the left-hand column of the order book, it became commonly known instead as 'Locomotion Number One' as it was the first job on the list.

1810

Friday 18th September

A short, stout figure stepped above the 50-odd men by standing on a chair brought forward by a more wiry fellow whose suit was cut tight under the arms and around the waist over a sky-blue and jasmine-yellow striped shirt, red waistcoat and a white silk cravat – a combination that made him look even more slender than he was. Neither figure bore the hallmarks of working men, for both dressed well and had scrubbed fingernails and clean hands, the man on the chair deliberately clapping his together with some effort and ceremony and watching the effect the echoes had as more faces turned until he had the attention of all.

'Gentlemen, gentlemen, my name is Leonard Raisbeck and we are here today to celebrate the opening of The Mandale Cut, a reduction of a loop of the River Tees by two and a quarter miles, reducing transport time to the sea by almost two days!'

A cheer went up and Raisbeck paused, looking towards the back of the room where a number of excited Stockton businessmen not directly invited had earnestly arrived only minutes before to the banquet at the Moot Hall to convey respects and attempt to tap into the energy of the event hosted by the Tees Navigation Company.

'18th September 1810 is a day I hope we remember for it is the day we open to the world. Yes, I say the world! We are not on the shores of the German Ocean, like Hartlepool and Sunderland, but we *are* accessible to trading vessels and, despite the threats of the French, *we – carry – on*!'

As Raisbeck emphasised these last three words, a patriotic cheer, shouts of 'Hear! Hear!' and a thunderous stamping of feet drowned out all other sounds for almost a minute then gradually died down so he could continue.

'Any friendly ship can unload here within an hour's journey of the sea and Durham and North Yorkshire can trade *if*', he paused for dramatic effect, and, like a soapbox orator, looked around the room at as many faces as he could, 'they can get goods here in sufficient quantities to make it profitable. So I ask you: what means can we provide them with to bring the fruits of their produce to Stockton?'

Raisbeck had studied rhetoric in his school days and found it useful now – despite a dry throat from the smoke of the Virginia tobacco and Cuban cigars that fogged up the room – to ask questions each man could answer for himself.

'Many are aware of the survey for a canal but the iron road is also gaining favour. My right honourable friend Ben Flounders,' Raisbeck glanced down to indicate the short, wiry man by his side, 'is an entrepreneur, like many who have come here today, all of whom stand with expectation of what more we might achieve. Therefore gentlemen,' Raisbeck paused and filled his lungs with enough air to bellow out: 'I motion a committee be appointed to enquire into the practicability of a railway or canal!'

Ben Flounders' voice followed immediately, a further incitement to the crowd of men already exploding with cheers, 'And I second that!'

1811

Thursday 25ᵗʰ July, St. James Day

'Well, George,' said Heppel standing by, 'what do you think?'

Kitchener Heppel, responsible for pumping out the thousands of gallons of water that often collected in the 160-miles' worth of galleries being worked at Killingworth Pit, north of Newcastle, wiped the sweat from his black forehead with a filthy handkerchief and studied the tired contraption. It was working, though clumsily. The exhausted rotative Newcomen engine and pump built by Messrs Smeaton, bought 11 years previously from Boulton and Watt in Birmingham, '1800 AD' cast in iron on its side, had been lethargically pumping for nearly 12 months and had become regarded not only as a failure but also an embarrassment. And Heppel hated embarrassment – embarrassment came out of incompetence and only people were capable of that.

'I reckon I can make 'er draw in seven days,' said Stephenson. In fact, he'd estimated it could be done in five, but seven seemed safer. His observation was simple: the pump's various parts mostly comprised wood, leather and iron and they were under constant use. It was, like the pocket watches he repaired in his spare time, in dire need of a good service, but because it had been bought out and not built in-house, nobody dared interfere: to wreck it completely was a sack-ble offence.

Heppel was struck by the confidence in his tone but said nothing and gave nothing away in word or look as he went to speak to Ralph Dodds, the Head Viewer, in his office. This was what his immediate boss Mr Dodds called 'management'.

'Geordie Stephenson, the Brakeman?' said Dodds. 'I kna 'e fixes timepieces in 'is spare time but this isn't like fixin' clocks n' watches!'

Both men knew of Stephenson's part-time job as a watch-mender but it was a Brakeman for which he was most well known. Like a rider masters an equine, Geordie Stephenson mastered his steam horse – as Brakeman it was a real skill to operate the lifting and lowering of the flimsy steam-powered platform that lowered men down underground from the surface and brought them back up again. Going up or going down, their tools were always collected in wooden barrels to reduce sparks, and the platform floor piled high with corves of excavated coal coming up to be taken away on wagons, washed and then selected for market. But shift change was always a tense time as hundreds of men collided in small, claustrophobic, poorly lit stalls and so knowing just when to slow the engine to minimise disruption and anticipate and soothe any of the short-tempered, short-term tensions that might arise was considered a job of merit: a bumpy ascent/descent made for grumpy workers.

'Well, at worst 'e could only fail, as everybody else 'as,' commented Heppel glumly, as Dodds leaned forward and peered through the dusty glass pane across the yard to where the bobbing heads of Stephenson and his mates could just be seen on the ridge. Dodds rubbed his stubbled chin.

'What shall I tell 'im?' asked Heppel.

'Nowt - thou leaves the talkin' to me,' said Dodds. 'Send 'em back to their posts. That'll be all, Mr Heppel,' and so that mysterious word 'management' came into Heppel's head once again as he returned to the pump to pass on Dodds' wisdom.

Later that day, with other business taken care of, the steam whistle sounded and the fore shift workers dispersed to their homes. Dodds caught up with Stephenson on the Shiremoor Road. It surprised Dodds that Stephenson seemed to be expecting him. The two men walked along the dusty lane, its hard mud dried around a thousand cart tracks and horses' hooves, Dodds looking down and selecting every careful step and Stephenson striding while looking up and around at the sunny countryside.

'Kit Heppel tells us yer think yer can put the engine at the High Pit to rights, George?'

'Yes, sir,' said George, 'I reckon I could.'

'How?'

'I don't rightly know, Mr Dodds.'

Dodds glanced across at him as if he was joking. So he laughed.

'Well, that's bold talk! You kna, Geordie, it's a fragile game keepin' your job round these parts, an' I've not wanted it broadcast we've an unproductive pit n' still don't. Do you understand me?'

'I think so, Mr Dodds,'

'If that's the case, I'll gi' yer a fair trial n' you must set to work immediate. We're clean drowned out n' cannot get a step further. The engineers 'ereabouts are all beat, so if you succeed in doin' what they can't, I'll make yer a man for life.'

'I'll start tomorrow then, Friday. My guess is it'll take about seven days. Do you want us to work Sunday as well?'

'Why, the sooner the better, hinny! I'll chuck in a couple of bob overtime if that's what yer worried about?'

'Only condition I ask is yer let us select me own lads,'

Dodds stopped walking, as did Stephenson who hesitated, wondering if he'd gone too far.

'There'll be jealousy tha knas?' said Dodds.

'Aye, reckon yer right, but I need a clean 'and, Mr Dodds.'

Dodds took a breath. He was out of options.

'Fair enough, I'll see to it tomorrow.'

He was about to turn to home when he remembered.

'By the way, canst thou fix my watch?'

Dodds pulled his pocket watch like a big gold plum from his waistcoat pocket and unhooked it from its chain. Stephenson took it from him and lifted the lid. Behind its glass cover, both hands were frozen at the Roman numerals for two.

'I tried winding it but it's just made it tighter inside and now I cannat do a thing wi' it,' moaned Dodds.

'I'll 'ave a look at it later,' said Stephenson and slipped it into his trouser pocket.

At home that night, after putting his young son Robert to bed, George got out his tool-kit, put on his strongest magnifying spectacles that had been made in Newcastle – two tiny glass pebbles set in a teak frame – prised open the pocket watch back and looked closely at the intricate parts under a quizzing glass. A fine inspection with a needle sure enough raised a tiny residue of greasy dust on the tip. The minute sophistication of the works made him marvel at the invention of men – to craft such tiny and delicate parts by hand and to make every single part dependent on the power it consumes and the power it passes on. Names of his workmates slid through his mind: he'd need men who'd take no offence at orders – considering they were equals, and men with imagination – not those who shook their heads and rubbed their chins pessimistically, *and* men who didn't object to working on Sunday as many liked to respect the Lord's day of rest. The oven was warm and the dry heat would speed up the evaporation of the grease clogging the parts. Five minutes later, having picked his team for the job ahead in his mind, he pulled it out with a cloth, let it cool, replaced the back cover and gently wound it by inserting a common key into the tiny hole at the bottom. It ticked perfectly all through that night.

Next morning, he carefully wound the watch again and then went to the pit where he selected his helpers as if selecting a cricket team, and together they took the engine entirely to pieces and laid everything side by side on the ground. Iron nails, screws and fittings were rusted and corroded and the wooden parts were worn and damp.

'I want to improve the vacuum,' Stephenson said to the assembled men standing on the hard, sun-baked mud near the pithead. 'The piston has to create a larger pressure difference, makin' it deliver more water, an' the cistern needs to be raised to create more force.'

One of the men blinked. 'Come again, Mr Stephenson?'

'Get yersel' a hammer n' spanner Joe, n' leave the talkin' to me.'

He first found replacements from the forge and then, measuring everything carefully, he sketched each item onto parchment with charcoal, using the measurements and sketches to assist the carpenters to reshape the wooden parts. The forge provided new screws, nails and bolts and the carpenters shaped a new framework and pump.

The necessary alterations were made in a day and a half and the pump was slowly reassembled. On the morning of the third day, with Dodds present, Stephenson sprung a lever and the improved engine, blasting steam from a freshly stoked fire, bounced into life. In the brick boiler house just beside the shaft, the heat boiled the water that made the steam that turned the large vertical flywheel that pushed the piston down and pulled it back up again repeatedly. The once-worn, leaky and threadbare surface materials tightened and hermetically sealed in an irresistible force through which the sludge at the bottom had no choice but to be displaced by the vacuum. From the sluice, filthy muck trapped for months at the bottom of the pit coughed out and into Wylam Burn, staining it black downstream until pouring into the Tyne where for days after, local fishermen told of dead fish floating on the surface that nobody dared eat.

'Instead of five pounds of pressure per square inch in the suction vacuum, I strengthened it overall and increased it to ten pounds per square inch,' Stephenson explained. 'The rulebook says I'm not supposed to, but I did it anyway and it struck me that many of these manufacturers have it within their interests to say that in order to keep themselves employed.'

'You said seven – you've done it in five. She's better than she was. She'll knock the 'ouse down!' shouted Dodds above the din.

By ten o'clock that night, a worker sent down on a rope to report the level said it had dropped 20 feet. The engine kept pumping for another day and a half and by Friday afternoon produced only a trickle, so the worker was sent down again.

'I'm standin' on the bottom!' he shouted up to the surface through cupped hands, though way above him the words were compressed into a single singing echo so he had to get pulled back up again before giving his news.

'How looks it?' asked Dodds.

The gangly young lad reached down with his filthy hand and touched his dirty left leg between the ankle and the knee. His shoeless feet were so begrimed with dirt they resembled horses' hooves.

'About 'ere, sir,' he said.

'Good!' said Dodds, who turned to Stephenson, relief and excitement in his voice. 'Well done, Geordie – this bodes well!'

With the action of the pump suspended, the constant hissing and sucking and clattering ceased and peace reigned once more. The polluted water stopped painting the burn black and the upstream brooks drew away the sludge in the folds of the currents.

Later, in his office, Ralph Dodds opened his cashbox and lifted out a large square of creased paper, on it the name of the bank of Richardson, Overend and Company and a short sentence that promised to pay the Bearer on Demand the sum of ten pounds.

'It's not much, I know, for what yer've done, so I'm goin' to appoint you Engineman,' said Dodds. 'If that works out, I'll recommend you supervise more pits. I'm grateful, George, very grateful.'

Dodds shook George's dirty hands and George pulled out Dodd's pocket watch and handed it to him without a word, still ticking.

'Marvellous! Bloody marvellous! How much do I owe you?' said Dodds, holding it up to his ear.

'A shilling?' asked George.

'A shilling?' Dodds exclaimed. 'This merits more than that, Geordie!'

George stepped out holding up the ten-pound note to the sun and marvelling at it. It was the first time in his 29 years he'd been paid in paper and he was determined it wouldn't be the last.

1812

Monday 25th May

One early summer afternoon in Felling, a pit village of about five hundred souls on the south bank of the river Tyne, a baby boy was born to George Lovatt and his wife Catherine, whom they named Lewis.

Both young parents had grown up in large families and seen brothers and sisters as adults, adolescents, and children and, more commonly, infants die in accidents or from diseases that mystified everybody and were interpreted as God's calling, though quite what use a busy man like God would have for small babies was incomprehensible to most. George and Catherine had met a year before, at the wedding of her brother in Wallsend. With all mutual parents dead except Catherine's mother in Durham, they needed each other for the fullness that came with friendship. He was a little older than her but had a reputation for working hard and keeping sober hours. She liked his blue eyes and he liked her laughter – that was all they needed. They married and she moved into his rented terraced cottage and learnt the life of the miner's wife.

It was miracle enough they hadn't frozen or starved to death in their first cruel winter, with inadequate heating, bedding, clothing and food or that George hadn't been seriously maimed or killed by the many accidents with which miners were exposed. George, who'd started out at 15 as a putter, had worked his way up to 'hewer' - loosening coal from the seam and helping the barrowmen load it for transportation to the pit shaft by ponies. It was backbreaking and only suited to short stocky men with supple spines like him, but it was better than pushing wagons laden with coal along tunnels four feet high in the pitch black, heads a patchwork of bruises and cuts and unhealed scabs scarring their backs.

In his loose jacket, vest and thick white flannel knee breeches, long stockings, strong leather boots he'd cobbled himself and a close-fitting, thick leather cap that tucked away his unruly curls, he was lowered with other miners on a wooden platform down a 600-foot shaft by the steam-operated winding engine.

'Nae baccy, nae flints, nae pipes – nae roasted miners!' was the chant from the Deputy who awaited them below, but there was rarely anything to declare: none wanted to be responsible for the spark that killed. All the same, the Deputy carried a whale-oil lamp in the pitch-black tunnels and a canary in a tiny cage, its constant chirping reassuring them.

Catherine learnt quickly to adapt to her new life as a miner's wife, though many of the tasks she was already familiar with from the five years she'd spent as a scullery maid in a big house in Durham. When her husband got home after each shift, Catherine would spend an hour boiling sufficient water to fill a tin bath on the parlour floor and scrub him with a hard brush and carbolic soap; sometimes in the summer months he'd strip off and submerge himself under the cold waters of the River Tyne to save her the trouble, but it was hard to get the coal dust off without soap, and anyway it made little difference to her reality: a constant round of scrubbing, wringing, sewing, cleaning, baking and cooking.

But on the morning of the 25th May, the village midwife had been called and though due to go straight to the pithead that morning, George sent a message via his neighbour he'd stay home. George spent most of the morning pacing outside, wincing every time Catherine screamed and the midwife told her to push. The labour wasn't easy: his wife was fragile and weak after the cold winter, living mostly on salted meat, potatoes and porridge, but other women aided the midwife and shooed George away every time he felt drawn towards the house.

'Why is it takin' so long? Does it always take this long?' he called out.

Around midday the midwife appeared in the doorway looking exhausted, wiping her glistening hands on her apron: 'We might have to fetch the doctor,' she said, unable to look him in the eye.

'What's the problem?' asked George. The lack of a reply and the woman's face said much and, perhaps perturbed by George's helpless features, she went quickly back into the house.

But as it turned out, the doctor wasn't needed. If it hadn't been for the imminent birth of his only son on that day, George Lovatt would have been in the mine owned by Charles Brandling, industrialist, landowner and MP for Northumberland, down one of two 600-foot shafts that worked what was called the Low Main Seam and generated a quarter of a million pounds profit for Brandling every year. George would have gone down at about half past eleven with 40 other men and boys, one as young as eight, all neighbours with large families.

The new shift and the old passed each other in the mile-long tunnel. A seeping pocket of methane gas – fire damp – from a fissure, crept along the underside of the roof of the tunnel and touched the naked flame of the deputy's whale-oil lamp. Even the canary didn't have time to react. With nowhere for the forces of the expanding air to escape, a mile of underground tunnel exploded, hurling soft human bodies and a dozen pit ponies like rags against the walls and ceilings, then crushing in their chests in a white-hot, suffocating fire that sucked the last air from their lungs. The flames raced up the main shaft, a man-made volcano spurting a mushroom cloud of dust, rocks and a thousand splinters above the pit village. Windows cracked, slates fell from roofs, the earth rumbled and it was at this moment that Lewis Lovatt was born, aided into the world by a bed that shook from one of the worst underground mining explosions ever recorded in the North East of England.

After the thunderous noise, wives in flapping skirts and headscarves and bare-footed children in flimsy rags emerged wide-eyed with terror and ran to the pithead. George was torn between wanting to go and wanting to help his wife. The midwife slapped the baby's bottom and cut and tied the umbilical as fast as she could before rushing out to find out what had happened to her husband and sons. George only ran up to the mine after seeing Catherine was awake and cradling their newborn, a tiny bundle of pink flesh with a tuft of blond hair. With tears in his eyes, George laughed with relief as he looked down at the little piglet-like creature they'd both created – his son, the tiny puckered lips searching for his wife's milk.

And then he ran out and arrived at a scene akin to what he imagined a battlefield might be from the stories he'd heard war veterans tell: splintered timbers, broken glass, lumps of coal and thick black dust. The brick structure that housed the winding mechanism and stood over the shaft had exploded outwards and bricks and masonry had blown out in a circle. A crowd had picked its way through the rubble and gathered at the edge of the shaft. A rope was brought and dropped into the less smoky of the two shafts with a canary in a cage tied to one end and when pulled up again it was still alive. There was hope. The winding rope had been blown from the block-and-tackle directly over both shafts and a new one was called for, so within ten minutes a basket was lowered containing two Viewers, faces wrapped in torn blankets soaked in burn water their only protection from the smoke. The crowd was moved aside and only essential rescue personnel allowed near its edge and even they had difficulty, their eyes streaming from the acrid smoke. Eventually the rope jiggled loosely in the block-and-tackle – the basket had reached the bottom. After some five minutes more, the rope jiggled again and was read as a sign to raise it, so the coils were wrapped around a donkey-operated turning wheel and a painstaking eternity passed as it plodded round and round the axle. Pushed, prodded and aided by frantic men and bellowing donkeys, the basket finally came into view containing four terrified miners caked in a thick paste of coal dust mixed with sweat, their red eyes vicious streaming rivers. These were the first of a dozen who'd been working a different part of the pit when the explosion happened, the force directed away from them. Wails of joy and sadness went up from the groups of women as some were recognised.

'The's bodies piled like dorty washin'!'

The basket was sent down a further three times to bring up the most fortunate miners, and then the two Viewers scrambled out retching and puking, their red eyes telling silently of the scene of horror that lay deep underground. The escaping methane was by then burning like a torch in a long jet and smoke made further access impossible, so on their word, the area around the pithead was cleared and the two shafts sealed to allow the methane to burn out.

For weeks, smoke rose like the spout of a smouldering volcano. Sometimes the wind caught it and scattered it across the rooftops towards the Tyne, but on breeze-less days it hung over the village like a pungent fog and was judged unlucky to breathe as some said the vapours contained the souls of the dead miners.

Six weeks later, the 92 dead were recovered, but it wasn't until the 19th of September that the final decomposing corpse was extracted. Brought to the surface in the positions in which they'd died, the doctor had the grim task of breaking the arms and legs of the corpses with a small hammer to fit them into their coffins. Identified by wives, mothers, daughters and sisters, they were laid to rest in the churchyard at Heworth, the green grass, daisies and buttercups trampled, row upon row of graves scoured out by gravediggers.

Felling drowned in a whirlpool of wailing and it was in that noise that young Lewis found his own voice – a few days after they'd had him baptised in St Mary's, the one occasion of respite for the reverend who'd been burying the dead all week. Lewis cried because he was forced into the cruel world and the widows and orphans cried because their loved ones had been forced from it.

And what a hard world it was.

The whole of Britain was in a state of high tension that summer following the assassination of the newly elected Prime Minister, Spencer Perceval, in the House of Commons by a crazed businessman made bankrupt by the Napoleonic war. A General Election had had to be held again and the less moderate Lord Liverpool was elected.

Talk of revolution was everywhere, so his new government's response was harsher punishments for milder crimes and then the Frame Breaking Act in February had seen the death penalty imposed on the Luddites who were attempting to halt mass unemployment in their own warped way.

In April workers had smashed West Houghton Mill to smithereens and burnt it to the ground causing £6,000-worth of damage. Their trial in Lancaster had begun on the day of the explosion in Felling. Internationally, wars were smouldering or being stamped out by various treaties with France, Russia, the USA and Scandinavia, and recruiting officers scoured the land for young men to go off and secure the peace.

One good thing came out of the Felling Disaster: the owner and Member of Parliament, Charles Brandling, wrote a letter to George Stephenson at Killingworth, whose reputation as a local engineer and inventor produced proven and practical profit at roughly the same time that the Rector of Bishopwearmouth wrote to Sir Humphrey Davey in London, a knighted and eminent university-educated scientist. Each man was independently asked to find a safe way, once and for all, to allow miners to work underground in gas pockets without suffocating them with coal damp or setting off explosions with fire damp. In short: a new safety lamp. A year later though, in the exact same mine in Felling, a similar accident repeated itself, claiming the lives of 22 more men and boys, settling the determination of all parties to find a rapid solution.

Meanwhile, being unable to read, and reliant on stories or tavern gossip, none of this meant much to George Lovatt. He was given an official release letter as a cheap form of compensation that guaranteed his freedom in words he couldn't read. He'd heard desperate gossip of work in lead mines, a profitable metal, as it was in demand from the British Army fighting Napoleon, so the young couple travelled to west Durham with two donkeys: one to carry the new mother and her baby and the other to carry their belongings over poor roads often clogged with farm workers, carts from the harvest or flocks of sheep. They shared the way with many other mules, donkeys, horses and carts carrying sacks of coal back and forth around the countryside. But eventually hedgerows, ditches, lowland trees and woods gave way to dry-stone walls, narrow burns and firs. They slept in a small canvas tent George pitched at dusk. He tried to make a fire on the first night but the tinderbox wouldn't light so they ate raw vegetables. They had had to negotiate several roadblocks of armed and ill-disciplined militia and the Brandling letter got them there by the skin of their teeth, as George was considered a prime candidate for soldiering.

In Evenfield, six miles southwest of St Helen Auckland, they sold the donkeys to the butcher and with the money rented a one-up, one-down cottage made of cheap bricks and roof slate quarried by Sir Giles Crockatt of Crockatt Hall, west of Bishop Auckland, home to the influential clergy known as the Prince Bishops. Crockatt Hall was remote and protected by a thick wood and a high wall of granite, and miners rarely ventured there. In one snug corner of the parlour-cum-scullery a Box Bed was partitioned off by a sliding panel. This was to be the newborn's eventual bed.

Evenfield was home to around 20 low-quality brick miners houses thrown up and crowded around a perfectly flat village green with a large oak at one end, a forge, a chapel, a few more substantial houses for more professional people and an inn called The Cleveland Bay and a general store that sold basic goods, cloth and even coffins. Local employment was limited to lead mining, sheep farming or the felling of timber to be shipped to the towns to make furniture. To the rear of the miners' homes were garden plots and a communal privy. It was built of brick with a wooden half door for privacy and erected over a sluggish beck that swarmed with insects in summer and which froze in wintertime. George saw immediately that the soil in his garden plot comprised too much clay to support anything but hardy vegetables, so after work, he laboured the mile to the River Gaunless and ferried barrows of inlet sand up to the plot and mulched it in, breaking down the clay and altering it to a fine tilth that would welcome vegetables like turnips, peas and swedes.

He took the Bond to work in the lead mine – a small affair employing only 50 men, sworn in by the mine's Head Man, Ben Hackett, and paid a guinea for his loyalty. It suited George to be panning around in bubbling streams for the bright shiny lumps of galena, though not hacking away at sheer rock in the gloom with nothing but the small flame of a guttering candle stub to see by and freezing water soaking his back. The mine, 500ft down one central, brick-lined shaft, was old and worn out, not only due to dwindling supplies of good-quality lead but also for lack of investment and poor equipment.

They'd been settled for a fortnight when Catherine was overcome by another weak spell and the village apothecary, 'Mad' Aggy, was called in. Everybody in the village delighted in telling strangers of her history: how she'd served her five-year apprenticeship to an elderly male apothecary with failing eyesight and, though women weren't allowed to train as apothecaries, how she'd cut off her hair and passed herself off as male for the full five years. In the end, her Master had gone blind and she'd nursed him on his deathbed, inheriting not only his knowledge but a sizeable amount of his potions and books.

'Yer wife needs to rest, she's not recovered from t'birth. I'll fetch laudanum – a few drops in 'r tea'll ease 'er recovery n' 'elp 'er sleep. Take this. Light it then extinguish it n' make sure she takes the smoke in – it'll 'elp 'er back pain.'

She handed George a tuft of thick, matted animal hair.

'Goat – it's a remedy from the old days,' she said.

'Does it work?' said George.

'Per'aps, or per'aps it works 'cos we want it to,' she hissed, winking and tapping her temple with a grimy finger.

'Can you come back n' look at 'er from time to time?' George asked hopefully.

'Divvent expect much – I've family o' me own,' said Aggy. 'Just make sure she gets rest 'n fed.'

'But 'ow will yer be able to work n' care for us at the same time?' his wife asked weakly after Aggy had left.

'Now don't you worry, pet, you leave that to me,' said George, though he did not know the answer. He lit and extinguished the goat's hair as instructed, but the stench almost made Catherine sick and as she recoiled her hand caught the lid on which it smouldered and knocked the contents to the floor, so that was the end of that.

The next day at dawn George climbed reluctantly out of the warm bed in which he'd passed the night with his wife and two-month-old baby boy and stoked the embers. There was plenty of coal from the various mines around and it was cheap and there was no transport involved as he wheeled it over in a barrow.

That morning, he tramped through the shivering dark the quarter mile to the mine where he found his new workmates and neighbours William Crosby, John Dawson and Thomas Carr standing in front of Ben Hackett. George explained his wife was ill. Ben Hackett saw no reason whatsoever to be a kind, respected and generous-spirited man – as far as he understood that was not how the pyramid of responsibility worked. For him, the further a man went up the pyramid, the harsher he should be. And so he was – to those men he himself had called comrades when he'd been one of them – and to his own wife and children.

'You shouldn't 'ave 'ad the kid if yer cannat look after it!' he scolded. 'Now, are yer workin' this day or not?'

George bit his lip.

'No, sir' meant he would never work in Evenfield again and if he lost this job, he may never work in the region again. As a newcomer he was in the lowest of positions and the most vulnerable, as he'd not yet proved his value.

Despite the high price of lead, profit didn't filter down to men like him. Without saying a word, he glanced through the dawn mist in the direction of home and took up a spare pick. Catherine would guess he had been forced to work and she would fend for herself.

For the rest of that shift, on his back in wet filth, hacking sideways at an iron stave with his hammer, George burned inside. How many times had he heard the chapel minister preach about Jesus who came to lead his people to salvation? Jesus never worked in a lead mine. If nobody was going to guide them, then maybe somebody should go about starting, but how? He couldn't even read or write.

1814

Thursday 24th March

George Stephenson coughed, but it was from nerves more than a bad chest. He looked down at the floorboards just in front of the man's bare feet and noted how splinters might prick the feet of lesser men, but these feet appeared to have the quality of tanned leather. The floorboards made up the small floor of his office as Engine Wright. A steep-backed drawing board near the window and a high stool furnished the room, and a fire burnt in the corner. It was that simple, ugly truth – a grown man in bare and filthy feet – that stuck in George Stephenson's mind. The sign of any man was that he did the most decent thing when passing from childhood to adulthood – he put shoes or boots on his feet. All men he knew made that simple effort, no matter what their profession or how lowly their status in the world. Shoes or boots defined a working man with sense from a working boy with a gawping face in need of orders. The figure before him was not the former.

'Do you know why you're here?' Stephenson asked as gently as he could.

'To answer for my fault, sir, I suppose,' said the man with little remorse.

Stephenson looked up beyond the dirty ankles to the grotty canvas trousers held up by knotted rope, the torn shirt and waistcoat and tight woollen coat heavy with patched repairs. Bright eyes looked out from a soot-stained face etched with resignation.

'I have seen thee about but have difficulty placing thee, lad,' said Stephenson.

''Twas me sent down to check the water level the day you fixed the old pump, sir,' said the man, brightening a little.

'Ah yes, I recall thee now,'

''Twas a day that set you on your road was it not, Mr Stephenson?'

Stephenson remembered the happy summer week a couple of years before when his gamble repairing the pump had paid off – two years later here he was in his new office. But being promoted had brought different responsibilities: now the title outside his little office door was 'Engineman' and he was also temporary foreman when Hedley wasn't about and it was on his temporary watch that the recent accident had happened and, as there'd been a serious injury, Stephenson now had to decide what to do with the man.

'Do you have a wife or children or a family?' he asked.

'No, sir,' said the man. 'I share digs with some pickers in the village.'

'How old are you?' Stephenson asked.

The man opposite him frowned momentarily.

'Nineteen, sir, I think, possibly twenty?'

'How long have you been at the pit?'

'Five years, sir, since my Dad died in a pit over Hexham. That's why I don't rightly want to work underground, sir. That's why I'm always working above ground, sir.'

'Lowering and raising colliery wagons?'

'Yes, sir.'

Stephenson sympathised – he had spent a few weeks underground himself at 11 as a putter, the worst of all jobs and better suited to the agility of younger men. Young George had hated it and once or twice had had secret panic attacks in the cramped space, frozen with terror, unable to move or respond. He got out of the work by showing an interest in the machines above ground, whereas this man's only idea of escape was to sleep.

'On the day in question,' said Stephenson, 'two wagons broke loose from six being pulled up the bank. Your job was to throw beams under the wheels to stop the runaway wagon.'

The hope fell from his voice like a breeze from the sails of a suddenly becalmed ship.

'Except you didn't run back to block the wagons because you were asleep and as a consequence of that, the wagons ran full pelt down the bank and smashed into old Joe Davidson who was picking up slag.'

Stephenson had visited old Joe in his hospital bed. It hadn't been pleasant – the old man had lost his left leg and his facial features had been re-arranged so he resembled a gargoyle.

'He will live but he has suffered badly. Why were you asleep?' Stephenson demanded.

To the accused man, the question seemed monumentally stupid, but as questions went, it deserved an answer and the only reasonable answer possible to offer was: 'Because I was tired, sir.'

The accused thought back to the moment he was awoken in his hammock, which was hooked up behind the boiler room door. He was angry with himself for some minutes for not having any chance whatsoever of inventing a plausible story.

'You know I must sack you,' said Stephenson. 'It's not a task that sits lightly on my shoulders.'

'Accidents can happen, sir.'

Stephenson disliked this part of the job – rendering men from their work took money from their pockets and food from their bellies and then they were outcasts in the region and had to move to where nobody knew them, or they turned to crime and then the Hangman's rope usually beckoned.

Stephenson fished into his waistcoat pocket and found a guinea coin and handed it to the young man, who fingered and examined it with a wide-eyed look of awe. George had given two guineas to Joe. Despite his lack of shoes, there was a flash of intelligence in this lad's eyes – he was no fool and might have done well at any pit, but having caused serious harm through negligence, his worth there was forever tarnished.

'That will help you for a little. Go now,' said Stephenson. 'And don't look back.'

The man looked at Stephenson with a beaten face, then turned heel. With the guinea in his fist, he stopped off at his hovel, gathered up his few belongings in a bundle tied to a stick and, as the sun set, made for the Roman road to Newcastle. He did not look back.

Friday 8th April

Edward Pease watched through the window of the Viewer's Office at Witton in west Durham as steam plumed out of the chimney. The thick ropes wound diagonally into its open side and the pit wheel atop the timbered derrick spun, pulling up the wooden platform on which stood its sole passenger: wiry William Coulson.

Although young, Coulson had been highly recommended by a Walker pit as having an uncanny ability to find coal. In addition, he worked like a Titan: a full shift at the pit then another shift as a trimmer at the Tyne docks. He came from a family of blacksmiths and was self-made: he could read and write and did both profusely though he'd never been to school or university. The prime reason Pease had brought him in discreetly and at his own expense was to confirm whether or not this coal drift mine near Woodhouse he'd recently acquired could be made profitable. The first test was to clarify if there was sufficient coal to be exploited. The second test was to know how to transport it efficiently from its remote spot to any place worth selling at a profit. Two steep banks stood between them and the hamlet of Shildon and close by was the competition – Etherley Colliery's mining interests, owned by the Stobart Family. The Stobarts were already talking of new sinkings in the area, but that was Pease's problem, not Coulson's. Still, young Coulson came with references and was cheap.

The wheel stopped turning as the platform drew up to ground level within the little brick house, and Coulson emerged and walked through the drizzle to the Foreman's Office with a skip in his stride.

Pease thought again about the letter that lay open on the desk of his study in his house in Northgate, Darlington: 'Dear Mr. Pease, the London Coal Company requests you send double your usual quantity of coal from your mines in County Durham. We know you are already sending as much as you can, but it is simply not enough.'

The 53-year-old Quaker businessman owned Darlington's largest cotton spinning mill, rented out warehouses and homes and shops, had shares in others, as well as a few small but productive coal mines near Shildon and Bishop Auckland and even part-ran a bank whose main account holders were Quaker investors like himself. The Peases were also involved in weaving, dyeing and supplying linen, yarns and wool by the ton for merchant manufacturers in Durham, Yorkshire and Cumberland and overseas export. They bought wool in bulk from farmers and ferried it in from the countryside and moorlands using their extensive network of drays and carts. The wool was then spun in the factories or contracted out to people who set up looms in their houses and back sheds. Darlington was famous throughout England for tablecloths and napkins but for centuries the only means of transporting both materials had been by mule, packhorse and cart over poor roads. The logic of economic progress was simple: improve the transport infrastructure and you improved the general standard of living.

His father had championed the call for a canal in 1767 but didn't live to see his dream fulfilled, dying in 1808, so the son felt a duty to carry on the idea: find some way to link west Durham with the sea. At Stockton, ships were built and goods traded and traders came from ports all over the world, especially London.

Coulson entered the office breathing heavily, his arms, hands and face streaked with coal dust and drizzle so he glistened under the oil light. He pulled his black woollen shirt over his head and peeled his filth-encrusted woollen pants down over tatty grey longjohns and his booted feet. From the trouser pocket he produced a few broken lumps of coal wrapped in a hanky that he put on the tabletop, and then he stuffed the dirty clothes into a sack.

Stripped semi-naked, his white skin contrasted with the patchwork of stains and streaks that swathed his body like some insane tattoo as he'd wriggled underground, sweating in the dirt. He unselfconsciously turned to the nearby table where a large porcelain bowl, a jug of cold water, a flannel, a fresh bar of carbolic soap and a white towel awaited their filthy customer. Coulson poured the water from the jug into the bowl, took the soap and started lathering his black hands. Pease looked at the lumps of coal and then at Coulson, no more than 25 years of age and all lean muscle.

'I am intrigued as to how thou arrives at thy verdicts, Mr Coulson,' Pease said.

'I can read and write,' said Coulson in a strong Geordie accent, without looking up. 'So I read – a lot. There's proof in fossils that the Earth is much older than we imagined and that strange monsters ruled our past long before we were here. If that's true, it could mean various plant formations passed this way also, and as we know, coal is a product of carboniferous activity. Now, I know of a colliery over to the east in Thornley rich in coal deposits and I know of the same as far north as South Shields where sea coal is as common there as all along the coastline. You're here at the most westerly part of that same band, like a large diamond shape if you will.'

'And what is thy verdict in my case?' Pease asked.

'It's my belief,' said Coulson, 'there's a thick band of limestone across most of this region and beneath it, though we may be talking of shafts as deep as 1,000 feet, a bountiful kingdom of coal lies undiscovered – including here at Witton.'

'So one could sink new pits from here all the way east to the sea?' Pease asked.

Coulson ignored the question. He knew better than to answer it. If his predictions were wrong and investments were wasted, 'they' would say: 'Ah but Mr Coulson said...' and his name and reputation would be dirt. Instead, he rubbed the soapy lather around his wrists and forearms and face and neck once more and immersed each arm to rinse off the dirt, but the water was grey by then.

'If my theory is correct,' he went on, the word 'if' being the strongest word in his arsenal of speculation, followed closely by 'could be' and 'think', '...the only other place in the whole of this country where there are such rich reserves is Wakefield down to Nottingham, around Lancashire and South Wales.'

Coulson took the towel and began drying his hands, staining it instantly. He saw Pease taking the bait of his own imagination. He had seen that look before in the faces of many other rich men.

'And do you know what that means, sir?' he asked, glancing in a shaving mirror to dab away the dirty traces of black from his face with the towel. Fascinated by Coulson's knowledge, Pease shook his head dumbly.

'Where there's coal there's often iron ore, so it means, sir, that you and others could be sitting on a Northern gold mine. Now, I shall take these samples away and break them down. A squirt of acid will have the sediment bubbling if my theory is correct, and I think it is.'

After Coulson had cleaned his face, oiled and brushed his hair and put on a clean shirt and trousers, he'd left by private coach having been paid £25. Pease had stood for a while and studied the mule-trains coming and going from his pit and the pitiful amounts they slowly carried over a tortuous route. He decided to be a mule himself to walk to Shildon, ordering his coachman to wait for him at The Mason's. He walked in an almost direct line up two significant inclines through fields of cows, cowpats, sheep, thistles and nettles and down the other sides, badly negotiating slippery stones to get across the River Gaunless and plunging his shoes under so his stockings were soaking wet and yet buoyed by the fact he was walking on solid wealth: as well as coal, there was limestone – and that made paint, wool dyes, glass and quicklime. It was also a top-notch building material and full of profitable ores, such as lead and iron.

So when Pease arrived at Shildon exhausted but elated two hours later, breeches and shoes muddied and torn by bramble thickets, he told his driver to wait a while as he himself took a bench in Dan Adamson's empty inn and a stiff brandy and surrendered himself to deep thought. He came to the sudden and startling conclusion that there was more money to be made in finding an efficient way to transport other peoples' coal than his own.

But profit would do nobody any good piling up in a bank and anyway, how much food could one man get in his belly and how many rooms could he sleep in? No, this was not about profit – this was about value. Pease believed he was sitting on a valuable mountain of potential hope for hundreds of people, but it was cut off from that potential by anything other than mules. His company owned almost 200 horses and 50 carts, their maintenance and upkeep a constant drain on finances. He knew of parallel rail tracks of a few hundred yards and he'd even heard of the Middleton to Leeds railway that two years previously had pulled eight loaded coal wagons ten miles in one hour. But Darlington was 12 miles and Stockton another 12 after that as the crow flew – 24 miles of track was unheard of anywhere in the world, *unheard of.*

1815

Sunday 18th June

Silas Scroggins stepped back from the mouth of the cannon and the officer gave the order: *FIRE!*

The fuse at the breech, lit from a burning torch of tar-soaked rags, coughed pungent black smoke, fizzed briefly and gave out a momentarily deafening bang as the cannon recoiled and a six-pound ball of pig iron impacted the massed French Infantry two hundred yards away, muskets across their chests their only armour.

'To it, you by-blows!' came the Gunner Sergeant's command, his right eye to his telescope. 'Pay attention, Yorkshire!' the Sergeant added glaring at Silas.

Silas's crew that had adopted him temporarily – half drunk on looted red wine and cognac from the nearby Belgian village of Waterloo – lay on and pushed the Blomfeld cannon back into position as across the valley the air rang to the percussion of thousands of other shots like hail on a tiled roof, swallowed up by the never-ending boom of drummers on both sides drilling their battalions into formation at varying speeds, the drone of bagpipes adding to the surrealism.

Until only an hour prior, Silas had been trudging – for there was no marching in mud - onto the battlefield with his Troop of Infantrymen from the 51st, 2nd Yorkshire and East Riding Regiment with whom he'd signed up only a year before after being persuaded by a Recruiting Officer in Eldon Square in Newcastle. The regiment took up position behind Houguemont Farm. He hadn't taken much persuading to join up. He had been slowly starving to death anyway so signing up for seven shillings a week with free food daily, for it was known the Duke fed his soldiers well, though Silas risked getting his head blown off, was better than a miserable end facing starvation. 'Risk, risk, gamble and risk' - life according to Silas.

He spent a full year building up his muscles with exercises, long marches carrying sacks of rocks, peeling spuds, digging and emptying latrines and conducting battlefield manoeuvres. He bought a second-hand red scarlet uniform – complete with stitched up bullet holes - a Brown Bess flintlock musket, a white bandolier and black Shako stovepipe hat and was then hurriedly shipped to northern France and then marched south into Belgium. Ordered up to their battlefield positions in the drizzling rain on the evening of the 17th June, Silas was then touched by the hand of fate in an event which, like so many throughout history, went unrecorded but remain unique, a sign that we must never judge the sense of something by the space between its lines. An Artillery team member had been brought down suddenly with dysentery and the Gunner Sergeant had randomly selected the first trooper who passed by who could answer confidently 'Yes, Sir!' to the question: 'Have you brains enough to brush out a spent breech?' Words were quickly exchanged between the Gunner Sergeant and their own officer Lieutenant Mercier and Silas was suddenly whisked out of his Troop, handed a wire-bristled brush and told and shown what to do and when and it was this simple twist of fate that plucked him from the role for which he had trained for almost a year. As luck would have it, the 51st were not unduly challenged at their holding position behind Houguemont and spent much of their time down in the wet grass where they occupied their patch of the battlefield but were reasonably safe from passing shot and shrapnel. On one occasion they were called to arms and then stood in the pouring rain for an hour as the battle raged some distance away. A few men made inevitable and tempting targets or succumbed to the mass of random lead bullets that crisscrossed the air like horizontal hail, but Silas was not one of them.

The crew went through the reloading, the air vent cleared of burning embers by a birch brush, a powder charge rammed into the barrel and another six-pounder rolled into its mouth and wadded-in.

'Yorkshire!' the Gunner Sergeant called him out loud as his cue to step forward and stick the brush into the breech and scrub out the burnt and congealed powder grains.

'Scrub it hard, for fuck's sake man or you'll blow us all up!' screamed the Gunner Sergeant.

Silas focused only on his singular job. The only other time in his life he remembered doing such a job was when he'd been at Killingworth Pit some years before and told to brush out cauldrons and kilns baked with soot.

The Artillery was closer to the action than the 51st so when he caught the odd glimpse of the enemy through the dense smoke, when he dared to look away for a second, it was to see bits of bodies flying through the air or to hear the terrible cries of wounded and dying men clutching appalling wounds. Musket and cannon balls weaved together a bizarre cacophony of spinning sounds sailing overhead, alongside or between them as they worked. He glimpsed the white uniforms of French grenadiers, trudging forward in a heads-down, determined manner, tightening up their centre ranks and trampling and stabbing all in their path, including wounded British soldiers pleading for mercy.

Calling constantly for any God that would give them refuge that day, he and the crew did all they could to reduce the number of rifles, firing all afternoon, taking fire a number of times but never retreating. Eventually, the officer, Silas's temporary comrades and the carriage-horses were all killed by a freak mortar shell. Silas had begged permission to move away only a few yards to piss and no sooner had he started than the bomb fell close to the cannon. When Silas turned back there was only thick white, acrid smoke and his former temporary team were all dead, laid flat on the ground, the Gunner Sergeant cut in half. He soon after heard: 'Retreat! Retreat!' in English and, confused, as 'Retreat' was a most uncommon word for the British Army, he stumbled confused away up the hill, picking up his as-yet unused Brown Bess and thronged among hundreds of others desperate to escape the terror of the sudden impact of a lead ball or the searing pain of a foreign lance in his back. They clambered through shrinking gaps of the British rifle phalanx and turned shoulder-to-shoulder. The Duke had chosen his terrain well – French Lancers and heavy cavalry stumbled as the last few steep yards drained the exhausted legs of the horses and, when they finally reached the ridge, half a dozen squares of 100-plus British reservists, muskets on all four sides bristling like death-spitting spines, opened fire. Hundreds fell at the first volley screaming in agony or falling wordlessly with surprised faces staring at stumps where hands or feet had been. Silas reloaded and fired until all the lead balls were spent and more were pushed into his pockets by young lads dishing out ammunition. He thought he saw Frenchmen fall under his shot but there were so many bodies there and so much smoke and noise that identification of anything was impossible. Horses buckled and stumbled, pitching riders onto the grass to be shot down and slaughtered and, for no gain whatsoever, the disordered retreat of the French began, breaking like a spent wave on a high beach, the British squares soon dissolving and chasing the Old Guard down the hill and back into France.

There was no order to ceasefire or if there was, few received it. Instead, gradually, over the course of the evening, the bullets and balls stopped flying and here and there groups of desperate men skirmished to the death, the French Old Guard defiantly refusing to surrender and being blasted to pieces.

Silas was almost dead himself from exhaustion, his face, neck, arms, hands all blackened with gunpowder, his threadbare jacket streaked with filth, his beard, eyebrows and hair singed with the heat of blasts, his fingernails broken, hands and arms cut, bruised and begrimed with black powder. He had a thirst the size of a whale. He slept where he fell and when he opened his eyes again it was a sticky and stinking dawn. A medical orderly no more than 14 or 15 years old was pouring water onto his swollen lips. He saw an officer approach on horseback. Picking his way through the carpet of dead with care, he looked down at Silas and said:

'Well done, that man!'

The Duke, barely a scratch on him, cast his eyes across the carnage and asked one of his generals: 'What are our losses?'

'Ten thousand and counting, your Grace,' replied a pale-faced general with a tourniquet on his stirruped bloodstained thigh.

'My God,' the Duke sighed painfully in a rare expression of emotion, 'If only we could have packed the Prussians into carts and got them here sooner.'

Silas, along with hundreds of other survivors in various states, staggered around, looking for a way out of the field of death and at the fields beyond - as far as the horizon was strewn with tens of thousands of dead. Finding even the smallest patch of land to place his foot was almost impossible, for the Earth seemed to weep blood and the bodies piled upon bodies were not unscathed but mutilated by modern ordinance, torn apart, blown open or made limbless or headless. Many wounded French were slaughtered by the late-arriving Prussian Cavalry. Silas did nothing to alleviate their suffering. Why should he? All day the British and Dutch had been pounded by the French but had held their ground - now it was time to settle scores. At one point, a Prussian Lancer rode towards him, his spiked lance painted red with blood, but Silas held up his hands shouting: 'English! English!' and the Lancer spat and rode on. Silas took a silver hipflask of cognac from a dead soldier's belt and drank it all then un-shouldered his Brown Bess flintlock and pouch, sparked and loaded it.

The groans of the dying and wounded were everywhere. He hardly knew where to look or to begin. The shock of seeing guts and intestines spilling out was only vomit-inducing the first time. Medical orderlies ran about with stretchers laden or stretchers empty. Most of the French were no further threat. Once, a wounded and enraged Cuirassier staggered towards him with sabre half-raised. Silas pointed the rifle at his chest. The ball struck the man clean, sending him reeling onto other bodies where he groaned once and then lay still. Silas spent a few seconds examining the man's dying face before stealing his belongings and then absently reloaded his musket and spent the rest of the day with others picking their way through the fields of dead while helping themselves to rings, pocket watches, gold and silver coins and chains and anything shiny.

On the battlefield many more men would die of their wounds where they lay that night and an eerie but almost beautiful, if it had not been for the sombre occasion, summer mist covered that place like a macabre quilt tucking them in for their final sleep. Only those that had borne the battle and lived had the misfortune to bear it once again at its saddest point – the end with the living dancing a final brief jig with the ghosts of dead comrades.

Silas saw his reflection in the silver armour of a French cavalryman's breastplate. He'd never been able to grow a bushy beard, only a patchy affair around neck and chin, but fine eyebrows suggested a spark of wit; thin lips and sharp, pointed nose meant a man of business or a man who meant business. But the eyes he saw that day seemed to belong to another man – his helmet long gone and his hair matted to his head, cheeks and forehead blackened with gunpowder smoke and the blood of other men. At the start of that day he'd been a relatively simple 20-something Northern English labourer recruited into His Majesty's Army over a year before, but at the end of 18th June 1815 he was a changed man, made decades' older by the horror he saw and helped make – a war veteran whose only claim to the title was that he wasn't dead.

It was at the point when he could no longer conceal the looted gold trinkets, earrings, bracelets, coins, wedding rings and brooches he'd already 'liberated', being the closest thing Silas would ever get to being in a goldmine, he wrapped his loot in rags to stop them clinking and carefully concealed them in the lining and hems stitched into his red uniform jacket. Once this was done and, looking around to make sure he was alone, he pointed the barrel of his pistol so it touched the very outer edge of his muddy left boot and pulled the trigger. In fact, what happened was not that Silas shot his toe off but that the powder charge in the breech, poorly rolled and set, exploded. The shock knocked him over and when he recovered and put his hands to his face, his nose recoiling from the pungent odour of burning human hair and wiped his eyes thinking they were clogged with soot but that caused a terrible burning, stinging sensation. He splashed water onto them from his canteen instead but it made no difference – he was blind. It took some minutes for the reality of the situation to sink in and manifested itself with a shock that seemed to steal words from his mouth and then an uncontrollable shaking as he adjusted to his new state and lastly terror as he realised with shock the consequences of his own stupidity.

The 19th June arrived on the back of a troubled sky; it painted the fields with a low mist like a sea through the surface of which the stiff arms and legs of the dead grasped for salvation. Already, groups of French fortunate enough to surrender to the British were being marshalled and, just as the crows arrived, these prisoners with spades began digging mass graves.

Wednesday 21st June, Midsummer Night

In northern England, 34-year-old George Stephenson was sitting in his office early laboriously reading a letter. Being self-educated at the late age of 18, he was finding it hard going. Numbers, plans and diagrams were easy for his eye to read and his brain to compute but letters and words were not.

'Robert, I need thee!'

His son entered from outside where he had been in the protection of the woodshed striking an iron bolt against a lump of quartzite to make sparks on the char cloth – his father had recently introduced him to the art of making fire using this method. He still hadn't mastered the knack, and preferred the traditional method of a spindle rubbed along a groove of sycamore with dried bark kindling at the end. His father handed him the letter. Robert glanced at it and asked: 'Who's Doctor Clanny?'

'He's been experimentin' wi' a safety lamp for miners,' said George. 'Think on the disaster at Felling Pit three years back at the Brandlin' mine: 90 men killed in one go, an entire village. And why? 'Cause they needed a flame to see by for men're not moles; better that they were for then they wouldn't need their eyes. What does a fire need to burn?'

'Combustible material an' air,' replied Robert.

'Or gas,' said his father. 'But supposin' the bad air could be filtered so the naked flame didn't burn any dimmer be'ind its casing but at the same time didn't ignite the dangerous air? Look at this,' He pushed a charcoal sketch into his son's hands of a large vertical tube fitted around a metal base, a flame inside and around the base, small holes covered with gauze.

'I'm 'avin' it made by a Newcastle tin man called Hogg, n' the glass is being blown by the Northumberland Glass 'ouse. It'll be ready in October and then I'll be going down the pit to test it myself and if it all goes well I'll be off to Newcastle to demonstrate how it works.'

The sudden sound of boots on the wooden steps outside preceded a knock and a young lad stuck in his head around the door.

'*Blucher*?' George asked the boy. 'No, sir,' said the boy, 'the rails.'

'Run along n' tell Mr Wood I'll be with 'im shortly.'

The boy left. George reached for his topcoat and went out through the grey smoke, Robert tagging on behind.

'She's come off the rail agen, George,' said Nicholas Wood, the Head Viewer.

'Best call the boys,' said George, familiar with the routine. All able-bodied men gathered around *Blucher*, Stephenson's first custom-built locomotive – each part beaten and forged by blacksmiths at Bedlington and fastened together here at Killingworth. It had been inspired by one of Trevithick's locomotives when it had arrived at Wylam and, while Hackworth and Hedley worked on *Puffing Billy* and *Wylam Dilly*, it gave Stephenson the chance to study the design for his own improved engine.

He simplified the transmission of thrust to the wheels by placing the unit on top of the boiler and also devised a system to cushion it against shocks and it had since pulled wagons from the pitheads to the staithes down at Sunderland docks very efficiently, though it lay now a little askew, its left back wheel of four buried in the stone ballast of the track, a shattered cast-iron rail having sprung its blocks. But its main limitation was weight. He'd heard plans to redesign the engine with four axels and eight wheels in order to spread weight but hadn't yet seen it, and anyway it seemed to George the main problem was the track so, once appointed Engineman, George had been given a free hand to tinker to his heart's content so long as he produced profit. For two painstaking years and while working a full-time job and bringing up his son, he'd helped design and build his steam engine and now profit was very healthy indeed.

'Malleable iron – it's the only solution. I've said it a hundred times,' said George wearily.

'But the cost!' said Wood.

'What price this?' asked George, indicating the stranded engine. 'The future's here, Nick. The engine needs improvin' n' rails strengthenin' but in theory it's all 'ere.'

With an almighty heave, the combined force of men, horses and steam power got the back wheel righted and the engine moved forward. Workmen gathered with hammers and nails and a new rail soon replaced the broken one, but few noticed as a boy ran through the smoke from the gate, pushing through the men to the front.

'Sir! Sir! News from London, sir!'

'What is it, boy?'

'Boney – Well'ton and Blucher ave beat 'im!'

A cheer went up from all the men

'Ha, I told you Blucher was a good name!' Stephenson shouted.

Nonetheless, fate should have dictated he might have been at that battle – he was the right age, but instead he'd bought himself out at considerable expense. He knew he could fight if he had to: a few years before he'd out-boxed a bully called Ned Nelson – but it was perhaps his frail parents and dependent son, combined with his inability to imagine himself murdering anyone that provoked him to abandon the call with the only honour available. In France, other men with just as many responsibilities had done their patriotic duty and brought a fragile peace to Europe. Men had died so he could live. Was he vain to presume he could repay their sacrifice?

Thursday 22nd June

Across to the west, in the direction of the fragments of the wall men said was built by the Romans and stretched across the neck of Britain like a stone noose, the village of Wylam on the banks of the River Tyne was home to a few hundred people, among them one Timothy Hackworth.

Twenty-nine year old Hackworth was in his forge at the Blackett Colliery where there were problems again with *Puffing Billy*, the steam engine designed by his fellow 'engineer', William Hedley, and built by Tom Waters and Bobby Hawthorn. Funded by mine owner, Chris Blackett, who'd also funded Stephenson's early experiments, it was painstakingly built from 1811 and was now successfully working the short lines that connected the colliery to the upper part of the Tyne.

The forge coals glowed orange and Hackworth, stripped to the waist except for a large leather apron and gauntlets, lifted out a bright orange rod of iron. He laid it on the smooth anvil, took his hammer and began hammering the glowing strip, tiny sparks bouncing off with every singing stroke. He allowed his grip to loosen a fraction of a second before the strike so it sprung back, but still every blow vibrated and inflamed his face. With sweat pouring from his brow and his mouth half-open with exertion, he hammered the rod until evenly flat then glanced at it but, not quite happy, slid the bar into the orange coals once more.

Wiping the less painful side of his face with the rough sleeve of one of his gloves, he wandered outside in the vain hope of a cooling breeze. In every direction the landscape was black: the black wooden scaffold that straddled the mouth of the pit, the black of the winding house, the black of the small slag mountain, black wagons laid on rails black with loads of large jagged black shapes and the line itself across the black earth and down to the staithes.

The slagheap was a small perfectly conical hill where widows and the elderly picked for discarded coal and staggered to their nearby homes with it strapped to their heads like strange bonnets. Men covered in black dust ladled the sellable coal onto black keelboats to ferry the black gold down the Tyne to the colliers waiting to sail to London, or to the coke works where coal was smelted, distilled and hardened. Coke was in rising demand by many ironworks who found it vastly increased foundry temperatures for less effort and cost and made iron ore more workable.

A small carpentry workshop stood alone. Old ships' timbers were brought up from the river into the joinery and sawn into props, then taken down the shaft and used to shore up the ceilings and walls of the mine.

Only the natural ring of green trees all around the site contrasted with the landscape. In the centre, proud and stubborn, squatted *Puffing Billy*, its chimney belching smoke, but immobile due to a broken connecting rod. He walked across and looked closely once again at the space where the rod he was currently beating should have been connecting a crank with one of the four wheels.

Hackworth had had toothache for three days, but he had not found the time to have it pulled, and instead soothed it with a constant round of garlic cloves. It had inevitably worsened and had begun to pass beyond the realms of something with which he could cope into something unbearable.

'Thou art Friday-faced this day!'

Hackworth turned. It was Jonathon Foster, the engineman.

'Hast thou righted 'er yet?' he added.

'Almost,' mumbled Hackworth, 'A little longer n' I should 'ave summat ready.'

'The boys's pressin' fer this load. The's a dozen angry keel men waitin'.'

'Well, they'll just 'ave to wait a little longer n' keep their tempers. I'm no man to rush. My father, God rest his soul, taught me that.'

'Fair enough,' said Foster.

The two men stood in silence for half a minute more. Foster decided to change the subject.

'How's the parson's mousetrap these days? Settlin' in to married life is she?' he asked of Jane, Hackworth's new wife.

Hackworth attempted a smile.

'Jane's fine n' askin' after you, Mr Foster.' Hackworth replied.

'We didn't see yer at work last Sunday,' noted Foster.

'Was my absence noticed?'

'Yer absence is *always* noticed on Sundays, Tim.'

'It's written in the scriptures. I cannot go against God, Mr Foster.'

'Indeed,' sighed Foster accepting Hackworth's plea. 'I 'ear Geordie Stephenson's doin' well at Killingworth. 'e's a new engine, *Blucher*.'

'An apt name for such a beast – the locomotive I mean,' said Hackworth. 'Let's hope the real General's livin' up to his reputation as we speak.'

Just then, the nerves in his face flared up and he groaned.

'What's up?' Foster asked.

'Toothache!' moaned Hackworth.

'I can fix that for thee in a tick if th'art brave.'

Hackworth knew what was implied.

'Come on then, let's get it ower with!' he said irritably.

They set off at a brisk pace to the forge, Hackworth immediately straddling the anvil as Foster selected the smallest pair of pliers. Hackworth opened his mouth and tipped back his head. Foster grimaced as he looked inside and identified the little knot of black and white decay set into the pink gum. He put his left hand hard on Hackworth's chest and with his right hand clutching the pliers, reached in, gently enclosed the fragments of broken molar, tightened his grip and pulled. Hackworth whimpered as the force increased and he pushed against Foster's hand. The pain was unbearable and Hackworth's eyes filled with tears. He groaned horribly and gurgled in his throat and would have screamed if his mouth and tonsils were not stretched wide by Foster's hand and the cold iron of the pliers pressing against his tongue.

'Just a little longer! Just a little longer!'

Foster suddenly tugged and fell back gasping, the shattered tooth held up to the light shining with blood and saliva. Hackworth cried out and tears rolled down his face and mingled with the spittle and blood dribbling from his bottom lip. He spat a number of times, wiped his mouth on his bare arms and groaned as the wrenched nerves throbbed. But the worst was over. He passed no more than two minutes there licking the hole and spitting blood. The pain was intense but would gradually fade and he just about managed to mumble: 'Let's get this engine fixed.'

Wednesday 13th December

Being found stumbling blindly around the battlefield by medical orderlies while desperate to rub his stinging eyes but unable to do so because it only made it worse, Silas had been taken to an Aid Station where he was forced to endure the horror of the shouts and screams of wounded and dying men. The only remedy for the screaming, said the MO, was to put your hands on your ears. Eventually an under-pressure, retired, alcoholic Surgeon studied him absently for a few moments and delivered the verdict: 'Invalided out! Send back to England!' before moving on to the next unfortunate.

Once Napoleon's last resistance had been snuffed out, the 51st Yorkshire and East Riding had shipped across the choppy Channel and plodded back to the Chelsea Barracks in London there to rest and freshen up before going on with the next part of their journey: a long march all the way back to the Regimental Barracks in Pontefract. But every minute of the trip back, despite being in the company of a few of his surviving infantry comrades and in the back of a cart, it was hell on earth for Silas as he was forced to come to terms with his new status: he was a blind man and as dependent as a baby on others for his every waking moment. This included the new humiliation of begging for help in eating, pissing and shitting.

'Life is guided by events beyond my control' he concluded calmly to himself as the panic munched away at the outer edges of his sanity. He prepared himself mentally as best he could for this reversal of fortune, which he was sure would see him dead in a workhouse by Christmas. For him, life was over. He couldn't even walk down a street without an arm to lean on, as helpless as a child. His soldier mates took care of him as best they could but they had lives of their own, some had wives, few had time for him and few knew him well as he'd been thrown into the regiment straight from basic training so had had little time to build links. Once or twice they offered to take his regimental jacket and clean it but he refused, clinging on to the sweat-laden, bloodstained, mud-streaked uniform and praying for a miracle as he knew any nosey parker would soon spot his loot and easily have the edge on a blind man. Mostly he wore a white handkerchief around his eyes tied with one knot at the back of his head – it didn't really protect him from anything as he couldn't see anyway but it was less unpleasant for others to look at the ugly black and red streak across the bridge of his nose and his upper face.

Invalided out only a few days before, he'd then arrived at Chelsea Barracks and the regiment was billeted down and given 24 hours grace. The very next morning would see him being given a second opinion and a final examination by another, less-stressed, teetotal and active Surgeon who would decide once and for all if Silas was repairable or permanently broken. He'd not slept that night because he knew that at dawn he might finally be forced to leave the Barracks for an uncertain future as a 'blind' man. But as the darkest hour gave way to a bright dawn, he realized he could see slivers of sunlight and then after he'd bathed his burnt lids with warm water, finally managed to open and operate them again. Objects were blurry at first and distance was hard to magnify but if he held up his hands in front of his face he could easily make out the dirt-lined fingernails and black-haired hands and arms. It was a right royal turn-up for the books, as the saying went: fed, boarded and trained by His Majesty for a year in England, sent into battle, survived, made reasonably rich, been blinded as divine punishment, been discharged from the Army and now the good Lord had seen fit to restore his sight! His wounds would heal and scab over but he'd be left with scars and what are scars anyway but marked memories? The relief was palpable – he cried tears with the sheer, child-like joy of seeing again as he'd since been resigned for five days to the end of the world. But then he stifled his words. He was alone. He had to keep his 'secret' safe and continue to play blind, so the very next day he replied plainly: 'Nothing at all, Sir' to the Surgeon's final question of 'Can you see the candle light I am holding close to you now?' Silas could very well see the candle's light but he didn't want to see the candle light at that moment because it meant the Army might keep their hands on him. He'd made his plan: he'd recover in a nearby Inn for a night and then quietly slip away.

And so it turned out. Morale restored in the Inn, 'recuperation' came within hours but he continued to pretend to be blind for the sake of the inn-keeper and his patrons and then on the following day walked out tapping his stick in front of him until he was well out of that neighborhood and was able to throw away the stick and scarf, but it took another few minutes to adjust to the strong sunlight.

He was able to unstitch the gold booty from his regimental jacket and found a tinker's encampment on the moorland outside Hampstead village (he could trust no blacksmith in the city, most would shout 'Thief!') where he was able to pay a shilling to make use of his fire and metal moulds. Not all his looted trinkets were of a good quality, some were mixed with tin or other metals for weight, but he was able to melt down at least two small ingots, each two inches long by one inch thick, no questions asked by the tinker who may have had his own reasons to stay quiet. Silas slipped him a shilling as payment and for good measure the tinker gave Silas a small, empty, wooden cigar box with the odour of tobacco still in it with a secret panel to hide his ingots. Silas had left the tinker and, his pack on his back, staggered and slid through the mud to a coaching inn near Golders Green as fresh snow began to fall.

Early the following morning, woken by the first cockerel, he bought a ticket to York and shared the journey with a corpulent woman toting a caged parrot and a fishmonger reeking of his trade and quickly began to wish he had chosen to ride outside the coach but was at least relieved the coach had decent Elliot-made springs. Lurching from Golders Green to Lincoln, stopping at Cambridge for new horses and refreshments, it took a long day, hampered as they were by lightly falling snow and sleet that made the roads slick and limited daylight. Silas had sufficient bank notes and coins to pay to ride inside until Lincoln that evening, when snow turned to rain. At Lincoln where they stayed the night, he'd managed to win an oilskin cape at a round of cards and sufficient money to ride with the driver and his mate up top but in the pockets of his newly won cape he unexpectedly found men's leather gloves and they did well for keeping his hands warm. Otherwise, it was bitter and he doubted he'd make it to Darlington alive if the freezing temperatures persisted. The trunks were arranged two on each side and one at the back with a slight hidden dip between. It wasn't comfortable but he was facing ahead and didn't get jolted about too much. He kept out of the cold with a borrowed blanket and scarf wrapped around his head. Within a short time they were clear and onto the Turnpike. Silas drank from his brandy flask and offered it to the driver and his mate, but they refused, saying it was more than their job was worth, so, rocked by the carriage and lulled by the soporific effect, he fell asleep and it was only the absence of the rocking that made him open his eyes about ten minutes later.

'I have a pistol pointed at your chest! Don't move – this is a robbery!'

He looked at the backs of the two drivers holding up their hands in surrender then pushed himself painfully up onto his aching, numbed elbows and caught a glimpse of a man in a dark cape, Tricorn hat low over his head, scarf wrapped around his nose and mouth and erratically pointing two flintlocks in the direction of the coachman but doing a poor job controlling his horse. Another highwayman was on the side of the coach Silas couldn't see. Neither knew he was there but he could locate them by the clouds of hot breath emanating from their and their horses mouths.

'I'll avail you ladies 'n gents of valuables 'n coins. My friend n' I are in difficult circumstances n' forced to desperate deeds. Think not unkindly of us – until recently, we were law-abiding 'uman beings as you are now.'

Silas thought the speech eloquent but the coachman's mate had obviously heard it before and started to reach down behind him. As he did, the highwayman pointed a pistol. The lock flashed, the powder cracked and fresh white wooden splinters exploded out of the paintwork of the coach. The Mate held his hands even higher, pleading not to shoot. Reaching forward unseen, Silas took the case instead and opened the lid and saw two loaded pistols with cotton tufts of powder charges stuffed into their pans. He cocked them both with loud clicks and struggled to his feet, one in each hand, reeling from the rush of oxygen to his brain. Registering the look of surprise in the robber's eyes, Silas levelled the pistol in his right hand, pointed, closed his left eye and fired. He could not be sure but it seemed the ball struck the robber in his upper body as he slumped in the saddle and his horse turned and pushed noisily into the dark forest. Hearing a shout and realising the other was behind him, Silas turned, pointed the second pistol at the second outlaw leaning into the window and pulled on the trigger. It blew his hat off revealing a bald head with wisps of long hairs around each ear and angry eyes. In return, he pulled a pistol from his belt and steadied his arm at Silas, who could do nothing but say:

'May God have mercy on my —'

The powder flashed and Silas was slammed backwards by the force of the ball onto the luggage at exactly the time the driver cracked the whip and the huge coach lurched. The Mate pulled a blunderbuss from under the seat, turned, levelled it and pulled the trigger. Smoke puffed from the trumpet-shaped barrel and a handful of lead pellets spat viciously in the direction of the bald highwayman, who held up his hand in vain, losing two fingers in the process.

The coach horses tumbled down the hill, a cacophony of churning hooves, creaking wood, leather and jangling metal amid the cries of both drivers and passengers. After a half mile, they stopped and nervously, reluctantly, got out and examined Silas who they'd seen take a ball directly in the chest but were stunned to see him open his eyes and sit up shocked and winded, his hand in his coat pulling out fragments of the smashed cigar box. The gold ingots had taken the force and there it rested: a small circle of flattened lead set into the brilliant yellow.

'You lucky bugger!' said the driver. Silas blinked at it and then laid his head back and looked up at the sky. He was alive.

Once they'd ensured Silas was as comfortable inside the carriage as his aching ribs could be, they pushed on hard for another mile until they reached a hamlet, where they eased the exhausted horses to a standstill. The red-caped coachman got down to reassure the other passengers: a woman had fainted and was revived with smelling salts and a bespectacled priest broke his normally strict abstinence rule and drank a brandy for medicinal purposes.

'What's your name?' they asked Silas, as they helped him climb down from the carriage rubbing his painfully sore chest. 'You're 'n 'ero!'

Feeling sick, his chest aching as if punched by a prize-fighter, Silas leaned over and vomited. He didn't feel like any type of hero. He couldn't believe it – after all he'd been through for His Majesty and to end his days like that, shot by the home side?

'Life is made up of events beyond my control' he thought again.

The first he'd shot at received a body shot and possibly a fatal, killing wound and where there were dead bodies there were always questions. Who had the answers to questions like: what was the difference between killing foreign Frenchies and killing British footpads? There wasn't a difference, he concluded: killing was killing. But all killing shared the same theme: killing was such an evil thing that he could never talk about it with anyone, not then nor for the rest of his days. And so he had to learn to live with this new version of himself. He began to realise that trying to be the man he was before Waterloo in order to retrace his original path – which he had thought would bring happiness – was pointless. This – where he was at this precise moment – *this* was his destiny. For better or for worse, his one true, constant ally and friend to the very end was his own destiny and it seemed to have an extraordinary and unpredictable way of showing itself.

For what they called his bravery and he called his luck he was allowed to ride inside the coach and a day later they entered York under the auspicious gaze of the Minster, passing the gallows and seeing the hanging, rotting corpse of an executed murderer being picked clean by crows. The sight filled the others with horror and disgust but Silas felt only a resigned fear: how many condemned men must have hungered to be put out of the misery of having to live with what they'd done?

He was offered free passage to any of the remaining stops on their journey as a reward for his courage. A journalist from a newspaper heard about the action and tried to talk to him, but Silas had no desire to publicise his deeds. He dodged the newspaperman and caught the next coach out, happy to finally disembark at Darlington later that evening as snowflakes fell heavily from a leaden sky. The journey from London had taken four days, a difficult voyage – the bruising impact of the lead ball on his chest causing considerable discomfort that didn't fade for some weeks.

As they'd pushed further north, he'd dreamed of buying a small sheep farm on the moors and made plans in his head that included fine clothes and a dream house, but as soon as the coach arrived at The King's Head in Darlington on that chilly thirteenth day of December and stepped into the slush, Silas sniffed the scent of beer and tobacco and in an instant accepted his dream it as the fantasy it was. He'd killed men at Waterloo. He was a hero and heroes belonged around firesides where they told stories embellished with white lies for the ever-changing rounds of guests.

Unable to find a pawnbroker with the £100 cash, for which one such had valued the ingots at £50 each, he managed to get them weighed on the scales at the recently opened Backhouse Bank on the High Row. The bank was able to furnish him with the money. Paying Richard Stott, landlord of The King's Head, £50 bed and board in advance, Silas then set up as a semi-permanent resident to weather the coming winter. But trusting nobody, he buried the sum of £10 in a leather waterproof pouch – as most people he knew did in those days - under a thorn bush in a field on the other side of the River Skerne and kept £40 for expenses. With the long hard winter, he knew he'd be a fool to leave the comfort of the town for an uncertain future on the moors and it was always prudent to put something aside for a rainy day.

He tried to find a music hall such as those he'd seen in Paris and London, but the Quakers allowed no such excess in Darlington, so instead he got drunk and told tales of Waterloo. He was often heard mocking the fact that he was 'Invalided out due to a clerical misfortune' and he passed Christmas in a drunken stupor and indeed he decorated the truths of his Waterloo experiences to such degrees that not only did people get tired of listening but he got tired of telling and there was a lifting of his spirits when in mid-February of the following year, with the last few shillings of his allotted spending money dwindling, the feeble spring sunshine brought out the first purple and white crocuses.

1816

Tuesday 12th March

Seamus Gallagher, an under-nourished and underworked young Irishman, stepped down from the collier *The Betsy* onto Steer's Dock and, shielding his eyes from the sleet stabbing almost horizontally on the stiff westerly wind, he looked about him.

Liverpool, England. Hundreds of ships crammed the harbour, a dense forest of masts, rigging and flags against the skyline, the quaysides crammed with people and cargo. Cranes, pulleys and teams of dockworkers extracted Scandinavian timber planking, barrels of whale blubber from Arctic waters, Jamaican rum, home-spun linen from Ireland, boxes of tea from India, thousands of bales of raw cotton from the southern states of America and sacks of brown sugar from Guadeloupe. Other ships were being filled with ingots of lead from Weardale, wool from Yorkshire, spun flax from Manchester and coal from Cumbria.

Soldiers in red coats filed through the otherwise grey mêlée like a stitch of bright thread. Sailors scrubbed the decks of warships painted black, white and yellow with speckled ribbons hanging from their spotless masts, the sides of their bellies bristling with portholes. Gulls swarmed and squabbled over dead fish floating among the sewage or tipped from the ships galleys. Squinting in the daylight, a file of men with skins as black as coal, metal manacles connecting one to the other by iron hoops around their necks, were led from the hold of a ship and pushed into pens to be sold as slaves. Despite slavery being outlawed in Britain, a blind and often bribed eye was still turned to certain cargoes that used Liverpool as a port of transfer before sailing on to the southern states of America.

And then came the boats from Ireland.

Two weeks on the road had taken Seamus further than he'd ever been in his short life: from the back lanes of Limerick on the shores of the damp Shannon, through a beautiful countryside waking to the touch of the first fingers of spring, to Dublin, with its newly erected Georgian avenues crowded on all sides by swelling slum dwellings. Filing past the gallows where a dozen Catholics hung, he had spent two days with other passengers on the open deck of a coal-carrying collier boat that traded lead and tin between Whitehaven, Dublin and Liverpool and occasionally took paying passengers who were quartered in a windowless hold with wooden bunks and who ate with the sailors. Seamus couldn't write his name but he believed in God and knew his commandments: it was all he needed.

He had been born in 1799, with his only brother Sean born a year later. The year 1798 saw Limerick wrecked by Royalist forces and hundreds of ringleaders hanged or banished to France; Seamus's father only survived by signing an oath of loyalty to the British Crown. But prospects were few – a life cutting peat, fishing or weaving for pitiful wages.

Seamus had taken his chance and ventured to England where he heard there was work, providing he could stomach the prejudice.

The blustering of the Presbyterian Mad King George and all the Lords of England who loathed the Irish along with everybody else 'below' their aristocratic standing meant nothing to Seamus – he was a young lad going to waste. In recent days he'd crossed the widest sea he had ever seen, wider even than at Loop Head at the westerly edge of the Shannon.

In Liverpool, uncertain what to do or where to go, he stood at a brazier burning wooden staves and warmed his hands. He heard a voice moving through the crowds.

'Work! Work! Who wants work?'

He called the owner of the voice over, a bearded man with black teeth and a fiery red face.

'What sort o' work is dat now?' Seamus asked in his thick Irish accent. 'You're a big strong boy,' the man lied. 'Do yer know one end of a wheelbarra from t'other?'

'Oi do, sir,' said Seamus, pleased at least to get a question correct.

'Show us yer 'ands,' said the man.

Seamus held out his soft, skinny fingers and grime-edged fingernails. The man grabbed his wrists, turned his hands over and looked at his grubby palms. He tutted – he'd seen worse.

'The Manchester, Bolton n' Bury Company's looking fer men to 'elp 'em dig canals. Wages is two bob a day except Sundays. Board n' lodgin's nine bob. Interested?'

'Oi am, sir!' said Seamus, surprising himself: he had no trouble realising he'd be three bob up a week.

'Good lad. Take this token to the gates of t'Old Dock n' get a dry place an' a bowl of lobscouse n' ale, n' yer can join a dray tekkin' men to Manchester in t'mornin'.'

He handed Seamus a square brass token upon which letters were stamped, patted him on the back and disappeared along the quayside repeating his call. Seamus wandered through the crowds to the dock gate where he handed over the token and was ushered into a dry room with a coal fire. Here he joined a crowd of mostly Irishmen, and a few Scandinavians too, who had recently arrived. He was given a wooden plate, a spoon and three ladles of beef stew with a hunk of hard bread. It was the first food he'd eaten in two days. After, he smoked clay pipes with other Irishmen, who took his scrawny arms in their fists, saying they'd have to put muscle on him if he was going to be a navvy. He would dig a tunnel to the moon and back if the Manchester, Bolton and Bury Canal Company asked him to, he said, and they all laughed.

Saturday 27th April

By early springtime, Silas found himself with no job and dwindling money. He still had £10 buried under the thorn bush for emergencies but he knew it was now time to use his wits. So he considered his prospects: he'd done a little mining and poaching as a youth and had then been recruited into the Army but all that had done was taught him how to fire weapons. A job in the militia was feasible, but militia were generally locals who knew little of warfare, were badly or irregularly paid and nothing more than hired thugs. Silas had some negative traits, but he was no thug. He didn't want to return to mining because he kept those memories locked away with his growing collection in a private place in his mind. He had even heard, on the many nights he'd passed at the King's Head, there was work down in the middle of the country where canals were being built, but it was gruelling labour reserved for the 'bastard Irish', as people referred to the immigrants 'invading' England. Uncertain, he returned to the King's Head Inn and tapped a drink from Richard Stott.

'Yer advance on yer room runs out the morrow – no more credit or I'll be callin'' in the watchmen,' said Stott, half-jokingly.

Silas didn't want any trouble with Watchmen: borderline scum employed by local magistrates to keep the peace with whatever force deemed necessary. A month prior, he'd watched ten from Darlington fight a pitched battle with members of a notorious gang called The Black Troop in the marketplace and lost a shilling gambling on the outcome. It wasn't that he was afraid of the Watchmen: sticking his fist into some of their ugly faces would have pleased him greatly, but he was afraid of what they represented: the power of the King and local magistrates and, having seen what the King could muster in the wars against Napoleon, Silas didn't want to be on the King's bad side.

'Can you not spare us summat 'ere, coachman or stable manager?' Silas asked.

'The servants'd be treatin' you harsh, I think – a man 'oo orders 'em about suddenly reduced to an equal footin'? Don't bode well for an efficient inn,' Stott replied dubiously.

Silas knew Stott was right – the war hero image had gone to his head.

'But I've 'eard say there's a vacancy over at Crockatt Hall, near Raby. The Head Gamekeeper's lookin' for 'elp.'

'You've long ears, Stotty,' said Silas.

'I do that,' said the landlord with a wink.

The next morning, Silas finally packed his carpetbag and took the road to Cockerton and Staindrop, climbing over stone walls and trudging across fields of spring lambs, passing a dozen coal-carrying mule trains and carts laden with wool and timber. His incentive was leaving that £10 safely buried, and his purpose was to refuse to leave Crockatt Hall without a job, whatever it took.

As he walked, he dredged up childhood memories of life in the massive Northumbrian forests and moorlands that coated most of County Durham and the Scottish Borders, following the keepers on their jobs, beating grouse and carrying things for rich men. He was no expert on the subject of keeping game but he was no stranger either, and he'd done his fair share of poaching rabbit – all many families had to supplement their meagre diets. And when he thought about families, he thought only fleetingly and with no emotion about his dead father and mother, both of whom were barely memorable now.

He stole an egg from a henhouse for breakfast, cracked it into his mouth and trudged through the spring rain to Staindrop and north again beyond Cockfield until he saw the little wood. It was on the side of a fell and seemed like a giant that held within its protective green arms the ancient manor of Crockatt Hall. Arriving muddy, wet, cold and utterly exhausted, for his lazy months in the King's Head had ruined his solder's strength and given him a paunch, he went around the back and asked for the Head Keeper. Silas stood up to his full six feet as the man arrived, much shorter than Silas.

'That's me, Hamish, Hamish Jones.'

Hamish Jones looked up and Silas Scroggins looked down below at the body the head was attached to and up again to the face but with sharper eyes – mid-thirties, a pink-skinned man with long wavy hair and an overall too-chubby-for-a-gamekeeper look.

'What can I do for you?' he asked Silas.

'I've heard there's a position going for Assistant Keeper, sir. I've come to apply.'

'I'm sorry but I've other men in mind for the job,' was the curt response.

Silas had walked a long way with hope in his heart. He wasn't going to give up yet.

'I work 'ard, sir, n' know the land, comin' down from above Plenmeller near Hex'am afore takin' the King's shillin' n' fightin' at Waterloo.'

'Waterloo?'

'Yes sir. – the 2nd Yorkshires,' said Silas proudly.

'Me brother William died at Waterloo,' said Hamish.

'More fool him' was Silas's immediate thought, but he knew if he chose the right words – like cards played in the right order – the job was sure. He waited – it was always better to let the other fellow speak first.

'He worked over at Raby,' said Hamish. 'Served at dinner, accompanied Lady Elizabeth on 'ouse calls, looked after lamps n' candles,' said Hamish quietly and then added as an almost embarrassed afterthought for want of better vocabulary: 'An' that sort of thing.'

It suddenly occurred to Silas that Hamish was one of the least likely Head Gamekeeper's he'd ever met – he wore authority like a wet towel.

'We was at war then,' Hamish went on. 'Government put a tax on a house wi' male servants and Lord Darl'ton kept 'im on 'cos of 'is wife wantin' to keep up the status. So 'e asked permission to go and Lord Darl'ton, a soldier himself, couldn't refuse. Caught a bullet right between 'is eyes they say. Did you – did you see Boney?'

'From afar, yes, though a dwarf 'e is in the flesh,' Silas lied.

'And the old Duke?'

'Well done that man', 'e said, close as you are now.'

'Bill was an infantryman in the Durham Brigade. Did you know 'im?' Hamish asked hopefully.

'I can't say I knew 'im, no, but the bravery of the 16th was very 'ighly spoken of.'

The job was his. He spent the night in the barn with the hunters and carriage horses, which was a step down from The King's Head but warm and dry and he was fed with a bowl of broth.

It was important that both his Lordship and the other members of staff knew his face, so the next day he met them in a line-up. Hamish took off his cap and stood dutifully to attention, head slightly bowed. But not Silas – he had fought at Waterloo and he'd killed men so that the likes of Sir Giles Crockatt could exercise their liberties. He felt he had every right to stand as tall as any 'sir', and Sir Giles – in his tweeds, a gleaming rifle over his arm and a monocle on his left eye – looked self-assuredly at Silas.

'Jones tells me you fought at Waterloo. Is it true?'

'It is indeed, sir – the 2nd Yorkshires and East Riding.'

'Commanded by?'

'General Morshead, sir,'

'You should address 'is Lordship as 'Milord'' hissed Hamish.

'This man fought for his country. He may address me as 'sir' if he so wishes,' Crockatt scolded.

Hamish, humiliated, nodded once.

'The Yorkshires are an infantry regiment are they not?'

'Yes Sir that is true but the Royal Artillery was under-manned that day so my self and others were pulled for duty. All I had to do was brush out the breech for fresh firing, not too difficult, sir. The Artillery regiments fared better than most that day, sir'

'Tell me Scroggins – did you meet Wellington?'

'I wouldn't say I met him, sir, but he did pass me by on his horse at the end o' the battle, sir and said: 'Well done that man' to me after I'd spent the whole day firin' cannon balls into the French, sir.' Silas declined to mention anything about being 'invalided out due to a clerical misfortune' as it felt like it would just complicate things.

' 'Well done that man', eh? I've a hero of Waterloo on my staff. A good choice, Jones - the Duke and I frequently brush shoulders in Parliament. I hope you'll be happy here, Scroggins.'

Stung by Sir Giles's rebuff, Hamish was never quite as friendly after that and their relationship soured almost instantly. But Silas noticed quickly that it wasn't personal – nobody liked Hamish much. Nor was he married. Who'd want him? He hadn't lived or developed a tongue to entertain as Silas had. He was a green and rather dull country boy with the air of a child who preferred to cry to his mother – who still lived in a pensioner's cottage on the grounds – than find his own way. So be it. That was the competition.

'I'll take yer to yer cottage,' said Hamish and they set off around the side of the manor house.

'His Lordship's only son died at Salamanca under Wellington, serving with Lord Darlington's son, Arthur, who also died. It is a sore point n' must never be mentioned,' advised Hamish.

'Sir Giles 'as no wife?' asked Silas.

'Died givin' birth, as at Raby,' said Hamish, 'So you see, a very sore point indeed. Heathcote is 'ead Butler n' the Cook is Alice.'

Hamish nodded at a small cottage on the other side of the kitchen garden.

'That's thine,' said Hamish. 'It'll need a sweep. You can get wood and coal from the bunker at the back o' the house. Get sorted and then come and see me and I'll show you yer duties.'

Silas inspected the house – it was no palace but it would do, so he cleaned away the cobwebs, brushed the stone floor, beat the mattress and carpets and stocked up on firewood.

He was then given the more serious job of repairing fox coverts to the south of the estate, and being left alone, he soon discovered, suited him greatly.

The estate was divided into two: a few hundred acres of lowland to the south and east and even fewer acres of upland to the west and north. In the upland, he worked the moors for red grouse, blackcock and deer. This was also home to Sir Giles's dwindling business interests: lead, coal and timber being his main sources of income. The lead mine at Evenfield had been abandoned the previous year as the price of lead had plummeted, and a nearby coal shaft sunk 20 years before had been re-opened, though it had taken a month to repair and pump out.

In the lowland, Silas worked in woods and farmland, concerned with mallards, partridges and pheasant. In spring and summer his main tasks were rearing young birds – keeping game safe from predators such as crows, magpies, mink, stoats and rats – and repairing broken fences, gates and stiles. Hamish showed him his tasks carefully beforehand. It meant Silas had to ask lots of questions and answering them didn't suit Hamish at all, especially as it had begun to dawn on him to think about getting rid of Silas for he knew almost nothing about the job. His popularity with Sir Giles also threatened him and got him to thinking Sir Giles might even replace Hamish one day with this arrogant newcomer and so he knew something must be done to preserve his position.

But Silas was a survivor, and within 12 months he proved diligent: the foxes produced large families and they in turn were torn apart by hounds and shot at by aristocrats, and the more that were shot, the happier were both their Lordships, Lord Darlington of Raby and Sir Giles. The happiness of these two men was in fact the singular pursuit and employment of most of the hundreds of people who worked for them or paid rent to live on their land.

Sir Giles kept no hunting hounds because he couldn't afford them, unlike his neighbour, Lord Darlington of Raby. Lord Darlington's hunts were legendary throughout Northern England. As with all aristocracy, Silas felt, both lords had a certain arrogance about them, the stuff that went about creating an empire for Britain. Silas felt, as he'd felt with the Duke of Wellington, he could put his faith in them. They were educated men and if educated men couldn't act in the best faith for all the people of Britain, who could? It was either: educated men, God or the demon drink – death held few surprises any more for Silas Scroggins.

In the grouse season, beginning traditionally on 12th August and finishing around April, he helped Hamish arrange shoots and hire beaters from the environs and pickers-up to collect shot game. Partridges began in early September and pheasants later in

October and November and other work included burning heather and clearing ponds and ditches. Beeswax was cultivated from hives at the edge of the estate, some to be made into candles or stored in the kitchens and the residue sent to town markets in clay jars where it always fetched a good price. Propolis, the resin used by the worker bees, was scraped off in tiny amounts into a balm jar and stored to treat cuts, and Silas collected many of those from his work with the tools he borrowed from the forge. He worked flexible hours according to the season and jobs that needed completing, all working time being outdoors in all weathers, but he still preferred that to working in a mine. His wage was £25 a year and he was paid in cash that he also secretly buried – the poor man's bank.

Silas had been both wise and lucky to be taken on in the early part of that year because it turned out to be one of the wettest summers anybody could remember, which in turn produced one of the worst harvests anybody could remember.

There's nothing like hunger to drive a man to madness and desperate acts. The 'riots' started as small affairs in outlying districts when a few angry youths, weavers and miners made unemployed by industrialisation or returning from Wellington's armies, got drunk and threw stones at Boss' windows. But as winter wore on, more and more coffins were ordered and the poor starved in their thousands; prisons and workhouses bulged to bursting. When *Habeas Corpus,* a judicial writ requiring a detained person to be brought before a court so that the legality of their detention could be examined, was suspended the following year, the shipping of criminals to Australia was stepped up: thousands of men spending thousands of pounds and millions of man hours transporting hundreds of thousands of starving people and dumping them on an already-occupied Australia on the other side of the world.

In parts of rural England, the Highlands of Scotland and in Wales, entire villages and communities with poor roads, mountains, a lack of turnpikes, deep ports or other basic transport infrastructure were decimated by starvation and emaciated bodies began turning up in rivers or ditches or hanging from trees.

January saw the Prince Regent's coach attacked as it returned from Parliament and February saw the last major Luddite attack in

Loughborough. That brought the Blanketeers March: disaffected weavers who had woven by hand for centuries suddenly made unemployed by steam-powered looms. They didn't get far – most were arrested and hanged.

British society was under siege as the government struggled to cope, the Napoleonic War having crippled Europe. Either another great war or a technological miracle that would occupy, pay and feed the millions of unemployed was needed, or, more grimly, a killer epidemic. Canals were springing up all over the land but wages were so poor only the mainly Irish immigrants – already starved in Ireland by Protestant landowners – accepted the work. All this went pretty much over the heads of people like Silas and his neighbours – they lived in a self-sustaining, insular world with limited traffic of reliable information. The seasons came and went and though thousands of haggard and lean men and women were traipsing the countryside, he was fed and boarded and only watched from a neutral distance when the villagers of Stanhope confronted and routed the Bishop of Durham's private army come to arrest poachers and the mayhem that followed of beatings and secret hangings. But it is otherwise safe to say that Silas Scroggins found some peace and his life probably would have worked out very comfortably until he grew old, had it not been for the arrival of the railway.

1818

Thursday 9th July

Edward Pease and Jonathan Backhouse of Darlington and Richard Miles of Yarm were sitting next to each other at the back corner of the cramped, smoky and crowded room and at the front, the Stockton engineer Mr Christopher Tennant was overseeing the pinning of a large yellow scroll of paper, drawn from a round leather map holder, to a rigid board set up on an easel in front of the gathered crowd of about 40 entrepreneurs and potential investors.

The July day had dawned cool but by 10 o'clock it had begun to warm up, forcing many to remove their topcoats and hats. The windows of the Long Room on the first floor of the town hall had been opened but brought little breeze and, for most, liquid refreshments brought from the bar below were the only means of staying cool. Fresh lemonade proved almost as popular as the port, wines and sherry on offer, but as usual Pease stuck with his customary tipple of warm beer, his pewter tankard topped up by one of the serving boys. Backhouse and Miles opted for lemonade.

They had listened intently to the brief introductory speech by Colonel Sleigh, the Chairman, who explained they were about to discuss the goodwill gesture of Christopher Tennant, who had paid for a commission to look at the results of a canal survey conducted by a Mr George Leather.

Tennant had only just taken delivery of the parcel of prospectuses wrapped in brown paper and tied with string brought to him by one the printers, Mr Jennet of Christopher & Jenet. He'd hurriedly cut the string and been greeted with the scent of fresh paper and printers' ink as he read the recently proofed front page, set in Roman italic type to give it 'a sense of urgency', as Mr Jenet had advised. It read: 'Address' in large letters and underneath: 'To the gentlemen, clergy, merchants and other inhabitants of Stockton and the neighbourhood', and it was at this last word that he discreetly lifted his eyes to glance at Pease, Backhouse and Miles.

At that moment they were allies and potential partners. They needed a more efficient way to get their coal, lead and ores from west of Shildon in County Durham down to Stockton, in order to ship them to other coastal ports, and it was a fortunate coincidence that he himself owned and operated lime kilns near East Thickley Farm just west of Shildon: a canal connection, geographically adjoining the railroad, would be to their mutual interests. But what worried him at that precise moment were the costs that Mr Leather had quoted for the construction of the canal and the fact that it circumvented Darlington by some miles. This wouldn't please the three Darlington representatives, so he would have to tread carefully, ensuring profits and advantages outweighed losses and disadvantages. His older brother, Tom, came alongside and asked: 'Everything ready, Chris?'

'As ready as can be, Tom,' the younger replied.

'It's going to be fine!' the elder assured the younger, patting him on the back. 'Strike straight and true!' and took his seat in the front row.

Tom Tennant was a rope and sail manufacturer who made a tidy living supplying and outfitting the hundred of ships that frequented Stockton Harbour every year. The brothers knew that if a canal were to be built, no matter what the cargo was, it would encourage more ships into port and that meant increased profit for their family business, which was a far more lucrative enterprise than that of their father who'd only scraped a living as a milliner. Tom looked at his pocket watch – almost 11 o'clock.

Pease and Backhouse held copies of the prospectuses in their hands. Their eyes had already traced the sinuous black line on the paper that wended its way from Stockton on the right-hand side of the page due east via the villages and hamlets of Bishopton, Bradbury and Rushyford and then through the Dene Valley around Ferryhill where it stopped at the River Gaunless near Evenwood. Notably absent from the locality of the thick black line was their own town of Darlington which, according to the map, sat alone and isolated and seemed to be there merely to indicate the canal's crossing of the River Skerne's source, located at Bradbury. Backhouse's shoulders sagged and almost at the same time Pease let out a sigh. Miles tutted and shook his head almost imperceptibly.

'Art thou thinking what I'm thinking?' Backhouse asked quietly but doubtfully, looking at neither of the men.

'I may well be,' replied Pease from the corner of his mouth.

'I certainly am!' whispered Miles.

'Let's see what Mr Tennant has to say,' Pease said.

Christopher Tennant took a sheaf of folded papers from his pocket, notes covered in facts and figures and then coughed, not because his throat was blocked or dry but as a gesture to bring silence to the room.

'Gentlemen, I thank you kindly for your hospitality this fine summer day here in Stockton, and of course for the fine selection of wines.'

These compliments were well received with murmurs of approval from the seated men.

'I am aware that this is the fourth time in a little over 50 years that a canal survey has been explored and discussed. Indeed, I bow with grace to those illustrious surveyors who have come before, namely Messrs Whitworth, Brindley and Rennie. You see here before you...' he turned his body towards the large map '...and you should also be holding in your hands, a simple map showing the route the proposed canal would take. Wherever possible, Mr Leather has taken into account the calculations of the previous surveys and made alterations to those original figures owing to the gradual but inevitable rising of costs for materials and manpower offset against potential profits in goods carried. Rather than go into a convoluted explanation of his methods and conclusions, and given the oppressive heat of the day, I therefore suggest you ask questions and I will answer them as succinctly as possible. Please raise your hands and we will begin.'

Leather, the surveyor, waited expectantly. A hand was raised in the front row.

'Yes, Mr Jenet?' Tennant asked the printer and bookseller who had delivered his prospectuses only an hour before.

'How long is the canal?' came the blunt question.

'It would be 29 miles and four fathoms in total, sir. Previous surveys have been, including branch canals, around 30 miles in length.'

Another hand was raised in the middle of the group.

'How many locks?'

'Fifty,' Tennant replied with little restraint.

Although the figure was impressive, all men there knew that would be an expensive order. The assembled group again allowed a murmur to pass among them – fifty locks meant an enormous amount of work.

The same gentleman asked: 'To descend to sea level, what depth are we looking at?'

Tennant glanced at his notes.

'Four hundred and forty-two feet, sir.'

As the group digested this figure, the murmur grew louder – 442 feet was no small drop. Fifty locks divided by 442 feet meant each lock would have to accommodate a depth difference of about nine foot. Negotiation of fifty locks would add considerable time delays to transportation and shipping estimates, which meant an almost non-stop, end-to-end fleet of barges and boats would need to be maintained and run – again increasing costs by the owners to the carriers and operators. More horses, more men, more boats.

Tennant anticipated it.

'I understand this number appears excessively high. However, to compensate for this, Mr Leather has increased the width of the canal at the top in order to accommodate two-way traffic; that is to say two longboats could in theory be strapped side-by-side and go in one direction and two others connected in the same manner could go in the other direction, each longboat being approximately 12-feet wide. Furthermore, the draught would be increased to six feet, which means that boats capable of carrying up to 60 tons each could safely navigate the canal.'

All assembled knew that one good horse could pull around 2-3 tons of coal in a good cart on a good and level plane. To have one horse pull 60 tons on a boat was impossible but it could pull between ten to 12 tons and this meant their current profit on one ton would be multiplied ten to 12 times. A boat capable of carrying 60 tons could just as adequately navigate rivers and reasonably calm open seas so the coal wouldn't have to be unloaded from a seagoing vessel to a longboat, it would simply pass through the locks straight from the river – a saving in time and money.

As more questions were asked of Tennant, Pease's mind drifted as he thought back to the efforts of the previous surveys. This meeting today was, as far as he was concerned, the last time he'd devote any time or attention to the building of a canal and if this survey didn't deliver what he wanted, then he and his allies would shift their opinion permanently from a canal to a railroad.

The first canal scheme had been in 1767 headed by his father Joseph and surveyed by George Dixon of Cockfield, who had even built a short stretch of working canal on Cockfield Fell to show potential investors how the canal might function successfully. Coming to nothing, another survey had been conducted by Brindley and Whitworth in 1768. Some 33 miles in length, it would have travelled from the River Tees near Winston in the west of County Durham to Walworth, Piercebridge, Darlington, Croft and Yarm and would have cost in excess of £60,000. In 1796, Ralph Dodd of Stockton had put together an interesting but vague plan for a canal from the Wear at Durham via Darlington, Northallerton, Thirsk and Boroughbridge. It would have been a foot deeper than the previous survey, to accommodate larger loads, but pushed construction costs up to £74,000. The impending war against France soon scotched that idea. Dodd was something of a visionary though, and had predicted a big demand for coal from the fields in the west of the county that would rival competition up around the Tyne and the Wear area once war had passed, such was the confidence bordering on arrogance of British men with their mastery of the seas, mastery of arms and the assured impregnability of their island fortress.

In 1800, another idea from a Mr Atkinson of Richmond proposed a canal from Boroughbridge in Yorkshire up to Piercebridge west of Darlington on the River Tees into which coal producers could tap with smaller branches connected to their pits, but nothing came of that either. At the now-celebrated opening to the Mandale Cut at Stockton in 1810, the proposal had been to look into the 'practicability of a railway or canal', but because development of the railway was still in its infancy and canal-mania was grabbing all the attention, the former had been largely neglected in favour of the latter.

There were advantages and disadvantages by the score, but the one stumbling block on each occasion were the costs. A railway or tram-road would cost half as much if not two-thirds less than a canal. Rail repairs and upkeep could be as much as half that of canal repairs and upkeep. A tram-road would not be affected by drought or by frost, especially in the winter when coal was most in demand.

Then there was the infamous Rennie survey delivered in 1815, but commissioned three years previously, which, due to a shortage of men and materials owing to the ongoing war against France, Holland and Spain, pushed costs up to almost £100,000. Quite why it had taken Rennie so long to deliver the report was a source of great aggravation to Pease. He had begun to suspect that Rennie had delayed it as long as possible to appease his wealthier clients. If it hadn't been for the financial catastrophe suffered by most of County Durham in 1815 due to the collapse of the Mowbray Bank in Darlington (subsequently bought out and replaced by the Backhouse Bank) and combined regional losses of some £12,000,000 sterling produced by the domino-effects of the recession that had wrecked County Durham, the canal scheme might even have been finished and fully operating by then. But such is fate.

'So,' Pease said, turning to Backhouse and Miles, 'Shall it be one of thee or shall it be me?'

Miles reflected for a moment and then dug his hand into his trouser pocket and pulled out a shiny florin. Balancing it on his upturned thumb, he asked Backhouse: 'Heads or tails?'

'Tails' said Backhouse. 'But I don't approve of gambling.'

'Me neither,' said Miles and flicked the coin so it turned only half a dozen times before he clamped it onto the back of his left hand. He had no need to glance at it. Pease had raised his hand.

'Your question please?'

'How much will all this cost, Mr Tennant?'

Tennant glanced at his notes again.

'Two hundred and five thousand and two hundred and eighty-three pounds,' came the reply. 'With another ten per cent added for unexpected circumstances.'

'Good grief,' Pease said through barely parted lips, raising his eyebrows momentarily in reaction.

'Oh dear!' added Backhouse, equally quietly.

The largest and most audible murmur swelled as all men present absorbed the immense number, and it had no sooner left Tennant's lips than Pease knew they would have to switch swiftly to Plan B. Backhouse didn't raise his hand to speak because Tennant and many in the room were already looking in his and his neighbours' direction, so he asked: 'According to your map, Mr Tennant, your canal passes north of Darlington. How many miles at the narrowest point would the canal be from the northern part of the town of Darlington – say around Harrowgate?'

Leather studied his notes and realised he had no answer, so he looked at the larger diagram on display and, using his own approximate scale, replied: 'Eight miles. But the turnpike road is in very good condition so coal carts carrying a ton each could make the journey in a matter of one to perhaps two hours.'

Yes, Pease thought to himself, but the turnpike road is expensive, so if they took the public highway, which was of poorer quality and already overcrowded with traffic, it could be three to four hours.

No, it just didn't add up. The scheme was good for Stockton but bad for Darlington. As the Stockton scheme was already collecting subscriptions, Plan B was to demand yet another survey, this time from George Overton, for a railway. Plan B had already been discussed by the Darlington and Yarm contingent and put into action some weeks previously. In September, the results of Overton's survey being then known, another meeting would be held looking at a part-railway/part-canal scheme but if still dissatisfied, and Pease felt he already knew the fateful outcome, they would hold a further meeting which would be devoted wholly to the proposition of a railway instead of a canal, a decision based mostly on the cost but also on the economic rivalry that would soon become entrenched between the Stockton contingent and the Darlington/Yarm contingent.

After that, their only problem would be who to appoint to construct the tram road and who to operate the horse-drawn carriages that would pull the coal to Stockton. It was completely logical and totally understandable that a shorter line could be drawn between Bishop Auckland and Stockton via Norton or Bradbury *but* would miss Darlington by eight miles.

Events were now moving very swiftly indeed, almost as if the war against Napoleon had been a barrier holding back a thoroughbred. With Europe put to rights, at last the industrial revolution could race from the starting gate.

Much talk was being made of engineers and blacksmiths up around Tyneside and Wearside who were already designing and building engines powered by steam that did the work of 50 horses but such fancies were more hot air and rumours than reality. Everybody Pease knew was still thinking of horses, not fanciful machines, pulling wagons.

Friday 13th November

Once all thirty of the cheaper tallow candles had been lit by candle-lighters around the walls, they illuminated the better-quality beeswax candles in the holders on the Board's table, the men of the committee taking their places around it in one of the cold rooms of Darlington Town Hall. Despite the freshly stoked coal fire throwing out heat, it warmed only a small portion of the high-ceilinged space, but Edward Pease was happy it was his side of the room and not the side where sat John Grimshaw, William Chaytor and Bill Cudworth. He felt the warmth reach his legs and run up through the back of his chair.

The evening's meeting had a number of items on the agenda, but overriding all was the means of traction and the route itself: horses pulling chaldrons of coal on rails or tramlines, or barges on canals? The difficulty wasn't simply the form of traction: it was the fact that both the planned lines and the canal avoided Darlington instead of going through it, and of course the costs of each.

Darlington was his home. He couldn't have cared less whether they chose a canal or a railway so long as Darlington was linked to the wider world. Back in 1813, the Rennie Survey's estimates had been astronomically high – over £200,000 – and had avoided Darlington altogether. But their own technical fumbling was inevitably coming to a head and, one way or another, they had to take the plunge.

He reflected ruefully that though the most practical system of common responsibility available to humanity – democratic procedure – was, in its dispensation of change, one of the most fair and equal, it was also the most inefficient and time-consuming. So here they were, yet another meeting. The members took their places facing a seated crowd of about 50 local businessmen. Doctor John Ralph Fenwick was Chairman.

'Gentlemen, this meeting is now in order. The following committee is my self, of course, Mr Edward Pease, Mr Leonard Raisbeck, Mr John Grimshaw, Mr Thomas Richardson, Mr Richard Miles, Mr Jonathon Backhouse, Mr Thomas Meynell, Mr Francis Mewburn, Mr Jeremiah Cairns, Mr Benjamin Flounders, Mr William Cudworth and Colonel William Chaytor.'

Each of the men reacted as their names were announced, but none offered a salutation.

'As we all know,' Fenwick went on, 'things have moved on apace since August when Mr Cairns and Mr Miles shared a belief that, according to the Welsh engineer, George Overton, a railroad or tramway was infinitely preferable to a canal. However, iron roads are untested when compared to the hundreds of miles of newly constructed canals we see operating successfully across the country. But before we enter into that debate, let us settle the item carried over from our last meeting of 4th September: the name of our company. Shall we be the Darlington and Stockton Railway Company or the Stockton and Darlington Railway Company? Does anybody have anything to say or add to this proposal before we take a vote?'

'Mr Chairman,' said Backhouse the banker raising his voice, 'given that the majority of the impetus for this enterprise is coming from this town, would it not be more fitting that we be known as the Darlington and Stockton Railway Company?'

Edward Pease raised his hand.

'That's a valuable point, I feel, Mr Backhouse, but pride is not a Quaker virtue, so I wouldn't feel it necessary to agree with thee. Like a man and wife, one does not exist without the other, so, if I suggest the name Stockton and Darlington Railway Company, I do so simply because it rolls easier off my tongue than the other way round.'

There was a chuckle from the assembly. Fenwick struck while the mood was favourable.

'All those in favour raise your right hand and say 'Aye'.'

The vote was passed almost unanimously and the Stockton and Darlington Railway Company was officially brought into being. Doctor Fenwick continued.

'Next is to determine whether a canal, railway or tram road should be adopted. I urge we resolve this issue as soon as possible in preparation for the submittance of our Bill to Parliament in the spring of next year.'

Just then Pease caught the eye of Jonathon Backhouse and then both caught the eyes of John Grimshaw, the rope maker. Earlier that afternoon, the three had met in a backroom of The Queen's Head and discussed a plan of action. A great many people would be at that evening's meeting, all potential subscribers to the railway project *if* they could be convinced of the superiority of the railway. What the trio wanted to know about wasn't 'public duty'; what they wanted to know was how much it would cost them and how much they would earn, so Pease decided not to waste a valuable opportunity extolling public benefit but get straight to the heart of the matter: money.

Backhouse raised his hand to speak and then gave detailed figures of estimates he'd made concerning expenditure and revenue. William Stobart, Managing Partner of Etherley Colliery, said he couldn't afford to put coals into canal barges for less than 15 shillings and nine pence a chaldron – three shillings and three pence higher than in the report of the Canal Committee.

It was Pease's turn to speak.

'Gentlemen, there was discussion at our last meeting to support Christopher Tennant's part-canal, part-railroad scheme from the coalfields to Stockton through Rushyford. After much reflection, I'd like to propose we do away completely with this idea as nothing but further dissention can come of it. Let him go his way and let us go ours. If we're to select a team to go to Parliament to lobby MPs we must all be facing the same direction.'

There followed mumblings of support and dissatisfaction in equal measure. Francis Mewburn, a Darlington solicitor, raised his hand.

'Mr Pease has a valid point. We're to launch our appeal to Parliament on the basis of George Overton's survey in which he clearly states that a railroad is preferable to a canal simply because – and I am quoting: 'whereas a canal conveys goods upwards or downwards, a railway conveys them with more facility downwards than upwards'. As your legal representative, I want to go to London, gentlemen, and will give heart and soul to make it happen, but I *cannot* do it with one hand tied behind my back, for that is what I would be doing if you asked me to only half-believe in something.'

'Thank you, Mr Mewburn,' said Pease. 'Therefore, gentlemen, I'd like to draw your attention to what I call 'My Five Per Cent'.'

At that, he stood as a servant lifted his chair from under him and another brought out an easel with a classroom blackboard. Pease stepped to the front of the desk, took up a chalk and drew diagrams with equals symbols, question marks and numbers as he spoke.

'Based on current turnpike costs for transporting coal to Darlington, it stands at half a penny a ton per mile, that is to say 12 miles divided by halfpence a ton. Per day, this ton produces annual revenue of £2,000. We plan to charge three halfpence a ton per mile, which will produce £6,000 each year. That is approximately five per cent of our total capital of £100,000. Yes, our charge is higher, but labour and carriage are slashed. By rail, ten tons can be carried in one trip in about half a day. It would take a horse and cart by road ten trips that is five full days, to do the same. There is ample room for speculation, but I'm quite satisfied with *my* five per cent. I have only made this statement to show that we can make a sufficient rate of interest by this undertaking, and all the rest may be taken as profit over and above five per cent.'

He chalked a large number five on the board and went over it three times to make it stand out and then sat down again. It had been an impressive performance. The murmurs that followed were approving and encouraging. Doctor Fenwick stood.

'I propose we adopt the recommendation of this committee and apply immediately to Parliament for an Act to make a horse-drawn tramway on the plan and estimates – current costs are recorded at just over £113,000 – given by Mr Overton.'

He sat again as Francis Mewburn stood and pulled the two ends of each side of his fulsome grey beard down as if trying to twist them into one: an annoying gesture for which his wife scolded him frequently. He disliked too being the bearer of news that might dampen the enthusiasm of that meeting, but wisdom came with age – somebody had to ask the difficult questions and that generally fell to old men.

'Gentlemen, my family have supported this project since the very beginning back in 1767. I speak selfishly, perhaps, but I feel I speak for all, each of whom has his own reason to see this project work. Overton's survey does something dangerous: it suggests we go perilously close to Raby land. I am of the understanding that Lords Darlington and Eldon, both of whom own land on which Overton's plan is based, are strongly opposed, and unless we make certain changes their alliance will work against us.'

'That's not the only opposition,' said Thomas Richardson, a Quaker banker from London with his own bank in Darlington. 'Up around Tyneside I've heard we can expect stiff opposition from mine owners. The two main ports, gentlemen, have every reason to seek to protect their interests. And who can blame them? Wouldn't *we* if our interests were threatened?'

He sat to murmurs of agreement. Doctor Fenwick looked at his pocket watch, sighed and rang a bell. He was tired. The endless meetings and arguments over a period of years had become irritating. He rattled out very quickly, as if he'd said it many times before: 'Gentlemen, I'd like to propose a short break during which refreshments will be served.'

On cue, the doors opened and servants came in with trays of wine and port.

Though a man of iron determination and discipline, Pease knew there was nothing like a drink to make men convivial. Nonetheless, he was worried: there seemed to be too much disagreement. They really weren't ready for Parliament but as this was their first foray, he wondered if it might be better to go ahead and fail so they could learn lessons and ensure the second attempt didn't. Of course, on the other hand they might win. William Chaytor of Croft-on-Tees, a few miles south of Darlington, approached him.

'Fine speech, Edward. If your five per cent is safe, I suppose mine must be too, and everybody else's. I've experience of strategy and more often than not you should give the enemy the impression he doesn't pose a threat, lure him into a false sense of security as it were. Can't say what will happen in Parliament though.'

'We Quakers shun war, Captain, as we shun the manufacture of arms. But we welcome debate,' said Pease.

'Perhaps,' went on the wily Chaytor, only momentarily conceding Pease's observation before pressing home: 'I could print up a little pamphlet that suggests we're only a small, insignificant enterprise wanting to serve a few farmers in North Yorkshire and would never dream of being serious competition to the Grand Allies. It might take off the pressure in Parliament.'

Pease's back always stiffened around Chaytor. As an old soldier, Chaytor was indirectly involved in the ritual war machine of slaughter yet Pease also recognised the best teams were made of people who embraced a variety of skills.

'Very well, but give a proof copy to me first. I may wish to add some notes,' said Pease.

'Which way do you think the wind is blowing?' asked Chaytor.

'I think the Stockton parties favour the canal and we at this end the railway, but putting Stockton at the front of the new company name is a good spending of Spanish coin.'

'We shall win them over,' said Chaytor, relishing the slang term for flattery and adding a touch of his own, 'We must not be sold a Smithfield bargain by the Stockton-ites!'

'I have a preliminary list of subscribers here,' said Pease, pulling out a square of paper from his inside pocket and fumbling to hook his tiny reading spectacles onto his nose. 'I think we're in business. Top-quality port, by the way.'

'Madeiran, I believe,' smiled Chaytor, warming to the subject. 'A drop more?'

'No. I shall stick to me homebrewed beer tonight!'

1819

Thursday 22nd April

The post rider came galloping over the hill. In towns and villages, he was forbidden to no more than trot, but on the moors he could do anything and he was paid well, for there were few occasions riders liked more than to be able to open up their horses, and there were few moments horses enjoyed more than to please their riders. He knew the horse well too – six years old put Apple on the far side of skittish and near to sedate: a perfect age for a galloper.

Arriving from Darlington at Raby, he showed the letter marked 'Immediate', Lord Darlington's name transcribed in elegant script on the front. As Apple pawed restlessly at the gravel, the Butler said: 'His Lordship is out hunting. You might try Newton Hall – he was meeting the Hunt there. Do you know it?'

The rider nodded, pulled the reins sharply over, jabbed his calves into Apple's flanks and pushed her into a trot, cantering out of the castle. Once on the road, passing a train of coal-carrying mules and farmers' carts, he found a low stone wall, urged Apple to leap over and then opened her up, riding along five fields and jumping three fences, two walls and a ha-ha beck before rejoining another track and trotting to Newton Hall. There he called out to a gardener. The elderly man laboured up the path and went through a door. A younger man ran down to the gate.

'Lord Darlington – urgent mail from London!' the rider called out.

'Up the 'ill, 'bout two miles over the moor – that's all we know!' came the response.

The rider rode up the hill at a gentle incline to save Apple's tired legs and at the top found a good panorama in three directions: Tees Valley to the south; treeless purpled moors to the west; and wooded valleys and rolling hills pocked with woods, dry-stone walls and pines to the east.

The strangled note of a huntsman's horn floated to his ears like a half-imagined dying cry intertwined with the staccato echo of barking dogs. He willed the horse round, seeking a visual pinpoint, and saw between two clumps of woodland half a mile away a thin file of chestnut and grey Hunters speckled with the colours of red jackets and white breeches. Just then, Apple started – a flash of russet: the quarry. He'd have no need to chase the Hunt – the Hunt was coming to him.

He waited as the first of the hounds came spearing over the wall like one long white-and-brown-skinned animal, incessant barking making his horse dance as instinct told her to run though her rider held her firm. Then horses came galloping up the incline and the post rider spurred Apple so she was forced to clamber through the beck, splashing as she climbed out of the other side.

'Get out of the way, man – you'll ruin the scent!' a rider shouted.

'I have urgent mail, sir, for Lord Darlington – from London!'

The rider turned just before the beck and looked back at him.

'What? *Now?*'

The rider knew this man was Lord Darlington – he rode at the front and was angry without consequence: only a Lord could behave like that. Nevertheless the rider had a job to do.

'My instructions are to find the addressee n' deliver it to his hands forthwith,' he said.

Just then a dozen men and two women riding side-saddle arrived. As yapping hounds milled frantically around the horses' legs, Lord Darlington snatched the letter and tore it open, barking a harsh command at his nervous mare.

'Dammit! I don't have my reading spectacles. What does it say, Giles?'

The man addressed as Giles rode alongside and took the letter, his accent defining his status.

'It's from London. Your solicitors say: 'Most strongly urge you to come to London immediately as Quaker influence for the Railway

Bill is much stronger than anticipated. Fear all could be lost without your presence.''

'Bloody Quakers! Oh, forgive me, ladies!' apologised Lord Darlington.

Lord Darlington impatiently pushed his horse around in a circle a few times, swearing under his breath, trying to focus not only on the pursuit of the fox but his entire day.

'Your Lordship?' said another rider.

'Shut up – I'm thinking!'

The riders waited.

'Jones, finish the Hunt! I must go to London, but I should be back within the week. Ladies, gentlemen, forgive me, I must sacrifice my sport against those city heathens who would mar our pleasure.'

At that, he rode back alone the way they'd come. A fat rider pulled a short trumpet from his jacket, blew it and galloped after the fox, followed by the other hunters.

The post rider watched them disappear and then dismounted, his job done. He led Apple to the beck where she lowered her sweating neck and drank deeply.

Tuesday 6th July

With a soft summer dew on the ground, Silas found himself out at the fox coverts close to the boundary that separated Sir Giles's land from the Raby Estate, stalking through the woods with a single-barrelled flintlock resting over one arm and a pick-axe in the other, ready to dig. The twigs brought down by a recent storm crackled underfoot and disturbed a stag that bounded away on legs like springs. The firearm made him feel safer – disturbances had broken out recently in Stanhope between lead miners and bailiffs and gamekeepers. Local families were suddenly divided over the right to hunt, stretching loyalties to breaking point. For many, rabbit was considered common quarry and was often the only source of protein.

Foxes had no natural predators to diminish their numbers other than men, either men who hunted or farmers who trapped. Silas's job was to encourage breeding. He did this by digging underground dens, but any wild animal would only follow its instinct, so he did his best to encourage them by increasing the size of tunnels, cleaning out dead branches and leaves or rebuilding them. True, they were wild, the foxes, but they were smart too and played games with hunters and led horses a merry dance.

From a distance he heard hooves and through the forest spied his master on a grey Hunter.

'Mornin', sir!' he called out.

'Are there plenty of the beggars about? I've friends coming up from London, want to give them a good show on Sunday,' Sir Giles demanded.

'No worries, sir. Saw a lovely stag earlier too, eleven hands by my reckonin', sir.'

'Excellent! Well, let's hope those damned railway men don't get in the way or we'll all be out of a job!' said Sir Giles.

Silas wanted to ask why that might be so, but if Sir Giles didn't want to waste his time explaining things to his staff, Sir Giles didn't. Instead, he grunted, pulled his horse's head away and disappeared into the woods, and it wasn't until Silas returned and enquired that he learned more from Heathcote.

'Developers want to build a length of iron track over land where t'foxes live,' said Heathcote. 'His Lordship's fightin' 'em in Parliament with Lords Raby n' Eldon an' 'avin' visitors from London.'

'So what's that to me?' asked Silas.

'Backhouse is putting money into the railway scheme. Lord Darlington has decided to try to break his bank,' counselled Heathcote. 'So he's asked all tenants – that's us - to pay their rents with notes issued by the Backhouse Bank with the intention of presenting one large sum to the bank which the bank by law must exchange for gold or be broken, hence the expression. Sir Giles wishes to make a similar gesture of support.'

Silas had often thought about the £10 he'd buried near the Skerne in Darlington and wondered how he might find the time to check up on it. His assistant gamekeeper's wages of £25 a year had doubled over his tenure and he now had £50 stashed in a clay pot under a loose clay tile under a cupboard near his bed. There were few distractions in the countryside for bachelors with steady incomes. He had enough food as the castle kitchens provided everything. Sewing repairs were done by one of the maids who'd taken a shine to Silas, though he remained largely indifferent to women. Prostitutes suited his needs rather than wives, an occasional expense being a discreet brothel in Barnard Castle; his only other major expenses were clothes and boots, but as he was usually outdoors in all weathers it became normal to wear things until they fell apart. His accommodation was included in the job and he cobbled his own work boots. Once he went to Barnard Castle and ordered some smart tan riding boots for £2 and 10 shillings but couldn't bring himself to wear them publicly, partly because they were too good to ruin but mostly because it could upset his status on the estate.

'Given your military experience,' said Heathcote, 'Sir Giles wishes you and I to accompany he and Lord Darlington tomorrow to help guard the banknotes.'

'Me?' asked Silas.

'Would you refuse your Master?' said Heathcote sarcastically, for Heathcote was no gull.

'*Me?*' repeated Silas with greater insistence and snorting a laugh once, no hint of irony in the hint of irony.

Wednesday 7th July

In the event, the attempt to break the bank was a failure. Lord Darlington was carried in style with the strongbox on the opposite seat in his carriage holding £15,000 in collected banknotes and £800 added by his friend Sir Giles Crockatt. Silas, in his arms a Brown Bess the likes of which he hadn't held since Waterloo, travelled up top with Heathcote the driver. They wended their way over the course of the day to Darlington's most prominent street, High Row, where they pulled up outside the bank. As Lord Darlington strolled in confidently, with Heathcote and Silas carrying the strongbox inside, Silas then exited again and waited by the coach wondering how he might be able to get away for half an hour to check on his buried £10. Just then he espied Richard Stott, landlord of The King's Head where Silas had spent the winter of 1816. Silas told him about his success at Crockatt Hall.

'So what brings you to town?' Stott asked gruffly.

'Come to break the Back'ouse Bank,' Silas gloated.

'You'll have a job,' said Stott. 'Backhouse was down to London n' back wi' a quarter ton of gold two days gone – it's the talk o' the town!'

Silas didn't quite know what that meant but was sure Sir Giles and Lord Darlington would have anticipated all likelihoods, but after only minutes Lord Darlington came storming out of the bank and straight into the coach, slamming the door, banging his cane on the roof and shouting: 'Home!'

Heathcote appeared moments later with the still-laden strongbox half in his hands and the other half dragging on the ground and with Silas's help they loaded it into the carriage and climbed onto the driver's seat.

'Backhouse skidaddled off to London and returned with enough gold to cover demand,' said Heathcote quietly. 'The journey's been completely wasted – and we're in for it now!'

Silas said: 'Those Quakers have really got that town sewn up, haven't they?'

'You could say the same about Sir Giles and all the other gentry,' Heathcote whispered with a rare flash of wisdom. 'It'll put Sir Giles in a bad mood, that's for sure,'

And it certainly did. He was foul-tempered for weeks, especially with the servants – he placed Stephenson in the same social class as them, despite their being forced to help their Master. It was frustrating for Silas too: he'd been unable to verify his buried £10 was safe.

Friday 23rd July

'How *did* I end up here?'

The armed soldier in his spotless uniform standing nearby did not respond to the rhetorical question.

Jonathon Backhouse eyed the reception room: the mirror gilded with stylised laurels and lions on a wall thick with plush damask, beneath his feet carpets as soft as a tightly mown summer lawn. As a Quaker, he'd spent much of his life walking on wooden or tiled floors of banks, offices and his own home. Being married to one of Pease's daughters, he didn't have much choice – every time his father-in-law visited, servants spent a whole day making the house as austere as possible.

He looked at the top hat in his hand and realised it was trembling because his own hand was trembling. Quaker religion decreed hats were never to be worn when praying but at all other times, even in the presence of kings, for fashion was a waste of spiritual effort. But did that decree also cover Lord Liverpool, Prime Minister of Great Britain and the Dominions?

Backhouse, with burgeoning bank branches in Sunderland, Stockton-on-Tees, Durham and Darlington, had come to the Old Palace Parliament in London by stagecoach, over three days of turnpikes, with other members of the company to persuade MPs to support the Railway Bill. The main sticking point was the aristocratic alliance of Lords Darlington and Eldon, who refused to countenance selling land to a project that may very well undermine their own high-profit margins by being in competition with their interests.

They had been defeated in 1818 and an amendment had been made to the bill after George Overton had again surveyed the planned horse-drawn line. Objections had been raised by Lords Darlington and Eldon and Backhouse had come up with adequate compensation proposals to keep both Lords happy, but the Lords had stubbornly objected. Much progress had been made moving into 1819, with a second attempt to get the bill through. They wanted to lodge it before Parliament no later than the end of September of that year, but without permission from these two Lords it was going to prove impossible. Backhouse felt sure both men could be bought, as all men had a price, so the maxim went, but how to make the offer without it looking or sounding as if an offer was being made?

So Backhouse had gone out on a limb. Telling no one for sheer terror of what they would say, he approached the Prime Minister's Private Secretary, Mr Brooksbank, with a preposterous conceit that could only command incredulity and contempt. The tactic was high risk – catch the PM on a bad day or don't conduct oneself with brevity and the whole trip could be a public-relations disaster. Correct protocol usually dictated that one would present a petition or a case to a local, in Backhouse's case, Durham MP Sir John 'Radical Jack' Lambton. The MP would then draw the petition to attention in Parliament for debate. But Lambton was widely known as an arrogant and foul-tempered man who made more enemies than friends and the last thing the railway venture needed was more enemies.

Lord Darlington's attempt to break Backhouse's bank two weeks before had failed because Backhouse hadn't waited for the inevitable – he had not even hesitated: when the King's Head spy brought him the news, he took his finest horse, galloped to Scotch Corner and paid top weight to rent fine racers from various coaching houses to London and then rented an armoured coach in London to transport the gold to Darlington, as well as two armed guards. In London, he'd borrowed aforesaid gold worth £32,000 which wasn't only to cover attempts to break the bank but also to deal with usual business and act as insurance against further attempts to break him of which he was as yet unaware. He had driven his armed coach non-stop back to Darlington eight days after leaving it, the last few miles with only three wheels owing to an accident and only the weight of the gold pushed to one side of the carriage keeping it level to drag it over the roads to High Row. For this bold adventure, he'd single-handedly saved the family fortune, business had trebled and he'd become something of a local legend for his exploit and so now he'd convinced himself he was addicted to spontaneity. Spontaneity seemed to cut through the staleness of fear like a hot knife through butter. Despite the demigod-like status heaped upon the Prime Minister by most, Backhouse was a Quaker and trained to penetrate the superficial finery meant to puff up the status of a PM so he calmed his nerves by telling himself Lord Liverpool was, after all, just a man.

Just then a door opened and Mr Brooksbank stood stiffly and said: 'Mr Backhouse?'

Backhouse took a few steps and suddenly the soldier stepped forward and looked him directly in the eye, laid his rifle against the wall and said: 'Arms out from the body now, please sir, there's a good gentleman.' The soldier carefully padded his hands against Backhouse's pockets to check for concealed weapons. Satisfied, the soldier took up his rifle and stood to attention, and Backhouse finally followed Mr Brooksbank into a room of red carpet where dark oil paintings of well-dressed aristocrats looked down from the walls. In one corner a magnificent grandfather clock ticked, and along one wall a coal fire with a mantel as high as a man heated the room.

Robert Banks Jenkinson, second Earl of Liverpool, had been Prime Minister since 1812 and he was a British legend, in part for his repressive measures to maintain order in a lawless society and in others for steering the country through the Napoleonic Wars, the Corn Laws, the Six Acts and the political damage of the Peterloo Massacre of 1819.

'Mister Jonathon Backhouse, sir,' announced Brooksbank. His role fulfilled, he retired.

The Prime Minister finished writing and glanced up, his brow lined with wrinkles.

'Some fool is talking of abolishing the slave trade!' complained the Prime Minister, stabbing his finger on the sheet in front of him. 'Your Mr Pease is forever lobbying against slavery. Fair driven me to distraction he has. I must put 'em right, Mr Backhouse. I must put 'em right. Now, you have exactly two minutes to tell me what on earth possessed you to have the impertinence to presume I would see you.'

Backhouse was suddenly aware he was trembling. His voice caught in his throat. It was as if he had suddenly woken from a dream. Liverpool misread the hesitation and said: 'Forgive the armed presence at the door – the Cato Street Conspirators of last year's little escapade. My advisors insist I have armed protection. They also tell me you have returned to plague us with yet another attempt to get this Railway Bill through Parliament. Darlington isn't known for its coal, it's known for its cotton, and now you want to change direction and construct a rail-way,' he made a point of dissecting the word into separate sounds in an attempt to weaken its importance' from where?'

'A t-town c-called Sh-Shildon through Darlington to a port called Stockton in the north of England, sir,' said Backhouse calmly. 'And I am a banker, sir, not a cotton man, but cotton puts clean clothes on working peoples' backs and stops typhus.'

'Yes, yes,' said Liverpool impatiently, glancing at notes on another sheet. 'And you're here in London to petition the Members into accepting horse-drawns and mechanical locomotives, is that not so?'

'It is,' said Backhouse. 'We've done beyond what has been demanded and yet still the Alliance between Eldon and Darlington remains strong. Unless that Alliance can be ... compromised, I'm afraid we shall fail again.'

'Hmm, nice choice of words,' said Lord Liverpool, smiling neutrally. 'His new Majesty George IV is all in favour of progress of course but our country is largely owned by wealthy landowners who don't take kindly to being forced to sell up or have hordes of Irishmen digging up their land. Much English blood was spent on the rebellious Irish you want to employ by the thousand. However, my advisors tell me that in theory your plan holds enormous potential. What makes so many cautious ... *is you!*'

'M-m-me, sir?'

'You and your damned Quakers! You seem to be harmless but you're not a step removed from the Jews with your secret rituals.

Millionaires, half of you, and you dress like farmhands. What's it all about? What's the point in making so much money and yet sitting on it like misers?'

Backhouse swallowed hard but didn't take the bait. He'd stomached the prejudice all his life. Besides, he was beginning to connect with the man underneath all the glitter and pomp of his title and position – the country was in a mess and Liverpool would clutch at any straw to get it out of a mess.

'Men need work, sir. As long as men have work then they are not sitting around idle, fomenting revolutions, starting wars or stealing.'

'Too honest for your own good and there's the rub!' snorted Liverpool. 'If – and I promise nothing, Backhouse – if I could do anything, what would you have me do?'

'Find some way to break this ... resistance?'

'I'm not in favour of breaking things, Mr Backhouse – I leave that to the Luddites. Eldon is one of the most powerful men in the land and a friend of mine.'

'Yes, I understand. But may I ask, where does your coal come from?' enquired Backhouse, indicating the fire glowing in the grate and determined to move on to familiar ground. It was his Plan B. He'd rehearsed his speech.

'I've no idea, the North? Perhaps Wales?' the PM guessed.

'Perhaps Wales? Perhaps Yorkshire? Perhaps the Midlands? Certainly, all places distant from London. If this railway goes ahead, the British people will be able to burn 100,000 fires for 10,000 years. There'll be such an abundance that the price will drop and where there's heat and warmth, there's security and growth, and where there's growth, there's enterprise and where there's enterprise, commerce. Your war cost a lot, but such growth will pull Britain out of the red within a decade. As a banker and something of an economist, I promise you that.'

'*My* war?' growled Liverpool, real menace in his voice, 'We were on the same side you know?'

Backhouse inhaled silently and defended his principles.

'My religion is opposed to war. Should we be forced to fight, we would passively resist, sir.'

'What gall!' snorted Liverpool with derision, but Backhouse's impressive speech had silenced Liverpool for a second and Backhouse was relieved the hours he'd spent writing it weren't in vain because he'd known his nerves would never have held nor his diplomacy be deft enough to persuade this wily old fox. Just then there was a tap at the door.

'The Lord Chancellor wishes an audience, sir,' announced Mr Brooksbank in a monotone.

'Speak of the Devil,' said Liverpool dryly, but his mind moved sharply.

'Backhouse - take the ottoman over there in the corner, away from the door, and sit. Say not a word, move not a muscle – if you're seen, acknowledge it without hesitation.'

Backhouse pushed the ottoman on its castors between two bookshelves, in a position that would be a visitor's blind spot, adjusted it and then bade Backhouse sit, which he did. Liverpool re-sat himself behind his desk and shouted for the Lord Chancellor to be shown in. The door opened and stout Lord Eldon entered looking flustered. He strode over to the Prime Minister without looking left or right.

'John, what brings you here in such a state?' the PM asked his friend.

'I've just been caught by the bally chaplain of the Lords chapel is what!' said Eldon exasperatedly. 'Everywhere I go it's 'railway this' and 'railway that'. I'm under pressure, especially from Henry, not to relent, but I don't see how I can't after what's just happened!'

'What has just happened, John?'

Lord Eldon leaned forward further as if afraid of being overheard.

'I'd some notes on the railway subject stuck between the prayer book pages in church and was glancing at 'em instead of reciting me scripture. I was so intent, I didn't see him looking. He waited till the service finished then told me he was outraged because I was regarded as the country's mainstay for the Protestant religion!'

'And what did you say?'

'I said: 'Damn it, you would be outraged too if you were worked to death as I am!''

'How long have we known each other?' Liverpool asked, smiling and leaning back in his chair.

'Why?' Eldon asked.

'When you eloped with Bessie in '72 to Scotland to marry her against her father's wishes, one might say you were no respecter of tradition, right?'

'What's your point?' asked Eldon impatiently, knowing his friend too well and knowing too that his oblique approach to the conversation had some ulterior motive.

'Where's your sense of adventure?' asked Liverpool.

'You think I should crack?'

'I think you should remind the world that you're still full of surprises. Anyway, I'm sure the backers of the railway could compensate you handsomely.'

Lord Eldon looked down at the carpet then stood up straight.

'This conversation never happened, George.'

'What conversation is that, John?'

The Chancellor left without looking up. Liverpool said: 'Now go about your business, Mr Quaker, and if you ever have such impertinence again, I'll have you hung from Big Ben!'

Backhouse hastened a retreat.

Saturday 21st September

At the age of seven, Lewis Lovatt wasn't yet of an age to be of much use to his family monetarily, but he at least dressed more like a boy: he had progressed from wearing a girlish frock to his first pair of breeches, handed down from his Dad. He put them on, fastened them around his bony knees and slipped on the wooden clogs with the leather uppers George had painstakingly cobbled on his last. Lewis had spent hours clattering on the cobbles in the street. He savoured what he presumed was an adult pleasure: scraping his new footwear on the boot-scraper set in a flagstone outside the door, even though the clogs were often mud-free. He was tall for his age too, and could easily have passed for nine.

It was just after he turned seven that his father introduced him to fire-making, his preferred method being the old-fashioned way: a willow-wood spindle and fireboard. George deftly rubbed the spindle vertically between his two palms, having first rubbed the tip of it over his face – 'Skin grease helps to lubricate the tip' he told his wide-eyed son – and, with the fireboard pinioned to the earth by George's feet, he spun the spindle time and again until the first wisp of smoke rose from the notch. Soon Lewis could espy a tiny orange ember. George transferred this tiny ember to the dry down he often found in birds' nests and took it to the stove where he gently blew on it and ignited it. George encouraged Lewis from that day to learn to make fire.

Still too young for the pit, Lewis managed to obtain a few simple jobs: Old Widow Harker kept a herd of a dozen dairy cows on common grazing land. Lewis kept them off the roads and every evening herded them into a shed and helped milk them. The creamy liquid was collected in wooden pails, to be sold by the quart or to make cheese at the chandlers alongside The Cleveland Bay.

He learnt too how to spud thistles, hoe turnips and, in October, pick potatoes. It paid him a few shillings he was able to give to his mother and she'd give him a penny back, though there was little to spend it on. With his father's wages of 20 shillings a week it meant they didn't starve, but almost all George made was spent back in the same shop and on the same goods owned by Sir Giles Crockatt: Crockatt owned everything.

George's diligence paid off on the Lovatt garden. The fine tilth had to be reworked every spring as strong winds would blow away the surface soil, but it regularly produced a healthy crop of leeks, shallots, parsnips, carrots, potatoes and onions and a little herb bed provided parsley, dill and chervil. The Lovatt house was always full of the scents of wild flowers or of lavender, freshly baked bread or apples.

The value of lead had fallen after Waterloo and lead mines closed in rapid succession, but as one industry shrank, another grew: coal. Sir Giles Crockatt had had an old mineshaft, abandoned some years before, pumped out after buying a third-hand Boulton and Watt pump from Killingworth.

For George Lovatt, lead mining had been a comparative heaven. Entrance to the mine meant walking upright through a semi-circular gate cut to the contours of the tunnel mouth and then a gentle descent by foot so fresh air was always close; either that or they panned in the streams and the open air. But the coal mine was different: the winding engine supported the weight of a six-man platform and it took them five full minutes of vertical descent to reach the bottom, the previous shift waiting their turn to be taken up to the cool fresh air on the surface where, even in the bitter cold of midwinter, they drank it in. Because the temperatures were hotter underground, George was often stripped to his underclothes, constantly sweating and caked in a layer of black dust. With only a small hammer and pick, he worked hard to maintain the size of the slabs, as larger ones produced most profit.

He had to pay a few pennies to the children of other miners to help cart his diggings on their sledges from where it was excavated to the main shaft where it was transported to the surface. Most of his mates had their wives and children to help them, but not George, not yet, but the day was coming when he knew he'd have to get his son down to help him.

'When will I go down the pit, Dad?' Lewis asked, knowing that going down with his father was a big step up from being a child to being a young working man, a promotion that all the boys in the village and some of the girls, revelled in.

At home with his son, George pre-prepared powder charges with black gunpowder grains given by workmate and neighbour Will Carr, who also worked as the official 'knocker-upper' who tapped on miners' windows to signal shift changes and starts for those who could not afford clocks or time-pieces. These powder charges would be popped into a cut length of straw, packed into crevices and ignited to dislodge the slabs. But accidents were common: as well as risking being crushed by coal tubs and rock falls or falling down shafts in the dark, there was deadly gas.

What definitively decided Lewis's destiny occurred one afternoon in early May: George was involved in an accident – a rock fall crushed Alf Mitchell and injured James Crosby, though George escaped with a few bruises. Many months later George said that fateful day was the day his troubles started, caused by a rock fall that in turn was caused by lack of investment in pit props, and that event was to have a curious domino effect on everything that happened after.

The small village felt a loss of life keenly. Almost the whole population turned out for funerals, lining the route between the cottages and the tiny graveyard encircling the chapel. The Reverend Prattman from Etherley conducted, when not attending his mining interests in Butterknowle and Copley. The local cemetery was potted with simple graves and wooden headstones. At Alf Mitchell's funeral, Tom Dawson, James Crosby with his arm in a sling, and Will Carr and his younger brother, John, shook hands with George. John operated the bellows that pumped fresh air into the tunnels underground.

'Your Da saved Mr Crosby's life,' his mother said to Lewis as they walked home.

'But not Alf's,' chipped in his Dad. 'It needn't've 'appened if Hackett had installed props – the price of a man's life measured 'gainst the couple of bob it'd've cost to fit out some decent timbers.'

'But what was it like?' Lewis asked.

In response, George stepped on a lump of dried earth on the road, crushing it under his boots.

'That's what it was like,' he said.

Lewis looked down at the tiny circle of flattened soil.

'Nobody cares about us – nobody,' George said to his son, 'Not the masters and not even God. We've only got each other down there – Alf had only me and a couple of others underground who care.' He wanted to add: 'That could have been me' or 'That could be me tomorrow, the day after or next week', and nod at the crushed soil, but he didn't want to scare the boy, so he tousled his hair and said no more as they walked home.

1820

Wednesday 15th March

'Look for yersel',' said Michael Longridge, indicating a length of track that stretched into the distance. 'Two miles to Choppington Pit.'

George Stephenson, body-length out on the grass, rested his left cheek on the cold iron and closed his right and left eye alternately, blinking at the rail.

'It's curved!' he noted.

'Of course it's curved. Curved is logical!' said Longridge, bending forward, resting his hands on his knees. 'Six months. You do the same amount of work on a cast-iron track under the same conditions an' tell us 'ow many 'old-ups?'

Longridge walked with his friend George Stephenson to the brick-built Bedlington Iron Works on the banks of the River Blyth, north of Newcastle. He was the owner and master of all he surveyed and yet, like Stephenson, if you passed him in the street you would hardly know it. He and George were men of little pretence and, if not yet self-made men, certainly in the process of being made. There was an unwritten understanding between them – neither could change who they were and from what lowly stock they'd originated just as they couldn't change their accents – they would never rub shoulders with men educated at Oxford, Cambridge or Eton. They never had their fathers' connections or money – they made their own, based on experience and skill, and were both in the right place at the right time and each in the right line of work. One of the greatest skills for a man in this world is to spot a good thing when he sees it – these men had that skill and if both played their cards right over the coming years and the world embraced railway transport, the market would explode and all those in that profession could become very busy and very rich.

Set back from the river, tall brick chimneys and kilns like tapering wishbones and stationary engines threw out great clouds of steam to be swept into the atmosphere by the breeze. Iron ore was mined along the riverbanks down specially built shafts and, with a plentiful supply of cheap coal coming from a colliery owned by Lord Barrington at Choppington every day, huge furnaces had been built and labour-intensive machinery installed to manufacture more iron. First the coal had to be smelted into coke, so part of the factory had been turned over to that process: a ten-acre site developed around tramway links to the distant pit and then the exit for the smelted coke and its immediate shipping to the furnaces of the nearby foundry. The Port of Blyth was just downriver, with access to the open sea and trade routes.

'What's the secret?' Stephenson asked.

'Ah,' Longridge joshed, reducing his voice to a whisper, 'That's confidential.'

'Gan on, man, I'll not tell nobody,' Stephenson joked.

'Well then: low melting point, good fluidity, resistant to deformation an' wear by oxidisation, an' needs about nine 'undred degrees,' said Longridge as they walked towards the gates of a workshop. 'It's the coke that does it – gets the temperatures up. Come inside!'

The intense heat hit them as they entered. About 20 men and boys, stripped to their waists, in boots, gauntlets of leather and heavy aprons, special metal gauze masks on their faces, wielded huge iron hooks and bars like giant claw-like extensions of their arms, hooked via an ingenious machinery of levers and chains. Loose streams of molten iron dripped bright orange magma into cold moulds as efficiently as a pastry cook pouring chocolate. The small army worked together: two rails at a time taken away to cool, two more loaded into place and a small team of smiths side by side beating and shaping on dozens of anvils as well as steam-powered presses, while up near the furnaces human-powered and steam-powered bellows flooded the fires with oxygen-rich air and pushed the temperatures to frightening heights so every sort of mineral the earth could spit out could be melted and re-shaped.

'The rollers turn concentrically,' Longridge shouted through cupped hands into George's ear. 'It needs dexterity to extract the material at the correct time, hence the labour costs, but it's the only way! Up the production side so big orders are feasible. My agent, Birkinshaw – it was his idea. We took out a patent!'

After a few minutes, they stepped into the fresh air, relieved to be free of the punishing heat, both men wiping brows with handkerchiefs as they walked to the river's edge where the redundant mill wheel idled uselessly.

'George, to keep up this kind o' scale I need big orders,' said Longridge. 'Birkinshaw's out on the road as I speak, up n' down the country with a cart, but samples like these don't fit into a carpetbag.'

'I wish we could see the likes of the *Savannah* on the Tyne, Michael,' Stephenson sighed wistfully in reply, looking at the river. Longridge knew he was referring to the steamship that had crossed the Atlantic from Savannah in South Georgia in America to Liverpool the previous year. Though part of its trip had been under sail, when winds were mild, steam-power had taken over. Steam power was suddenly all the rage as the industrial world woke to its possibilities.

Longridge had a gem of a piece of news to pass on. When he'd learnt of it, he'd tried to imagine going for the contract himself but he knew he couldn't. It was a contract for the creation of a railway link between two towns in south Durham. What appealed to him was the idea of casting thousands upon thousands of rails, but the contract was also for the building of the engines that used the rails. He knew nothing about that but his mate George Stephenson did.

'I've 'eard there's a feller down Darl'ton way putting together a company to build an iron road to link towns, not just pits and ports, but whole towns. Just think – 30 mile o' track! That's what I call a good order.'

'Where'd you get this information?' asked George.

'Birkinshaw 'as big ears,' said Longridge plainly, paradoxically tapping the side of his nose. 'Why not go n' 'ave a word? I think the' speak English down Darl'ton way!'

Saturday 26ᵗʰ August

Catherine Lovatt first heard of Mr Leakey while picking up the gossip at a cricket match a fortnight before. The mine was always slack in the summer months and so George and other men – with the help of grazing goats – had turned flat the village green that gave its name to their village into a cricket pitch. A game was in full swing with George having a solid innings, marking 50 not out. Lewis, sitting under the huge oak tree at one end of the green, its ancient branches offering some shade, watched occasionally, but was often distracted by his own thoughts, such as how strange it was that in this world blessed with golden sunlight, the same men playing cricket burrowed like rodents in the black tunnels underground.

'Who's the old man over there?' Catherine asked Mary Crosby.

'Schoolteacher,' said Mrs Crosby, looking up from her knitting. 'Just opened up a classroom.'

''Tis a good thing an education, I've heard,' said Catherine.

'No use for the likes of us,' tutted Mrs Crosby.

Conversation drifted to other things but Catherine didn't forget. Her husband was finally caught for 72 from a ball bowled by Will Carr's brother, John. George disputed the delivery. John argued and the umpire and other miners gathered round, taking sides. Finally, George accepted the decision and was taken into the inn, so Catherine took Lewis's hand and they left the green. An old man with almost no hair, a wrinkled face and kindly eyes, Mr Harold Peregrine Leakey, chuckled as he read the newspaper and looked up at her from his chair in his tiny front garden set back from the green by a dirt track.

'I'm reading about His Majesty's coronation last month. Lady Caroline was turned away from the ceremony – imagine the humiliation for the poor woman!'

Catherine stared, having no idea what he was talking about. He took off his spectacles.

'Are you the schoolteacher?' asked Catherine.

'I am. Harold Leakey; retired,' he replied.

'Can you teach my son to read n' write?'

'How old is he?' Leakey asked, looking at Lewis.

'Eight,' she replied. 'But he looks much older, as you can see.'

The old man glanced at Lewis only momentarily.

'An advantage for employment. It's thruppence a week. That entitles him to two visits. I teach in the evenings from teatime to sunset in the summer and Saturday mornings and afternoons in the winter. He doesn't need anything – I've slates, chalks and a few books. Will he want Latin and Greek?'

'I just want him to know 'ow to read an' write. When can 'e start?'

'Monday after next?' suggested Leakey, 'If your husband is in agreement.'

'He will be,' replied Catherine decisively.

At supper that night, she spoke about her idea with George who was in good form, having basked in cricket glory and sunshine and with a good dinner in his belly.

'Three pence a week?' said George, pausing from peeling his apple for afters.

'He cannat do much else at the moment. He could learn how to read n' write,' said Catherine.

'What'll 'e do wi' readin' n' writin'?' George asked.

'Boys that can read an' write get took on as apprentices,' said his wife. 'They eat well an' can afford nice clothes an' doctors when they're sick.'

'But in a year or two he'll be old enough to go down the pit,' George objected.

'He's not goin' down the pit,' Catherine said, her tone turning cold.

'I shall remind you 'oo's the man in this 'ouse, woman,' said George.

'Don't go givin' me that flannel!' scolded Catherine. 'If God wills we shall 'ave no more bairns, we must invest all our 'opes into the one we 'ave.'

George remained doubtful, being uneducated himself, but they could afford three pence a week. He turned to his son.

'What do you think about that, son?'

'Can I read you n' Mam stories?' Lewis asked.

'Aye, I suppose so. But listen, thruppence is a lot fer Mam an' me, so don't go wastin' it on daydreamin'.'

Young Lewis started school as the sole pupil in a tiny room with four worm-eaten pine desks with inkwells set in the top left corner of each. His own seat was a hard bench. Mr Leakey's desk was inches away, behind it a blackboard set onto the dark wood wall. A small window was the only source of daylight – six candles and an oil-lamp burnt almost non-stop.

'Where most of your thruppence goes!' Leakey noted sardonically.

On the walls were a large map of the world and a smaller map of Great Britain.

Britain's shape fascinated Lewis: he had never seen it before.

'It looks like a begging dog,' he noted.

When Leakey indicated the world map, Lewis saw for the first time its shape and learnt it was round like a big ball floating in the heavens.

'But 'ow does it stay up, sir?' he asked. 'And 'ow does the moon stay in its place?'

'It moves round our planet on a fixed pattern called an orbit, just like the planet we live on moves around the sun in an orbit that lasts a whole year.'

To help Lewis understand better, Leakey drew diagrams on the board.

'But I see the sun rise in the East every mornin' n' then move across the sky n' fall down beyond the 'orizon,' Lewis said.

'No, it's not the sun that's moving – it's us.'

The next day, as he herded the cows, Lewis studied the sun's passage across the sky until sunset and yet couldn't see how the Earth was moving but Leakey had said it was so. He also learned later that week that a Sir Isaac Newton in London had discovered something called gravity that glued them all to the Earth so they didn't fall off. When people dropped something on the ground, it didn't just fall because it was heavy; it fell because it was attracted by a magnetic force. Lewis practised letting an apple fall from his hand to try and understand better. 'That's India,' said Leakey, moving his finger across the map at another lesson, 'part of His Majesty's Empire, where we teach the painted-face savages how to read and write and know the good Lord's work. That's the desert,' he added, changing his finger's trajectory, 'a world of sand and animals called camels with humps on their backs. It's from here that wonderful stories come to us as well as being the Holy Land.'

He drew another straight line with his finger.

'This is South America – jungles, wild animals and legends of golden cities and palaces.'

'An' this?' asked Lewis, pointing to a shaded shape surrounded by sea.

'Australia,' said Leakey, 'Discovered only 50 years ago by Captain James Cook from Cleveland way, a desert land of people with skin as black as coal – Australia that is, not Cleveland and where we send our criminal classes, which is where I'll be sending you if you don't get on with your alphabet!'

Leakey drilled Lewis and taught him how to recognise, write and speak the alphabet, make sounds and put together words. Lewis practised for hours at home with his chalks and slate. Though often frustrated and angry, after much dedication he was finally able to write I LOVE MAM AND DAD on his slate and show it to them. George and Catherine were as proud as punch.

1821

Thursday 12ᵗʰ April

Francis Mewburn finished his quail in parsley sauce, boiled potatoes and a selection of French cheeses, washed it all down with strong coffee and retired to his hotel room where he'd been resident for two weeks co-ordinating the campaign.

He lit a cigar and exhaled the purple cloud and then looked at the papers strewn across his desk. As the sun began to paint the skyline crimson, he watched lamplighters go about the business of threading together the darkest pockets of London with pearls of bright flame from the newly installed gaslights.

He thought of the bright sunlight of Darlington and how much he missed the green fields and clean air. At that moment his family would probably be sitting by the fireside reading or playing piano and he wished he could be with them. Instead, he was in London, alone, where the smoke and crowds were unbearable, where seemingly never-ending queues of horses and carts flowed through surely endless roads, where buildings sprang up, crushing and squeezing out all traces of vegetation and where a thousand times the population of Darlington seemed to spill out from hidden places before sunrise and swamp it. He'd seen poverty and hardship in the Poor House in Darlington but here in London it was as if a gigantic Poor House was turned inside out.

In 1819 he'd been in that same hotel in a different room, but he'd not liked that room. It'd been too small and he'd never looked forward to being in it. Though in no way could his choice of room influence decisions in Parliament, he felt a change would bring fresh air to their counter-attack – the first Bill was defeated by 106 votes to 93, but they weren't dismayed by the defeat. On his return to this, the Northumberland Hotel in Tottenham Court Road, he'd insisted on choosing his own room. He wanted to do everything right the second time that he didn't do right the first. The S&D Railway Company was footing the bill as before, and this better laid-out room cost no more than the other, but it felt right. 'Hasten With Caution' was his family motto and he followed it assiduously.

He'd half-known two years before then that the Bill wouldn't pass. He'd tried to warn the committee and even though they'd recruited the likes of Earl Grey to their cause it had made no difference – aristocratic blood was thicker than common water. All the gentry in the neighbourhood of the railway were either opposed or deeply suspicious, as were the Turnpike trustees and the proprietors of coaches and wagons, while on the extreme margins some farmers thought it would render their fields uncultivable or that their cattle, hay and corn would be pilfered.

He and Thomas Meynell had accompanied one another everywhere back then. The opposition had been well organised – Lord Darlington's solicitors had urged the old curmudgeon back to London from hunting just to be on the safe side. But the S&D hadn't been organised – even the papers they'd submitted were hastily put together: loose sheaves, unfinished maps, scribblings in margins: all very unprofessional. They'd learnt from their mistakes soon after and started to push for another debate on their revised bill with its many amendments for the spring of 1820, when suddenly the old King had died in January and so, out of respect, they had agreed to postpone their attempts by a year.

But now they were back. They had come to terms with Lord Barrington, another landowner affected by the revised route that (finally) avoided Lord Darlington's fox coverts. They had pacified the Hale family with an offer to buy out their shares in Coxhoe and Quarrington colleries that would otherwise suffer a loss of profits. They had satisfied the turnpike commissioners and conciliated nearly everybody who had a voice in high places. Even Lord Eldon had cracked and enough pressure had been put on Lord Darlington to accept compensation. What more could they do?

Mewburn carefully unwrapped the crisp, immaculate sheets of hand-made paper upon which he'd been painstakingly writing out the Act for some weeks. On one wall he had erected an 8x6-ft picture frame empty of its artwork. Pinned to it were dozens of small cards with various ideas, and by this process he had been able to marshal his thoughts and begin the laborious task of putting together the wording of the Bill. It currently stood at 36 pages but he guessed it would go as high as 60.

He took off his frock coat, hung it on the back of the Queen Anne, found his pebble spectacles, breathed on and rubbed them, donned them and studied each of the cards again. He finally settled on one. He read aloud: 'For the purpose of facilitating the transport conveyance and carriage of Goods, Merchandise and other articles and things upon and along the same Roads, and for the conveyance of Passengers upon and along the same Roads.'

Which meant what? This meant locomotives. If Stephenson's predictions were correct, horses would be redundant within five years.

But something niggled him. Perhaps the quail – had it been fresh? Getting fresh food into London was fraught with difficulties given how quickly game decomposed after slaughter. No, it wasn't the food. There was something else. This was what his former employer and father-in-law Mr Smales, to whom he'd been articled as a clerk 20 years previously in Durham, had drummed home to him time and time again.

'Relax, laddie, have a dram, read, sing a song, go for a walk and just as surely as looking for something, that something will sure as not find you when you are least expecting it.'

Passengers? It stood to reason that men would be required to drive the locomotive and operate the brakes. Technically, they would be passengers. It seemed ludicrous to insert 'and people' into something that seemed so obvious. And what about 'export of coals'? He'd been warned by Darlington's MP if he included the word 'export' it would be rejected by Tyne and Wear. So he'd simply omitted the three words with a bold flourish.

What was missing?

Nothing. Nothing was missing. It was simply a question that had to be aired.

He wandered across to more papers and looked at printed notes produced by Parliament, studying the tiny words by holding them very close to his quizzing glass.

Suddenly his eyes passed a sentence, rolled over into the following one and then back again.

'Compliance with the standing orders of the House requires that four-fifths of the amount of the share-capital should be subscribed before the Bill goes into committee.'

He lifted his head, stared into space, blinked, brought out the bank book and statements and began to tally up. Within a short time the sun set and he fumbled irritably to light the candelabra to scribble out his total with the goose-quill pens he favoured. Finally, he was left feeling as if his stomach, full of the rich food he'd just consumed, had opened up and fallen onto the Turkish carpet. He chuckled. But it wasn't born of amusement. It was shock. Some 30, less – 20, 15 minutes before he'd been sure the plan was flawless. Now, his world was spinning: they were short £7,000.

He felt only marginally fortunate he'd been alone when he'd discovered the error: it was a shatteringly expensive mistake and could have been highly embarrassing. But that was the only good news. The bad news now had to be urgently communicated to Edward Pease in Darlington. He pulled the bell for room service.

Thursday 19th April

The man's thinning and almost transparent white hair was brushed to his collarless black tailcoat. In one hand he gripped a walking stick while the other rested against the mantelpiece, his well-fed bulk balanced between the two as he stared vaguely into the flames.

Rich, dark-wood wall panels soaked up the heat and reflected a golden tinge. Outside, a steady rain fell over Darlington and occasionally the sky flashed silver, followed by a rumble.

Two days before, at an emergency meeting held in Yarm, Edward Pease had proposed to add £7,000 to his bona-fide subscription of £3,000: 'The said £7,000 shall be considered as lent upon mortgage on the intended railway or be taken as shares as the said Edward Pease may determine' as the small-print said. He'd then signed a cheque that had taken the considerable sum of £7,000 from his personal savings to save the S&D's progress through Parliament after an error discovered by Francis Mewburn, solicitor of the S&D, who was temporarily quartered in London.

Upon making his discovery, Mewburn had ridden by coach across the bleak fens to Norwich to the Gurney Bank to try to raise the money, but had failed. He had then gone through London Stock Exchange contacts but all drew a blank. Next, he had written to Pease in Darlington to say he must return home unless he received the sum within three or four days.

The cheque arrived four nail-biting days later. For those four days he and his fellow lobbyists in London had coerced and lobbied as many MPs as possible, none aware that he himself was playing for time. Mewburn hadn't known was that in paying the money, Pease had dented his personal account: the last refuge of the besieged businessman. When that was plundered, there was nothing but debtor's prison. Rats would leave the sinking ship in droves simply because they could not afford not to. If the venture failed its second reading, his company might go to the wall and have to start selling assets, perhaps even the Old Mill itself in Darlington. In signing the cheque, Pease became the virtual owner of the S&D Railway Company, but one error – if the bottom suddenly fell out of the linen market or war was declared – and he'd be ruined. These were realities he kept from everybody, especially his wife Rachel, his daughter Elizabeth and his four sons, Joseph, Henry, Arthur and Isaac.

Just then a door from an adjoining room opened. It was the youngest.

'Art thou well, father?' Isaac asked.

'Of course my boy; only thinking, that's all, only thinking,' his father replied.

'About what?'

'Us, human beings, business, the world, how we can change it and questions such as *should* we change it? Everyday reflections of a good Quaker,' he chuckled. 'At what point does: 'Art thou doing a good job?' change to: 'Hast thou done a good job?' and 'Did thou do a good job?' I've seen some remarkable changes since I was in leading strings: I was 16 when the Montgolfier brothers flew a balloon, 31 when Dr Jenner cured smallpox, 38 when Horatio Nelson died at Trafalgar and 48 when Napoleon Bonaparte was defeated. And yet all these…', he searched for the word, '...significant moments fade to nothing when I think on our current problem: do I want to fund a railway line at all?'

'I don't understand, father.'

'Just because thou canst do something, doth it mean thou *should*?'

Isaac searched to understand. His father went on.

'When I was born, the world was a collection of parishes: everybody knew everybody, often by first names. *C'était une grande famille!* Men, women and children ploughed fields as they had done for centuries. But over the past few years, mechanisation has put thousands out of work: Tull's seed-planting machine, a harvesting machine, Hargreaves' multi-looms, Arkwright's Spinning Jenny, Watt's steam engine – what next, I wonder? Men and women we knew by name have been replaced by nameless, faceless workers moving around the country all struggling desperately like millions of ants. Yes, we're reaping enormous profits from inventions but we are few and the workers that make us rich are many.'

'Mr Adam Smith's *The Wealth of Nations* states that the greater good is served by individuals pursuing self-interest, father,' said Isaac.

'Yes,' agreed the father, 'but then thou hast men like Mr Locke talking about the responsibilities between government and the governed. Here in Darlington we are eagerly pursuing these new methods but thankfully we've not yet created the conditions I've seen in these new towns like Manchester and Leeds. There, men, women and children survive like animals while their masters live in luxury. I tell thee, one day there must be a reckoning.'

There was a knock and the door opened. A servant entered and announced the arrival of a Mr George Stephenson and a Mr Nicholas Wood.

Pease furrowed his brow.

'Who?' he asked, searching his memory for the names.

'They say they've come from Stockton and Newcastle to propose a matter of great importance, sir.'

'Have they now? Have they indeed?' spluttered Pease, taken aback by such impertinence. 'Well, due to the fact that I have never heard of them nor do they have an appointment, and given the late hour, you must tell them I cannot see them at this time!'

Hilda, a quiet and dignified servant known by her more formal family name of Rose in the Quaker household, hesitated.

'What is it, Mrs Rose?'

'They – they say they have travelled a long way and they are both bedraggled and wet,' she added, having felt some sympathy for the two men when she'd answered their knock at the scullery door.

Pease hesitated too because he realised then that it wasn't the first time he had heard the name of Stephenson but his turning up like this out of the blue and unannounced was uncharacteristic of how Pease preferred to do business. Nonetheless, the man named Stephenson was now under his roof and desired an audience, and Pease's curiosity simply could not resist.

'Alright, show them in and tell them I cannot give them more than a few minutes – I am expecting my son back from London at any time!'

The servant left momentarily and Pease realised both men had been standing in the hallway, not in the scullery, and had clearly overheard all he had said. The two men appeared in the doorway, their shadows ballooning against the walls and ceiling by the light of the flickering candles. They wore sodden capes and hats and boots that dripped onto the wooden floor. Their outfits were of simple wool or cotton. Their brown trousers were spattered with mud and rainwater but their boots looked surprisingly clean.

'Mr Stephenson, Mr Wood, *bienvenu chez nous! Entre, entre!*'

Stephenson and Wood stared blankly. Pease chuckled.

'Forgive me, gentlemen, I have made a study of the French language and use it whenever I can. This is my youngest, Mr Isaac Pease. Hast thou come far?'

Pease shook the hands of both guests and instructed the servant to take away their coats and fetch refreshments and a mop and then ushered the men towards the fire.

'Yes, sir, we caught a coach from Newcastle to Stockton early this mornin' and then walked here from there,' said Wood.

'Walked from Stockton? Good gracious! You must be exhausted! What can I do for you at this late hour?' asked Pease.

'My name is Nicholas Wood. I am Head Viewer at a pit near Newcastle called Killingworth. This is my friend and Engineman of Killingworth Colliery, George Stephenson. He's in charge of the operation of all the steam engines at the colliery.'

'Well,' said Pease, 'that all sounds well and good, but why?'

'We think we can help you build a railway connection from your winnings up around Etherley and Witton, down to Shildon, on to Darlington and then across to Stockton, *and* build the moving steam engines to travel on them', said Wood. 'So we took a coach down to Stockton this midday and thought it'd be a canny idea to walk the planned route here to Darlington to get a feel for it.'

Wood's faith in Stephenson was unshakeable. Only two years before, Wood had been down a Killingworth tunnel inspecting a fall of stones and, with only the naked flame of a candle in his hand, had climbed to the top of the heap. A big pocket of firedamp had gathered in the now vacated space where the roof had once been and when it made contact with Wood's naked flame there was a huge whoosh. He'd got off with singed eyebrows and burnt hands, but he swore he'd never go into a tunnel again without one of Geordie's lamps.

Nicholas Wood slipped his hand into his bag and brought out a sealed folded paper.

'The Overseer at Killingworth is Mr Lambert. He's written this for you, sir', said Wood, handing Pease the reference he had taken out.

Pease broke the seal, reading for half a minute. It was a reference of good character for George Stephenson. No such meeting had been pre-arranged with either of these two men, especially at this late hour, so clearly they had come of their own volition, but this reference had come from an authoritative employee in a well-known and productive Tyneside pit and it vouched for them both. Pease liked that approach. He folded the paper and placed it on the mantelpiece.

'And what can I do for you, gentlemen?' Pease asked.

Stephenson hesitated so Wood said: 'Mr Stephenson is an advocate of the steam engine, Mr Pease.'

'I see,' said Pease. 'Why so enthusiastic?'

'We're using steam engines to transport wagons from the pitheads down to staithes at Newcastle and many others are too,' said Stephenson. 'Next year we plan a line from Hetton Colliery to Sunderland.'

'I've heard they are slow, dirty, unreliable and expensive,' Pease said dubiously, but George had heard these rumours before, so he waited for whatever other doubts might come from the mouth of this conservative Quaker in order to answer many questions at once.

'I've also heard that knowledge of the building of such machines is still very limited. The horse, for example, is cheap and reliable and barely a man or woman alive doth not know something about them. More people in this world own horses than steam engines. It seems easier, therefore, for anyone enterprising to hitch their horse to a carriage and pull it between Shildon and Stockton surely?'

'We've 'eard you're be'ind a venture to raise funds to connect yer pits at Witton-le-Wear to the docks at Stockton usin' a rail track n' horses,' interrupted Wood. 'Now we think a unique opportunity exists for everybody, right 'ere n' right now and we're here to suggest you create the line for 'orses but also include steam engines in yer remit.'

'Why?' Pease asked.

'My locomotive is worth 50 'orses but wi' 'orses we'd 'ave to build a railway line from Shildon to Stockton 100 yards wide to accommodate such loads as my steam engine can do on three yards wide or less,' Stephenson said confidently.

'Thou art proposing to turn the traction over completely to this steam engine?' Pease asked.

'I'm suggestin' the steam engine can work alongside the 'orse,' said Stephenson. 'Look, the only fact I know to be true is that steam engines at our colliery can pull 30 tons of coal – maybe more, n' one horse two or three tons. It takes almost three days to get from Witton to Stockton with one horse. Based on tests at Killingworth, an engine could do that distance in about eight hours. It'll transport anythin' from any place to anywhere providing there's sturdy track. A hundred years ago we just had iron, but thanks to science we now 'ave malleable iron n' cast iron. One is good at temperatures but bad at endurance, the other, the opposite. The engine iron is temperature n' the track iron is endurance.'

Stephenson paused as Pease digested his words, and feeling encouraged by the lack of objections, he decided to volunteer his second observation.

'The route too can, I believe, be improved. I've taken the liberty of studyin' George Overton's route.'

Both Peases and Wood sat at the table while Stephenson remained standing. The servant entered with a tray of pewter tankards and port, Madeira, Marsala and sherry from Jerez in southern Spain and a jug of homebrewed beer. The elder Pease took a plain white pot of the beer he had had a hand in brewing in his cellar – a drink of which he partook regularly as it was safer than drinking water, the younger took a glass of port and Wood a sherry, but Stephenson declined all and instead unrolled two scrolls of paper from a brown leather wallet, bringing over a candelabra for illumination. Pease tilted his head and studied the diagram etched in Indian ink onto the rough paper surface.

'This,' said Stephenson, placing his finger onto one side of the paper, 'is George Overton's railway survey: School Aycliffe, Harrowgate Hill, Morton, Yarm Bank n' Stockton. The dotted line is mine n' you can see it takes pretty much the same route but away from School Aycliffe, crossin' Darlington near Whessoe, then across to the Fightin' Cocks Inn n' then the same route up into Stockton.'

Edward Pease saw a rough line that snaked its way from a circle called SHILDON down to a circle marked DARLINGTON to the meander of the River Tees via various landmarks to a circled STOCKTON.

'Why have you done that?' Pease asked.

'I believe I can trim Overton's survey n' bring the line closer to Darlington, but I'd 'ave to survey the route first to prove it.'

'That's very enterprising of you, Mr Stephenson,' said Pease, impressed. 'And th'art quite convinced it's possible for one of thy steam engines to power its own motion and to pull great weights?'

Wood then spoke: 'There's been a widely held misconception that smooth wheels wouldn't run on a smooth track, but we've discovered the key is to make the track gradient almost zero, that is: no hills. Ten years ago, Murray and Blenkinsop used a complicated system of traction called the rack railway, but it was inefficient and then later on William Hedley connected the wheels so if one pair began to slip it would be counteracted by the other and so we've studied all these eclectic ideas and analysed them and come to certain conclusions.'

'The main conclusion is that the biggest expense isn't the engine,' interrupted Stephenson, 'The biggest expense is buyin' the land n' transformin' the landscape.'

Pease turned his back on the men and looked into the fire.

'Other businessmen are willing to put money into this but thou will need to attend a meeting and convince them,' he said.

'I can do that,' said Stephenson confidently.

'And part of me wants to support this as a businessman and part because I believe it will be good for all,' added Pease.

'There's interest in the plan from other towns,' said Stephenson, 'so the idea will not die, but immortality, as we all know, is lent only to them who get in there first, not second.'

An uncomfortable silence followed what was meant as a joke.

'Look, why not come to Killingworth an' see fer yerself?' suggested Wood, attempting to break the ice.

'Very well, gentlemen' said Pease, a master at changing the subject effortlessly and, warming to Stephenson's directness, 'Now, you must be hungry after your journey. How does pigeon pie sound?'

Both Wood and Stephenson were hugely relieved at this invitation – they were both ravenous and doubted they had the energy to get back to Newcastle that same night without sustenance and it was too late to stop off at an inn. So the men dined on asparagus soup, pigeon pie, pressed beef and boiled potatoes and fruit, washed down with beer, as was Pease's custom. Stephenson talked more about his background and upbringing and stories of how he'd walked to Scotland and back to study steam engines. His manner was natural but polite. He was amusing too, though rarely intentionally. He portrayed himself largely as an honest, shy and modest man who often found himself in worlds beyond his imagination and people related to him because they saw him as they saw themselves: wide-eyed and gaping at the wonders of these new worlds.

Stephenson and Wood left around nine. They said nothing about their mode of transport and Pease presumed they would be staying in Darlington overnight but was mortified to learn later they'd been too proud to mention they had neither fare nor board to pay anyone so they'd had to walk to Durham.

After they'd left and just as the servants were blowing out the candles, there came a furious knocking. Barely into his nightgown, Pease was called and in the hallway, he found his eldest son Joseph, exhausted but elated, his topcoat and boots saturated with rain and filthy with mud from his long ride north from Parliament in London.

'What ails thee, my son?' the father asked.

'The Bill – it passed, father! It *passed!*' Joseph gasped.

Pease sat down heavily, his heart beating like a drum in his ribcage. Years of struggle, but finally they'd done it. The railway was going to happen and George Stephenson, the Geordie who'd convinced him a steam railway could work, had walked into his life only hours earlier.

Saturday 8th September

George stepped from his coach, held out his palm and cast his eyes skywards. The rain had stopped but clouds still blanketed the horizon behind Stockton. He mounted the duckboards laid down for the wheelbarrows, stopping at the end and looking along the length of the string tied between two short stakes ten feet apart.

'Give us your spade,' he said to Seamus Gallagher, the ganger boss.

Seamus, at the head of a group of damp navvies, handed Stephenson his spade, impressed by the bossman's lack of ceremony and fear of getting dirty. Stephenson stepped off the gangplank and his leather boots sank up to his ankles in mud. He slid the edge of the spade into the earth, raised his heel to the shoulder and pushed. The blade sank to the shaft. He worked the spade and it dragged out a plateful of sopping earth and grass to be deposited in a wheelbarrow. A ray of sun peeked out.

'Never let it be said we 'aven't made a start!' shouted Stephenson. 'Now, boys – show the English what the Irish are made of!'

Seamus and his mates fanned out across the boggy plot and began digging. Up ahead lay a sizeable hill through which they were going to carve a flat-bottomed trench and then cart the hundreds of tons of excavated earth further along the line to shore up an embankment.

1822

Thursday 4th January

'Three miles!' said Robert Stephenson excitedly. 'Almost three miles!'

'Because I employed John Dixon: 'is uncle worked the Mason-Dixie County Line in America - it's in 'is blood!' added George his father.

'We'll have to return to Parliament,' warned Robert, 'to add clauses.'

'I'm sorry I wasn't able to do it sooner,' said George. 'We'd Christmas to get past n' all measurements accurately calculated. I'll present the full report to the board on the 22nd.'

George and his son Robert had recently arrived at the Peases' from Shildon where, despite the snow and mud, they'd been surveying the route of the line together. Almost as soon as they had warmed their cold hands at the fire, George unrolled a map and spread it across the table, Robert carefully moving the fruit bowl to accommodate it.

'There's very little to Aycliffe,' said George, 'No need to stop there. Bringin' the North Road crossin' closer to Darl'ton makes more sense in findin' a market for coal so it seems better to concentrate loadin' possibilities there rather than Aycliffe. Overton attempted to take advantage o' the narrow gap ower the Skerne south o' Haughton but he moved away from Darl'ton. If we go past Whessoe we can build an extension say five 'undred yards long n' offload near Westbrook. Spend a little more n' we can bridge the river 'ere.' Stephenson placed his finger on the map, 'Three hundred yards west of Hill Top Farm.'

'Then it means we ought to start buying up land around this area,' said Pease, sweeping his hand around to the left. 'That's Backhouse land, easy enough. But as we go east we move onto Eldon's.'

'We only need three n' a quarter acres,' said George. 'From 'ere we go across to Haughton village n' the Red Hall n' across to the Fightin' Cocks at Dinsdale n' then rejoin Overton's original route around Oak Tree.'

'But according to Overton we'd have to ascend 25 feet over two miles,' said Robert interrupting, 'And our engine would lose a third of its power in doing so. The new route would require far less work cutting through the hills.'

'Well certainly Chaytor's a lot happier,' said Pease. 'He resigned in '19 because Mr Overton's route omitted Croft and he was most upset seeing as how his family had supported the project since the start. Needless to say, with thy re-inclusion of Croft he's back on board.'

Behind them as the men talked, Pease's only daughter Elizabeth was sat on the edge of her chair in front of the fire carefully embroidering plain white handkerchiefs with her mother, Rachel. Still, Pease was unhappy with his daughter. A few days before, he'd discovered a copy of a book by a girl called Austen – *Pride and Prejudice* – two words of which the Quakers disapproved. The book had been confiscated but she'd already read it. Her punishment was sewing.

George noticed and suddenly said: 'May I join you? It's been a while but I've never forgotten.'

He crossed and took up the handkerchief and needle. As Elizabeth sucked her fingertip, she and her mother watched fascinated as the Engineman expertly threaded the needle.

'Picked up some years ago when I used to cut an' stitch for the miners at Killingworth. They talk nonsense those who call it 'women's work', for it takes great skill,' said George.

Stephenson cut the thread with his teeth and sewed the loose end seamlessly into the material.

'Thou mentioned something about delivery of the steam engine, Mr Stephenson,' said Pease, bemused by Stephenson's deft movements but feeling hungry and wanting to move on.

'Won't you call me, George, Mr Pease?' said George a little irritably but smiling nonetheless.

'Alas, Mr Stephenson, our religion advises we use full titles and not Christian names,' replied Pease.

'Oh. I see,' said George, breathing in to camouflage his *faux pas*.

'Well, Mr Pease, we lack space to make engines just as we lack workmen to manufacture parts n' joinin' them together. I - was plannin' on my old friend Bill Losh – Mr Losh- but I'm afraid we fell out over the need for malleable instead o' cast iron. I was a partner in the cast-iron patent with Bill so I diddled mesel' out of a monkey in the process n' made n' enemy of my former business partner.'

'A monkey?' said Elizabeth.

'I beg your pardon,' George said, correcting himself, 'A monkey is slang for £500. The problem was 'e was the man whose factory also built my steam engines.'

'But we gave that contract to Bedlington Iron Works, didn't we?' said Pease.

'Cast iron,' Stephenson went on by way of answer, 'Is resistant to temperature change, but very brittle. Our locomotive's boiler is made from it, whereas malleable iron has a high tolerance of deformation on uneven ground.'

'Thou – thou means to tell me thou deliberately robbed thyself of £500 in order to prove malleable iron worked?' asked Pease raising his eyebrows.

Stephenson shrugged and held up both palms.

'It was an expensive error of judgement but not the end of the world. Now, I've seen land near Forth Street in Newcastle where I've speculated buildin' a workshop. I lack all the capital but could put up the thousand given me for the Safety Lamp. Such a factory could provide good remuneration for a wise investor.'

'How much more?' Pease asked, wincing a little.

'A thousand?' George suggested.

Pease drew in his breath as if a tight financial corset already squeezed around him had been re-laced. But it was feasible.

'I could scrape together half and I've a friend, Mr Thomas Richardson, who might be interested in the other half. Who would run the place?' Pease asked.

'Robert,' said George, casting a glance at his son.

Pease shifted his head to look up at Robert Stephenson.

'Thou art very young. No disrespect, but it's true.'

'None taken. I can't deny it – I will be 19 in October,' said Robert.

'But 'e can read an' write n' has a solid knowledge of engineerin',' said George. 'We work well together. We can build it in six months n' 'ave it up n' runnin' by next year. First order: Locomotive Number One, but our working title will be Active. Give or take about a year to build then test 'er. Early Spring 1824 for an openin' possibly?'

'Yes, but why build one when thou canst build two at the same time and usually for half the cost in my experience?' suggested Pease.

'Two engines at the same time? That makes sense. What shall we call the second?' George asked.

'Hope!' Elizabeth blurted out.

The three men and her mother looked at her.

'Hope it is then,' said Pease.

'Mr Stephenson,' added Elizabeth, 'Would you consider it inappropriate of me to ask if ladies will be permitted to ride your train: a carriage of some kind with cushions perhaps?'

Stephenson was about to reply but Pease's hunger was at his heels.

'Food for thought, food for thought,' he murmured, 'And speaking of food, ladies, *une peu dejeuner*, I think. These gentlemen can be off to Stockton and I must attend to pressing matters at the mill.'

After a hearty but brief dinner, Stephenson and his son walked to Stockton that afternoon, taking advantage of a rare burst of winter sunshine before it set too soon for them to see their way. They followed the lines of picket fences staked out by navvies, George with compass and triangle stopping occasionally to measure and Robert glancing at his barometer to gauge air pressure.

'Can yer keep a secret?' George asked his son. 'Pease told us back there they're meetin' in their new offices in Darl'ton on the 22nd and 'e's going to recommend me for Engineer at £660 a year.'

'Six hundred n' sixty? That's tremendous, father!' said Robert.

'Not bad is it?' said George. 'And I'll need it 'cause I want you to go to Edinburgh University for a bit.'

The news stopped Robert in his tracks.

'Edinburgh University?'

'It would be Oxford but I cannat stretch it. Edinburgh's still as good, closer n' not so dear,' said the father. 'Anyway, us Unitarians are not allowed in English universities so we have to make do.'

George was referring to his own chosen religion and that of his son: Unitarianism, a relatively 'new' belief that stated that religion and science, reason and dogma, could exist side-by-side. It suited George's temperament well.

'But you never went to university?' Robert said.

'No,' said his father, 'And I was lucky to get the S&D job. I doubt I'll ever get one so easy again. The well-educated men are the builders of tomorrow, not miner's sons who started shavin' before they learned to read. A term or two at Edinburgh'll do you the world o' good.'

George approached his son and put an outstretched arm on each shoulder.

'When I look at thee I see yer mother,' he said.

He paused for just a second too long and Robert saw his father's eyes glisten.

'There's not a day goes by I don't think about 'er. So don't let me or Mam down will yer?'

They walked on in the rapidly fading light, intent on commandeering a company cart to take them on to Stockton, higher spirited for their emotional exchange but were dismayed just outside Yarm to discover vandals had been at work: a section of picket fence had disappeared and the line of staves uprooted and scattered.

'Of course, we've a way to go afore we can please *everybody*,' sighed George.

Tuesday 22nd January

Edward Pease held up the newspaper and read: 'To the astonishment of all present, the engine conveyed with the utmost facility, upon a railway having an elevation of one eighth of an inch to a yard, 20 laden coal wagons, the correct weight of which, with the engine itself, may be estimated at nearly 100 tons, with an amazing degree of rapidity and with an effect upon the whole which beggars description, etcetera, etcetera, extraordinary talents, etcetera, etcetera.'

He lowered the newspaper and glanced at the assembled committee in Darlington Town Hall.

'In brief, from every source we receive reports of Stephenson being an intelligent, active, experienced and practical man, assiduous in attention and moderate in his charges. From him we've received detailed estimates and changes, as well as personal sacrifices he hath made simply to gather the minutest information. From Overton we've had a survey that failed to get us through in '19 and with steeper costs. Overton may be a good surveyor but he does not know engines. Stephenson knows both. This means if we employ Stephenson, we get two professions within one person and for half the cost, in theory. I hereby propose we appoint George Stephenson forthwith and look at returning to Parliament for a change in the clause.'

Thomas Meynell rose.

'I'm deeply concerned we're wasting money and I believe Mr Mewburn, could he be with us today, would agree: the Act made no mention of a deviation.'

'It will cost more if we don't get it right, Mr Meynell,' Pease suddenly snapped in such an unfamiliar way that all who knew him were surprised. 'I beg thee, consider the facts: neither Overton nor his assistant Davies hath supplied us with a sufficient report or specifications to enable us to enter into contracts for the execution of a railway or justify the purchase of land. Detailed information needs to be supplied before the work can be properly entered upon. In fixing upon Stephenson, I am influenced solely by the high character I have received of him from various quarters. Ask me to go against every instinct in my being and I would rather walk away from this right now than go along with it!'

He sat down heavily with exasperation but it had been worth the effort. None could stomach the idea of Pease walking away, especially now he was Chairman and main shareholder of the company into which they'd all sunk their money and reputations. The proposal was passed: George Stephenson was appointed Chief Engineer and the company's solicitor instructed to prepare an Amendment to the first Act to alter the original route. None was more relieved than Pease. For years he and his friends had been fumbling in the darkness, unable to see what they needed to make their dream become reality, but George Stephenson could see, George Stephenson could see very well indeed.

Wednesday 28th March

'The letter is from your brother Ernest … your mother … died … of typhus a week ago,' said Lewis, his initial burst of pleasure at being able to read to his illiterate mother and father trailing to a whisper at the final words, the letter from Durham in his hands.

'That's all it says? Nothin' else?' snapped Catherine. He turned the sheet over and shook his head quickly. Catherine went very quiet and George and Lewis waited apprehensively.

'There was little love lost,' she said. 'Because there was never much shown. That's why I'm determined our 'ome will never ...' and she started crying throwing an arm towards her husband. Lewis had never met his grandmother or uncles or aunts so he was more upset his mother was upset than by the death of somebody he barely knew.

George arranged for Lewis to spend two days with Aggy while he continued to work, leaving Catherine free to travel from Evenfield to Durham for the funeral with a cousin of Mr Leakey who took a herd of sheep to market. The trek took a full day. When she returned, Catherine brought with her a nasty chesty cough and went straight to bed. Little was said about the funeral in Durham and Lewis didn't ask.

Thursday 23rd May

The first rail was laid in Stockton High Street. Bunting was hung half-heartedly from a few windows, a church bell rang, the small river port's population of 4,000 took a holiday and Union Jacks flew from ships in the harbour. At about 3 o'clock some men formed a procession and, music courtesy of Yarm Brass Band, it marched to the edge of town where Thomas Meynell, Yarm solicitor and one of the main shareholders, was drawn along in a carriage pulled by a team of singing Irish navvies. Seated alongside Meynell on board were Benjamin Flounders and the reverends Storey and Bradley of Stockton and Yarm respectively, later joined by Mayor Jackson and Mr Leonard Raisbeck and all then transported to St John's Well. There, they helped lay four lengths of malleable track fresh from Bedlington, taking time to hammer in the wooden nails.

'A few words!' cried a voice. 'Speech!' cried another.

Meynell took up his position near a small brick house adjoining the line; the mayor, Mr Leonard Raisbeck and local dignitaries stood opposite. He thought of a few choice words but knew he'd be pilloried if he said: 'Why is it that so few residents of Stockton have put money into the project?', and so he said nothing and thought: 'Let future historians note I was silent this day and a few men of wisdom may guess why.'

The 300 or so navvies who were settled in makeshift camps near Bowesfield were led to the Black Lion Inn for a free meal of cheese, bread and ale and given the rest of the day off. Seamus Gallagher, ganger for his crowd of 30 boys, was among them.

When off the boat at Liverpool only six years before, he'd been a naive and spindly boy who couldn't write his name. But he'd persevered and had made his way over to Manchester where he'd been thrown in with a gang of Ennis boys, digging the canals around Manchester where it seemed to rain even more than in Ireland.

At first, they laughed at him and deemed him too puny to lift a spade, let alone fill it with earth and wheel it away, so they put him in the mobile kitchen and he spent some weeks carrying sacks of potatoes and barrels, gradually building up muscle while eating regular meals. He'd been introduced to the pick and the shovel, and like most beginners believed it was muscle power that did the work, until an old timer showed him it was the tool that did the work, not the man. All man had to do was hold the tool, let the shoulders do the work and the tool do what it was designed to do. After that advice, he forged ahead. Working the kitchen was an important job too, as he got his education into the life of a navvy.

The gangs elected foremen to negotiate with contractors and surveyors. The navvies made money, but spent much of it on ale, gambling and cockfights, but the smart navvy kept for a rainy day exactly one half of what he wasted on a sunny day when the pub was open. They taught him much especially the importance of friends, discipline, loyalty and pride. He often fell asleep with exhaustion on the floors of tents, but little by little the foreman upped his wages until eventually he was paid as much as the rest and renting a raised camp bed. Work on the Manchester, Bolton and Bury Canal had finished by the end of that year so he'd learnt of the Bridgewater diggings and spent two further years there. By

1820 he was watching 72-foot narrow boats make their way along the massive system in which he'd had a hand.

There'd been much talk of the new railway work and though less labour-intensive, as it largely involved cutting lines and building up embankments rather than digging ditches, he wandered over to the North East in a convoy of carts, complete with women, kids and cooks and even a navvying Catholic priest. They made their way to Stockton and camped near a place called Bowesfield. On their journey, some villages barred them and soldiers were called in to protect the travellers, though more often than not the soldiers stood around laughing while kids stoned, spat at or taunted them, even though they were digging canals for the benefit of all.

It was O'Shaughnessy, the navvying priest, who taught Seamus to sign his name and it was in Stockton that Seamus was joined by his young brother Sean, who like him, had tipped up at Liverpool docks, an innocent and gullible underfed Irishman, and made his way to the Tees Valley where he found his brother whom so many knew.

For Sean, Seamus had become a legend and the reality didn't disappoint him: his big brother was taller with legs and arms like tree trunks, feet like hooves, a long mane of straggly black hair and prickly black whiskers. In awe, Sean set about becoming educated by his big brother.

'We pay a shilling a week to de cook. He cooks us all a big meal of meat n' potaters every noight. We eat in de same tent, at de same table, at de same toime. A navvy's work is hard, so he needs to eat well. Here it's preferred you buy your tools n' take care of dem. If dere's a breakage we've a blacksmith. You sleep in a round tent in de shanties – floor or bed: – nutten's free. For tree bob a day dey work us five n' a half days a week, half day Saturday n' off all day Sunday. You can do de church ting if you want but oi'm not bothered.'

Sean was shocked.

'Seamus, you would never dare say such a ting if you was in Oireland!'

Seamus laughed.

'But oi'm not in Oireland, boy! Now shut yer trap n' listen: board n' lodgin's eight bob a week plus one good shirt washed. Let me have a look at ye.'

Sean's bare feet and legs were filthy, his breeches were torn; upon his scrawny torso was a grotty shirt and a frayed and tight frock coat.

'You look like de bogtrotter you are, so you do! Oi'll fix dat. De Master on dis job is a feller called George Stephenson. He's a big man, ex-miner, fair an' decent, no airs an' graces, loike so many of dese feckin' English. But we've to be in place wit shovels on de ground to begin work de very second de day's first rays come, an' den work hard till its down again. The paymaster's Quakers, a queer lot, but dey pay on time. Down Manchester dey'd pay us in de local inns, de same inns dey bloody well owned, so half de time Micks'd blow half dere lolly straight back in de Master's pockets. Oi loike a drink but oi know when to stop n' oi put a little by every week. Don't end up in de local Lock House. A few oi've known got de rope for stealin' – de English justice don't like de Irish. Can you remember all dat, Sean?'

'Er, oi tink so,' Sean said uncertainly.

'Bejasus,' said Seamus, putting on an upper-crust English accent: 'What an awfully tick Mick you are, brother Sean!' They both laughed as a small crowd of Stockton-ites looked on suspiciously yet fascinated by the wild Irish navvies who'd come to their town. Seamus had been asked to be one of the lads who pulled the toffs in the private coach because horses were scarce that day and somebody somewhere had thought it would be amusing to have the carriage pulled by navvies at the laying of the first rails at Stockton, but he'd politely told them to take a jump – they paid him to be their donkey but he wasn't going to be their horse.

Almost none of the Stockton-ites could read, so they were completely reliant on the words of others and, from the embellished stories, had begun to imagine the mechanical beast really would be a cross between a wild bull and a machine. The four smooth iron rails on separate blocks laid by Meynell could just as well have been a game of dare to see how far they could walk along them as balancers without falling off. The idea that these rails would extend in one long flowing row 26 miles west into the coalmines around a town they had heard of but few had visited was beyond their imaginations.

Friday 14th June

They initially thought Catherine's continual chest cough was a result of 'damp air', but then the first spots of blood appeared on the sheets in mid-May. Aggy had been called and Lewis sent outside, not that it made much difference, as he inevitably heard everything that was said anyway.

'I think it's the consumption,' growled Aggy.

George knew almost nothing about consumption except that when somebody died of it, other family members would die one after the other. Tales from the old days still lingered: he'd heard the word 'vampire' mentioned: the dead drained the life from others as they entered Hell. They had red, swollen eyes, disliked bright lights, were pale and lean, and they were forced to attend revels with evil spirits at night, evidenced by their tired and wasted appearance by day. And they coughed blood, suggesting they had to replenish their supply from other sources.

Aggy whispered: 'You need a proper physician or surgeon.'

'I can't afford a proper surgeon!' George said desperately. 'I can't even afford a butcher!'

Aggy thought for a second and said: 'Over at Shildon there's a navvy camp. Fridays the Quaker physician visits, Peacock I think his name is. They send him to check the camps stay clean. And he's free, paid for by the Quakers.'

'But I'm not a navvy,' said George. 'He's not goin' to 'elp me.'

'It's the consumption,' said Aggy urgently, 'It's serious!'

George thought about it.

'It'll take me an hour to run to Shildon.'

'John Carr – he's got long legs – he can do it in 'alf,' she said.

And so it was that John Carr, who was an older boy and one of their neighbours, ran to Shildon, found Doctor Peacock and arrived back in Evenfield within two hours perched on the back of the doctor's pony and trap. The well-dressed Quaker stepped down under the scrutiny of the watching neighbours and went into the Lovatt household with his leather bag. Physicians like he had trained with other would-be physicians, often in well-to-do houses where they'd observed them at work and gradually been allowed to partake in return for payment from the trainee or the trainee's benefactor. One step down from his own profession were the barber-surgeons who had generally learnt their craft in the army or navy and who were responsible for cauterizing wounds with hot brands or cutting off damaged limbs. Peacock had trained to make diagnoses and this diagnosis confirmed it: 'galloping consumption': the most virulent form of the disease.

'What – what can I do?' gasped George, as he fell back onto the edge of the table.

Peacock studied the shattered miner with compassion. The man's options were limited. Peacock knew consumption was a contagious disease but he knew little else. Physicians were not even sure if it was one disease or a number, and apart from 'consumption', as it gave the impression the victim was being consumed from within, it still didn't have a medical name, a thought that depressed Peacock from time to time.

'I can only tell you what little I know: she has entered the final stages. I am dreadfully sorry. All you can do is wear this mask at all times and isolate her to one room.'

He took out a small square of cotton with two strings tied to each corner and a bottle of camphor and put them on the table.

'You must avoid being close to her, especially if she sneezes or coughs. Always wear your mask and avoid facial intimacy. Soak the mask in camphor from time to time. She must be allowed no visitors, not even family, unless wearing a mask or from some distance away.'

George only half-listened to Peacock.

'Once the victim has passed on, interment must be immediate and the body wrapped by the sole attendant through the victim's illness, which in this case I presume would be yourself?'

George's eyes glazed over as he managed to whisper: 'Yes.'

George watched his beautiful wife wither away rapidly like a rose in winter – no time to prepare. Hackett, the Evenfield Head Man, grudgingly gave him compassionate leave and George spent the last few days with her, trying to feed her and keep her warm; prolonging the inevitable.

Lewis was called in to see her only twice – once near the beginning when she wasn't so bad, and then just close to the end a mere five days' later, when he thought he saw the ghost of death hidden in the curtained room waiting to take her. He wasn't allowed to kiss her.

'Swear Lewis will never go down the pit. Swear it,' was the last coherent sentence he heard her say. After that, he ran as far away as he could until he could no longer hear the coughing fit that overwhelmed her. Even if he hadn't left voluntarily, his father would have ordered him to leave, for he knew her last night had come.

Lewis returned home at dusk and entered the silent house. He sobbed himself to sleep in his father's arms until they woke the next day in the intense silence.

'Is Mam asleep?'

'Yer Mam's gone to 'eaven, son.'

George paid three shillings for the cheapest coffin at the village carpenters: a pine box cut from wood from Sir Giles's timber in Hamsterley. Lewis was sent away for the day to Widow Harker's and George bought five yards of white linen from the general store. He began to wash his wife's dead body but he was unable to finish the job – he broke down and his sobs brought Aggy, who came and finished the task. Catherine spent her final night at home in the closed coffin and Lewis and George said their farewells to the lid of the box.

The next day, Aggy and her family, Mr Leakey, George's workmates William Crosby and his wife, Tom Dawson, Will and John Carr and their elderly mother attended the service in the local Methodist chapel, carried the coffin down to a cart and wheeled it slowly down the lane to the cemetery pulled by Leakey's pony. Almost all the people who weren't working that day stood outside their homes as a sign of respect and children stopped playing as they saw Lewis walking stiffly along beside his broken father. At the chapel they unloaded the coffin and walked to the hole in the ground. The Reverend Prattman conducted the ceremony in Latin and the coffin was lowered.

George had had a letter written by Leakey to Catherine's family in Durham just prior to it but there was no reply and none came to the funeral. A few pennies bought a fine plank of pine and in the backyard he carved her name in neat letters and the years 1796 and 1821. A few weeks later, he and Lewis fixed it into the ground at the head of the newly turned grave and at the top put wild flowers in a glass jar.

Monday 15th July, St. Swithin's Day

'That's Blucher,' Stephenson said, pointing at the fat iron animal wreathed in a heavy veil of pungent black smoke about half a mile away. 'It's being driven by me brother, Bobby. Bobby and me are in the same line o' work – he does my job when I'd down at Hetton and then I take over or join in – however you want to see it – when I'm here.'

'The Hetton Line, near Houghton-le-Spring? What are you doing down there?' asked Pease.

'Designin' n' buildin' an eight-mile track to take eight wagon trains up and down some fairly steep hills to get coal down to the boats. Bit by bit, we're buildin' up longer lengths. We can go n' 'ave a closer look but first - I want you to meet me wife, Lizzy!'

A comely woman stepped forward from the gate of the cottage at Killingworth Colliery where she had been maintaining a dignified and respectful distance from the two men. She curtsied to Pease. Pease bowed his head formally.

'I've heard much about thy cooking, Mrs Stephenson,' said Pease.

'I 'ope you'll consider comin' for tea then, Mr Pease?' she replied.

'I shall be happy to,' replied Pease. Turning to George, he winked and said: 'Let's get our business out of the way and then I can get down to the more important work!'

The two men wandered away from the house a little, watching the trains pulling their loads. Pease removed his topcoat and folded it across his arm, wiping sweat from his brow with a handkerchief.

'Its strength and vigour is impressive,' noted Pease.

'Something I picked up from Trevithick,' said Stephenson. 'Twenty tons of coal over one mile in ten minutes. Now, from what I've seen, it's 26 miles from Shildon to Stockton, another two from Shildon to your pit at Witton: four hours to complete a journey that'd otherwise take 150 hosses three days. And that's not all: I believe we can reduce the 26 miles to 24, savin' about £15,000 in costs.'

Yet again surprised and satisfied with Stephenson's sacrifice and enterprise, Pease felt there was little more to be said. His mind was being made up by the evident facts. The men sauntered back to the cottage where the second Mrs Stephenson was hanging out washing.

'Right then, Mrs Stephenson, I am all thine!'

After dinner and on a full stomach and his head buzzing with figures, Pease walked with Stephenson to have a closer look at Blucher, where the workings of the machine were explained to him in greater detail.

Pease had then finally returned to Darlington in his private coach, arriving late in the evening exhausted, letting himself in the front door without waking the household and going to the dining room. He'd been surprised to find Isaac sitting alone in front of the fire in his dressing gown, nursing a glass of brandy. It was a warm evening and the fire seemed out of place.

'How was thy day, son?'

'Mr John Coates and I went to Sockburn to witness a Will with Mr Mewburn. Tell me, whom did you meet at Kilingworth?'

'Stephenson, of course. Why?'

'Did you by any chance meet a Mr William James?'

'Who is Mr William James?'

'I wanted to show you these.' Isaac produced some letters. Pease sat, hooked on his spectacles and held the letters up close to his eyes.

'I'm surprised you didn't meet him, father. He was at Killingworth.'

'Many people were at Killingworth,' Pease replied, looking at his son's face rather than at the letters.

'Mr James is a canal man mostly, but he's met Mr Watt, no less. It's said he saw Trevithick's original 'Catch-me-who-can'. Anyway, if you look to the second letter you'll see he believes Stephenson is a genius on a par with Watt.'

'Yes,' the father said to the son, suddenly realising how tired he was. 'His estimates are very good, very thorough.'

'I'm no politician, Father, but it strikes me the Overton Survey ought to be let go and the Stephenson Survey be brought in,' suggested Isaac.

'I'm way ahead of thee, son, but mightily pleased thou art moving in the same direction. Come now, 'tis late – bed!'

Thursday 22nd August

Lewis cried often. His Dad did his best to put on a brave face, saving his own pain for nighttimes in his cold and empty Box bed.

The mourning period lasted a year according to custom and was visible by the black armband George wore. The miner's club had paid George ten shillings a week for the first month so he wouldn't starve, but after one week sitting around morbidly depressed George returned the money and went back to the pit. He gave away his wife's small wardrobe of dresses, gloves and hats to the neighbours, burning what remained in a bonfire. From this, Lewis rescued a dainty white cotton glove with a fur wristband and every time he smelled her scent she returned to him. It wasn't that George was heartless but that life was heartless and he had to survive for himself and for his son. Work filled his mind and occupied his focus and the summer passed them by as father and son drifted hazily through an unreal and empty life. In September, Leakey had paid another visit to ask if Lewis intended to continue his education and George had eventually agreed. The subject had not entered his life since before her death but now it seemed to reawaken and reinforce him to honour the agreement he made with her.

'We've doubled your hours, son, for schooling,' he told Lewis later that night.

'Why?' Lewis protested. Some independent instinct inside was surging suddenly to the newfound strength in his growing limbs. 'I could work, like you!'

George wanted to say 'No. Because I could die down there underground and you'd be adrift and in the workhouse in weeks and it'd have all been for nothing' but instead he said: 'For your Mam,' as if that explained everything.

And so, though at times he felt strongly compelled to find a job, Lewis Lovatt lived and studied and grew faster in that short time than ever before. He learnt about verbs, nouns, prepositions of place and movement and conjunctions and was soon able to connect and compose long sentences made of many adjectives. He could add up to 1,000, subtract, multiply up to 12 and divide. He learnt about angles and the existence of sums of money larger than the few shillings his father was paid every week and, just as he'd promised, he learnt to read.

One day in August Leakey lent him *The Thousand and One Nights* and though he didn't know it at the time, that book would change his life, prising open his stubborn young brain and pouring into it all the golden possibilities the wider world could offer a young gifted boy with imagination.

'Translated into French by Antoine Galland,' said Leakey, 'I managed to find this on my last trip to Newcastle: an English translation poorly done – not even an author's name. They call it the 'Grub Street' version.'

Lewis took the book home and later that night started reading the stories that helped take his Dad out of his depression and enter into an imagined world of deserts, legendary beasts, mythical creatures, camels, romantic warriors, fine cushions and silks and spices. As the heroine, Scherezade, stayed alive night after night by telling stories to the sultan so the Sultan would want to hear more the following day, and the same stories gave George the same daily hope.

George learned to cook too, as best he could, but the dishes were repetitive and bland: pease-pudding with bread, soup with bread, beef and mutton puddings with bread, potatoes with bread, bread and butter, cheese and bread, porridge and tea. In spring and summer it wasn't so bad, what with the supply of fresh vegetables, but in autumn and winter their diets were much plainer. So he spent another two shillings a week paying Aggy to cook their dinners two or three nights and have Lewis collect them between hot plates wrapped in a towel. He paid another few pennies to elderly neighbour Mrs Crosby or to Granny Carr to wash and sew their clothes when the repairs were difficult or they needed something knitted, and a shilling a week for the Club – a common fund for miners who for whatever reason were unable to work for any length of time. George didn't have much left from his wages, but he and his son managed to live without too many discomforts and because Lewis was now almost as tall as his father he sometimes had to wear Aggy's childrens' cast-offs.

Rumours went around the village that George ought to go to the Miner's Annual Gala in Durham and look for a new wife but he was a long way from wanting to do that. Finding a wife was one thing but finding a wife *and* stepmother to his son was another.

Monday 18th November

'We sunk the first two pits in 1819,' shouted Nicholas Wood, as the wind whipped his words away. 'At 109 fathoms it looked promisin'. At 148, it was in the bag, and pits were sunk all over east Durham thanks to Master Sinker William Coulson. The next problem wasn't extraction, it was transportation. The nearest port to here Sunderland is eight miles gentlemen, from flat plains to steep levels, with becks n' valleys between and the highest point o' the whole route is where we are now – Warden Law.'

At the end of his speech, Nicholas Wood pulled his collar up around his neck against the cold November wind and the small crowd at the crest of the forbidding, treeless hill at Hetton did the same. From their vantage point, they saw a number of timbered pithead derricks dotting the horizon like ancient siege towers and, in different stages of operation, two of Stephenson's patented steam engines, two 60 horse-power reciprocating engines and five self-acting inclines. Shacks and cottages were already springing up to house the miners that had begun to drift in from neighbouring areas. Within a few years they would become villages and if coal were as abundant as Coulson claimed (and he was rarely wrong) these would turn into towns.

But for now the hilltop had been stripped of obscuring trees and bushes, leaving a wide-open landscape where two locomotives, one behind the other, pulled a dozen wagons each in one direction while another two in the same order went the other way. Over to their right, wagons pulled by a fixed engine tucked away in a brick-built engine house gave the impression they were moving under their own locomotion and on another hill more were descending with brakemen controlling the descent while empties rose. It presented an impressive picture to those watching, among them Edward Pease, his son Joseph and Jonathan Backhouse.

Wood set off at a brisk pace towards the line, arriving within ten minutes, the observers loping behind, many using staffs and sticks to pace themselves over the uneven ground, the becks and stone walls, their faces numb with cold. They intercepted one of the two colliery engines pulling six laden wagons driven by George Stephenson, the wind blasting the thick smoke away. Most of the men managed to climb onto a wagon behind the moving vehicle, except the portly Pease, who was helped up.

'Grand, isn't she?' beamed George. 'I don't think y've met my brother Jimmy?'

He introduced his brother on the far side of the noisy steam locomotive. Streaked with soot, grease and coal dust, Jimmy thought about offering his dirty hand to Pease but offered his elbow instead and Pease tapped it with his knuckles.

'Down at the staithes we'll meet me other brother, Bobby – 'tis he surveyed the route n' built most of it. Jimmy also works at Blenkinsop's,' said Stephenson.

George propped his arms on his hips and stood back, legs apart like the proud owner of a horse.

'Does it have a name your engine?' asked Pease.

'Nay, an' it's not breakin' any speed records, but it is doin' the job of 100 hosses. We're pullin' aboot 50 ton 'ere now! Iron wheels, iron rails – nowt up me sleeve, haha!'

'What speed are we doing?' asked Backhouse.

'Seven or eight is my guess,' said Stephenson. 'Without the wagons we could push 'er up to ten or 15! You see, when the engine starts cold, all the metal parts acting against each other put up a sort of resistance. But when those parts have been running for a while they start to heat up, thus making the resistance gradually less and in turn this increases the efficiency of the engine.'

'I've stubbornly held out that this railway we've asked thee to build would be mainly horse-drawn.' said Pease, 'But I am beginning to come around to thy way of thinking.'

'Good! And by the way,' said George, 'I've looked closely again at the Act and there's nothing concernin' passengers.'

'The average man has never given any impression he would benefit from travelling away from his home over any distance,' said Pease. 'Most people are born in their homes, work in their neighbourhoods and are buried in their parish graveyards.'

'I was 30 before I even saw the German Ocean, Mr Pease' said George, 'But once I saw it, I never forgot it. To light so many thousands of fires is one thing, but why shouldn't this be available to anyone who can afford a shillin' to take a journey in wagons? This mode of transport gives a kind of liberty to every person.'

'I'm dubious', Pease said, 'But I'll speak to Mr Mewburn. It'll make no difference to lobbying but it remains to be seen if thou art right.'

'I'm right!' said Stephenson. 'I know I'm right!'

1823

Thursday 17th April

By spring of 1823, Lewis was almost 11 years old, though he looked older. Spending life at home, at school or out in the fields surrounded by nature, he developed a love for animals and birds, and although the land around was mainly for grazing, there were glades here and there where he found nests. Sometimes he fished, but rarely with success, except in autumn when anyone could catch sleeping salmon coming upstream to spawn: they were easy to find in the shallows and made a welcome change from potatoes and mutton.

Each spring he'd raid the birds' nests and take one or two chicks home, set them up in the shed, feed them and watch them grow and take flight. He often kept the down for fires-starting, as his Dad had instructed him. One blackbird became so tame that after flying about all day it would take up roost on his bed-head until his father banned it because it left droppings on his pillow.

The Lovatts kept rabbits and chickens, fattening them for three months before slaughter, and Lewis had to learn how to kill them, as well as show them compassion. He continued to visit Mr Leakey for lessons, and his progress came on exponentially, but he was ostracised by the boys in the village: most of his age were working down the pit with their fathers and brothers. None could read or write. The other boys sometimes mocked and bullied him, accusing him of having ideas above his station because he did not work underground and because he studied, but mostly because he wasn't as dirty and dishevelled as they were.

He had no brothers or sisters to defend him, and was often found undertaking what many considered a 'girl's role' in keeping house while his father worked underground, but from what he had observed over the course of his young life women were the heart of any home. Without their constant work and care and attention, most households would collapse within days and he thought it very unfair that so many women in the village were treated so harshly by their men, for without their women the same men would likely starve or wear rags or be forever drunk or imprisoned. Nonetheless, Lewis learned to be a loner and to make the most of his lot rather than allow it to beat him.

He even learnt how to cut hair and visited the village forge with the Lovatt knives for sharpening. He measured his father's locks between fore and middle finger and snipped anything unruly with great care as his Dad did for him but sometimes they both had to shave their heads because of fleas from other people. For dental care the two brushed their teeth with frayed twigs and hot salted water but they were rare – many poor people had all their teeth pulled in their 20's to save on future toothache and doctor's bills.

Traditionally, in the schoolroom Leakey should have taught Lewis Latin or Greek, but Leakey could see no use for it whatsoever in Evenfield and environs, so mostly they talked a lot, with Leakey telling Lewis facts about the outside world that Lewis's own father, George, had no knowledge of then supporting his claims with passages from books.

'Now,' said Leakey, 'What is the capital of England?'

'London?'

'Yes, a Metropolis of almost a million souls,' said Leakey.

'How many is a million?' asked Lewis.

'A lot, boy, a lot!' exclaimed Leakey. 'A number one with six nothings after it. London is like a ravenous dog barking day and night to be fed. But where does it all come from? From us! From the countryside, farms, towns, villages and cities of England, Scotland, Wales and Ireland. And how does it come? It comes by packhorse, by cart and by ships that travel around the coast and barges dragged along the canals. But all that may be about to change, for at this moment up at Shildon a long track of two iron rails is being laid along which horses will pull wagons laden with coal in a matter of hours instead of days. And that means even more to feed the hungry dog.'

'Is it like the turnpike?' asked Lewis.

'The turnpike is a private venture – the railway will be a public venture,' said Leakey doubtfully, knowing every time he used terminology the boy didn't know, he'd have to explain. 'The turnpike is run for personal profit but the railway will be owned by the government because the government is more cushioned against profit and loss than a private company. Anybody willing to pay the fees to travel on the iron road will be able to do so provided they follow the rules.'

'But they can do that now, Mr Leakey,' Lewis said.

'A turnpike is limited to carts carrying a couple of tons each at most,' Leakey warned. 'The railway is supposed to be a steam engine on wheels pulling 40 or 50 times that. Now, to get a public railway means going to Parliament and persuading all the MPs – that's men like Mr Lamb and Mr Brandling – to allow it. Educated men vote for these MPs so they can represent our needs, but it often means forcing people who own the land to sell it.'

That night Lewis asked his father if he voted.

'No, son. I'm not allowed.'

'Why not, Dad?'

'Only rich men can vote, son.'

'You told me Mr Brandlin' owned the Felling pit where all your friends were killed the day I was born. How could a man who's supposed to take care of people like us allow us to work in such bad conditions?'

'Brandlin' didn't cause the gas to escape that caused the explosion, son,' said his father.

'Did God do that then?' Lewis asked innocently.

George didn't know what to say, except: 'It's late. Go to bed.' Education enabled his son to ask such questions but he couldn't answer them for lack of it. He would never be an educated man. Indeed, if things went on as they were, pretty soon his son would know more than he: son would outpace father. But in this world, a man also needed everyday, common knowledge too – how to cobble, sew, make furniture, skin a rabbit and cook and pray. Those skills were worth passing on and he at least gave his son a layman's knowledge of these. His own needs had always been secondary after Lewis's birth, he knew that, but he hadn't always understood how his late wife must have felt and then one day he did: he had to be both father *and* mother. Education was an unknown for George, but honour – in this case to his wife's memory – was second nature. And he was compelled to honour his promise.

Friday 23rd May

Backhouse, Mewburn and Pease were dining in a restaurant near The Strand in London, celebrating the Royal assent given by King George IV to their Amended Railway Act that very day. It had passed the Lords on 12th May with the important changes to the route that would take it from Witton to Shildon to Darlington to Yarm to Stockton. But none had wanted 'conveyance of passengers' inserted as much as George Stephenson – only Pease knew that.

'When our amendments were submitted to Lord Shaftsbury's secretary,' said Backhouse, 'he could not comprehend them. He thought it was some strange, unheard-of animal and struck the clause out!'

The men laughed, though it was more in relief the long process was over rather than amusement at the incompetence of a befuddled secretary.

'Francis sent Brandling and I over to explain it to him. Poor chap felt most foolish!' said Backhouse.

'Under the powers of this amended Act,' said Mewburn more seriously, sipping claret and wiping his mouth with a napkin, 'the directors are able to make the alterations recommended by Stephenson, extend to Croft Bridge, reduce capital, use locomotives *and* fixed engines, charge an extra shilling per ton for goods and levy sixpence a mile on every coach, chariot, chaise, car, gig, landau, wagon, cart or other carriage. A tall order! I must confess, it was initially difficult to persuade me to return to Parliament to make the amendments given mainly the cost of sending us and based on past experiences, but I must now say I am pleasantly surprised. There have been applications for a number of other Railway Acts across Great Britain as other committees study our progress. The world is waking up to the potential.'

'I agree.' said Backhouse. 'Unfortunately, others will profit from our mistakes: the politicians will know better the questions to address, the surveyors and engineers will know better how to carve up the countryside and the shareholders will know better how to raise capital and spend it.'

'And the humble navvy will know better how to apply himself to the undertaking and at what fair rate to sell his muscle.' added Mewburn. 'Meanwhile I propose a toast, gentlemen.'

'Whom are we toasting, Mr Mewburn?' asked Backhouse.

'Leonard Raisbeck of Stockton,' said Mewburn empting the silver decanter of its contents. Each raised his crystal glass to form a glittering mid-air chandelier of thick, strong wine. 'It is Leonard I have to thank for helping me overcome my nerves when it first came to addressing the House of Commons – I froze in terror at the prospect, gentlemen, I have no shame in saying so. Leonard rushed to my side and stiffened my sinews and it is to his resilience we drink today. To Leonard!'

The others chorused his name and drank from their glasses and then the three educated men reflected for a moment, but none dared voice their concerns at what failure could mean. Only Pease began to worry about the extra finance. Despite the reduction of the capital, the next 12 months would be critical. He reluctantly looked at the bill: dinner 17' 6d, ale 5' 11d, sherry 5' 6d wine 15'/- brandy, rum and gin 9'/-. It was more than most miners made in a month.

Friday 19th December

For weeks on end the River Gaunless west of Bishop Auckland in northeast England, heavy with autumn rain from deluges over the North Pennines, mangled everything in its path, washing around the foundations of Stephenson's little metal girder bridge that rested on three stone piers, installed only a few months before.

The snow had come early, thawing out and re-freezing, imposing more stress. The terrible winter continued, until the Great North Road was cut off between Darlington and Durham and neither mail nor passengers could get through for a week. With the ground frozen and the winter days short, hundreds of navvies were laid off and though a lucky few were assigned to snow clearing, for the vast majority there was little to do.

Some enterprising Darlington-based navvies were allowed by the S&D Committee to club together to marshal the first of two winter convoys of decrepit mules in order to make their way via the villages running parallel with the turnpike to Evenfield, and there they bought a ton of coal for six shillings and broke it up with hammers, loaded it into baskets and set off back. The coal was needed for the workers' ovens and for their forges, as it only burned well in enclosed spaces, not on open fires. They lost a mule on the return trip, loading its coal onto their own backs before abandoning it by the roadside and returning through treacherous mud to Darlington, a cold, wet one-day journey fuelled by apple whisky, black bread and tobacco.

Edward Pease often paid a doctor to go into the navvy camps to ensure workers were nourished, stayed on the useful side of healthy and no diseases were given sanctuary. Being Irish, all were Catholic and mostly respected churchgoing – the local churches were as full as other denominations: warm places on cold days. But prejudice continued. In the streets, navvies were often insulted and more than a few took exception: brief, bloody battles fought in public or in private, boxing or wrestling matches where scores could be settled and money won. At least two navvies went too far: one was executed at Durham for poaching rabbits and the other fined for stealing potatoes and put in the stocks for three days. After the first night, he was liberated by friends and never seen again. The punishment often depended on how prejudicial the magistrate was and how much the S&D Company interceded.

Seamus and Sean Gallagher, Sean having filled out almost as much as his brother, were well known around Shildon by then. Neither were big drinkers, as so many of their fellow navvies were, and both always had a hand to help anyone in need. Seamus showed initiative and would often go out of his way to anticipate problems and report them to the men in charge of the decisions.

This trust placed in him by the S&D Company enabled him to travel freely up and down the length of the entire line with messages for contractors and their gangs. It worked to his advantage because he was able to understand better how much other workers were paid and so demand better terms for his own men, as well as learn more about the basics of navvying and a few light-engineering principles.

'You must come an' look for yourself, sir,' he told Stephenson. Seamus didn't want to be responsible for passing on bad news and anyway, the truth was he was no engineer. He didn't know if it was serious or not, but it didn't look healthy.

They walked up the treacherous mud of Brusselton Incline to the crest of the hill, all around them the fields streaked with intermittent slivers of thawing snow and earth reclaiming the light of day after weeks being buried. They crossed into the Gaunless valley where the metal girder bridge held the two lines of hills together, a tidemark of grass and straw showing how the water level had dropped the previous day. Down at the first of the stone foundations of each of the three legs, Seamus pointed. George examined it closely: a diagonal crack about an inch wide and a foot long had appeared on one side. He put his finger into the gap.

'Bugger it!' he muttered.

1824

Friday 27th February

For the people of Evenfield, winter was a matter of life and death, but at least there was work, for everybody needed coal in winter. Big families fared better than smaller ones as they often slept two or three to a bed and older sons could get work at the pit.

Lewis and his father slept in their clothes, nightgowns and socks. Old coal sacks were also used as rough-hewn blankets. George was given two cast-off, threadbare cardigans by Aggy and every night he poured boiling water into the glazed ceramic bottles they took to warm their beds. Every morning they'd wake to icy traceries on the inside of the windowpanes; the surface of the water barrel under their outside drainpipe was often frozen solid. As in all houses, coal fires were rarely allowed to go out, burning day and night. Rags were stuffed into gaps at the foot of doors. As the cows were all in their sheds, there was no work to be done for Lewis so he filled his days with reading.

Ten people died of the cold that winter in the village, the youngest a baby boy of nine months born sickly, the oldest an ex-miner who lived alone in a hut behind the inn; the only reason anybody knew he was dead was the lack of smoke from his chimney.

Another death was Ben Hackett's wife, Maud, from an alleged heart attack. After her death, some said she was lucky to be in a better place and rumours spread about the cause of death but nothing could be proven. Few attended the funeral but many lined the route out of fear of heavenly retribution. As for the other deaths, they perished from cold or an inability to survive due to lack of sustenance, despite neighbours doing their utmost to help.

It was in late February that one of the navvy winter convoys came to town. George was underground but Lewis stood on the step, as did other families. The idea of disliking strangers rather than welcoming them was odd to him. Prejudice had never shown itself in his father but in other families it seemed to be encouraged. Soon, children were shouting insults and throwing snowballs as the navvies plodded through the white snow streaked with black traces of the seemingly never-ending traffic of coal-carrying mules.

Once inside the compound, the pelting stopped. They paid for their ton: six shillings at source – it would have been 18 if they'd bought it in Darlington. They weighed it and smashed it to fit in the sacks. Nothing was wasted. After half an hour, they set off back, enduring more snowballs and insults from a zealous knot of small boys. Just beyond the village the oldest mule's legs collapsed. Lewis watched as they relieved it of its load and one of the navvies, after gently stroking its head and whispering in its ear, held it in place as best he could while his mate brought down his coal hammer between its rolling eyes.

When the convoy disappeared, a butcher was called, dragged the steaming corpse onto the cart with the help of some boys and took it to his back-garden slaughterhouse. Within an hour he was selling strips of meat for next to nothing to an eager crowd of women.

'Read me another story,' George asked his son that night after a meal of tough donkey meat and potatoes. Lewis read *The Adventures of Bulukiya*, occasionally casting glances at his father's transfixed face as he thought of the Garden of Eden and Hell, distant galaxies of worlds populated by mermaids, talking trees and serpents and a place where there were no kings or rich people or money.

Friday 26th March

Jonathon Backhouse's coachman brushed down the black mare, lifted each of her hooves to lever out caked earth and straw, pulled the harness over her dipped, obedient head and backed her into the traces. The carriage hosed and the mud wiped from the paintwork, it left very early under a clear blue sky for the two-hour run over to Stockton on the turnpike where it picked up Thomas Meynell, the Mayor of Yarm and an S&D investor.

By midday, the carriage was back in Darlington where it was steered to Northgate to collect Edward Pease. At about the same time, Francis Mewburn, the S&D legal expert, arrived in his private coach and the servants showed them through to the drawing room of Backhouse's villa, West Lodge, set back from Cockerton Road. Backhouse's coach drew in behind Mewburn's and discharged its passengers, and a final coach arrived: Reverend William Prattman of Barnard Castle, owner of mines in Butterknowle and Copley. Each of the drivers warmed his hands by the kitchen fire. Their passengers gathered in the drawing room with its fine command of a large front garden. All sipped port, except Reverend Prattman.

'Weather's turned,' said Mewburn, as they looked at the melting ice and snow in the garden.

'About time,' sighed Meynell.

Backhouse called the semi-official meeting to order.

'Gentlemen, I've called you here to discuss a number of important matters, some of which we can share with...' He hesitated. 'Reverend' was a forbidden word in Quaker vocabulary, but as with his doubts about wearing a hat in the presence of Lord Liverpool there were times it seemed impossible to avoid. '... Reverend Prattman and some of which we can not. As you know, we're to return to Parliament to ask for a third Amendment to our Railway Act. Our original plan in '21 was to build an extension from Norlees to Evenwood to embrace as many collieries as possible in order to encourage investors. However, not all collieries have seen things our way. In fact, some have been most unsupportive, indeed, opposed. I'll mention no names.' At this point he thought about Giles Crockatt. 'Reverend Prattman has suggested we drop completely the Norlees–Evenwood extension and replace it with the Haggerleases Branch that would open up his collieries. Gentlemen, your thoughts?'

'Some papers to draw up to make it official,' said Francis Mewburn.

'It doesn't affect business over in Stockton or Yarm,' said Thomas Meynell.

'Providing, of course, the concerned party understands on the day of the opening,' chipped in Pease, 'our intention is to connect Witton with Shildon, Darlington and then Stockton. That must be our absolute priority. The extension will follow as soon as physically possible afterwards.'

'Of course,' said the Reverend, dryly amused to think his title of address challenged a Quaker.

Edward Pease was accepting of other religions and their representatives but only because his principles demanded it. The Reverend Prattman represented the Church of England, that is, the powerful and patriotic branch of thinking that saw the King as the head of the Church and not the Pope in Rome. The Reformation had been the cause of a dozen major wars and widespread massacres across Europe in the name of God. It perplexed him how a religion saying it is dedicated to peace could incite so much bloodshed.

The Quakers had no bishops dining on fine foods while their parishioners starved and nor did they have pompous ceremonies. Quakers met at designated places and at designated times and sat in silence waiting for inspiration and could talk about anything without restriction. They were in favour of freedom for all and tried to create things that helped people – such as jobs. At the same time, they liked to drink as much as the next man. They opposed slavery and war and the manufacture of arms but they mistrusted dancing and frivolity and this odd selection made them appear to be zealots and fanatical. How could any religion promote alcohol but not dancing and singing? For most people the three went hand in hand.

But their principles also made them trustworthy and this generally produced profit, and for this they were gradually accepted. For the three preceding centuries, they'd been marginalised, prosecuted and even put to death. With Christian Protestants or even Catholics, you just knew immediately where you all stood and what you were fighting for, but with Quakers you had to readjust the brain and think in a different fashion – and that wasn't easy for many British people at that time. So few people could read or write that those who could dictated how the world was run and those who couldn't followed with blind and often misguided faith.

'Very well, gentlemen, I will take my leave. I have a sermon to prepare for Sunday. Any advice?' asked the Reverend.

'Seek and ye shall find?' Pease suggested, smiling.

The Reverend held his gaze for a second for a hint of a double meaning, but finding none, smiled, shook various hands coolly and left. As his carriage pulled away and headed down the drive, the tension unravelled.

'Where the hell is Stephenson?'

'Myers Flat is a disaster!'

'What's happening with the engines?'

'What news of the Tees and Clarence?'

'Mr Backhouse, where do we stand?'

'Calm, gentlemen, calm,' said Backhouse. 'Now, there's good news and there's bad: winter has been unusually testing, almost as if nature has pushed everything against us to see how we cope. But better now than later, I say, though it doesn't help that Mr Stephenson is spending time down at Manchester.' At this, he dared cast a glance at Stephenson's closest ally, Edward Pease.

'He's surveying a line from Leeds to Hull,' chipped in Pease supportively. 'But we can't blame Mr Stephenson for the winter.'

'The Gaunless Bridge needs urgent repair work and compensation claims have rocketed,' Mewburn added.

'Did you hear about Captain George?' piped up Meynell. 'Old sea captain – demanded we built a single arch over the track on his land. Made a real Cheltenham Tragedy of it! Twice we went to court to contest, twice we lost; the third time we were forced to accept, but it cost him more to dispute it in legal fees than it cost us to build it!'

'So,' said Pease, patiently, 'We are to go back to Parliament…'

'Yet another expense!' said Mewburn, wringing his hands.

'…to ask for a change on one of the extension lines and to raise more capital. Is that the long and the short of it?' asked Backhouse firmly.

'How much more?' Meynell asked.

Backhouse's hesitation and lack of emotion did little to pave their way for a comfortable reception to his bad news: 'Fifty thousand.'

Mewburn sat down heavily. Meynell's lips opened and closed but no words came out. Pease closed his eyes and formed a steeple from his hands that covered his nose and mouth.

'But its not all bad news,' Mewburn countered. 'Through our Quaker contacts we've managed to secure a loan from the Gurney Bank in Norwich for three-fifths and Tom Richardson for the rest.'

'But *fifty thousand!*' exclaimed Meynell. 'That's twice the original. Where is Stephenson to answer for it?'

'Three days ago, Parliament rejected the Tees and Clarence Railway Bill, Christopher Tennant's project,' said Backhouse. 'There'll be no more Acts passed for the moment. So let's focus on us: the winding engines are built and Robert Stephenson has made a start on the two locomotives, but we only need one locomotive to open the one line: one locomotive, a dozen wagons full of coal and some sturdy track to run it on. That's all we need, gentlemen.'

'When doth thou expect it to go up before Parliament?' Pease asked Mewburn.

'Mid-May. It'll pass,' Mewburn replied confidently. 'It has to – something like twelve and a half million has already been speculated on the Stock Exchange. Indeed, some ambitious but unrealistic gentlemen in London have even talked about a line to connect London to Edinburgh.'

'Hah!' mocked Meynell.

'Thou laughst,' said Pease, 'but this has always been Stephenson's point. Until recently we all imagined carrying goods to London meant a struggle to adapt our transport to our environment, that is: finding something powerful enough to negotiate our fields, rivers, valleys and gorges. Look at what the steamship can do on a flat ocean. But our little revolution is about forcing the environment to adapt itself to the railway, not the other way round. So don't you see, it is as possible to connect London and Edinburgh on one flat length of track as it is Darlington and Stockton?'

The others said nothing. Pease continued more soberly.

'Everything is on us. So stand to thy posts, gentleman. I'll ask Mr Hackworth to come down and see if we can't get things moving at the works. Good day to thee.'

At that Pease stood, bowed stiffly and went out to the waiting carriage. Few could argue with him – he was the main shareholder. As he passed the scullery, the under-butler ran to the driver in the kitchen who grabbed his hat and ran out to open the carriage door for his passenger. Pease had wanted to mention at the meeting he'd heard William James, the once rising star of engineering, had fallen dramatically from grace and was now in debtor's prison as a declared bankrupt, but he thought it diplomatic not to – nothing was to be gained by it.

Monday 28th June

In the morning, Pease and his wife Rachel visited 42 avenue des Gobelins in Paris, and saw for themselves a selection of the great tapestries that depicted hundreds of biblical and pastoral scenes.

They had left Darlington by coach a week before and travelled to London. From there they had travelled via Canterbury to Dover and taken a steamer to Calais. Their journey was a combination of holiday and work in the sense of God's work – for Pease this meant petitioning and lobbying the French government for the abolition of the slave trade, something which had been made illegal in Britain though traces still lingered in negative attitudes. He had counted on his good friend in London, William Wilberforce, to steer the legislation through.

At the Manufacture des Gobelins, Pease was struck by the complexity of the weavers' work, noting how strikingly similar were the colours of the dyed material to the original paintings from which the scenes were taken. Back home in Darlington they could never hope to match the intricacy, the finish of the material, nor the richness of the colours. They would have had to have lived in London to even vaguely attempt to manufacture such beautiful tapestries and even then, unless as was the case in France where the chief client was the State, would have woven to order. The work would have had to be done by hand whereas the looms at Pease's mill were all steam-powered. Anyway, tapestries were luxuries and out of reach for most ordinary people even if he could find a skilled weaver.

After a delicious lunch at L'Auberge du Moulin near La Bastille, Pease and his wife wandered the more salubrious regions of the neighbourhood, constantly amused or bemused by the thronging mass of colours, nationalities and languages of those who crammed into the teeming alleys and streets. In many, the upper gables of the towering wooden houses almost touched, while down below only a putrid ditch of stagnant water flushed away the human filth that leapt occasionally from the windows to explode below. The hotel staff tried to guide he and his wife to visit a perfumer so they could mask many of the unpleasant odours of the city, but Pease explained in his poor French that as Quakers they had no use for perfumes or fashions and when the manager of the hotel actually noticed their plain grey clothes and un-starched shirts he looked at them disdainfully and tutted his lips as if scolding naughty children while trying to explain Paris was a city of fashion.

Pease was frequently able to practice his poor French. However, almost everyone he addressed had to ask him the same thing two or three times until either they understood him or he understood them: his English accent was as thick as porridge and he was unused to their dancing, singing syllables.

Having no coal or wood, the Parisians mostly used charcoal for cooking and the Peases were not only struck with how abundant were the stoves and tiny braziers that produced the charcoal itself from small bunches of sticks but also by how much clearer the air of Paris was, unlike London where a blanket of smoke perpetually clouded the skies. It also seemed almost every Parisian family roasted its own coffee – they observed many people holding small tin cylinders fixed over smouldering charcoal in the streets. The odour of coffee was one of hundreds they savoured.

On the second day they called at the Hôtel du Ministre and met the Bishop of Quimper from Brittany and requested he accept a tract on the treatment of Negroes – the prime purpose of their visit to France. The Bishop seemed reluctant to accept the tract and possibly only did so out of politeness and it struck Pease how mixed were the individual reactions of certain French people, even those of a religious nature who, it seemed to him, should by their very nature be deeply concerned for Negroes unfortunate enough to be treated as slaves.

'What about the shipbuilders at Nantes?' Pease asked. 'Can nothing be done to outlaw the fitting of holding pens and manacle bars with which they transport their abominable cargo?'

The Bishop raised his considerable eyebrows.

'My dear Monsieur Pease, it is very easy for zem to claim zese fittings of which you speak 'ave some practical use. Zere is much money to be made from zis slave trade and bribes for 'arbour-masters are commonplace.'

'The British Consulate in Nantes is deeply interested in suppressing the trade,' Pease defended.

'I 'ave no doubt about it Monsieur Pease, but do not forget it is less zan ten years since you British destroyed Napoleon's Army and many of ze hopes of ze revolution wiz it. Ze Nantais are no supporters of Napoleon – our soldiers killed thousands of Bretons in the Vendeen Wars but alas, it is all politics, Monsieur Pease, all politics.'

The same afternoon, while his wife strolled along the Champs-Elysees to see the flower markets, Pease went alone to visit Monsieur Villele, the French Minister of Finance.

Pease had fiercely opposed the slave trade since first understanding and learning about it at the end of the previous century. As a Quaker, it was his duty to do all he could to help lift his fellow man out of the dirt and stand with dignity. He did this in Darlington via his position – employing loom operators at the Priestgate Mill and dozens of weavers in their cottages, as well as miners at the various pits around the North East. The Poor House and the Workhouse were dependent on contributions from the

Quakers, and two or three thousand employees and associated trades, half of them with families, were dependent on his benefaction for daily survival. He was proud of that fact.

He felt he treated his workers well and maintained their health with free medicines and food and in return, that investment in humanity repaid him and his companies with solid profitable work – the two elements went hand in hand. Why couldn't this Utopia also be applied to men of different hues and cultures? The conditions he'd seen on the slave ships at Bristol and Liverpool had given him visions he doubted he could ever erase. Count Severin Tonnerre, Marine Minister, whom they had visited two days before, had recounted a slave auction he'd witnessed in Nantes some years previously. The overpowering stench, he said, had caught in his throat from a quarter of a mile away. He said that slave ships at sea could be smelled before they could be seen. Over 300 men, women and children were shackled and crammed horizontally into what amounted to a labyrinth of low-ceilinged shelves where human bodies had been packed like boxes and cases in a warehouse, without recourse to sanitation, light or decent sustenance. Pease learnt that at least 20 had died on a voyage from Senegal from where they'd been kidnapped and their bodies thrown overboard. Once sent into the holding pens at Nantes, each was stripped and hosed and inspected for disease or lice. If they had the latter their heads were shaved. Fathers were separated from wives and mothers from children and then sold. Pease's fervent imagination pictured these images to such a colourful degree that, upon leaving the Ministry, they put him off his lunch that day.

Monsieur Villele glanced perfunctorily over the sheets of notes and signatures handed to him by the Englishman and gave him a neutral smile. Pease wanted to mention an ironic quote by Villele's countryman Jean-Jacques Rousseau: 'Man was born free, and everywhere he is chains' but judged it too impertinent.

'Could you not make slave trading a criminal offence, Monsieur Villele? It would greatly discourage slavers would it not?'

Pease noted Monsieur Villele shrugged in the manner all Frenchmen did when they wanted to react without taking sides.

'Zis will only exasperate ze traders and per'aps lead zem to greater acts of cruelty. Zey will feel zey wil 'ave nozzing left to lose. It is very difficult to get zees men into a tribunal and even more difficult to convict zem. All we can promise you is to be more vigilant, stop zis activity when we can and confiscate zere property and ships, and if your England wishes to try to stop slave trading completely, zen I suggest you look at colonizing ze west coast of Africa instead of ze East.'

Later that afternoon Pease, subdued, strolled back to his hotel near the Tuileries, reflecting on whether his journey had accomplished anything. He was uncertain. He *was* certain he'd left England with the hope of changing the stubborn minds of stubborn men and even if he was just one tiny insignificant pawn in the game Christians called chess, his accomplishment was that he had acted for the general good. It was this same motivation that fuelled his plan to connect Witton to Shildon, Shildon to Darlington, Darlington to Stockton and Stockton to the world. Yes, of course he would make money, but a man could only get so much into his belly or so many clothes on his back. What should he do with this money other than invest it back into humanity?

Tuesday 6th July

Francis Mewburn laid the first 5lb sandstone brick into a clay bed of what would eventually be the Ignatius Bonomi Skerne Bridge and tapped it lightly with a trowel. It was a hot July day and he had wandered up from Darlington along the North Road with various workmen and Joseph Pease for the small ceremony.

Earth brought from other parts of the line where entire hills had been removed had raised the lowest height of the valley to the same level as the ground above, along which the line would be laid from Whessoe to Eastmount Hall, where hundreds of navvies reshaped the stone bridge. Where once had been a wide, open sloping bowl was now a gigantic wall of earth and stones with space for the river to pass through.

After the stone-laying ceremony, Mewburn contrived to be in private with Joseph Pease to unburden himself of the bad news he carried.

'You know, your brother Isaac is a very gifted clerk, Mr Pease. I'd every hope he would go on to become an associate but…'

Joseph frowned in anticipation of what would follow.

'He has consumption, Mr Pease. He has known for some time but tried to keep it secret from almost everybody I believe, but that's no longer possible. He was taken very bad a week ago in my office. I called my personal physician who gave him a thorough examination and confirmed it. I'm sorry. I don't know how to tell your father and nor does he. That's why I'm telling you now.'

'Thank you, Mr Mewburn,' Pease said quietly.

Mewburn walked on, leaving Pease alone. He leant against a tree to steady himself, masking his grief as best he could. It was wrong: they were the richest family in Darlington, they worshipped with zeal, gave to the poor, strove against poverty, opposed war and bloodshed, loved and respected strangers as family members, were educated well, clothed well, fed well and to top it all today was a beautiful summer day! Why now? Was it another of God's tests?

Tuesday 14th September

Throughout the hot summer of 1824 the Gallaghers and their gang worked ceaselessly at digging the cuttings and raising the embankments between Aycliffe and Darlington. The work was offered – in lots – to groups like his who'd formed temporary partnerships. In Seamus' gang the job of negotiating had fallen to him and he was waiting for the arrival of the contractor, James Potts, a former keelman, to negotiate over a section of land proving hard to extract from the ground.

Seamus chewed tobacco with Sean, the pair lounging on the grass with around 50 other navvies, spades and wheelbarrows idle for a time. Jugs of fresh water passed between them. A gang of younger lads sat apart from the older men – they looked after the hammers and nails to nail the chairs to the blocks of stone. Even the carters responsible for going back and forth to Brusselton Quarry for more blocks or down to the Aycliffe junction with the Great North

Road to pick up the rails from Bedlington were doing nothing but waiting for a resolution to their grievances. Almost all the men except the carters were stripped to the waist, muscles glistening with sweat, mud and exertion. The laid iron rails leading from Shildon halted abruptly in a field, one horse idle in its traces with a chaldron of tools and six more empties with horses standing like equestrian statues, swishing tails batting flies. Another cart contained an arranged pile of the iron brackets that would hold the rails in place, and yet another held a dozen iron rails ready to be laid. At least two other carts held three dozen of the 75-lb stone sleepers that would be placed in the ground for the iron rails to rest on.

Seamus had recently discovered he had a gift for numbers and figures. He didn't know where this skill originated. Certainly he had no education in Ireland and could just about sign his name, but give him a verbal tally of numbers and figures and he would remember them a week later. This skill was very useful to Mr Potts, who could entrust him with calculations and he could, instead of being laden with papers, store them in his head and work at the same time. This combination was already earning him five shillings a week more than the others and yet didn't lose him respect on account of how hard he worked. He'd come a long way since stepping off the boat at Liverpool.

'How many oak blocks again?' Sean asked, referring to the foundation blocks on which the rails were fixed.

'1,996 sawn-up timbers off old ships from Portsea brought up de coast to furnish de ground between dere an' Darl'ton an' 3,520 stone blocks quarried from Brusselton to secure de rails from Etherley,' replied Seamus confidently. 'The stone blocks are from the pit to Darlington and the wooden blocks from Darlington to Stockton. The stone blocks weigh 75lb each – just heavy enough for one man to lift, they say' said Seamus, 'But if it was a pound or two over, it'd take two men to lift and that extra man would have to be paid for and dese tight-arsed bastards don't want to pay a penny more than they can keep for demselves. Now tell me, Sean, are dese not slippery English fish we're dealin' wit here and do dey not deserve to be treated with caution?'

Sean listened but didn't understand what his big brother was hinting at, so he asked:

'Whoi is dat?'

In reply Seamus rubbed his thumb and fore-and middle finger together - funds.

'And what about de rails?'

'Fifteen and 12-foot lengths from Bedlington ferried down through Newcastle and by cart to Shildon den Darlington an' den all places along de route.'

'How heavy?'

'Very heavy – ten stones each. Dat's two strong men each and one in de middle to lift.'

'Do you ever miss de old country?' Sean asked suddenly.

'Change de subject whoi don't you?' said Seamus.

Seamus thought about Ireland. It'd been almost ten years since he'd left. Thanks to the arrival of Sean and the largely Irish company he kept, he hadn't lost his accent, but when dealing with the English bosses, Seamus had learned to speak as the Englishmen spoke: it seemed to make the English treat him with a little more respect. Sean stuck to his accent as a matter of stubborn patriotic pride. Stubborn pride, Seamus thought, was like being at war with the world and in the end the world always won and their world was the English world. Nothing more insulted an Englishman than showing him how unimportant he is. Better to turn his back and walk away.

'If you ask me do I prefer my loife now to moi life den, I'd have to say yes. It's too easy to get romantic about de past, Sean. You can tink about Limerick in a rosy way, you know, but de reality was dat awful damp an' de Protestants treated us loike dirt. Nobody would have paid me so well for shovelling dere shit in Limerick as dey do here, Sean.'

'But you're gonna make some money an' den go back, roight?'

'Oi'll go where de work is,' said Seamus.

Just then two riders trotted down the lane in the distance, hooves signalling their arrival. Seamus stood up.

'Better get up, lads,' he said to the men, 'Creates a better impression.'

The navvies got to their feet, except one who seemed to be deliberately ignoring the order.

'Hennessy!' hissed Seamus. The man of this name got to his feet mumbling under his breath.

'What's the problem?' asked Potts, dismounting, wiping his brow with a scarf and shielding his eyes. Blinking into the bright sun at the other rider only briefly, Seamus said in his Irish-English accent:

'It's hard goin', Mr Potts. The clay is baked hard and the season hot and dry. You know us boys're not afraid of a little hard work but we're not donkeys. The spades'll break first before they get a handful of dirt worth shovellin' onto a cart.'

'Well now Seamus,' said Potts, 'Prayin' to the good Lord might bring a bit of rain to loosen the ground up for yer but tell me fairly now: what do yer think we could do to rectify this situation?'

'Well,' said Seamus carefully, 'I've heard a gang 'twixt the Skerne and Coatham were getting four pence a yard and dug 4,000 yards but threw it in 'cause other gangs were being paid five pence, yet de clay is as hard and de ground as dry as it is up here. *And* there's the limestone bed up at Middridge we discovered by chance: that'll be making some Englishman rich now.' He was referring to the limestone quarry the workings had accidentally uncovered – an unexpected bonus for the S&D to exploit.

'Give 'em a penny a cubic yard more!' called the voice of the man on the other horse.

Everybody looked at the speaker.

'The man himself,' Potts said quietly. 'Stephenson.'

'Then they'll go on cheerfully, one 'opes,' Stephenson added.

Seamus looked at Potts for a moment and then crossed to the other horse and looked up at George Stephenson. He spat symbolically onto his hand and held it out.

'A handshake means as much to an Irishman as it does to an Englishman oi believe, sir?'

Stephenson took the hand and held it firmly, leaning forward in his saddle.

'Potts speaks highly of you, Mr Gallagher. I'll 'ave need of such men down at Manchester.'

'With de greatest of respect, sir, let me see that this handshake means something first before oi enter into any more negotiations witcha for de future.'

'Point taken, Mr Gallagher,' Stephenson said. 'I'll make a note now,' and he made a pencilled note in a pocketbook. Potts remounted and he and Stephenson rode off.

'Right boys, back to work! But Mr Stephenson referred to me boi name – Mr Gallagher he called us, so from now on I want you all to call me *Mr* Gallagher, is dat clear?'

'Even me?' asked Sean.

'No Sean, not you, boy.'

Monday 13th December

Michael Longridge lifted the latch and opened the smaller door in the wooden gate. He and Hackworth cast expert eyes over the workshop. Without a forge and workers, it was no more than a room filled with iron junk. The specialised workforce had been laid off some weeks before: 20 useful men who'd all served their seven years, at home languishing or playing draughts over tea and clay pipes. At the far end of the building was Active, its wooden-panelled boiler horizontal on a four-wheeled chassis but lacking the pistons to apply power. In another corner the big wooden drums of two winding engines stood awaiting delivery.

'When did yer last work in 'ere?' asked Hackworth.

'I was left with enough instructions to get the windin' engines finished and do what I could with the locomotive but then' – Longridge stepped over to the office and produced a sheet on which was scribbled a pencil drawing – 'I 'ad to stop ... here.'

He pointed at one part of the drawing. Hackworth studied it.

'Hmm,' said Hackworth. 'I suppose these two yoke-like devices above transmit the power down through these rods via coupling rods rather than a chain.'

Hackworth glanced from the window across the valley to the buildings huddled on the river's edge of Gateshead, where the smoke of nearby chimneys was being beaten out of shape by the wind and weaved into the dotted masts of the black-sailed, black-hulled keel boats jostling like the ends of busy knitting needles, tangled up in an endless round of shipping coal from the upriver pits to the waiting boats in deeper water around South Shields. It always seemed to remind him of the time he'd been out one wintry pea-souper of a day: seeing those sinister keels sailing silently out of the mist had sent a shiver running through him – it was, he mused, the nearest an ordinary man could get to seeing the Ferryman taking the dead across the River Styx.

Robert Stephenson meanwhile had gone to Colombia in South America to supervise the digging of gold mines four months previously, an offer he'd taken up from Thomas Richardson, the Quaker banker. Hackworth knew that Robert had felt a need to cast off the long shadow of his father, but regretted that this show of independence had come now at such a critical time.

He glanced in at the door of the foreman's office: charcoal sketches and half-finished letters littered the desks, and writing quills sat in dried-up inkwells. The designs for the two stationary engines, one of 30 horsepower for Etherley Hill and the other of 60 for Brusselton, were laid open on the office desks.

'Let's get that fire started,' said Hackworth.

Longridge brought out the tinderbox, iron spigot, quartzite and char cloth and soon a thin finger of smoke rose from the wood shavings. Within minutes the fire was burning.

'I'm expecting John Dixon any moment,' said Hackworth. 'He's my assistant from Wylam.'

'I 'eard about yer disagreements with Wylam,' said Longridge.

'Yer mean yer heard they fired me 'cos I wouldn't work on a Sunday,' Hackworth laughed.

'Summat like that,' said Longridge.

'They did,' Hackworth said proudly. 'And that makes me a man of principle, prepared to surrender all if he doesn't believe in something. I respect Dixon and Dixon respects me and Dixon's a good man. When he gets here I don't want to see that fire out until the summer of '25. We'll lay some private track, about 200 yards,' he indicated the open land beyond their workshop. 'That way we can test the machines to see 'ow they cope wi' pullin' loads. She'll have two vertical nine-and-a-half-inch-diameter cylinders with a 24-inch stroke and four wheels coupled by two side rods and will weigh about 11 tons.'

'That's a very accurate proposal, Mr 'ackworth.'

'I'm a very accurate man, Mr Longridge. Now, how's that fire? First item on the agenda: tea. And then let us set to building ourselves an engine!'

1825

Thursday 20ᵗʰ April

Tempers were fraying but Francis Mewburn was used to it. To those unfamiliar with law, it was always a testing time.

'I told Mr Longridge technically he was in breach of the law to alter or change the shape of the physical road, so I ordered my men to dig it out again!' said red-faced Major-General Aylmer of Walworth Castle, one of the trustees of the turnpike where the railway crossed the Great North Road.

'But this was the second time in a week,' complained Longridge. 'We *had* to fill in that hollow in order to maintain an even bed for the track. We felt we improved the road by doing so. I cannot see why the Major and Mr Allen are objecting.'

'We were objecting because we felt it would be remiss of us *not* to object,' said Allen, another trustee and local magistrate.

As a magistrate, Allen was finding himself under increasing pressure since the arrival of the railway. As the number of strangers had swelled dramatically and crime had increased, he'd come under scrutiny from the gentry to be firmer with the law and with punishments.

'It was our duty to order our workmen to dig up the soil and stones the railway company had filled in – twice – as we felt the only way to provoke a firm resolution were to get in front of this panel and let them decide, not us,' concluded Aylmer.

Navvies from the two opposing gangs sat quietly at the back of the Darlington courtroom looking uncomfortable, stiff in suits, hair oiled, summoned as witnesses but not yet called. The spokesman for one of the gangs, Seamus Gallagher, had been in consultation that morning with the company solicitor, Francis Mewburn.

'I'd one of my boys hold up traffic comin' into Darlington for five-minute periods,' Seamus had said. 'We timed with watches while the rest spread soil and stones and den switched for five minutes, so traffic leavin' Darl'ton could do so. It was the only way oi could see o' getting' the hollow filled and traffic flowin' at the same time, sir. I was very surprised at de 40-shilling fine.'

'Did you, at all times, stay calm and not lose your temper?' insisted Mewburn.

'On the grave of my mother, sir, an' you can ask any of the boys, sir.'

'The important thing then,' said Mewburn later that afternoon as he addressed the Commission, 'is not to waste time trying to establish who owns that section of space, given that the railway track owned by the S&D Company passes directly over the road owned by the Turnpike Trust, but to find a compromise, is it not, gentlemen?'

Mewburn left the question hanging as the panel consulted in whispers. He discreetly crossed his fingers under the tail of his coat. The Head of the Commission turned to Mewburn.

'After consultation, the Commission feels that it isn't worth pursuing this case as it would be a matter of some considerable expense. We therefore rule that Major-General Aylmer and John Allen, JP of Blackwell village near Darlington were quite justified, as indeed was the Stockton and Darlington Company, but we urge both to maintain amicable relations and reach compromises suitable to the public good.'

Mewburn uncrossed his fingers.

'What does dat mean, Seamus?' whispered Sean at the back.

'Dat means we got de rest of de day off, boys. Who's for a pint?'

Saturday 21st May

George Stephenson and John Dixon walked the 24 miles from Shildon to Stockton, every step seeing signs of their great undertaking: ballast being spread, sinkholes for the blocks measured accurately by a Foreman and re-checked by his apprentice and marked by a wooden stave placed in the exact centre of where the half-sunken block would be. All the work along the way was supervised by patrols of ex-miners and ex-weavers carrying heavy sticks, as rumours were rife that landowners were determined to see the venture fail. The pair made their way east to The Fighting Cocks Inn for refreshments and then walked to the village of Dinsdale and across a flat marsh a mile north of the old Viking river port of Yarm.

'This is where the strength of malleable iron comes into its own,' said George. 'It can adapt over hard and soft ground but not break with the weight of the load.'

They then walked to where coal drops were being built and then back again, crossing the turnpike into Eaglescliffe and working their way along the outer border of Preston Park, where workmen were tearing down the rotten timbers of the medieval mansion that had stood for almost 300 years to rebuild it for an industrialist.

Arriving in Stockton later that evening, they went to The Black Lion, ordering mutton stew and a bottle of French wine. Stephenson uncorked it, poured it into two crystal glasses and spoke.

'Now John,' he said to Dixon, 'I think we'll live to see the day when railways supersede almost all other methods of conveyance in this country. It'll be cheaper for a workin' man to travel upon a railway than to walk on foot. I know there are great difficulties ahead but what I've said will come to pass as sure as I speak. This time next week I'll be in London standin' afore the Prime Minister championin' the cause of the Liverpool to Manchester link n' leavin' with a successful Act in my 'and. 'ow can they say no?'

The men clinked glasses.

Wednesday 1st June

George Stephenson looked from the windows of the room onto the Thames flowing beneath the window, a line of boats moving upriver and another downriver, while on the south bank, in

Lambeth, the coal smoke of thousands of chimneys rose and lay a suffocating blanket over the city.

It had been ten days since the Parliamentary Committee had opened on 21 May, grilling witness after witness and expert after expert, none of whom left without having endured Edward Hall Alderson, the barrister brought in to sway the vote. Five days before, George had taken his position in the chair. Giving his name in response to Alderson's customary first question had been about the only thing he'd got right. It was downhill from there on. The second question was: 'Profession?'

'Engineer' he'd answered.

'Recognised by which authority?' had come the innocent-sounding reply.

'None,' he'd replied equally after a slight pause. But as soon as it had tumbled from his lips he knew it was a trap.

'None?' was returned with an exaggerated air of outrage. 'Are we to understand that an Act is being asked of the learned Lords and Members of Parliament for 63 bridges, a double line of track 31 miles long, geographical changes that will carve up the English countryside like a Sunday goose, displace thousands, be lit and paraded as a beacon of industrial power, raise share capital of half a million from hard-working investors, all placed in the hands of a man whose title is recognised by no academic institution in the land? Is that what you are asking us to accept, Mr Stephenson?'

Stephenson hesitated.

'I've been entrusted with the survey of the Stockton to Darlington Railway and –'

'But you're not here to talk about the Stockton to Darlington Railway, Mr Stephenson!' he interrupted aggressively, 'Did they not mention in the invitation? You're here to answer questions on the feasibility of the Liverpool to Manchester. In fact, no, let us look, shall we?'

He searched in an exaggerated manner through documents in front of him, plucked out one and read: 'An Act for making and maintaining a railway or tram road from the town of Liverpool to the town of Manchester, with certain branches there from.'

He laughed. 'Are the 'certain branches' an extension to travel 150 miles across the Pennines to link up with Darlington? No? Well there's no mention of Darlington or Stockton in this application, is there?'

'No, sir,' said Stephenson.

'*No, sir,*' repeated Alderson. 'Your initial survey was carried out by William James by trespass on land belonging to the Duke of Bridgewater, one of the most respected earls of the realm whose magnanimity has enabled thousands to benefit from the goods that pass daily along his canals. *Trespass,* Mr Stephenson – William James now languishes in debtor's prison in Southwark!'

It was about then that Stephenson began to realise what a monstrous circus act Parliament really was as the MP's actually cheered and jeered Hall Alderson's words and he himself seemed to speaking as if onstage and entertaining rather than informing.

'You relied on your son, Robert, another self-styled 'engineer' with only six months education at Edinburgh University, to survey the Liverpool to Manchester, but where is he when we call him to act as a witness? Oh, he's in South America chasing his personal interests in gold mines! And your figures and calculations on the proposed Irwell Bridge are, frankly, laughable – a child of ten could have done better. All in all your claims seem to add up to a Banbury Tale, Mr Stephenson!'

The Whigs and Tories on both sides of the Commons were swept along in Hall Alderson's entertaining rhetoric, and riding this groundswell he finally delivered the *coup de grâce:*

'I submit to the committee that Mr Stephenson is *not* qualified for the undertaking!'

This was the state of affairs for much of the remainder of the inquiry: Edward Hall Alderson, a former Charterhouse pupil who'd built a substantial reputation as a lawyer on the feared Northern Circuit and who represented as one of his illustrious clients the Marquess of Stafford who was making over £100,000 a year from the canal, versus a few common, self-made millionaires or 'new money,' as they were referred to, men of limited education and very little breeding but who employed thousands on subsistence wages in Manchester and Lancashire. The LMR was founded on 24 May 1823 and whipped into shape due to the over-zealous recommendations of William James. It represented a more serious economic threat than the Stockton to Darlington. The only thing to Alderson's credit was his dislike of capital punishment.

On the afternoon of Wednesday 1 June 1825, the House of Commons finally voted. Stephenson was waiting for the result in the Clubroom that overlooked the Thames. He and Lord Darlington had spotted one another and a silence descended as the two men shared the same space for a few minutes. Stephenson mustered up his dignity and prepared to shake his opponent's hand as he approached, but Darlington gave him the cut direct: a cursory glance in his direction. It was a very public humiliation. Stephenson had memories of his time underground when the workers had had to build brick walls from floor to ceiling and two lengths wide in fewer than five minutes, to seal off firedamp; his team held the record for building brick walls in record time. This image was embedded in his mind as he waited for the result of the vote.

The cries of lobbyists listening through the door to the Commons carried to George the news that Alderson had had his day – 103 to 93. But Stephenson wasn't as perturbed as he'd expected. The writing was on the wall. Shortly after, Hall Alderson and he met by chance in the corridors of power, Hall Alderson full of victory. George appeared to be grinning, a state that disturbed Hall Alderson who was not used to seeing those he defeated so buoyant.

'No hard feelings, Stephenson?'

'None at all, sir,' said George. 'We'll be back in the spring after the inevitable success of the Stockton to Darlington. Within five years you'll be travellin' on my trains on my lines n' payin' my fares to do so. All of this is but a temporary hiccup.'

Hall Alderson, undeterred by Stephenson's seeming arrogance, closed the gap on the formidable stature of Stephenson and said: 'I hope I *will* be travelling on your trains on your lines and paying your fares, but I'll sleep better in my bed knowing that I won't be sinking into Chat Moss or falling off a poorly designed bridge and breaking my neck in the process. Good day to you, sir.'

Sunday 31st July

One hot afternoon in Evenfield, Ben Hackett, foreman at the Evenfield pit where George Lovatt worked, stepped forward, flanked by two 'clearers' used for the odd unskilled job. He'd come fresh from Crockatt Hall where his Lordship had informed him the pit had scraped only a slight profit, down from the previous year. Sir Giles had explained that a combination of financial problems plus the traditional lack of demand for coal in the summer were causing difficulties. His Lordship had advised him to inform all the men immediately as Sunday was traditionally a day of rest and therefore the only time all men could be together above ground to hear the news.

Clearing his throat to address the miners, Hackett said: 'Owing to difficulties with the coal markets, Sir Giles must announce a temp'ry cut in wages of one shillin' a week.'

A murmur of unrest emanated from the assembled men at the front, swiftly turning to anger as the news filtered through the crowd. It was a pay cut. His bodyguard closed ranks around him and as some miners pressed in with objections. He raised his hands.

'This is only – this is only a temp'ry change expected to last no more than a few months. Don't act so suprised – we all know demand slackens in summer months! In the meantime – in the meantime, we don't want you to starve, so we're issuin' tokens!'

There was uproar and Hackett's pleas were lost as angrier younger men gave vent to feelings that were calmed by older men before all dispersed grudgingly with only one topic on their tongues at dinner.

That night, after tea, George Lovatt went to the houses of James Crosby, an Overman, Tom Dawson the engine driver and finally Will and John Carr, hewers like George. At the Carr's, young

John asked what it was all about. When George told him they were going to meet to talk about what they could do, John sarcastically said: 'I've a mind to take me shotgun, stick it up Hackett's arse an' pull the trigger!' but his elder brother told him to watch his mouth.

In a corner of the parlour George said: 'This cannot stand, lads, Hackett thinks we're as cork-brained as he!'

'But what can we do?' asked Crosby. 'We've taken the bond. Sir Giles is our Master.'

'We must form a combination,' said George.

The men looked at each other and then at George.

'I've 'eard it's forbidden to form a union, by law,' said Dawson.

'I've no immediate answers, lads,' said George, 'But there must be educated men sympathetic to our cause.'

'I 'eard of a man in Durham called Wilson 'oo helped form a combination of pitmen an' successfully negotiated wi' the owners,' said Carr.

'Well, I propose this,' said George, leaning forward and lowering his voice, 'Wi' the 'elp of me son, we'll write to this man n' ask 'ow to proceed. I suggest we pledge to swear to hold secret all that has passed between us at this meetin'. Agreed?'

George put his palm down on the centre of the table and the hands of the others closed around it. Nobody asked Lewis but he placed his on top of Crosby's.

'Ask Mr Leakey fer a few sheets o' foolscap. Yer can tell 'im you want to practise yer writin' at home n' that's not a lie, right?' said George to Lewis when they got home, having had Will Carr scratch down the Durham address.

The next day, Lewis arrived home with three sheets of yellow parchment and watched as his Dad mixed ink using coal dust. He took his knife to a feather he'd plucked from one of the chickens and fashioned a nib. Testing it a few times, he laid out the papers on the kitchen table and handed Lewis the plume.

'Right,' said George, 'Where do we begin?'

'Dear Mr Wilson...'

After ten minutes, Lewis showed his father a six-line message that said his Dad represented miners in Evenfield at the Crockatt mine, and that they were unhappy with pay; he sought advice on what they could do without breaking the law. Ideally, George should have signed it but because he couldn't write, Lewis signed it as George Lovatt. He also scratched their address as 'House Number Four, Paradise Row, Evenfield, County of Durham' in the top left-hand corner. The sheet was folded, the join sealed with candle wax and tied with a ribbon. Lewis carefully inscribed 'William Wilson, 6 North Road, City of Durham' on the front.

'Go over to Shildon on Monday morning to Daniel Adamson's inn. Tell 'em you want to send this letter to that address n' then pay the carryin' fare.'

George went to the drawer where he kept his tin moneybox and handed Lewis a half-crown coin with a picture of the King of England stamped on one side.

'But why not post it from 'ere, Dad?'

George wanted to say: 'Because everybody'll know George Lovatt's writin' to somebody n' everybody knows George Lovatt can't write,' but simply said: 'Run over to New Shildon. Make sure it gets to the 'ands of Dan Adamson 'cos it's he alone entrusted by 'is Majesty to take care of the mail.'

For the time being, Lewis would obey without question.

Monday 1st August, Lammas Day

Lewis's father woke him early and said he was going to work but not to forget about Shildon. He left the half crown and letter on the table.

After breakfast of hot tea and bread and butter, Lewis slipped the letter into a cloth pouch, donned his coat, hat and shoes and walked through the village and out onto the main road.

He'd hardly left Evenfield in the 13 years of his life so after a short time it seemed to him as if he'd been walking forever and twice he had to ask directions, once from a shepherd and then a coal-carrying muleteer near the turn-off to the neighbouring village of Evenwood. He arrived in New Shildon about midday. An isolated hamlet with a population of fewer than 50, it had just five standing houses, but there were pits around and large quantities of coal regularly passed through on caravans, packhorses and mule trains. Toll roads were supposed to reduce journey times but they had to be paid for and to save money, coal was diverted through Shildon. The biggest influence in the hamlet at that time was Dan Adamson, owner of the only building that seemed to be thriving, at various times known as The Mason's Arms, at others simply as Adamson's.

Outside the Inn stood a newly arrived black and red coach-and-four and the driver and his mate loaded trunks on the carriage and a smaller group stood nearby preparing to board. What struck Lewis as odd were the iron rails laid down in a long line in front of the inn stretching off into the distance in both directions. The natural world around was so full of deviating shapes and yet here was this man-made metal, so rigid and straight, announcing its presence on the ground.

Lewis went into the busy inn and asked for Dan Adamson and was directed to the end of a queue and as it moved forward he saw at the front a big man with a red beard sitting behind a table, one child in his arms and two clinging to his legs. The room was full – people crammed around tables drinking tankards of ale served up by a scrawny woman, behind her a dozen fat barrels with taps. Some smoked clay pipes, children ran around shouting, dogs barked and Lewis blinked to see two soldiers in bright red uniforms carrying muskets. In front of him an old woman was shrieking to her neighbour.

'I'm not one to gossip but I 'eard say Stephenson's lordin' it like 'e's the King of England. Twelve miles in an hour indeed! They say yer 'ead'll fall off if you go at such speeds!'

There was the sudden uproar: a fight, brief and brutal. Soldiers waded in, took the culprit and threw him into the street.

Suddenly, Lewis found himself being stared upon by Daniel Adamson.

'What can I do for you, boy?'

'Please sir, I want to send this letter to Durham.' Lewis handed over the letter. The big man took it, looked at the address, put it on the scales, studied them for a second and said: 'That's tuppence. 'ave you got tuppence?'

Lewis handed him the half crown. The man handed him two shillings and four pennies change, which he pushed down into his trouser pocket.

'What 'appens now?' asked Lewis.

'It gets took to Durham,' said Adamson. 'Next!'

Lewis went out, momentarily proud, but uncomfortable temptation moved in swiftly. He looked around enviously at the various stalls: some sold apples and bread while girls stood holding trays of oranges for a penny each, a cheap-jack sold watch chains and knives, a costermonger fruit and vegetables, another bootlaces, a packman lengths of dyed cotton to passing ladies and a pie man's stall boasted pastries, the savours of which made his mouth water. But he didn't dare spend anything.

'Land Navigators!'

Lewis heard the two men next to him talking.

'Land navigators!' repeated the older to the younger, rolling the words around his mouth and then spitting them out like apple seeds. 'We got dat name diggen all dem canals.'

They spoke in a strange tongue Lewis had never previously heard.

"'Is it not a canal you're diggen here?' 'e says to me.' 'No. It's de foundation for tracks,' oi says. 'Tracks for what?' 'e says. 'Tracks for an oiron horse,' oi says.' 'An oiron horse?' 'e says. 'Oi've never seen an 'orse wid wheels for legs. And what sort o' manure does an oiron horse have anyway? Nuts n' bolts?''

The men laughed again and Lewis followed them as they were walking back along the same road by which he'd entered the village until they turned into a field where the hedgerow abruptly ended and revealed an encampment of round tents, smoking fires, women labouring over steam-wreathed cauldrons, bare-bottomed babies tottering around and horses tied to trees. Over to the right in wooden shacks he saw blacksmiths beating iron on makeshift anvils, butchers chopping and carving sides of meat, women up to their armpits in tubs of suds and younger girls feeding clothes through mangles and hanging them out on dozens of lines. Carpenters sawed and planed blocks of wood, carters in a seemingly never-ending convoy arrived with loads of small stones, and dozens of men with dozens of wheelbarrows darted around purposefully. The industry took his breath away and the images stayed with him until he was back in Evenfield, passing numerous mule-trains of coal, some laden and some empty. Having picked up dinner from Mad Aggy, he met his father coming out of the pit.

'Did everything go well at Shildon?' his Dad asked.

'Aye, Dad. I posted the letter n' there's two shillings n' four pence change.'

'Good lad,' said George, proud of his son and throwing a dirty arm around his shoulders. They walked together as Lewis told him about all he'd seen at Shildon that day.

Saturday 6th August

Silas was sitting in front of his dead fire doing a clumsy job of skinning a rabbit.

His thoughts had been turning around memories of Waterloo nine years before. He wished he could understand why it was those thoughts returned so suddenly and at such odd times? Perhaps it was because he couldn't talk about or share them? Memories were like so many arrogant, desperate men jostling to reach the front like workers at the factory gates shouting 'Pick me!' but it seemed to Silas as long as he was busy with something there was no time to worry about the past. But a voice in his head kept repeating the same question to him so often that he started chanting it quietly to himself: 'Why me?' This was perhaps why he was doing such a clumsy job of skinning the rabbit.

Heathcote's head appeared around the half-open door.

'His Lordship'd like you to attend him in the Great Hall.'

It was unusual to be invited into the presence of his Lordship at this time of day, the evening usually being reserved for his Lordship's leisurely pursuits: business was normally conducted during the day.

'Might want to get yourself cleaned up – you look like shit,' Heathcote suggested drily. Heathcote had good reason – Silas was a mess.

Recently, Silas had been having the same dream: a nocturnal landscape of never-ending tumbledown ruins, home to countless thousands of itinerants, a million candles burning like fireflies across a horizon of walls broken through to link a labyrinth of gloomy and vague corners. He found himself holding all he held dear in a suitcase he'd put down for a minute to ask directions and when he turned, the suitcase had disappeared. He ran after the thieves through the ruins, but in vain: he was never able to catch them, only glimpse them ahead. By the time he thought he'd caught up, they'd moved a little further away and never seemed to tire whereas he grew exhausted.

He had also entertained morbid thoughts, frozen-in-time images, of arranging a tragic accident that would rid him of Hamish and leave the road open for his promotion, but despite opportunities, he had not tried. He'd wrestled with the dilemma: at Waterloo it was war – kill or be killed and on the Coach run near Lincoln he'd defended himself against somebody who would surely have shot him. But this was different. This would be a premeditated act against an innocent and unsuspecting man. Nonetheless, the more he tried to suppress or obliterate the fantasy, the more it returned, taunting him to take that damning step, teasing him to push Hamish down an old mineshaft or hold his face underwater and call it an accident just for the sheer thrill of the risk. There was that sobering moment just before Waterloo started when his heart was in his mouth and he thought 'Well, this is it. Farewell cruel world,'; that 'heart leaping out of its cage in sheer terror' feeling was what he felt then and what thought about doing for Hamish. It was powerful and addictive.

But for that moment, he stuffed his shirt into his pants, pulled on his braces and threw water on his hair to slick it back, though all it did was fall limply into his eyes and look worse. Swilling a mouthful of cold coffee, he spat into the fire, pulled on his boots and jacket and walked across the courtyard to the kitchen, passing through to where Heathcote was waiting outside the door of the Great Hall.

'What's it all about?' he asked Heathcote.

Heathcote remained silent. He tapped the side of his nose and knocked on the door and on the muffled command of 'Enter!' Heathcote went in followed by Silas.

At one side of the Great Hall was a large billiard table where Sir Giles and another aristocrat were toting large glasses of brandy while smoking fat cigars.

'Come in Scroggins, don't be timid, man. That'll be all, Heathcote – you may go to bed,' said Sir Giles as if he were talking to a child. Heathcote closed the door behind him.

'This is Lord Darlington of Raby. I've been telling him about your experiences with Wellington,' boasted Sir Giles, the worse for drink.

Silas studied Lord Darlington. This wasn't the first time he'd met him up close – Silas had guarded the carriage that had escorted the strongbox to Darlington to try to break the Backhouse Bank back in 1819. He obviously didn't remember a lowly hired thug. Silas muttered: 'Your Lordship.'

'Never mind Wellington - what about Stephenson? Far too high in the bloody instep that dog,' snapped Lord Darlington, also the worse for alcohol.

'I'd a battle getting the bugger to divert his invention away from my foxes. We've Scroggins here to thank for how productive *they* are,' said Sir Giles.

Silas smiled perfunctorily.

'I won't have his safety lamp down my pits!' Lord Darlington cursed. 'If miners are to have lamps, I've ordered them from Sir Humphrey Davy. It's absurd an uneducated coalminer can invent a lamp that burns safely – Sir Humphrey is one of the country's leading scientists. If anyone knows what he's talking about, it's him, not some jumped-up Geordie labourer!'

'In what manner may I assist your Lordship?' asked Silas looking at his employer.

Sir Giles slipped his hand into his pocket, pulled out a crumpled brown envelope and threw it onto the green baize.

'Can you read?' he asked Silas.

'A little, sir.'

He had had to pick up some basics to understand signs and notices in London and France.

'Read that then - looks as if it was written by a child anyway!'

Silas opened the torn envelope and unfolded the letter. It took him a minute to make out its contents. He looked up at Sir Giles.

'This letter,' said Sir Giles, 'was sent to a man in Durham called Wilson – a most dangerous character – seeking help to form a union, but it was written in Evenfield and Evenfield is my village.'

'Why don't you have the man arrested, sir?' Silas asked.

'Yes, well, I'm coming to that,' said Sir Giles, gulping back his brandy and exhaling cigar smoke.

Lord Darlington put down his glass, picked up a cue and lined up his next shot. Silas was aware of how Lord Darlington was studying him despite being seemingly pre-occupied.

'I could do that: have him arrested, but he's not alone in this business and I doubt he'll tell the authorities who else is involved.

Tough, dogged lot these miners. But what if somebody were to invite himself to one of their illegal meetings in Evenfield?'

'Has this Wilson read the letter?' Silas asked.

'It was intercepted before delivery but the words are clear: 'I do not know you but have heard you have helped other men in our situation.' Therefore, Wilson knows nothing about George Lovatt and there's no reason he ever should.'

Silas suspected what was coming next but saw no need to put his neck into the noose. However, he did notice that neither man seemed to have the courage to look him in the eye as they concocted their nasty little plan – a sure sign of their deceit.

'So I'd be very grateful,' Sir Giles continued, 'if a man with military experience were to penetrate this 'secret society' so I can bag them all like a brace of grouse, what?'

'Speaking of which, the season started a few days ago, your Lordship. We're all so busy...' said Silas seeking a way out.

'I'm aware of that. Jones can run the show.'

'But wouldn't the Evenfield miners know that I wasn't Wilson?' asked Silas.

'When was the last time you were in Evenfield, Scroggins?' Sir Giles asked.

'I've never been, sir,' said Silas. 'There's been no reason – everything I've needed has been here on the estate.'

'Perfect, no?' said Sir Giles, raising his eyebrows.

'And how would this arrangement be of benefit to me?' Silas asked, by now aware his head was in the noose and he had little left to lose. Sir Giles and Lord Darlington looked at each other.

'What do you want?' Sir Giles asked bluntly.

'Some improvement in my position would be useful, sir.'

Lord Darlington looked at the billiard table, lined up his cue, potted the black in one swift stroke and said: 'And he did wonders with the foxes, Giles.'

Sir Giles said: 'That'll be all, you'll be informed when you're needed.'

'Yes sir, thank you sir, good evening gentlemen,' and at that Silas bowed his head respectfully and exited the Great Hall.

'You know,' said Sir Giles, 'I'll let him do his job and then get rid of the bugger!'

'Absolutely,' said Lord Darlington 'Can't have commoners getting above their station.'

Wednesday 10th August

A few days later, Hamish saddled one of Sir Giles's chestnut mares and was told to tie it to the gatehouse and get scarce. He did what Sir Giles ordered but curiosity got the better and he lurked in the bushes nearby. He saw Silas approach the gate, glance around, untie and mount the mare, dismount again and adjust the stirrups for his longer legs before remounting. Just then, Sir Giles appeared and the two exchanged words Hamish couldn't catch. Silas was handed a letter and Sir Giles slapped the horse's rump. She clopped across the track and out into the wood.

A flash of envy coursed through Hamish. He had no idea why Scroggins was being given this preference or what his task was, but either way he didn't like it. Scroggins had to go. He was becoming a threat. The oldest trick in the book would do it: plant an object of value about their person or belongings when they were out, then report the valued object stolen. That was how he had got rid of people who had annoyed or crossed him in the past.

Silas, meanwhile, was enjoying his temporary status as a steed-mounted gentleman. It made him feel superior and he secretly hoped he'd meet some locals so he could milk his importance, but he realised that the less people knew his face, the better, considering the long-term implications of what he was about to do. He rarely rode horses: he spent most of his working life on his own two feet. Galloping or even trotting was an unpleasant feeling. Walking was safer but much slower, so it wasn't until mid afternoon that the ten-mile trip had been closed to one and as he approached the outskirts of Evenfield his jauntiness had all but disappeared. He said nothing to the salutations of the many muleteers and coal-carrying carters he passed in both directions on the way, so engrossed was he in his deception.

He didn't know if Lovatt was on the fore-shift or the back-shift. If the fore-shift, he'd have to be woken up and if the back-shift he'd be underground at least until evening. That meant he'd not be able to organise the others until even later. Even if they were all on the back-shift, they probably wouldn't be able to get together until dusk and he wouldn't be able to leave until after sunset. It was too dark to travel on an uneven road with no light and he didn't want to spend the night with them – he'd never keep up the pretence.

The cottages were simple brick affairs and, glancing at the chimney from which he could see no smoke but only a faint trace of heat, he counted down four and dismounted. Spotting a water pump, he tied his horse to it, went to the side door and knocked. No answer. He went to the front window and, cupping his hand to the glass, looked in to see orange coals glowing in the grate, though that didn't necessarily mean anyone was home. He took out his flask and swigged, and just after he'd replaced it, he found himself looking into the face of a boy.

'Can I 'elp you, sir?' the boy asked.

'Is this the 'ouse o' George Lovatt?'

'Yes, sir. I'm 'is son, Lewis.'

'I'm – ' Silas hesitated. 'My name's Wilson. I'm from Durham.'

The name shot into Lewis's memory like a spark from two struck flints: this was the man he'd heard his father talk about, the union man, the one he'd written to! But his father had also made an oath of secrecy, so he was cautious. He did not look like a lawyer but then Lewis didn't really know what a lawyer looked like other than a gentleman. This was a rough-looking gentleman with a wild beard and different shades across his eyes and face as if once burnt.

'Does that name mean owt to yer, son?' Silas asked.

'No, sir. Are you a friend of my father's?' replied Lewis.

'Sort of,' said Silas. 'Can we go in or do we 'ave to stand out 'ere?'

They went into the parlour where Lewis stoked the fire and added more coal then filled a copper kettle and put it over the flames. He took down the best china cup from the hook and a saucer from the drawer, put both on the kitchen table, ladled a spoonful of tealeaves into the teapot and stood uncomfortably, unsure what to say.

'When's your father due back?' Silas asked.

'When work finishes, sir. He's on fore-shift.'

'You don't work down the pit?'

'No, sir. I 'erd cows n' do odd jobs.'

'What about yer Mam?' asked Silas, looking about the room.

'Dead, sir, four year ago. My Dad's the miner.'

Silas tried to think of something to say in the guise of someone he was pretending to be and Lewis waited.

'Come far, sir?' Lewis asked.

'Aye,' said Silas, warming to the pretence. 'Durham.'

It would have been rude to ask his business, so Lewis decided to see if the visitor volunteered.

'Do you know 'oo I am n' why I'm 'ere?' Silas asked.

'No sir. Should I know?' replied Lewis innocently.

'Can your father read n' write?'

Lewis hesitated.

'A little, sir, not much.'

Silas simply said 'Ah'.

'But I can,' the boy went on. 'I've been learnin'.'

Just then they heard the distant singing of the mine's steam whistle.

'That'll be me Dad on his way back now, sir,' said Lewis.

'How old are you, son?' Silas asked.

'Thirteen, sir,' said Lewis, trying to stand tall.

'What happened to your mother?'

'The consumption, sir.'

'And you've nae brothers or sisters?'

'No, sir.'

The two shared the silence until the kettle whistled. Lewis took a rag and lifted it onto the table, struggling to pour the boiling water without spilling any. He returned the kettle to the grate and put the lid on the teapot. Silas mulled the consequences of what the boy had told him: to Sir Giles and Lord Darlington it was of no consequence, but if the father of this boy was imprisoned, the son would be put into beggary and all the reading and writing in the world wouldn't save him. Lewis poured the visitor's tea, careful to limit the tealeaves, and Silas sat down.

'Don' yer wanna be a soldier? Most boys wanna be soldiers,' Silas said.

'Were you a soldier, sir?' Lewis asked.

Silas's back straightened.

'Indeed I was, son: Waterloo 18th June, 1815.'

He regretted it as soon as he'd spoken because it was him talking, not Wilson.

'Waterloo?' gasped Lewis. 'Did you meet the Old Duke?'

Silas was saved by the sound of hobnailed boots. The door opened.

'Father, this is William Wilson of Durham.'

'I saw the 'orse n' wondered,' said George.

George Lovatt was caked head to foot in coal dust. The only parts with any colour were the whites of his eyes and teeth and the pink of his gums and tongue which gave his facial features an almost comical look. He blinked twice and said: 'Lewis, run out an' play - me an' Mr Wilson 'ave things to discuss.'

'I've put the kettle on, for you to wash an' for some tea for Mr Wilson,' said Lewis.

'Good lad, run along now.'

Lewis went outside to pretend to play but in fact he listened to the voices at the door.

'You got me letter then Mr Wilson?' asked George.

'I did, an' thought it wise to come straight over n' talk to you.' was the reply.

'I'm very grateful, though I didn't expect you so soon,' said George.

Lewis heard splashing water as his father washed; periods of silence punctuated with speech.

'Can yer 'elp us?' asked the father.

'Us?' asked Silas.

'Mesel' n' three other men from the village, all from Crockatt's pit. We've formed a union. Well, I say formed, but it's nowt official – just four blokes holdin' meetins wi' plenty to moan about but little to do.'

'Can I meet these other men now?' asked Silas.

'Well, I was wonderin' what you thought about the conditions that 'ave been forced on us recently? Are you aware of 'em?'

'Tell me now,' said Silas.

'Crockatt's knocked a bob a week off wages except for the Head Viewer, Hackett. We were all wonderin' 'ow we might be able to negotiate wi' pit owners wi'out breakin' the law.'

'The sooner I can meet 'em the better,' said the visitor with some urgency. 'I must try to get back to Durham tonight afore sunset.'

'It'd be better if you put yer 'orse round back – she'll attract attention. *Lewis!*'

Lewis opened the door far too quickly and for a moment it looked like his Dad was going to get angry and accuse him of listening at the door, which would embarrass his Dad in the company of the educated man he was trying to impress.

'Take Mr Wilson's 'orse round the back n' throw a blanket ower the saddle. Then run to Will Carr, Tom Dawson and Mr Crosby n' tell 'em the' must all come 'ere, but not why, you understand?'

Lewis did as he was asked and as he threw the blanket over the saddle, he noticed the letters G and C embossed in gold onto it and wondered what they stood for. He didn't think about it for more than a few seconds because he had to run off to his father's friends' houses, and within minutes the three, half-washed and still in their work clothes, were seated around the kitchen table with William Wilson. Lewis was sent out again but again eavesdropped.

Many questions were put and Silas-as-Wilson did his best to answer but replied often and regularly: 'I'll have to look into that' or 'I'll see what I can do.' Then Silas suddenly announced it was time to leave. Lewis listened. James Crosby was dissatisfied and pressed him but Silas again said he'd 'look into that' and got to his feet, the chair legs scraping harshly on the stone floor. George advised Crosby not to be impatient then more voices and the final words of Silas whom he'd presumed was Wilson as he left: 'You'll be hearin' from me!'

They watched through the window as Silas untethered his horse with irritability and urgency.

'He seems keen to get away?' suggested Crosby.

'Prob'ly wants to get started soon as possible – it's drawin' on dark,' George suggested.

'Why didn't 'e answer the question about negotiations?' asked Tom.

'He's an' educated man. We must trust educated men,' said George. 'I'm sure 'e's goin' to look into our case n' come back with 'is suggestions. We must trust 'im.'

'Well, I dunno about you,' said the cynical Will Carr who was known for his doubting ways, 'but if that's an educated union man then *I'm* a monkey's uncle. I've learnt nowt!'

The men exchanged mixed farewells and returned to their homes. Lewis finally went back in and saw his Dad sitting at the table. George too had been disappointed with Wilson, but had to give him the benefit of the doubt.

'Will Mr Wilson help, Dad?'

'I trust him,' said George. 'The others aren't so sure.'

The moment Silas mounted the horse he began to panic. It was irrational. After all, for the miners he was the 'educated man' and could easily have dictated anything. What let him down was that he'd felt he'd become a Judas. The miners weren't innocent, spotless men like Jesus but they were honest and hardworking with wives and children and seeking only to better themselves. At a certain point, he couldn't stomach his self-loathing and had had to get out and away from that place, and though he tried to stay calm as he untethered the horse, even she could sense his evil mood and pulled away as he climbed onto her back. He rode straight to Crockatt Hall, doing half the distance in dusk then dismounting and walking when night fell. When he finally got back, he took the horse to the stables and unsaddled her and Hamish was sent to inform him to attend Sir Giles. Hamish hissed: 'What you up to?'

'Business beyond your understanding!'

In the Great Hall, Silas saw Sir Giles waiting with another man, certainly not an aristocrat. Hamish was dismissed.

'Is it done?' demanded Sir Giles.

'The leader is a man called George Lovatt,' said Silas.

'I already know that! He signed the letter, you idiot! Who are the others?'

Silas swallowed hard.

'James Crosby, Tom Dawson and Will Carr, sir. They all took an oath a few weeks back to 'ave secret meetin's an' try to find a way to communicate wi' William Wilson to enlist 'is help in negotiatin' wi' you for better pay n' conditions.'

'And there are no more? Just those four?' Sir Giles asked.

'From what I gather, sir, no, no more.'

Sir Giles wrote the four names in ink onto the Arrest Warrant and blew on it.

'I know 'em all, sir,' said Hackett, standing.

'Hackett, get men who'll do anything for a bob and keep their traps shut.'

Hackett, thought Silas, was the one of whom George Lovatt had spoken.

'I can find such men but the grouse shoot starts in four days, milord,' said Hackett.

'That's true, sir, I'm occupied hirin' them as well,' said Silas.

'How's business at the mine?' asked Sir Giles.

'Very slack, sir,' said Hackett. 'Only 'alf workin' n' very little demand.'

'We'll wait 'til the grouse season gets underway before dating this warrant,' Sir Giles commanded. 'Then get your miners and take them to Darlington.'

'Can Darl'ton 'andle such cases, sir?' queried Hackett.

'Darlington will handle what I tell it to handle!' Sir Giles snapped. 'I'll give you a hunting rifle and you can say you found it in Lovatt's kitchen to make it official, then we can get them on at least two of the Six Acts: 'Misdemeanours' and 'Seizure of Arms.' You may go, Scroggins, but keep your trap shut.'

Silas waited for more, but nothing came, so he nodded and left. He had to trust educated men, however harshly they sometimes talked to or treated him. But on the walk to his cottage, the world turned blue and white by the light of the August moon, he began to wish he was somebody else, somewhere else and, like many hard-drinkers, could think only of one thing: a clay jar of cheap Irish poison that passed for alcohol behind his kitchen cupboard and oblivion.

Thursday 15th September

'Thank you, Coates. Show them in, please.'

Mewburn looked from his office window in Darlington marketplace. It was mid-afternoon and only a few people were about. The news he was about to convey was bad but it was 'just business'. His delivery would be impartial. Its reception would be taken, he hoped, with suitable impartiality and a lack of emotion. But what troubled him most was how Pease would handle it given that his son Isaac had no hope.

Pease and Backhouse entered the small room, their leather shoes making the varnished floorboards squeak. The three shook hands and Mewburn sat again, as did his two friends, Pease standing his stick against the edge of the desk. Mewburn picked up the teapot and poured. He glanced at Pease.

'Why are we here?' asked Pease through gritted teeth.

'We're in a bit of a bumble broth,' said Mewburn, unsettled by the curt query but sympathetic as to why it was so. 'At the beginning of this year there were at least 20 national railway schemes underway, representing a combined speculation of almost £14,000,000. We should have launched ours six months ago. The world is impatient and the press and Parliament are beginning to turn. Influential people have gone out on a limb and yet we have little to show. What's the financial situation, Mr Backhouse?'

'Land purchase and compensation has cost us £18,000 more,' said Backhouse in a low voice, and went on: 'Repairs to the Gaunless and the building of the self-acting plane at Etherley and the diggings have swallowed up the 50 from Norwich. We haven't built the staithes at Stockton, the depots or any engine sheds and we haven't even started on the extensions to Croft, Coundon or Haggerleases. We're in the red at £7,500 and rising by about £100 a day.'

'And today I received this,' said Mewburn, leaning back in his chair and looking at the letter. 'Richardson's Bank wants the £50,000 repaid by 9th February, six months from now. As a shareholder, Richardson gives his full support but he is only part of a Board who remains less convinced.'

'Is the line traversable from beginning to end?' asked Backhouse.

'Stephenson assures me the locomotive can be put on the line next week,' said Pease.

'Then it appears we're forced to play our hand,' said Mewburn. He picked up a copy of an almanac and turned the pages to September. 'May I suggest … Tuesday the 27th?'

'Is it enough time?' asked Backhouse. 'It's very short notice.'

'We can prepare locally but we must send word to ambassadors in London today so they can appeal for representatives and journalists. I'll write an announcement for the newspapers. That gives us just under ten days. Twenty-seventh day, ninth month?'

asked Mewburn, familiar with the Quaker custom of not calling days or months by their Roman origins.

'I suppose it must be,' said Pease distantly, wondering why the date rang a bell, and it suddenly struck him it was the date Dr Peacock had estimated when asked how much longer Isaac had left to live.

Friday 16th September

As Lewis and George were on their way to the Evenfield chandlers to trade in their food tokens, they passed a small knot of people gathered around a notice pinned to a board outside The Cleveland Bay and stopped to look.

'What does it say, son?' George asked.

Lewis stepped up closer to the printed declaration and studied it.

'Somethin' about the railway - the official openin's 27th, up at Shildon.'

'It's nowt to do wi' us. Come on!' said George.

Queuing with other miners' wives clutching their food coupons was a depressing and humiliating experience. But George was buying a quarter pound of nail tacks too – he was busy making Lewis his first pair of leather shoes. The old clogs were worn down now and he noticed that even when he wasn't wearing them, Lewis traipsed his bare feet as if he still had them on and that would deform his stance and natural gait. Besides, it was a symbol of maturity passing from clogs to shoes – like passing from childhood to manhood. It was mostly women shopping but there was no woman in the Lovatt household and when George finally got to the front of the queue it was to be handed one undersized stale loaf, a sack of flour that contained a few wood shavings and a quart of sour milk – flour from Sir Giles's mill, milk from Sir Giles's dairy and bread from Sir Giles's ovens.

'Milk's bad, bread's stale an' flour's got weevils,' George muttered. 'At least the tacks's sound!'

'Should consider yourself thankful – could just as easy let you starve,' said Mrs Cole, the shopkeeper's wife.

'His Lordship should consider 'imself lucky he's coal to heat his house this winter, we could just as easy let 'im freeze!' snapped George and strode out with his shoe tacks wrapped in a twist of brown paper, leaving the wives gossiping at his audacity. His father's nimble reply had excited Lewis but as they walked back with their meagre rations, George was very quiet.

'I could get a job at the pit,' said Lewis. 'I could take care of the ponies. A surface job isn't as bad is it, Dad?'

'I gave me word to yer Mam,' said George.

'But I'd not be goin' *down* the pit if I worked on the surface, would I?'

George thought for a moment and shook his head.

'No. Your Mam is watching us all the time. She'd not like it.'

'But how am I ever going to know how bad it is unless I go down myself?' complained Lewis.

'Because once the Devil gets you in his backyard, he never lets you go,' said George.

'What does that mean?' Lewis asked.

They arrived at their cottage.

'I'll show you,' said George.

George put the bread, flour and jug on the table, lit the stub of a candle and told Lewis to get into his Box bed, pull the blanket over his head and lie perfectly still, not moving a muscle. After the boy had settled, George asked softly: 'Now, what can you see?'

'Everything's dark,' whispered Lewis.

'Can you feel the material pressin' against yer skin? Don't move now, not an inch! Feel all parts o' your body it's touchin' against – legs, arms, feet, sides, shoulders, 'ead. Can you feel all that?'

'Aye, Dad, I can!'

'Now imagine that place where the cloth is touching you is the weight of a mountain.'

Lewis suddenly drew breath, panicked and threw aside the brown cotton blanket to find his Dad sitting close by with the lit candle in one hand and a look of surprise on his face.

'Are you all right?'

'Is that 'ow it was when you saved Mr Crosby? Were you scared?'

'Aye, I was scared!' said George.

'But – but men shouldn't be afraid, should they?' Lewis asked.

'All men are afraid of something, Lewis. Some men are afraid of violence and fighting. Some men are afraid of love. The big, tough ones – them that's always full of bluster – they're usually afraid to be sensitive and caring. Stupid men are afraid of clever men and clever men are afraid of stupid men. Fat men are afraid of hunger and thin men too. Everybody is afraid of something or someone. It's life. We all just have to find a way to live with it and not let the things that can make us afraid take over our lives and ruin us completely.'

As Lewis read himself to sleep, George sat for a while in the parlour, watching the moon caress the black and blue forms of the trees and fields beyond the window. The memories of his wife were still as fresh as ever but they seemed to be settling on a handful of particularly strong images and always she had a huge smile or was laughing. He treasured memories of her soft touch and warm embrace.

Drawing the thin blanket tight around his slight form, Lewis pulled his nightgown over his feet, knees up against his chest and closed his eyes. He dreamt of a world where men wore feathers and animal skins or worshipped the sun and hunted lions and elephants; where all people had money, choice and dignity, bread was fresh, flour smelled of the fields and milk was nectar. He'd never tasted nectar but it sounded lovely. With only the ticking mantle piece clock for comfort, George rocked gently in his chair staring into the flames while Lewis slipped into dreams of a land of roses and honey on a magic steam box cart on wheels.

***

'Out, out, o-*o-o-o-o-u-u-u-t-t-t!*'

Strong arms dragged him to the floor, down the stairs – legs bouncing off the treads – out into the black night and rain where his Dad was already on his knees, arms pulled behind his back by dark shapes of men, alongside Crosby, Carr and Dawson.

'Dad!'

George broke free. A masked figure lunged and Lewis saw his father's fist crunching with force into the man's jaw. He reached for Lewis but others clubbed him down. He curled up. Lewis screamed for them to stop and it seemed to work but only because they wanted to ransack homes, crashing, smashing and splintering as they searched for money and spoils as fast as they could.

Just then Hackett, wearing a long and fearsome black overcoat, arrived, dismounted and went into the Lovatt house, re-emerging moments later holding a shotgun aloft like a trophy.

'James Crosby, William Carr, Tom Dawson, George Lovatt: you're under arrest on suspicion of the contravention of breach of the Six Acts. You're to be took to Darl'ton.'

Along the road, wails from wives and mothers filled the air as the hired henchmen gathered Crosby, Dawson and Will Carr together. Will had blood flowing from his mouth and John Carr, his brother, was held back forcibly by neighbours to protect him and stop him making matters worse. George and his fellow captives stumbled to the village green where they were loaded into a wooden box a few feet high. The masked men mounted horses, sometimes two to a saddle, and as the prison cart pulled away Lewis followed, as did the wives and other children.

'What shall I do Dad? Dad, what shall I do?' Lewis pleaded.

'Go to Durham! Find Wilson! Number 6 North Road!' George gasped.

Two of the riders forced short bursts of pace from their mounts to discourage followers before swerving sharply after the carriage and then they were gone, swallowed by the night. Those that remained stood in fear and shock.

'How did they know who to arrest?' shouted John Carr angrily at the fearful faces as he struggled from his neighbours' grip. 'How did they know?'

Lewis staggered shakily to his house. The door was open and inside wasn't too badly damaged – they'd spared crockery and furniture but had searched for money: drawers were rifled and clothes strewn about. A rough hand had cleared the mantle piece in one swipe so the poor old clock was smashed beyond repair on the stone floor, the tin box was empty of its few coins and their one burnished mirror now in silver slivers. Even the panel on his Box bed had been opened and the hard mattress upturned and stabbed and squeezed for hidden belongings so that straw spilled out in places. Standing there for what seemed an eternity, Lewis saw then the shoes his Dad had finished for him only days before. They sat neatly together under the crockery cupboard. He reached under and lifted them out with one hand. The scent of the leather was strong. He managed to right an upturned chair but couldn't control his shaking limbs. He heard a tap on the door. It opened slowly. It was Mr Leakey.

'Oh my poor boy!'

'Why am I sh-shakin', Mr Leakey?'

'Partly because it's cold but partly from shock I should think. Come and sit down here.'

Leakey stoked the embers, gently laid a coat over Lewis's shoulders and sat him down on the righted chair. His old face pained as Lewis told him what happened, finishing with: 'But how did they know?'

'In small places like this, everybody knows everything,' said Leakey dubiously. 'First, tell me what *you* know and what has happened here?'

With dry kindling on the fire as well as a few lumps of coal, Lewis slowly warmed up and Mr Leakey pulled up the other chair to listen to Lewis's story about William Wilson, the union and the letter.

Eventually, Mr Leakey said: 'Hmm. I see. I have a plan: I think we should go to Durham and find this William Wilson first thing in the morning.'

'Do you really think that's possible?' said Lewis, desperate for hope.

'Yes. There simply must be some misunderstanding,' said Leakey.

Saturday 17th September

The following day, the road took them to Shildon. Lewis had dressed in itchy wool and was wearing his new leather shoes; they fastened across the top with a small buckle and were stiff. They felt tight and chaffed him but Mr Leakey assured Lewis that would soon pass. Already, as Lewis moved around he felt extraordinarily light and freer.

'Shildon is seeing such changes, Lewis. They say the steam engine is arriving today from Newcastle,' said Leakey.

Lewis wanted to comment but his heart was heavy. Any attempt to profit from the moment was thwarted by thoughts of his father.

After Shildon, they chose the Heighington Road. In both directions and as far as the eye could see were mule-trains laden with coal or travelling to collect coal. The young mare was fit and trotted well, but the gig had seen better days and it jolted, creaked and rattled, making speed risky. Leakey pulled over as another cart came into view loaded with large blocks of coal. At the front sat a bundle of black rags.

'Are we on the good road to Aycliffe?' Leakey called over.

The driver spat black phlegm onto the grass.

'Aye, left takes you to Shildon, right to Darl'ton. Aycliffe straight ahead.'

'Come far?' Leakey asked.

'Cockfield. Going to put up near Darl'ton n' finish journey tomorrow. Giddup!'

Both drivers slapped black sticks on the rumps of their respective horses.

From a distance, Leakey and Lewis saw a crowd around a dray and a team of six Shires, and as they approached, they could make out the name 'Pickersgill' painted on the side in elaborate gold and green lettering. The cart had blocked the road to Aycliffe. Sitting atop was a bulky white tarpaulin covering a square shape as big as a small house. Above the dray an arrangement of poles had been set into a tripod and under the crown a large wooden pulley and block. From this hung four chains tied to the object beneath the tarpaulin and a little distance away half a dozen men pulled on four ropes.

'I know you must be impatient,' said Leakey, 'But I've determined to get you to Durham and get you to Durham I will.'

At the crowd's outer edge a large man with rolled-up shirtsleeves climbed onto the dray and he and another man pulled back the tarpaulin.

Lewis knew of the winding engine at the Crockatt Pit in Evenfield but this was like a horizontal barrel: at one end a large chimney pointed to the sky and above the barrel was a complicated arrangement of metal rods and bars.

'Stephenson,' said Leakey, pointing at the big man in the shirtsleeves.

Stephenson gave an order and the workers heaved the ropes, their feet digging into the earth for leverage. The bulk of the engine lifted a few inches above the dray at a speed almost imperceptible to the eye. The horses and the dray were led forward as the body of the engine hung above the track. The order was finally given to lower. Stephenson watched from all angles as it descended and the four wheels finally touched the rails. Satisfied, Stephenson waved his hand – the way was free as pedestrians and carts surged across in both directions.

Leakey and Lewis returned to their gig and soon were trotting along to Aycliffe Village. Leakey was excited about what he'd seen and wanted to talk about it but Lewis remained tight-lipped. At the turnpike, Leakey paid some pennies that allowed them on and they turned north, towards Durham. There were less coal carts and mule-trains here as the Turnpike's tolls were beyond the reach of many ordinary carters and badly affected their profits. Lewis had never been this far from home before, nor had he seen the Great North Road, but despite his self-imposed austerity, he couldn't resist asking: 'Is it true this road connects London to Edinburgh?'

'It does indeed,' said Leakey. 'Two hundred and seventy miles to London and a hundred and fifty or so to Edinburgh.'

'Have you ever been to either of them?' Lewis asked.

'Yes, when I was a younger man. Edinburgh is not as big as London. London is enormous and the sky black with the smoke of a hundred thousand chimneys.'

Lewis noticed how busy the Great North Road was: a seemingly never-ending trickle in both directions pushing or pulling handcarts, passed continually by wagons, riders and mule trains transporting coal or crops or sheep, cows or geese. The road was rarely clear. Twice all carriages and flocks were forced to pull over or part for the Mail Coach. The traffic thickened as they crossed Ferryhill, Croxdale and nearby Tudhoe Collieries spilling out more mule trains and convoys. Once over the Wear at Sunderland Bridge the horse tired as it began the long ascent up the bank to the edge of Durham and, at a slow pace, they descended into the city.

For the first time in his young life Lewis saw the mighty fortresses of Durham Cathedral and Castle towering over all. The city was full of people calling for custom, children playing hoops and ball on the cobbles, bells ringing, horses and carts, the wretchedly poor alongside the indubitably wealthy, servants attending masters, schoolboys and schoolmasters and university students side-by-side marching in uniformed regiments – life, life, everywhere life. Suddenly, they turned into a marketplace and found themselves on the edge of a dense milling crowd. Leakey tried to urge his horse forward but she was spooked, and they'd only gone a few yards when they heard the sound.

'Listen!'

Leakey didn't speak – he knew exactly what it was. The crowd reacted to the drum calling them to follow and follow they did – a human mass surging away from the marketplace and swarming around the front of an imposing stone building. Curiosity getting the better of him, Lewis jumped down and was immediately dragged by the impetus and density of the people around a corner to the gates of the building where a wooden gibbet stood, four nooses hanging from the crossbar. Aghast and realising what it was he tried to turn back, but it was too late: he couldn't penetrate the writhing mass.

A gate opened in the side of the building to a roar of clapping and cheering, the drum beating as four prisoners filed out led by a soldier pulling on a rope tied to their wrists: three men and a woman. At the rear, a priest chanted and prayed. On they stumbled, one of the men trying to keep his eyes closed, another mumbling prayers as the human train mounted the scaffold and was positioned alongside the respective nooses.

Lewis couldn't hear the words the chaplain mumbled from the pages of his Bible but watched fascinated as a man in a black suit and cap read the list of names, crimes and punishments from a scroll. As each of the prisoners had hoods fitted over their heads and their ankles tied together, the hangman shouted:

'James Boyd: for stealin' several items o' wearin' apparel, includin' a silk tie, cotton britches n' gold-buckled shoes: death!'

'Nicholas Urwin: for 'avin' carnally known Mary Dodds against 'er will.'

A wave of dirty laughter rippled across the crowd.

'Death!'

A huge cheer went up.

'Ann Scott – for pickin' pockets *despite* bein' whipped on *two* previous occasions.'

A mocking 'Ooo!' of false horror rose up.

'Death!'

Cheers and hoorays.

'Henry Dove: for stealin' an 'orse: death! And may the Lord 'ave mercy on yer souls!'

The chaplain stepped away, leaving the condemned with hands behind their backs and nooses around their necks. The trembling legs of the woman gave way and she slumped to her knees. A soldier rushed forward, carefully positioning his feet around the trapdoor, to hold her up. The drumbeat picked up speed and volume and then suddenly stopped. The executioner pulled a lever and the trapdoors fell open simultaneously, the condemned woman ripped from the grip of the soldier as she and the others dropped into the void and jerked sharply on taut ropes. Most of the crowd cheered and some laughed out of fear, revolted and fascinated. The many became one, like a savage dog suddenly sedated or satisfied and called by its owner. Lewis noticed dark liquid dripping from the feet of the hanging woman and he felt a sudden knot in his stomach. He doubled over as he vomited up his meagre breakfast of bread and honey and tea that Leakey had made for them both before they'd set out.

'I did try to warn you,' Leakey said quietly. Lewis stood up and wiped his mouth and though still feeling queasy climbed up onto the seat, ashen-faced. Leakey flicked the reins and the horse moved slowly through the subdued and dispersing crowd. They didn't have far to go.

'What number was it?' Leakey asked.

'Number six,' said Lewis.

Leakey stopped the cart and nodded at a white door across the road.

Lewis climbed down. He couldn't immediately walk as his legs were still trembling, so he gingerly climbed the steps of the house. He began now to feel the new leather of his shoes hurting his feet and it was distracting him but he hid it well as he felt a man should at such times. A metal hoop was affixed to the left of the doorframe. He tugged at it and heard the distant sound of a bell. A moment later the door was opened by a tall wiry man with bright russet hair either side of his balding pate and spectacles on his bony freckled nose.

'Yes?'

'Please sir, can I speak to Mr Wilson, William Wilson?' Lewis asked.

Leakey joined Lewis.

'I'm William Wilson,' said the man. 'How can I help?'

'But you're – you're not William Wilson,' said Lewis, confused.

'I certainly am,' said William Wilson.

'Forgive me, sir,' said Leakey. 'My pupil and I have travelled from Evenfield near Shildon. Is this the home of William Wilson, the union man who helps miners?'

'This is the home of that gentleman and I am that gentleman,' said Wilson.

'But you're not the same man who came to my 'ouse a week ago to talk with my father about troubles at the Evenfield mine!' said Lewis.

'Is there trouble at Evenfield?' Wilson asked.

'I wrote a letter on behalf of me Dad some weeks ago askin' your advice. My father cannot write yer see, n' I wrote the letter for him.'

'Perhaps you ought to come in,' the man said, inviting them first into his hallway and then ushering them into a side room. Once they were seated, he said: 'Explain exactly what happened.'

A little way into their story, Wilson rang a small bell and an elderly woman entered. The householder ordered tea. Lewis continued to tell his tale. The story was interrupted temporarily as the servant returned and tea was poured, but finally, with the tea drank and the story told, the man lifted his spectacles from his nose.

'I *am* a lawyer, gentlemen. Four years ago I was in Wallsend near Newcastle when the miners at the colliery there suffered an accident. I lost a brother. Many of the miners were my friends. I argued for compensation and managed to secure five pounds per family. Now, whenever working men have problems with their employers they come to me and I do what I can, often for free. I can make no promises of a successful outcome – I am one man against a mountain – but it seems to me the greatest stumbling block to freedom of the miners is the bond. Can you read?'

'Yes, sir,' said Lewis.

'Good. Look at this then,' said Wilson, handing him a folded newspaper.

Lewis slowly and painstakingly quoted: 'Masters offer rewards for k-k-' he showed the word to Leakey who said: 'Knowledge' and Lewis continued: 'knowledge of the whereabouts of runaway miners and will prosecute whoever might employ them.'

'You've probably not noticed but across the street is a gentleman in a doorway,' said Wilson.

Lewis and Leakey looked at one another and Lewis got up and stood near the curtain. Across the street he saw a man in a once-sky blue but now-faded overcoat and ragged black top hat who seemed to have no obvious reason to be standing in a doorway looking towards them.

'I've found it curious I've received so little mail these past few weeks,' Wilson went on, 'And what I have has been tampered with. I suspect your father's letter was intercepted and whosoever came to you claiming to be me was in fact a spy.'

'A spy?' asked Lewis.

'But why? Who would do such a thing?' asked Leakey.

'The highest bidder I should think,' said Wilson. 'I have many enemies. Or perhaps I should say: justice has many enemies.'

A flash of a memory of the face of the man claiming to be William Wilson suddenly came into Lewis's mind. He'd never forget it.

'What might the outcome of a trial be?' asked Leakey.

'Sentences vary,' said Wilson.

'Can you do anything?'

'Sir Giles Crockatt is a friend of Lord Darlington of the Raby estate,' said Wilson, 'And both are as opposed to the emancipation of workers as much as they are opposed to the Stockton and Darlington Railway, which is completely irrational for if, as rumoured, it will increase the shipment of coal, then that can only be profitable for all. You say they're being held at Darlington lock-up? That's irregular – Darlington doesn't usually try such cases – it's used to petty pilfering, vagabondage or drunkenness. Aye, something is rotten, something is rotten. I'll go to Darlington on Monday morning and find out what I can.'

'I'd like to go with you, sir, so I can see me Dad,' said Lewis.

'Can you meet me in Darlington on Monday outside The King's Head Hotel?'

Leakey explained that it was he who'd brought Lewis to Durham in his carriage and though able to take him back to Evenfield that same night, he would be unable to take him down to Darlington the following day: Lewis had no other transport save his feet and no funds for hotels.

'Ah. Then you shall stay here with me,' said Wilson, after a moment's reflection.

'Are you sure that won't be an inconvenience to you, sir?' asked Leakey, surprised.

'Not at all - I feel partly responsible for your being here. The intention to contact me and seek my advice was an honest one, only it appears we were both hoodwinked. But if we do what we can, then we defeat those who aim to defeat us. We are in the right. Where is your carriage, Mr Leakey?'

'Down at the bridge,' said Leakey.

'I would suggest you leave now then, before nightfall,' advised Wilson.

Leakey finished his tea, shook Wilson's hand and thanked him. He turned to Lewis and told him he'd keep an eye on his house in Evenfield until the boy's return. Lewis promised he'd return as soon as possible, even if it meant walking from Darlington. As they reached the front door, Leakey said: 'I've been helping Lewis to read, Mr Wilson. If you've books, it'd help.' The elderly servant let him out.

As Leakey disappeared from view, Lewis suddenly felt alone.

'Are you hungry, Lewis?' asked Wilson.

'Not at all, sir,' Lewis lied, not wishing to be impolite. 'But my feet are hurting. I think I have blisters!'

'Well *I* am hungry!'

Wilson rang the little bell again and the old serving lady again appeared.

'Mrs Hudson, we have a guest. Dinner for two!'

Wilson didn't own the house, he explained over dinner, he rented the ground floor, but it was a proper home to Lewis: a wooden floor and wallpaper were luxuries to him. Gilt-framed paintings of members of Wilson's family – all stern or wearing powdered wigs – adorned the walls. The furniture too was brightly coloured, and ornaments and strange objects like stuffed foxes and birds cluttered the spaces. After the meal of mutton, potatoes and hunks of bread, Lewis tasted his first few sips of red wine, and raisins lingered on his tongue afterwards. After dinner, Wilson led Lewis along the coloured spines of books that stood in regimented order on the shelves.

'*Gulliver's Travels*' by an Irishman called Swift,' said Wilson. 'It is called a satire, a form of writing that makes a mockery of politics.'

'What is politics?' asked Lewis. 'Is it a place?'

'Ah no, no,' smiled Wilson, 'It's the science of government. Politicians practise politics and make laws used to govern a nation. And with those laws come punishments for those who break them.'

Wilson moved to another book.

'*Frankenstein*', Mary Shelley – a sawbones brings a dead man back to life by stitching him together from parts of other dead bodies – most gruesome but most enlightening. This is *Hamlet* by William Shakespeare, an Elizabethan playwright, dead two hundred years. It's a play, you see? Look.'

He opened the book randomly and showed Lewis the markings of the characters' names in bold ink and then the words they spoke following on in poetry or prose.

'Have you ever been to the playhouse or music hall?' Wilson asked.

'No, sir, there's nothin' like that in Evenfield, only an inn. What's *Hamlet* about?'

'Well,' said Wilson, 'It's about a prince who suspects his father, the king, was murdered by his uncle for his throne. This same uncle then marries Hamlet's mother. Hamlet then has to decide what to do about it. You must have heard the words: 'To be or not to be?''

'No sir, can't say I have,' said Lewis, 'but it must be a wonderful thing to watch men tell stories in such a way, movin' round speakin' like that.'

'Indeed, yes!' said Wilson. 'This is Doctor Johnson's Dictionary. It starts with A and then moves through the English language listing each word that starts with each of the 26 letters. The whole world is in this book.'

His forefinger tapped along the spines.

'This was written by a lady called Austen and has done much to illuminate us to the constraints forced on women. This last is one of my personal favourites, by Lord Byron himself: *Don Juan*, marvellous satire. His death last year in Greece was very sad. England lost a hero. Did you read about it?'

'No, sir, I didn't,' Lewis replied, bemused Wilson could presume a miner's son so well informed.

'I could read something from one of my books. What would you like?' Wilson asked.

Lewis sat fascinated as Wilson read parts of *Gulliver's Travels* and saw in his mind's eye strange worlds inhabited by men no bigger than a fingernail and tiny people in a world of giants.

Later, Mrs Hudson showed him to his room where another bowl of hot water awaited his poor feet. He spent five minutes sitting on the mattress rubbing his palm against the smooth white cotton sheets. The bed had a board at one end carved with an intricate pattern of laurel leaves. He pressed his face against the clean sheets and drank in their scent. As his head touched the pillow it was as if it were a cloud and just as he managed to mumble: 'G'night Dad' he was fast asleep.

Together, Mr Wilson and Lewis passed the Sunday reading a few words in each of the other books to understand their meaning and their content, over a bacon and egg breakfast of course, Mr Wilson read more of *Gulliver's Travels* to him, or walking around Durham City, along the placid River Wear and then up to the Cathedral. With perfect and disarming innocence, Lewis confessed to Leakey it was the biggest building he had ever seen and Leakey chuckled and said it was the biggest building most people had ever seen. Despite the nagging background circumstances, for Lewis it was a welcome way to pass a Sunday, all topped up by Mrs Hudson's cooking.

Monday 19th September

After a breakfast of scrambled eggs and sweet tea, Wilson and Lewis walked to the stable at the rear of the house and together they harnessed the horse to a two-seater gig. Wilson wrapped himself in a cape and put on a top hat and gloves as Mrs Hudson passed them a bundle of hard cheese, apples and a jar of hot tea. The old lady's kindly eyes seemed to flicker with concern for a second and his own eyes reassured her in a code known only to them.

'Go and see the Bookseller, and explain everything to him – I'm afraid we shall have to move again, perhaps Sunderland. I'll return later this evening.'

Mrs Hudson nodded understandingly.

As the gig rolled noisily over the cobbles, Wilson said to Lewis: 'Mrs Hudson has been with me for many years. She has no family. She treats me like a son and I don't object. Anyway, this will not be the first time we've uprooted and moved our affairs elsewhere. And the Bookseller is a man who sells information, not only books.'

Wilson glanced at the young boy's face – did he understand? Lewis said nothing. There was nothing more to be said.

The journey was swift – within two hours they were passing through Aycliffe.

'I think that's where we saw the steam engine loaded onto its rails,' said Lewis.

'Yes it is. I'm sure it will bring increased industry, but where there's industry there's always exploitation,' Wilson said ominously.

They shared an apple and two hunks of bread as they ran on, encountering farm carts laden with hay, apples and pears fresh from the orchards and herds of pigs fattened for slaughter, as well as columns of farm labourers in single file, men carrying scythes like crude muskets and women with babies tied to their backs. On approaching Darlington they were held up three times, first by a herd of cows, then a flock of sheep.

'It's market day,' Wilson commented.

The gig ran slower down the road, the mid-morning traffic increasing in volume, sloping fields left and right dotted with shaggy-coated sheep ready to be sheared, their wool washed and turned into cloth at the many mills. Finally, they came to a premature stop behind a long line of stationary carts laden with fruit, vegetables and baskets of poultry, as well as the habitual mule-trains transporting their black gold in saddle sacks – the third of their delays – the road ahead blocked by a gate. Just then swathes of black smoke rolled through the trees on their right.

'Is there a fire?' asked Lewis.

'What's the hold-up, man?' Wilson called out to a packman.

'It's the railway, sir – the steam engine!'

So, thought Lewis, for the second day in a row, the iron horse was delaying them. The crowd pressed forward, eager to get a view, their own needs temporarily forgotten as grey smoke rose from the trees like a big mushroom curling in on its self and the 'iron horse' revealed itself. First the tall chimney appeared and then a horizontal barrel, which his father had once explained to him when he'd asked about the steam engine that operated at the Crockatt Mine was called the boiler – a bizarre and almost comical arrangement of vertical rods and pistons like the elbows and legs of an emaciated man moving from side to side, backwards and forwards and up and down, pushing big flat iron wheels, jets of white steam spurting out from various joins and joints. Lewis counted at least ten of these vertical rods until he gave up. Perched on one of the ledges was George Stephenson in his shirtsleeves. The wagon behind shared the coal-storage space with a wooden barrel and behind that yet another coal chaldron with 'Stockton and Darlington Railway Company' painted in grey on its side, full of men carrying pickaxes and shovels. The train of waggons trundled laboriously in front of the turnpike and as soon as it had passed, the gates were wheeled open by navvies and the crowd surged across from both directions.

Wilson and Lewis saw the iron road disappearing into the distance, both sides swarming with men labouring with shovels and picks. The gleaming sandstone bridge joining two man-made embankments was taking shape. Fields were churned and trees uprooted where carts of stone slabs were hauled up in slings and pulleys, while to their right an entire field had been flattened and the iron rails were channelled across the top of a row of brick archways. Workmen here manhandled chaldrons amid numerous crashes, as the hoppers opened and test stones tumbled down.

They passed over the swiftly running Cocker Beck on Northgate to their left ramshackle wooden huts revealing huge wooden vats of soaking cloths being stirred with outsize wooden paddles, clacking spinning machines and reeking tanners' yards awash with animal blood. Drying on dozens of lines ranging down to the river on their left fluttered a hundred rainbow-coloured freshly dyed blue sheets like a navy message in pennants. On their right, a thin row of dilapidated cottages and a large boulder set incongruously to the side of the road.

'What is that?' asked Lewis.

'I believe there is a Town Crier called Bulmer who stands on it and tells of the latest news and I believe the house on the left there is the home of Mr Pease, one of the men building the new railway and also a big cotton man here in Darlington.'

Lewis looked at the fine house, well-kept garden and orchard rolling away to the river. At the end of the garden he saw what appeared to be a small building made entirely of glass.

'They call it a glasshouse or green-house,' said Wilson. 'It captures the rays of the sun and makes the inside much warmer than the outside by heating up the humidity in the air and turning it into steam. In this way, exotic plants grown in hot countries can be grown in cold countries like ours. They say Mr Pease is the fairest man in Darlington and that he has the greenest fingers!' added Wilson.

It was only the second time in his life Lewis had seen so many people, the first being the day before. Evenfield had two rows of detached houses with gardens around a village green. By comparison, Durham and Darlington were cities! Within seconds, the gig's iron-rimmed wheels joined a dozen others as they rattled over cobblestones and finally pulled up near a building where a projecting sign read 'King's Head', between a terrace of high-fronted narrow buildings boasting shop frontages with their insides turned out onto the street to attract commerce.

'The town gaol's where we'll go first,' said Wilson.

He parked the gig among others and an old man offered nosebags of oats along with water for the animals. Wilson paid sixpence and took up his saddlebag. Farmers gathered around a collection of sheep pens where a fast-talking auctioneer sold off animals to waiting buyers and they also passed stalls selling apples, pears, potatoes, turnips and carrots, bread and pies, cloth, silks and satins and cheeses.

There was a sudden commotion to their left and the crowd parted and Lewis found himself staring down a confused cow that had bolted from her herd, scaring passers-by, but he had had experience with these animals – as a young boy he had looked after cows for his neighbours and knew how to deal with them. He stood stock still as the animal lumbered towards him and then it halted as it realised Lewis was not going to budge, rolled its big head from left to right and let out a low moan and, just as Wilson, who had taken a step back, had the terrible thought the animal would knock the young man down, the herder rapped its hide with a stick and it turned back to its drove. The crowd closed as quickly as it had parted and Lewis motioned Wilson to lead on, which he did. They passed an apothecary selling clay jars of potions, while a man on a shoebox appealed to the crowd to buy bottles of a brown liquid he claimed cured everything. There was a candle maker too, a tanner selling all manner of leather goods from belts to whips, shoe shiners and a barrel-organ grinder. Women with buckets queued at a water pump. A whitewing and his boy worked hard with brushes and shovels to keep the ground cleared of the copious amounts of manure. Lewis felt a hand tugging at his sleeve and looked down to a legless man pushing himself around on a cart with wooden wheels.

'Spare a penny, lad – I lost me legs at Waterloo!'

Pulling a horrified Lewis away, Wilson and the boy passed a market cross cluttered with ragged boys and men and saw the word DISPENSARY painted in large letters on a wall and a queue waiting for cheap medicines. The old Town Hall, Dispensary and Gaol were all part of the same ugly building, stairs without rails leading up the outside to a door on the first floor. They climbed the steps and entered a small lobby where a soldier was smoking a clay pipe, a dirty, shoeless girl with straggly black hair perched on his knee.

'Who's in charge here?' asked Wilson.

'See the Clerk,' said the soldier and jerked his thumb at the double doors.

They passed through and found a room thick with pipe smoke. Ragged and filthy men coughed while women and children chatted or wept on wooden benches. Part of the room was fenced off like stable stalls, and at each end stood constables who wore black hats, had uniforms with big brass buttons and long black truncheons tucked into their belts. Set into a wall was a small window of bars behind which sat an elderly man who took names.

'How may I help you?' asked the Clerk.

'You have four men from Evenfield Colliery. I wish to speak to them,' said Wilson.

The Clerk peered at them oddly and said: 'Just a minute.' He slid a little wooden door across the hatch.

Moments later the side door opened and the same man appeared with a much bigger, stouter man behind him.

'What do you want?' the stouter demanded, weighing them up suspiciously.

'I want to see the four men brought from Evenfield Colliery and I wish to know the charges,' said Wilson firmly.

'And who are you?' asked the man rudely.

'William Wilson, practising attorney in Durham. And you, sir?'

'John Allen, Magistrate. What do you want to speak to them about?'

'That is for me to know and them to find out, Mr Allen,' said William Wilson stiffly. 'All accused men in this country have the right to a defence.'

'All accused men in this country only have the rights that educated men grant them, Mr Wilson.' Allen boomed.

'Since when did a small town like Darlington try men accused of a Contravention of the Revised Combination Act?' Wilson asked.

Allen's tone changed – his impertinent visitor was not as cognisant with the facts as he thought he was.

'They are being held in a provincial jail under one of the Six Acts: 'Misdemeanours: suspected possession of firearms with the intention of intimidating others.'

This news tripped Wilson. He turned to Lewis. 'Did your father own any firearms?'

'No,' said Lewis honestly and repeated the denial with greater emphasis.

'Has there been a hearing?' asked Wilson.

'No time!' barked Allen.

'Then could you tell me, Mr Allen, when their trial is likely to be?' asked Wilson.

'We've too many today. Next trial will be Monday the third of October,' said Allen.

'May I speak with the accused?'

'Return with a correctly presented case and I will consider it,' said Allen defensively.

'These men have a right to a lawyer!' protested Wilson.

'I didn't say they didn't,' said Allen, controlling his voice as some faces in the room turned to them. 'But we can't have any Tom, Dick or Harry walking in off the street making claims. Put your request in writing and state your case. The court will decide.'

Defeated and deflated, Wilson and Lewis went out and wound their way through the waiting-room crowd, down the steps and, on Wilson's initiative, into the Market Tavern where, sitting on high-backed wooden chairs in a discreet corner, Wilson called for coffee.

'Are you absolutely certain your father owned no firearms of any sort?'

'Absolutely not, sir!' said Lewis. 'I would have known about it, I'm sure. If I understand correctly, Mr Wilson, does it mean that a gun was put in our house to make it look like my Dad was going to use it against somebody?'

'Yes, yes it does,' confirmed Wilson.

'But – but that's impossible! That's – that's – unfair! It – it's a crime! Why would anybody do such a cruel thing to my father?'

'It could have been put there the night they were arrested,' said Wilson.

'There were lots of masked men crashing about in our house,' said Lewis.

'It almost unquestionably was done that way,' agreed Wilson, 'The point is proving it. This oath taken with the other miners, do you remember if your father wrote anything?'

'My father can barely write 'is name,' said Lewis. 'I told you – I wrote the letter but my Dad told me what to write.'

'For many years the creation of a union was illegal,' said Wilson. 'As of this year, it's not, but strict conditions have been put in place and the words 'obstruct justice and intimidate others' have been inserted. But the problem is how one man's idea of obstruction might be another man's idea of defending himself, you see?'

Just then a serving man came by with a tray set with a silver coffee pot and china cups. Wilson poured two hot cups of the pungent brown liquid whose odour swirled in Lewis' nose like a musky perfume.

'What about the others? Did any of them have any guns, even for shooting snipe?'

Lewis suddenly heard the angry voice of John Carr in his memory.

'John Carr might 'ave 'ad a huntin' gun,' said Lewis.

'Hm,' said Wilson. 'But a hundred thousand English men own hunting guns. No, the only witness, it seems to me, is the *false* William Wilson. The whole case rests on him. You met this man, you say? Would you recognise him again if you saw him?'

'Certainly,' said Lewis confidently. He sipped the hot, strong coffee, rolled the coarse grains on his tongue and swallowed. Almost instantly he felt his heart pick up its beat in his chest.

'You have never drunk coffee before?' asked Wilson, smiling.

'No, sir, only tea. How strange it tastes!'

'What did you talk about when you two were alone, you and this man claiming to be me?' Wilson asked, serious again.

Lewis thought back.

'He told me he was a soldier at Waterloo!'

'Indeed? Well, that narrows it down. Anything else?'

'Nothing I can think of. What do we do now?' Lewis asked.

Wilson looked at his pocket watch.

'We keep our eyes on the Gaol. Mr Allen seemed startled when I told him my intentions. Let's wait here a little while.'

And so they waited. When Lewis wasn't watching the Gaol, Wilson was and when Wilson wasn't, Lewis was. But there were lots of distractions. As it was September, the market was flooded with an abundant harvest of quince, apples, pears, plums and cherries, potatoes, turnips, carrots and bales of hay. At one point, a crowd gathered when a greengrocer prised the thin lid from a wooden box and revealed a hundred bright oranges. They rarely saw such colourful fruits so far inland, for they came from faraway countries and were difficult to transport. Lewis watched dustmen cart buckets of cinders and ladle them onto wagons in great dirty clouds and laugh as they were cursed by packmen who'd set up small trestles nearby with rare silks. But after two hours more, the sun had moved across the sky (though technically Lewis knew it was the other way round) and started casting long shadows over the emptying marketplace. They drank more coffee and ate bread rolls with cold ham that Wilson ordered and paid for.

Wilson opened up his saddlebag at one point and took out a sheaf of documents. He glanced at each one as if looking for something in particular and, unable to find whatever it was, he went through them again with more meticulousness. On his third fruitless attempt, his shoulders drooped.

'How very, very stupid of me,' he muttered.

'What's wrong?' asked Lewis.

'Can you hold out here for two days alone?' he suddenly asked Lewis.

Lewis blinked. 'What do you mean?'

'I mean, can you survive here until I can get back?'

'But where are you going?' Lewis asked.

'Durham. I am concerned for Mrs Hudson's safety on the one hand and on the other, it would assist us greatly if I had been clever enough to remember to check my documents for my certificates and various references to show Mr Allen before we left. I'd be wiser to leave now before its dark and come back replenished, tomorrow if possible, Wednesday if not.'

Wilson began to bitterly regret not packing his diplomas and references. It had been on his mind but so had many things. Lewis began to feel uneasy at the sudden change of circumstances.

'But what'll I eat? Where'll I sleep?' he protested.

'The next sitting is on the 3rd October,' said Wilson. 'That gives us time to prepare for the hearing. I'll give you what funds I can spare for tonight, though I'll need somethin' for the turnpike.'

He opened his wallet and counted ten shillings into Lewis's palm in four half crowns.

'But Mr Wilson, sir, I cannot accept it. I cannot pay you back!'

'You can pay me back when you're rich and famous,' joked Wilson, but Lewis only looked confused. 'You can use this to buy food for the prison guard to give to your father but remember: just because you've got it in our pocket, it doesn't mean you have to spend it. You'll also have to find a cheap place to sleep – I recommend the Talbot in Post House Wynd. Speak to Mr Atkinson. Come to the Bulmer Stone in Northgate at about – '– he paused as he studied his pocket watch and made some mental calculations – 'four or five o'clock on Wednesday. Can you do all that?'

'I think so, sir,' said Lewis uncertainly. Everything was changing so quickly.

'Meanwhile, keep your eyes on the Gaol, and if you see our man – the big chap we clashed with, follow him. If he's on horseback or a cart, take note which road he takes.'

Wilson backed the horse out and climbed into his carriage.

'But Mr Wilson, sir, you – you are coming back, aren't you?'

Wilson asked Lewis to give him his hand. Wilson took it in both of his and looked into Lewis's eyes and said: 'I swear to you, I will be back. Be strong now!'

Wilson would like to have added more. The thought that he was abandoning this naïve village lad to the temptations of a big town like Darlington wasn't something he could dwell on as he had a long journey back to Durham before nightfall. But the boy was 13. Boys younger than that fought in battles or dug coal underground. Wilson had to get back to Durham. He was concerned about leaving Mrs Hudson alone, suddenly aware that perhaps their foes wouldn't limit themselves to spying and letter interception but also to housebreaking and he had many sensitive papers lying around. Besides, he needed to find his diplomas with which to furnish Allen upon his return. He cursed himself for his stupidity.

Lewis watched until Wilson disappeared along Northgate then looked around bewildered at the mass of nameless people. He was not one of 'them': he had the 'look' and he knew it – the country boy on his first visit to town spends hours looking at every item in shop windows because he has never seen so many shiny things. Despite his years, he still dressed like a peasant. When Lewis saw two young and pretty girls giggling at his appearance he felt ashamed, but then hunger growled in the pit of his stomach and hunger not vanity became his main priority and he bought a meat pie for a shilling. He pulled the pie in half and ate one portion, licking his fingers clean, and persuaded the pie-seller to wrap the remainder in a sheet of newspaper, then returned to the Gaol and asked the constable to take the pie, delicious fat by now running through the greased paper, to George Lovatt. The Constable shared the pie with his mates but Lewis never knew that, of course.

Lewis then descended the stairs and pushed through a herd of sheep being driven to the river to be washed. He was about to set off to find the Talbot Inn when a gate at the side of the Gaol opened and John Allen, the big man they had been speaking to, emerged on horseback. Oh if only Wilson had stayed a little longer! Mr Allen cantered out along Blackwellgate and past the end of Skinnergate, which hosted many of the butcher's shops and into which hapless sheep, cows and pigs were already being herded to their doom. Lewis walked and ran at a discreet distance behind Allen's horse, dodging the many mules that were transporting coal back and forth along the road but soon the town gave way to fields and Allen spurred his horse and broke into a trot. Lewis picked up his pace into a run and followed as far as his lungs could manage to an inn marked The Salutation but by then Allen had all but disappeared over the horizon. Lewis, breathless and doubled over, looked up and saw the mirror reflection of a snaking river down to the left in the middle distance and asked a passing carter its name.

'The Tees, lad,'

Once the stitch in his side had gone, Lewis walked slowly back into town along the muddy road and, as the shadows of trees and buildings grew longer, he went to find the Talbot Inn.

* * *

In another part of the County at about the same time, Sean spat the oily brown saliva of soggy tobacco into the grass, pulled a fresh chunk from his pouch and pushed it into his mouth. He was nervous. Beside him was his brother Seamus. They were on the banks of the river, not far from the metal girder bridge that crossed the small River Gaunless at the unusual angle of 27 degrees. Sean remembered the number because it was the gaffer – Stephenson – who had mentioned it to Seamus once as he'd stood there wondering at the odd angle and Seamus had mentioned it to Sean. George Stephenson was using every hour of daylight to ensure everything worked perfectly on the day, but until Stephenson appeared at the head of the test train, Seamus had a battle of his own to fight.

Trouble had been brewing for a good while now. Pat Hennessy from Galway had started to be temperamental about some of Seamus's commands. Seamus was fair and his men respected him and Hennessy worked hard too, but he was a bully and his peers feared him. Right was on Seamus's side but it meant nothing in the world they shared: it was all about strength – and exclusion was the usual verdict for the loser.

The challenger and his seconds stepped forward, Hennessy bare-chested and shadow boxing and Seamus stock still and steady as a rock. Sean said: 'It's no hittin' below de belt, kickin' or bitin'. De winner's declared by a knock out of his opponent or his opponent submits. Agreed?'

Seamus and Hennessy mumbled 'Aye' and stepped back. Sean took out a dirty hanky, held it above the ground and dropped it. Seamus's fist smashed instantly into Hennessy's face, breaking his two front teeth, bursting his lip and stunning him before he hit the ground. There was a silence. Hennessy's supporters looked down in complete shock at their unconscious man.

'Now, anybody else want to challenge me as leader?' Seamus asked.

Silence.

'Good! Now clean dis man's face an' let's get back to what we're paid to do!'

He shouldered through them, picked up his shovel, pulled on his shirt and stood directly under the bridge, ordering his men to cross the river. The lookout from above signalled and though they couldn't see anything, they heard the arrival of the chaldrons and then a big figure appeared and descended the steep path at the side.

'Mr Gallagher! Are you there?'

'Here, Mr Stephenson!' called Seamus.

'I want you up here! Allocate one of yer men to 'andle your gang!'

Seamus had little time for grudges and he needed every able-bodied man he could find. Hennessy, who had opened his eyes and showing signs of rapid recovery, was one such man. It was better, Seamus reasoned, to pull him back in or at least offer him the chance, than lose him. It was a long shot, but worth a try.

'Hennessy,' he shouted, 'When oi give de signal, take de lads up top, roight?'

Hennessy, who was groggily washing away blood in the river, his pride crushed and his tongue licking the empty, raw space where his two front teeth used to be, looked up, stood up unaided and managed to half-shout through an unnerving lisp: 'Fuck you, Mithter Gallagher!'

As Hennessy strode away in the direction of the camp to collect his belongings, he spat blood contemptuously. Seamus bristled but swallowed and called out: 'Sean – when oi give de signal, you take de lads up top, roight?'

'Aye, aye, *Mister* Gallagher!' said Sean.

***

Later that evenin, Silas finally walked through the back gates of Crockatt Manor and into his cottage, having crossed from Raby where he'd discharged a dozen beaters hired from the surrounding neighbourhoods to flush out game for the joint hunting party, paying each two shillings. They'd been a surly lot, young and poorly disciplined. A number of times he'd had to threaten one, John Carr, an argumentative lad itching to fight, with real violence. The altercation had been potentially dangerous and only John Carr's friends saved both from a nasty moment. It shook Silas. It was the first time in years he'd felt a resurrection of the same violent intent that had enabled him to dispose of Frenchies at Waterloo and highwaymen outside London.

Finally home and glancing only briefly at a large man trotting away from the hall on a horse, he pulled off his muddy boots and he slumped down exhausted. The door opened. It was Hamish, equally exhausted and equally muddy.

'I want a word with you,' said Hamish.

'Well, what are yer waitin' for, an invitation?' Silas snapped.

'The beaters you took on were a poor lot. His Lordship's guests were complainin' the' only bagged a dozen brace but my lot bagged three-dozen. Why?'

'I don't know why!' snapped Silas, irrated. 'Maybe the' was less birds over my end? Or maybe you already knew that so yer did yer best to send us to the shittiest place possible?'

'It'd be just like you to blame somebody else!'

'If yer've summat to say, say it,' said Silas,' 'cos I don't do foreign languages. Thou 'ast more air than wit, Mr Jones.'

Hamish grunted and was pulling the door to when Silas shouted: 'I've a question!'

Hamish looked back.

'Why is it you didn't fight for yer country, eh? Why's it people like me n' yer brother went? I'd like to 'ave met yer brother. I bet 'e was a real man.'

Hamish's face reddened and he slammed the door behind him. Silas laughed, lifted a bottle from behind the copper kettle and drank, falling onto his bed. He'd only just closed his eyes when there was a knock.

'That bloody Hamish!' he hissed, ready to give him a piece of his mind as he lurched to the door. But it was Heathcote.

'Sir Giles urgently requests your company.'

Swallowing his rage with grunts, Silas pulled on his boots, jacket and hat and was shown into the Great Hall. It was empty. Tallow candles burnt on the candelabra. He sat and waited and was glad to be able to catch his breath and calm down. He looked around at the arms, shields and paintings and wondered how his life would have been if he'd been born into such an illustrious family. Sir Giles arrived a few minutes later. Silas stood as he entered.

'The Evenfield business,' said Sir Giles, abruptly, 'It's unfinished.'

'In what way, sir?' Silas asked.

'In the way that I'm going to tell you: I want these Evenfield dogs taught a lesson. *I* decide what goes on in my mines, not them.'

'As it should be, sir, as it should be,' agreed Silas.

'Return to Darlington tomorrow and attend a special session of the court,' Sir Giles ordered.

'A special session, sir?' gulped Silas.

'Give your name as William Wilson, lawyer from Durham. Tell the court you received a letter from Lovatt, went to Evenfield and discovered Lovatt had planned to use firearms against me and distinctly said it was his intention to obstruct the law. You felt it your duty to report to me. Simple.'

Silas was stunned. There was nothing simple about it. He'd been happy to go along with Sir Giles's wishes as a favour to Lord Darlington and he'd happily ridden to Evenfield, taken risks and ridden back having given the names of the 'conspirators' because they seemed to have promised him a rapid way to gain promotion.

No contract existed and never would – it was one servant's word against two masters. Silas just wanted to wash his hands of the affair and return to his cottage where he felt safe and protected.

'Do I 'ave a choice?' Silas dared ask, absenting the customary 'Sir' which did not go amiss with Sir Giles.

'Soldiers don't flinch in obedience to the demands of their superiors, or do they?' asked Sir Giles, directing the question directly at Silas. 'My boy Arthur volunteered,' said Sir Giles, 'Sandhurst Military College, first lieutenant. Brought him home from Spain in a box - what was left of him. Shock killed his mother.'

Sir Giles glanced up at a portrait of a young man with similar features to his own. He stared at it for what seemed like an eternity. Finally, he breathed deeply as if suppressing some emotion and said: 'Monday morning we'll have a horse ready. You should be in Darlington by midday. Ask for Constable Ralph Morrell and simply say: 'Evenfield'. He'll do the rest.'

Silas, exhausted and irritable, left and returned to his cottage to dwell on his destiny. A wiser man would have packed his bags and left that night but Silas was a gambler – he would risk he hazard of the die. With a bit of luck, he might just come out ahead. Well, one useful thing at least would come out of his unexpected trip to Darlington: he could finally reclaim the £10 he'd buried almost seven years ago! He drank his brandy until he was unconscious, slept fully clothed and snored all night.

* * *

Lewis, meanwhile, passed the first night at the Talbot on a full belly.

Despite the owner, James Atkinson, raising an eyebrow at his youth and lack of luggage, his half crown was real enough and it secured him a bed as well as one meal a day in the evenings. His tiny room high in the inn had a view across the rooftops. Far below, Lewis watched as coaches entered the narrow yard from one end to discharge or load passengers or parcels at the Posthouse that was incorporated into the building and horses were changed and passengers fed, or exited through the archway to continue their journey. From afar and sometimes closer, he would hear the muffled cry of 'What-ever-o'clock and all is well!' being shouted by night watchmen in various parts of the near-silent town. The sound of whinnying horses in the stables of the Posthouse below filled his ears too.

He'd gone to the Gaol again and looked at the candlelight that burned in the upstairs windows, knowing his father was somewhere inside. He wanted to hear a few kind words but there were none, just barking dogs, the odd fiddle tune, the cries of babies and swearing drunks. The darkness was profound and frighteningly dense beyond the marketplace, only the occasional tiny light in a window indicating life.

'Goodnight, Dad,' he'd whispered before returning to the Talbot, climbing the flight of narrow wooden stairs, finding his attic room and curling up in bed with his fingers between his thighs to keep them warm.

Tuesday 20th September

On Tuesday morning, the early pealing of church bells called people to prayer. Lewis opened his eyes. The first few seconds were bliss but then he remembered where he was and he was immediately sad. After the bells stopped, he washed his face in the cold water in a bowl, descended the narrow creaking stairs and let himself out into the early-morning streets. His feet hurt less now that the new shoes were wearing in.

Some people were out already, sweeping falling leaves into piles, and Lewis lost himself in the labyrinth of alleys around Post House Wynd, one minute squeezing between workshops and buildings a few feet wide and the next entering open spaces, or between holding pens for cattle waiting for slaughter or passing by householders who glanced at him as they emptied their fire ashes or slop buckets into compost heaps, pig troughs or chicken runs. He took some time to examine The Bulmer Stone in Northgate where they'd been yesterday, running his hand over the well-worn granite boulder. He waited for a while to see if the fabled Town Crier after whom it was named might make an appearance, but he didn't. The only visitor the stone had was an impatient woman who wanted him to go away so she could use the stone to flog her flax.

Opposite, he spied the house Wilson said belonged to the fairest man in Darlington and then he descended the bank that ran parallel with the Pease garden – marvelling at the glasshouse Wilson had mentioned – and arrived at the river. There, he crossed a footbridge and traipsed absently, following the flow upstream to where the water was quite still and home to dragonflies and pond-skaters. Cottages opened onto the river with idle looms on their back porches. Brown-leaved trees were snagged with tufts of white flax. He wandered back to the centre of Darlington and crossed a fine three-arch bridge that led to a row of cottages crouched around St Cuthbert's churchyard, its trees' branches a thinning canopy of golden leaves protecting myriad tombstones. Parked at the front of the church gates was a variety of carriages and horses. He ghosted among the graves, glancing at the names and ages of the dead and accidentally disturbed sleeping figures piled up in blankets or beds of leaves.

Just then the church doors opened and the beggars emerged from their hiding places looking abject as worshippers scattered, some to waiting carriages, others into town or disappearing into doorways around the marketplace. Lewis followed to where a grand row of shops stood, most with blinds drawn though still revealing their goods: a sweet shop with jars of lollipops and candies; an apothecary full of medicines, potions, jars of white powder marked quinine, ammonia or bromide, an ironmonger's with tins, cans and tools for cutting and hammering and an undertaker's advertising funerals for five guineas that included a hearse, mourning coach, elm coffin with silk lining and pall-bearers with black hatbands. There was a jeweller selling pocket watches and clocks that ran from one to eight days, and at least four drapers displaying damasks and sideboard cloths with prices given by length and prices in pounds, shillings and pence, along with nightdresses, nightshirts and Turkish towels fresh from the town's weavers. There was a barbershop where men of business were having hot, white towels lifted from their faces and then their whiskers were shaved with sharp blades operated by dextrous barbers. There were bookshops, too, where the rhythmic clatter of foot-operated printing presses churned out literature. There was a wine merchant. There were carpenters and coffin-makers. There were grocers calling out prices of their fruits and vegetables by the pound. And not forgetting the butchers too where great sides of red flesh hung from hooks and attracted buzzing flies. He kept thinking of Wilson's counsel – just because you've got money, it doesn't mean you have to spend it, how it controlled his temperate actions now. Lewis bought another hot meat pie and ate half for breakfast. Soon, he told himself, Wilson would return from Durham like much-needed reinforcements at a battle, with his documents and certificates, and all the doors would open and the good men of Darlington would be up in arms over this injustice! His father had always sworn by 'educated men', as he called them – men they could trust as they had everyone's best interests at heart; that's what his father had clung to and if this motto worked for George, it would work for Lewis too. He went to the Gaol but it wasn't yet open so he half-sauntered away and then spotted a young gent struggling with an armful of leather-bound documents.

'Could you help me, boy?' asked the gentleman.

He handed Lewis two or three leather documents as he fumbled for his key, selected one and unlocked the door. Lewis followed, mounted a few stairs and found himself in a small room in which stood a desk and a number of bookshelves and fatter, bulging wallets tied with string. The young man took the documents from Lewis and put them onto the edge of his desk. In a glass frame on the wall was a slogan reading 'Periculum Privatum Utilitas Publica'. Lewis asked what it meant.

'Latin – private risk for public service,' said the gentleman. 'You're in the offices of the Stockton and Darlington Railway Company, Jonathon Backhouse Junior at your service. That pie smells good.'

'It's for me Da, sir,' said Lewis.

'Lucky man. Here's for your trouble,' and he tossed Lewis a sixpence.

'Well, thank you, sir. Er...'

Lewis hesitated. Backhouse waited.

'Yes, what is it?'

'Excuse me for askin' sir, but it's twice now I've seen the steam engine in action. Could you explain 'ow it works, sir?'

Backhouse glanced down at the boy and then at his pocket watch and said: 'Come back after lunch. I might have time then.'

'Yes sir. Thank you, sir.'

Lewis went down the steps and out onto High Row, turning to remember the number, then walked across the marketplace and into the churchyard where he sat down with his back against the gravestone of one Michael Windale. The pie was still warm and he guiltily ate another quarter. As it was midday, according to the chiming clock on St Cuthbert's, he returned to the Gaol and asked a guard to give the last quarter to the Evenwood men. Once again, the pie never arrived at its intended destination.

For a little while Lewis stood outside warming himself at a burning brazier near stalls called The Shambles, reflecting on everything he'd seen so far. It didn't take much imagination to thread together all the elements, memories and observations: up in places like Evenfield they were digging coal out of the ground and ferrying it on mule trains down to places like Darlington. The new railway invention was planning to do that too but there had to be a much, much bigger world beyond Darlington and Durham or else why would all these men be going to so such great lengths? Leakey said London had a hundred thousand fires. The expanse of the world beyond Darlington, on the places marked on Leakey's old map, dawned on the young man as he stood there but more than wanting to puzzle or recoil from it, he wanted to see it for himself. He studied the workmen and boys around him in the market and wondered: did they think about things like he did? Or had they never been to school and never realised? Was he wrong to think such things? Should he accept what he was and go down the pit?

He worked through many thoughts as he sat there aimlessly near the Bulmer Stone for almost two hours. He timed it by the church bells – midday to the toll of two. Wilson had said four or five and Wednesday but just in case, every cart that turned the corner towards him a hundred yards down was scrutinised for details that would offer hope. At four chimes, Lewis suddenly remembered his rendezvous with Mr Backhouse and without thinking turned and ran as fast he could, without attracting suspicion, until he was once again outside number 9 High Row.

As he could find no bell and the door was ajar, he mounted the wooden stairs. They creaked. Ahead of him, muffled by the backs of other men leaning in through the doorway from the hall, he heard Backhouse's voice: 'And that was published a week ago. We've taken delivery of the printed tickets. Three hundred: one for every shareholder and one extra for every ten shares. Otley and I will spend the next few days organising distribution. Put out word they're here to be picked up from tomorrow. The rest will be posted!'

Lewis waited as one by one the men congratulated each other, turned and descended the stairs, ignoring Lewis. A remaining elderly gentleman did not ignore him and bluntly enquired of Lewis his business.

'Mr Backhouse said he'd explain the steam engine if I came back, sir.'

Backhouse, his head buried in the same newspaper he'd been reading from, looked up and saw the young man who'd helped him that morning. Otley went to the fire and took down a cloth with which he was about to lift the boiling kettle to pour its contents into an open teapot.

'Otley, may I ask you to defer from pouring tea until I have demonstrated the principles to this young man?'

'By all means, Mr Backhouse,' said Otley, releasing his grip on the handle and standing patiently aside.

Backhouse tore a strip from the side of his his newspaper and held it in front of the funnel of steam jetting from the kettle's spout. The gentle thrust made it flutter.

'You see that?' Backhouse asked Lewis. 'Air, when heated, expands: that is, it pushes outwards. Now, imagine we build a very strong box and fill it with steam: steam will push outwards in all directions but if we can channel it in one direction, then we can harness that energy and transfer it to a repeated movement. In principle, we make a hot fire, expose it to water, make lots of steam and then – are you following?'

'But how does it make the wheels go round?' Lewis asked.

Backhouse explained how everything was set at certain speeds and joined together by connecting rods and small compartments that admitted steam and then ejected it again and in doing so was able to create – in lightning fast moments – movement based on pressure and vacuum. He instructed Lewis to hold out his open palm in front of him and then he himself placed his own open palm against Lewis'. He said Lewis' palm was the piston and his own palm as the steam. He then asked Lewis to push his palm against his own and then Backhouse suddenly slid his hand aside so Lewis tilted forward, and then Backhouse replaced the palm in its original position against Lewis' by taking hold of Lewis' wrist with his other hand, making Lewis right himself.

Backhouse repeated: 'Steam pressure, no steam pressure, steam pressure, no steam pressure!'

Once they'd established this clumsy pattern and repeated it, Lewis began to feel how that backward and forward tilting produced a solid movement of one object against another. At the end of his explanation, Backhouse again asked: '*Now* do you understand?'

Lewis furrowed his brow and said: 'I *think* so. Thank you, sir.'

'Tuesday next – come to the opening,' said Backhouse, 'see for yourself!'

'In one ear and out the other,' reflected Otley, who finally got to make tea as Lewis descended the stairs.

'That's how Stephenson explained it to me, Mr Otley,' said Backhouse. 'And it took me some time to understand. Besides, today's young men are tomorrow's engineers.'

Standing on the High Row in the rain, Lewis had heard Otley's parting remarks but wasn't offended and he particularly liked the idea of being a young man in Backhouse's eyes and not a child.

Anyway, he'd seen the steam engine in operation and already had a rudimentary grasp.

Meanwhile, the rain continued and muddy rainwater coursed down from the yards leading up from High Row and ran across the cobbles where it quickly gathered in pools before spilling down Tubwell Row in torrents to the river. He ducked under the parapet of the Shambles and watched as horses and riders brushed past. One in particular caught his eye and made him turn back and look harder and longer - despite the turned-up collar and turned-down hat, it was the man who'd claimed to be William Wilson, the man who'd betrayed his father and his friends only ten days ago at Evenfield! The blackguard was astride a horse near the Dispensary! Lewis watched as he dismounted, exchanged a word with the constable on guard who opened the gate and then entered. Lewis slid over to the constable.

'What's going on 'ere today, sir?' he asked.

'Bugger off,' muttered the constable.

Undaunted by the rebuff, thoughts piled up in Lewis's head. Why was this man here? Why had he returned to Darlington? Was it an old enemy of his father's? Did his father have enemies? Certainly none had ever been spoken of. Their family got on with the other families except perhaps Hackett's, but nobody got on with Hackett. And then a more familiar and reassuring sight emerged from the rain: it was Mary Crosby, James Crosby's wife, on a mule led by John Carr. Relieved to see somebody familiar, Lewis stepped out of the shadows, took the reins and dragged the animal under the relatively dry protection of the Shambles.

'What news from Evenfield?' Lewis asked.

'Hackett's demanded we pay up the rent arrears or we'll be out,' said John sourly.

Lewis told them how Leakey had taken him to Durham and met the real William Wilson and how he'd been waiting for his return.

'Five minutes ago the impostor arrived n' went into the jail, the man pretending to be William Wilson!' Lewis exclaimed.

'A cock-and-bull story!' said Mrs Crosby.

Lewis wanted to shout and be angry. He wished they would believe him over 'William Wilson' but none of them had been present the night the impostor had visited to his house. Crosby, Carr and Dawson would have told their families when they returned to their homes after they'd met William Wilson, but nobody else could dispute his identity because none had seen him. Only five people had: four were in prison and the remaining person was himself. Besides, there was a feeling that the fate of the other miners had been accepted and nothing the families could do or say would change anything. Lewis felt as if he was in a very lonely place all of a sudden – nobody was on his side and nobody could help. Only John Carr seemed uncertain and looked at Lewis doubtfully before asking the others: 'But what if he's right?'

* * *

Justice of the Peace John Allen returned from his mysterious sojourn in the countryside, met Magistrates John Clutterbuck and Frederick Clapp and all three were briskly seated. Constables Taylor and Morrell escorted the prisoners to the courtroom from the cellar. The Evenfield men hadn't bathed, shaved or changed clothes since they'd arrived almost five days before, having shared a mud floor with rats and cockroaches and only old bread and water for sustenance. They looked so beaten, haggard, exhausted and desperate that sentencing seemed merciful. Each man had gone over a dozen notions as to why and how they had been betrayed and only by elimination did George begin to realise it had something to do with the letter. But for the other men the word 'traitor' had filtered into their imaginations and it was hinted by Will Carr that perhaps Lewis had talked. George grew angry at this suggestion and a dividing wall sprung up between he and Carr, with Crosby and Dawson taking sides and trying to keep both men calm.

They were directed into the dock, surprised to see no public or family. The windows allowed them their first significant light in five days and they blinked at it. Only the rain drumming on the roof told them the day was wet. The little artificial light came from candlesticks placed on the high desk of the three magistrates.

'You are accused of breaking the Reformed Combination Act of 1825 and suspected of harbouring firearms. How you do you plead, guilty or not guilty?' Allen asked.

'Not guilty' said each of the men in turn.

'Call the witness,' Allen ordered. The Guard left the room and returned followed by Silas Scroggins, wet from the rain. When George saw him he shouted:

'Mr Wilson, you've come! It's all right lads, it's Wilson, 'e'll get us out!'

Silas looked away from the four men and Allen as he was asked to give his name.

'William Wilson.'

'Again?' said Allen.

'William … Wilson,' Silas said a little louder, the lie catching in his throat.

'Profession?'

'Lawyer,' he lied.

George blinked, utterly confused.

'Residence?'

'Durham.'

Constable Taylor held out a Bible and Silas touched it.

'Do you swear to tell the truth, the whole truth and nothing but the truth, so help you God?'

'I do,' Silas lied again, expecting a bolt of lightning to strike him down, but none came.

'What is your relationship with the accused?' asked Allen.

'But Mr Wilson!' George tried to protest.

'Er, they wrote to me n' asked my advice to form a trades union.'

'And did you give them advice?'

'Er ... no.'

'What did you do?'

'Um ... I went to visit them at Evenfield.'

'And what did you learn from that visit?'

'Erm ... that they ... um ... that they'd took an oath and vowed to obstruct justice to achieve their ends.'

'And what were their ends?'

'Erm... intimidation of the owner of the mine.'

'Belonging to?'

'Sir Giles Crockatt, I believe, sir, of Crockatt Hall near Bishop Auckland.'

'And what did you do with this information, Mr Wilson?' asked Allen.

'Um... I ... I ... reported it to Sir Giles Crockatt 'imsel', sir,' said Silas.

'What??' George blurted out, unable not to.

'You heard these men say they'd taken an oath that used the word 'obstruct'?' Allen pressed on as if desperate to get this macabre fiasco expunged like some sort of bad dream.

'Yes, sir.'

'And which of the accused was the ringleader, in your opinion?' asked Mr Clapp.

'I sensed Lovatt was the ringleader, sir, for we met at 'is house in Evenfield and he did the most talkin'.'

George was speechless. Dawson, Crosby and Carr looked at one other too terrified to say anything but confused as to why George was denying it. But Dawson spoke up gruffly and said: 'We never said nowt about intim-datin'!' and then Constable Morell banged his truncheon hard across Dawson's knuckles and he whimpered and said no more.

'Mr Wilson, what're you sayin'?' asked George.

Clutterbuck then asked: 'And did you meet the other miners or only Mr Lovatt?'

'Lovatt at first,' said Silas. 'The others came after.'

'Can you repeat the word 'obstruct' in context, Mr Wilson?' asked Mr Clutterbuck.

Silas did not know what the expression meant.

'I'm sorry sir, I don't ...!'

'Repeat exactly what was said,' Clutterbuck ordered impatiently.

Silas blinked and coughed. 'Erm .... '

Allen interrupted: 'Mr Wilson, did Lovatt say it was his intention to obstruct and intimidate the mine owners?'

'Yes,' said Silas finally, and to burnish the lie added: 'That's exactly what 'e said, sir. 'e said it was 'is intention to intimidate the mine owners by acts of wanton vandalism n' Dawson said 'e had a shotgun an' would shoot anyone who tried to stop 'em.'

'You lyin' bugger!' shouted Crosby.

'You're condemning innocent men!' shouted George, grabbing the front of the witness box. Morell rapped his knuckles with his truncheon too and he too pulled back.

'Silence in court!' ordered Allen. 'Mr Wilson, no more questions. You may go!'

Silas looked confused for a moment, not used to being called Mr Wilson, but quickly understood and found himself back in the empty waiting room, face-to-face with Ben Hackett, the foreman of Evenfield.

'You stuck to the story?' whispered Hackett.

'What've they promised you?' replied Silas. 'Thirty pieces of silver?'

Hackett studied Silas, his face screwed tightly in, doubting whether or not Scroggins would change his camp and just then they both heard: 'Call in the evidence!' followed half a minute later by: 'Mr Lovatt, are you or are you not the owner of this weapon?'

'Never seen it before in me life!' they heard George say. 'Your Honour, this is all wrong! These things are not true!'

'Call Benjamin Hackett!'

Hackett pointed a finger into Silas's face as an unspoken warning and went in. Silas stayed behind the door and heard the magistrate ask Hackett to identify the three men. He was then asked to identify the gun held by Constable Morrell and Hackett said he'd found it in Lovatt's kitchen. Again the four accused men started to shout objections.

'Thank you, Mr Hackett that will be all!' commanded Allen.

Hackett came out grinning.

'If they don't swing for this I'll jump the moon!' he smirked.

So Silas Scroggins and Ben Hackett continued to listen through the door but they heard naught because at that moment John Allen was silent, looking down at the hardwood desk in front of him and reflecting how many times he'd sat and condemned the guilty through far fairer processes than the one he was now conducting. In his heart he was struggling with loyalty. Sir Giles wanted a harsh punishment for Lovatt but the evidence was flimsy apart from Scroggins' and Hackett's testimonies – both in the employ of Sir Giles. Clearly both were lying, but now Allen too was caught up in the farce and he felt ashamed. He would retire doomed to a mediocre place in history, so much promise resigned to so much complacency. He would never be an Edward Hall

Alderson now. All it took was three signatures to have the men sent away.

Clutterbuck whispered: 'Looks like an open and shut case, John – there's evidence, there's a witness, there's a crime. I just can't see why, if it were Lovatt's intention to use violence and firearms he would then ask for a lawyer and confess as much?'

Clapp added: 'But then these men are ignorant, working class, uneducated types, baseborn, one might say. Lovatt's in up to his neck, if the evidence is anything to go by, though he hasn't hurt or killed anyone. But I see little against the other men.'

Allen spoke to the accused men in a monotonous, hurried voice: 'Criminality is a disease passed down through the generations. The cure for this disease is punishment, so it is the decision of this court that Dawson, Carr and Crosby be fined 50 shillings each to teach them the folly of being associated with any form of illegal union.'

He lowered his eyes and took another breath.

'It is my judgement that Lovatt be transferred immediately to York then Hull where he'll be placed on the next prison ship bound for His Majesty's Penal Colony in Botany Bay, Australia for seven years hard labour. Court closed.'

At that, Allen rose and shuffled into the back room followed by Clutterbuck and Clapp. He knew Crockatt wanted hanging for all the men but he couldn't do it and get away with it and had told him so two days before. Besides, a hanging would have to be done in public and up at Durham the proceedings were far more rigorous – details of the case would come under scrutiny and then the whole pack of lies they'd concocted would come crashing down. His loyalty to Crockatt and his loyalty to the law had been over-stretched – harsh fines, periods of imprisonment and transportation were the only choices. Clutterbuck and Clapp removed their black gowns. Clapp inquired who would write up the records of the trial and Allen said he'd write them later. We must presume they have yet to be discovered.

The four condemned, meanwhile, stood in stunned silence and then Morrell and Taylor ushered them out and George was separated from the three other men.

'Take care of my son!' he said, before being pushed down the stairs to the prison cart, stumbling badly and splitting his knee on the cobbled floor. He climbed into a wooden prison box four feet square with three vertical bars over one hole.

'What's to become of us?' asked Crosby, as the constable lifted the trapdoor.

'You'll stay 'til you pay. If not, it's six months 'ard,' he said.

He prodded the men down the wooden steps into the darkness, slammed the trapdoor over their heads and bolted it.

Outside, meanwhile, Lewis, Mrs Crosby and John Carr were still wondering what to do when the door of the stables opened and out trundled the wooden cage on wheels, pulled by two horses driven by a soldier with a musket. As the cart passed they noticed the square hole at the back and then saw a face.

'Da! Da! What's 'appened? Where they takin' yer?' Lewis shouted.

'Sir Giles's be'ind it, I'm sure of it, son,' said his father. 'He's put Wilson up to it! Crosby, Dawson n' Carr got fines but they gave me seven years in Australia! Listen son, I don't 'ave long: yer must get out o' Evenfield n' go to Durham or Newcastle. Yer can read and write! That'll save yer!'

'But – but what about the house, father?'

'Sell everythin', use it to get to the city, boy!'

'But that wasn't the real Mr Wilson!' Lewis shouted.

There was a moment's look of understanding on his father's face but just then the soldier's head appeared.

'Clear off or I'll rattle yer lugs!' he spat.

'You 'ear me, boy?' cried George. 'Stay away from work'ouse n' pit!'

Lewis slipped and fell onto the wet cobbles as John Carr ran forward to help him.

On the other side of the gate Silas suddenly pulled his hat low across his face, mounted Sir Giles' horse and spurred it through, having already spied Lovatt's son and seen him chase after the prison cart. He estimated he could turn casually right and disappear among the traffic and rapidly put distance between himself and this place, between conscience and memory, perhaps even finding time to trot over the Stone Bridge and reclaim his buried loot. But he was over-confident and had never felt comfortable on horses. This one hesitated and lifted its forelegs in protest. Everyone looked – a rearing horse was dangerous. Silas felt the eyes of the boy on the ground but it was John Carr who leapt in front of the horse.

'I know thee! Th'art at Crockatt Hall!' shouted John.

'You're mistaken!' snapped Silas.

'No, I'm not!'

'You're mistaken, lad!' he repeated.

But Silas recognised the young grouse-beater he'd almost punched days before, panicked and dug his spurs into the horse's flanks carelessly. The horse lurched with painful shock, shouldering Carr to the ground as it skittered away, slipping and scraping on the wet cobbles. With all eyes on Silas and his horse, nobody noticed Benjamin Hackett leaving in the other direction.

John Carr lifted frail Mrs Crosby up in his big strong arms and coaxed her onto the mule.

'Wilson said 'e'd come back tomorra an' meet me 'ere,' Lewis said desperately.

'Give it up!' said John Carr, defeat in his voice.

'We must get back n' raise the money to get our men out!' insisted Mrs Crosby through her sobs. 'It's the only way. We must be thankful they're not swinging from a rope!'

'But I gave me word to William Wilson,' said Lewis, hesitating.

John Carr hissed at the mule and poked its backside with a stick. He turned away and did not look back.

Just then the clock struck four. As fast as his legs could carry him he ran back to The Bulmer Stone and waited for two hours in vain. There was no sign of Wilson. He had suggested the following day, Wednesday, he would return if not today, but nonetheless Wilson's absence and Lewis' general state did not improve his mood.

For a short while Lewis, getting more drenched, stayed in the same spot. He was confused, shaking, uncertain what to do, think, follow, say or feel. It was all he could do to stagger through town, soaked by the rain, across the river and pass the Poor House where orphans trod the wooden treadmill. There he fell blindly through a hedge, crawling into the long wet grass where a blank-faced cow watched him. How could his life have changed so dramatically and so quickly?

He crawled beneath a tree that did little to protect him from the rain and tried to cope with the emotions that seemed to be raging inside him in a way he had never experienced before. A cloud drifted aside and a September sun spread its warming rays. Lewis heard a voice and looked up. There she was.

'Thou art a study in brown today, my boy,' she said.

'Dad's gone! You're gone!'

'We're not gone,' she said.

But he looked away in tears and when he looked back she *had* gone. For the rest of that afternoon Lewis could do nothing more positive than at least not cry, and he stared into the clear still waters of the Skerne as the minnows darted beneath the surface and a rainbow garlanded the sky. He thought about his father. He thought about his mother. He thought about all the faces he'd met and conversed with in recent days and weeks. He thought about life and he thought about God. Finally, he thought about alcohol and wondered why it was so many men drank it? To get drunk of course was the answer – but why? He had seen men drunk – sometimes it had been unpleasant, but it had often been funny. The devil-may-care humour that rolled off men's tongues after being coated with wine or rum was always ribald and comical, especially the way in which they walked or had difficulty aligning movements with words. He made up his mind. As the sun set, he drifted back to the Talbot, spent two shillings on a small cup of sweet rum and drank it up in his room after throwing off his wet coat and lying on the bed. He felt a little light-headed and coughed as it burnt into him but then his head fell back and he was asleep almost immediately.

Wednesday 21st September

He woke on the floor, fully dressed, with a terrible headache and a horrible feeling in his gut. Within seconds of getting to his feet he stumbled dizzily as oxygen vacuumed up behind his eyes. He lurched, but managed to grab hold of the table edge and duck out of the window to puke down the rooftop. A servant had left a jug of water, but instead of using it to wash, he drank it.

Later, after a slice of bread and cheese and returning the key to his room, he left the Talbot Inn for the last time. He had been waiting at the Bulmer Stone for almost two hours, convinced Wilson wasn't coming yet again, but finally, on the stroke of four, he glimpsed the old cart coming down Northgate and the relief wasn't allowed full vent until he'd actually seen Wilson's face close up.

'Lewis, Lewis, Lewis, my boy, forgive my lateness,' he said, 'So many carriages on the road. How is your father? Have you managed to speak to him?'

'You're too late. It all happened yesterday,' said Lewis flatly and then quietly told him what had happened. Wilson was dumbstruck.

'But that cannot be!'

To Lewis, hope beaten out of him like dignity at the hands of a bully, Wilson's words were meaningless.

'I saw it. I saw me Da took to York in a prison cart. 'e's on his way there now if 'e 'asn't already arrived. Why? Why to York?'

'Allen, the magistrate from the Gaol, did you follow him? Where did he go?' Wilson asked urgently.

'I lost him near a place called The Salutation Inn,' replied Lewis.

'The Barnard Castle road?'

'There was a river on the left - the Tees. Why are they taking him to York?' Lewis repeated.

It was moments like these that made Wilson wonder why he bothered to help downtrodden workers at all. Life would be more secure if he sought only to work with the wealthy undertaking divorces, inheritances and land purchases.

'Prisoners gathered at York are taken to Hull,' said Wilson, 'Sometimes loaded on ships bound directly for foreign ports or to southern England and then transferred to boats bound for foreign ports, like Australia.'

Lewis remembered the image of that huge, flat, largely unexplored expanse known as Australia on his world map.

'How many miles is it between England and Australia?' Lewis had asked Leakey.

Mr Leakey had looked up the distance in a book.

'About fifteen thousand?' he had said, 'Three months or more at sea.'

Lewis had repeated the number as if it was on fire in his mouth.

'I've been to Shildon an' that's five miles, so 'ow many times would I have to go to Shildon an' back to cover the same distance?'

'Work it out!' said Leakey. So he worked it out with chalk – he would have to go to Shildon and back one thousand and five hundred times over a period of three months!

Lewis then looked at the large house across the street.

'You said the man that lives in that house was fair. Fairer than Sir Giles Crockatt?' he asked.

'Edward Pease? He virtually owns this town.'

'But you said he was fair,' said Lewis.

'Most Quakers are fair,' said Wilson. 'They work hard and have few vices except drink, which is unfortunate, as most of the population of England is in its cups every day of the week.'

Lewis thought it wiser not to mention the rum. Avoiding the carriages and carts as he crossed, he went up the steps to the plain front door and pulled the iron hoop and as an afterthought scraped the heel of his clogs on the boot-scraper.

'But – but we must go to the Gaol!' pleaded Wilson. Clearly the boy was in shock.

Lewis pulled the iron hoop again. Wilson realised Lewis was intent on attracting the attention of the most important man in Darlington without an appointment. Lewis seemed to be unaware of the import of what he was doing – and why should he? He'd lost his father.

A driver in black livery objected to Wilson: 'This is the Pease stand, sir.'

'We have business with Mr Pease,' Wilson lied, climbing down, taking his saddlebag and going over to Lewis.

The bag held papers and documents proving Wilson had been a lawyer for years and cited some of the cases in which he'd been involved, as well as his rather fine legal diploma from Edinburgh University.

A servant appeared. Wilson was about to speak when Lewis took control.

'An injustice 'as been committed in the court at Darl'ton n' a fair man's judgement is urgently needed. Mr Pease is considered the fairest man in this town. I seek 'is advice on a very important matter, sir.'

The servant, an elderly woman with a kindly face, looked at both the younger and the older man and realised they were in earnest.

'Do you have an appointment?' she asked.

'I'd respect, sir, that you relay this message to 'im forthwith,' said Lewis boldly.

Wilson cringed: the tribulations of the previous few days had turned the naïve boy into a bossy young man, but the servant said: 'Wait here,' and went back inside. In the front window, a curtain parted and closed again. The servant re-appeared.

'Mr Pease requests you come in, but he doesn't have much time.'

Wilson meekly followed Lewis and they had a glimpse of the entrance hall with its polished parquet floor as they were led into a small side room with straight-backed chairs and a plain wooden table. A coal fire was dying in the grate. After the servant left, Lewis shook the coal scuttle onto the dying embers and stoked it.

'What are you going to say?' asked Wilson.

'It's what you're goin' to say that matters – you're the lawyer!'

A door opened in the entrance hall and they heard steps, as well as two voices.

'Well what am *I* going to say?' Wilson whispered to Lewis.

'Tell 'im what I told you! This is wrong!'

The voices in the hall grew louder. They listened.

'Can you come up to Aycliffe Lane where the line crosses about noon on the 26th?'

'May I bring Tom Richardson an' Bill Kitching?'

'Is that the Kitchings who've been providin' us with the nails?'

'Aye. Will there be space?'

The words were lost in more murmurs and steps and creaking doors and then the hall door closed again and a well-built man in his late 50s came in. He wore white stockings and britches and a long black coat simply made with a dozen buttons from the top collar to the bottom hem covering his size. He had a round face and a mop of white hair. He looked exhausted.

'Gentlemen, my servant passed on to me thy eloquent message. I don't have a great deal of time but I appreciate poetry. How can I help?'

The three sat and Lewis and Wilson quickly relayed the events of the past fortnight and the previous day. They told him about the mistaken identity of William Wilson and the 'impostor' and only what they knew were verifiable facts. Wilson was careful to interrupt Lewis frequently and put into more sophisticated language all the raw and undisciplined prejudices that spilled out. But they didn't and couldn't have known that Sir Giles Crockatt was behind it. Pease grimaced at certain points as if he found what he heard unpleasant and distasteful until finally he paused then said: 'I am sorry to hear of thy situation; most unpleasant. I could speak to John Allen, of course, and get more details. What more wouldst thou expect from me?'

'It's spoken widely that you're a fair man,' said Lewis.

Pease was about to comment when there was tap at the door and the servant re-appeared.

'Sir, the doctor is here.'

'Thank you, I'm just coming.'

Pease stood up.

'I try to be fair, young man. I don't always succeed,' he said. 'I don't know any man that does. Forgive me, my son Isaac is gravely ill and I am full to bursting with business connected to the railway: so much sacrifice. I will do what I can but please don't expect too much, and if I cannot deliver what thou needs, then pray.'

He seemed disposed to say more but instead shook their hands in his own plump fingers and turned away as the servant showed them out.

'He won't do nowt,' Lewis said with an assured certainty outside on the steps, feeling inevitability gather like a cloud. Although reason shouted for justice, compassion and mercy, distress would change nothing. He was no longer concerned with righting a wrong. He was only concerned with his father. As each minute passed the distance between them grew.

'Come along! We have an appointment to keep!' barked Wilson, who had set off at a brisk pace towards the town.

'Where are you going?' called Lewis. 'What about your carriage?'

Wilson did not answer. He was a man possessed but in reality it was already half-past four and they would soon be closing up for business. Lewis ran after him and caught up, saving his breath as he strode briskly alongside, for Wilson had quite a stride on him. As they passed the King's Head, Lewis realised Wilson was heading straight for the court – where George had been loaded into a prison cart and separated from the other Evenfield men the previous day. Wilson rapped on the door with the butt of his riding whip. A soldier answered.

'We're closing up!'

'I wish to speak to Mr John Allen, the magistrate – open up!' Wilson demanded.

'He ain't here, he's upstairs in the Court Offices, sir.'

Wilson looked up at the upper floor and so carefully made for the steps leading up the outside and, pushing aside with his feet those that were using the stairs as a seat, he climbed up. Lewis followed, coldly apologising to those he'd disturbed. Wilson thrust himself into the waiting room where they'd spoken to Allen a few days earlier and it was as packed now as it was then. But

Lewis saw Wilson had no need to take the battle to Allen – Allen was waiting for him, barring the door to the court back offices as his bald, bespectacled clerk stood by meekly. Wilson had the bit between his teeth.

'Am I to understand that you oversaw a court that sent an innocent man to Australia?' Wilson demanded.

It was the threat in Wilson's voice and not its content that drew a silence over the crowded room as the two educated men had a discreet set-to in a very English manner. Allen's face and whiskers bristled. Wilson went on.

'My name is William Wilson. I am a lawyer from Durham. Here in this bag are my credentials from Edinburgh University. We met last week. According to this boy, you tried his father yesterday, instead of the 3rd October.'

'I remember you,' Allen whispered.

Wilson unbuckled the strap that held the flap of the saddlebag closed and brought out a stiff-backed frame of brown velvet with a black tassel hanging from the spine. On the elaborately decorated scroll was his name in flowing script.

'*I* am William Wilson and if I am William Wilson, who pray, was the man who went into that witness box yesterday, falsely gave my name as his and in so doing had you send a possibly innocent man to Australia? And why did you preside over a political case like this in a provincial court? I demand to see a written record of the proceedings!'

Allen looked down ashamed, unmasked but hid hidden reserves of pride and said: 'I don't need to prove anything to anybody. Crime has increased dramatically since the railway business. We are invaded with thousands of Irish. They lived like rats when they were in Ireland and they bred like rats and they do the same when they are here. Have you any idea what it is like to have two or three *thousand* Irishmen, their invariably drunken Irish colleens and their flame-haired army of Catholic offspring running wild, habitually homeless and penniless around your town for months on end and at every hour God sends, Mr Wilson? Evidently not, for you are an Idealist.'

'But these are not Irish men, Mr Allen – these are Englishmen born and bred!'

'When a man is on board a ship at sea,' said Allen, desperately seeking a way out of his predicament with pride intact, 'and he chooses to marry his fiancé there and then, is not the Captain of the vessel authorised to marry them in the stead of a priest such as they would find on land?'

Allen looked hard at Wilson – it was a serious question.

'I believe that is so, Mr Allen, yes,' Wilson replied.

'Then I hope you will consider me the Captain of my own small neck of the woods while I aid my storm-tossed navy by not imposing on her precious time and resources.'

'I shall tell the world,' Wilson warned him.

Allen suddenly closed the gap so that his mouth was close to Wilson's ear with a smile and such a mix of charm and menace it was difficult to distinguish the difference. He said: 'I have heard of you – the lawyer from Durham – word gets about. I did you a favour, Mr Wilson!'

'How so, sir?' asked Wilson incredulously.

'The gentry wanted them on the Northern circuit or the county court,' said Allen, 'We both know the judges on those courts have the power to give death sentences and we must of course thank Sir Robert Peel for reducing the number of hanging offences dramatically since he became Home Secretary. My point is, if I'd allowed that to happen all four men would be hanging. Fines and transportation are funds for the national coffers but they get to keep their heads on their shoulders, their shoulders on their active bodies and their active bodies down the mine digging coal for the rich.'

Wilson considered this and saw some uncomfortable truth in it. Allen went on.

'If you'd used that imagination of yours, perhaps you would understand that history itself doesn't record everything. There are always some details that get through the net and we're left for the rest of our lives chasing a great past that never really existed but was in fact all just a life of transition, like all lives in all times.'

Allen sighed through tight lips, the small climax to a philosophy that surprised him as it came from nowhere. He looked at Wilson with intent and then steered him to a corner away from Lewis.

'You can either pursue this course or let it drop. The choice is yours and the consequences will also be yours.'

'Is that a threat?' asked Wilson.

'Not at all,' said Allen, 'Merely a reality.'

Wilson appeared about to address the people in the room as if wanting to expose Allen as a fraud but his shoulders slumped just at that one moment and then Allen knew he'd won and turned and let himself through the door. Wilson and Lewis looked at one other and after some moments Wilson led them both thoughtfully out of the building, down the steps, across the courtyard and onto Northgate where they stood in the setting autumn sunlight.

'My Dad never owned a gun but the gentry own plenty, and the mine owners do an' those Lords in Parliament in faraway London do too. Is that not so, Mr Wilson?' asked Lewis.

Wilson's mouth opened and closed but he said nothing.

'Don't blame yourself, Mr Wilson – you tried.'

They eventually arrived back at Bulmer's Stone where Wilson's horse and trap was tethered.

'You've 'elped me understand things I'd never 'ave done if I'd stayed in Evenfield,' said Lewis.

Wilson put his hand to his cheek, looked at the ground and spoke: 'Supposing I had miners on my estate who wanted to create a union and as a landowner I didn't like that or didn't want a union? A union means negotiations, and a breakdown of negotiations, as is often the case, would mean a strike, and a strike means loss of profit. Supposing I'd already lost money speculating on some other investment like the Tees and Clarence Railway? I couldn't afford to take chances with disgruntled miners. So what could I do? I could coerce certain employees to frame the miners and using my influence have them taught to think twice before forming more unions. I could be the instigator of this idea and our imposter could do the dirty work. The trial was set for the 3rd October, but after we saw Mr Allen last week he brought the trial forward to Monday. So we must presume that he – Mr Allen – is in on it as well. The night they were arrested, did you recognise any of the men?'

Lewis thought back and said: 'Ben Hackett, the Crockatt Mine Foreman, he read the arrest warrant!'

'If your father had no firearm, Hackett could easily have planted it,' suggested Wilson.

'What does all this mean, Mr Wilson?'

'It means,' said Wilson, 'you could be at the centre of a scandal that undoubtedly includes Sir Giles Crockatt and possibly John Allen JP and almost certainly expendables like our imposter and this Hackett character. It also means, sadly, we're going to be pressed to bring down these respectable men for the sake of four miners.'

'But my Dad is on his way to York!' Lewis said exasperated.

A depressing realisation drained Wilson of all enthusiasm. Of course it all rested on Lewis. If Wilson pursued the case further it would make Lewis vulnerable but if he didn't pursue it then George Lovatt's sentence would be carried out and the gentry would once again get away with it. So, thought Wilson, now is the time I must make a heroic, self-sacrificing and moral decision. Now is the moment to play the hero.

'You must leave Evenfield and follow your father,' he said quietly.

'That's all you can suggest?' Lewis felt the wind had been knocked out of him.

Wilson nodded, beaten more than he was fighting, and looked down. He wanted to add stuff about hope and miracles but said nothing, deciding to allow the silence to speak. After what seemed an eternity, Lewis slowly said: 'My Dad said I should go to Newcastle or Durham n' find a position because I can read n' write.'

Wilson's face brightened – perhaps the boy would accept the reality he couldn't change? He could read and write, more than most boys his age, the poor ones anyway. Perhaps he himself could help with a letter of introduction to business contacts? It meant the four guilty conspirators would get away scot-free of course, but transportation and fines were better than hanging, as Allen had said. Better the son survives far away in a place like Newcastle or even Edinburgh or London, where nobody could threaten him than end up face down in a ditch with a knife in his back.

'I may be able to help you find a position in Newcastle?'

Lewis looked down at Wilson and felt sorry for him. But Wilson was preoccupied with his own skin. Lewis saw that. Night would soon be falling.

'I will consider what you have suggested, Mr Wilson. I need some time to think now. This walk will do me good. Thank you for your kindness n' your money which I do not know how I will repay an' for your support. I will promise to contact you via your bookseller.'

'Ah yes! The name is Butterfield's of Durham. Don't forget it! You can always find me there!'

Lewis scooped up the few remaining shillings and pennies in his pocket and offered them to Wilson but Wilson shook his head and said: 'Forget the money. Keep it. But shake my hand at least, Master Lovatt.'

He held out his hand and Lewis shook it limply. Lewis turned and walked a little way and then heard his name. He turned back and Wilson handed him a book.

'*Hamlet – Prince of Denmark* by William Shakespeare,' said Wilson. 'Full of good advice, I find, in times of difficulty.'

Lewis smiled and took the book.

'Thank you, Mr Wilson, for everything, for trying, at least. I hope you and Mrs Hudson will find the sanctuary you seek.'

Wilson said nothing further, so Lewis turned away and walked up North Road. He took Wilson's advice and didn't once look back. He didn't have far to go.

'Is it true that if I follow the iron road I shall come to Shildon?' Lewis asked a workman fixing a picket fence.

'Aye, but walk alongside, not on it!'

For almost a half hour he plodded through the twilight, dazed in a confusion of thoughts. How bright the stars twinkled in sharp but gentle contrast between the heavenly, natural world and the ugly, cruel world of men. As if on cue the skies clouded, blanking out even the thin guiding light of the moon, reducing the land to blackness. A tiny light flickered in the dark bulk of the shadow of a farmhouse nearby. Lewis reasoned he must rest until morning but should he curl up quietly in a barn or seek a warm bed? He had a few shillings still. He climbed a low stile, the shapes of cows moving slowly around him, to where a lantern burned bright and steady above a door. Peering in through the small dirty windowpane, he saw the glow of a fire and shivered as the autumn night closed around him. He went to the door and knocked three times. Hearing the shuffling of feet and then a latch being lifted, he found himself looking at a shrunken beldam carrying a lit candle.

Lewis leaned forward and said: 'I'm travellin' to Evenfield. I'm very tired. Would it be possible yer could offer us lodgin'?'

Just then the door swung wider and Lewis was staring down the barrel of a blunderbuss. He jumped!

''e seems polite, Henry,' the woman said reassuringly to the man.

'Forgive me, boy,' said the man. 'We've 'ad many new faces these last few years – it's the Irish buildin' the rail-way.'

He lowered the ancient weapon and ushered Lewis in.

'Come in n' sit at our table. Our food's simple but honest.'

'Where shall I wipe my shoes, sir?'

'A bit of mud never did anybody any 'arm,' said the old man.

Lewis stepped onto the worn stones of the uneven floor. It was warm and smoky, a light breeze occasionally causing a downdraft that puffed more smoke into the already smoky room. Two rocking chairs were set before it and a fat black cat was curled in a wooden crate. A large clock ticked resolutely, rapid chimes giving the time as eight. The man mounted his gun on two nails above the fire. The woman brought bread and cheese to the table and laid a wooden plate.

'What brings you to us on such a night?' she asked.

Lewis glanced at them, wondering if he should tell the truth. It would have done his heavy heart good to unburden itself to older people. They generally had wisdom and advice to pass on. But these people were still strangers and he'd trusted many strangers in recent weeks and few had repaid that trust. The woman slopped a wooden ladle of broth into the bowl.

'I've been to Darl'ton to seek work,' he lied.

'And what line of work would that be?' asked Henry.

'Now don't trouble the boy so,' the woman scolded. 'That is his affair.'

'I can read n' write,' said Lewis.

'Oh!' said the man, half-statement, half-question.

''e looks 'bout the same age as John,' said the woman, smiling at Lewis.

'John?' asked Lewis.

Her husband looked at her darkly.

'Now wife, don't go on 'bout that.'

'He went to Darl'ton too, but caught 'imsel' typhus. Such a dirty town is Darl'ton,' she hissed.

As Lewis ate, Henry told of their only son, John, whose job was carrying lead to Stockton by mule. One night he'd stopped in Darlington, contracted typhus and died shortly after, aged just 18. After the lead trade fell away, Henry moved to Shildon where he'd heard men were being hired to dig the land to lay the new railway. He was taken on as a digger.

'It wasn't all plain sailin' though – I lost two mates,' he reflected. 'Alderson and Briggs, two years back. A cuttin' fell on 'em; Briggs left a widow n' five bairns in Teesdale.'

Henry cut small chunks of hard cheese with a very old clasp knife and handed them to Lewis. One lump fell from the plate onto the floor but Henry picked it up, crossed himself and put it back on Lewis's plate.

'Myers Flat just up the way was devilish 'ard work, a boggy piece of land,' he went on. 'Well, 'ow many times did we fill it wi' stones n' 'ow many times would it sink again?'

'It was the fairies,' said his wife earnestly, 'Jenny-o'-the-lantern 'aven't been likin' all this tearin' up of their land so I wen' out last 'arvest n' made a little offering to the Green Man.'

'Me wife's a simple woman,' Henry said to Lewis and, when she was looking the other way, caught Lewis's eyeline, winked once and tapped the side of his head twice.

'Have you seen the engine?' Lewis asked.

'Indeed I 'ave, young sir; all the locals 'ave,' said Henry.

'She's impressive in't she?'

'I dunno about impressive,' Henry said dubiously. 'It stopped just over the way there one time n' the fire went out! Next day a navvy called Metcalf from Darl'ton who carried wi' 'im a burnin' glass 'e used to light 'is clay pipe 'ad to use that to get the fire started again. Well, I do that every day – nothing impressive about that!'

Lewis also told Henry he'd gone to Darlington to look for work in the mills, but unable to find any had decided to return to Evenfield.

'Evenfield?' said Henry. 'Will you go down the pit? I'd not recommend it, not if you can read an' write.'

'How much further on foot is it to Shildon?' Lewis asked.

'About three miles,' said Henry. 'Will you be wantin' to stay with us this night?'

'If it wouldn't be an inconvenience,' Lewis said. He had considered finding a barn to rest in but a bed would be more welcoming. He still had a few shillings left from Wilson's funds to pay for a cheap bed.

He felt a sudden ache behind his eyes. He was exhausted and, after some food and warmth, knew sleep was close. He wondered if the rum was still in his system? The old woman noticed he seemed unsettled and asked: 'What ails thee, boy?'

'My head aches a little: it's been a long day. I'll retire now if I may,' he said politely.

'By all means,' said Henry. 'Mary'll show you where.'

'Thank you. G'night, sir,' said Lewis.

'G'night, John,' said Henry. Lewis blinked at the old man's error but Henry didn't seem to realise he'd made one as he gazed into the fire, puffing on his pipe. His wife led the way up the half dozen steep wooden stairs with a candle into a square room with an uneven clay-tiled floor. In the corner was a low wooden bed, like a cot, with a mattress of straw and a blanket. By the side of the bed was a pair of clogs and a carved walking stick.

'Belonged to John,' said Mary. 'Do you have chilblains? John 'ad chilblains – eggs, old wine n' some fennel root rubbed on works wonders. What about baldness? I've an old Saxon cure for that involving bees.'

Lewis smiled, got her to leave the lit candle, said goodnight and persuasively closed the door to her. He looked down at the shoes and stick and stuffed them out of sight, lay on the hard bed, pulled out the leather-bound copy of *Hamlet* and opened it at the first page. A folded piece of paper fell out. He unfolded it and found himself looking at a banknote for the sum of £1. Had Wilson forgotten about it? Was it a gift? In the centre was a drawing of a buxom young lady in a flimsy dress standing beside a lion and behind them was the unmistakeable spire of St Cuthbert's Church in Darlington. He gently refolded it and as he slipped it back into the same page found a weak circle around a few lines that read: 'What a piece of work is man: how noble in reason, how infinite in faculty, in form and moving, how express and admirable in action, how like an angel in apprehension, how like a God, the beauty of the world, the paragon of animals.'

He then read the first scene on the battlements of Elsinore Castle in Denmark when they saw the ghost of Hamlet's dead father. Lewis thought about his own father and, to curb the emotion welling inside, stopped reading and blew out the candle. For a little while he listened to the inevitable tapping of the clock downstairs, straining his ears to hear if he might be the subject of conversation for the odd couple who'd given him their hospitality under the apparent misunderstanding that he was their long-lost son. And then he closed his eyes.

* * *

George Lovatt's journey, crossing the Tees at Croft, had taken him first to Northallerton and then Thirsk, two small market towns midway between Darlington and York but the horse never got up more than a trot on the better stretches and a walk on the worst.

As on other occasions in his life, George reflected repetitively over how he was powerless to fix the course of his destiny. He went over the last words he'd exchanged with his son: 'You can read and write – that'll save you!' and then his son's final words: 'That wasn't the real Mr Wilson!'

There was no justice for the likes of him and never being an overly religious man, he nonetheless prayed. Had he done a good enough job as a father? Would Lewis know the difference between right and wrong, between a lie and the truth? Jesus had been 12 years old when he'd passed from boy to man. Lewis was 13. Was it enough?

As they approached the outskirts of Northallerton, passing the seemingly never-ending stream of coal-carriers as they went,

George contemplated escape but he knew he'd not get far and the guards took no chances. The soldier levelled the barrel of his musket at the door of the cart as another man opened it.

'Get in!' ordered the soldier, and into the space climbed the other prisoner, shackled at the ankles and wrists.

'George Lovatt,' said George, introducing himself.

'Bill Williamson. What you here for?' Bill asked, slumping against the wooden wall.

'The Six Acts, but I was framed – seven years transportation,' said George. 'You?'

'Long story – I wouldn't mind but they all 'ad three legs anyway.'

'Ah,' said George, 'Horses?'

Bill looked at George. They were about the same age but Bill had longer hair and his face was pockmarked.

'Smallpox, in case you're wondering,' said Bill.

The soldier and the carter locked them in and they went off to the inn. Silence settled on the prison cage.

'Where you from, Bill?'

'Bedale originally, then Leeds. You?'

'Tyneside, then west Durham.'

'You a collier?' Bill asked.

'How can you tell?' asked George, frowning.

'What else is there to do in Tyneside apart from dig coal or build boats? I had a fifty-fifty chance of hitting gold!' he laughed.

George smiled.

'What's going to 'appen to us?' he asked.

'York first, then Hull,' said Bill assuredly. 'Ever seen the ocean?'

'Saw it from the beach at South Shields once,' said George.

'Standin' on a beach n' standin' on a boat's two different things,' said Bill. 'Ocean shows no pity to them what can't keep their breakfasts down.'

'You've sailed?' asked George.

'Under Nelson, powder monkey many moons' ago, but got mesel' into bad ways after. No, this part is luxury: once they get us in the belly of a boat tossed like a pine cone in a tempest n' in tropical climes, you'll be wishin' you was dead. Mind you, we've a toff to thank we're not dumped in prison hulks!'

'What toff?' asked George.

'Mr John Howard. 'e wrote a book. And no, in answer to yer question, I can't read. But it was read to me by an educated lady of ill-repute. Mr John Howard writ a book called *The State of Prisons* some fifty year back and it's thanks to him they stopped dumping us in old prison hulks offshore 'cos they was a nasty, nasty place to end up.'

Bill's voice was laden with layers of sarcasm and invective that invited questions for which there were no answers and neither of them spoke much after that – George was in his world and Bill in his. But George was impressed with how much his new cell mate knew about that world and just as saddened by how little he himself knew.

The prison cart travelled down to Thirsk once the carter returned from his lunchtime drink and by the time they stopped at the Gaol it was night. The soldier found lodgings and left the cart with the two prisoners out in the courtyard with a few dozen braying mules standing with their coal burdens deforming their backs. Both men suffered badly from the cold weather and hard floor. Around midnight, a hand threw half a loaf of hard bread through their window and they shared it as they listened to the sounds of laughter, shouting, fiddle music and drunken singing punctuated by shouts, the smashing of furniture and breaking glass. They slept. At dawn, with cockerels crowing nearby, the wooden walls were suddenly subjected to clattering sticks.

'Stand back!' barked the soldier.

Both George and Bill roused themselves but stayed back as the door opened. The soldier stuck his head in.

'You got a visitor, ladies,' he mocked. 'You – take 'is arms!'

Other men humped in an unconscious body – face bruised, bloated and cut, gaping maw toothless.

'Some Paddy,' said the soldier, 'Gave us a lot of verbal so we beat six ways of Sunday out of 'im.'

'What's 'e in for?' asked Bill.

''e stole an egg!' came the mocking reply.

The door of the cage was locked and the soldier laughed and repeated: ''e stole an egg!'

Bill looked away from man's bruised face, laughed drily and said: 'Christ, 'e stole an egg, you get framed an' I nicked an 'orse with three legs! When we gonna get lumped in wi' some *real* criminals?'

Thursday 22nd September

Henry was sitting at the table cutting pieces of cheese from a block with his clasp knife once again and chewing them with his remaining black teeth. The room was already smoky and in the hearth the fire burned poorly under a copper kettle, a weak jet of steam dancing from the spout.

'How did you sleep?' asked Henry.

'Very well,' Lewis lied.

It hadn't helped that it felt as if an irritating ghost had decided to prod him all night muttering: 'Are you going to take my place? Will my shoes fit? Do you like my stick?' and he wondered why William Shakespeare didn't think of such words for *his* ghost?

'Sorry 'bout the smoke,' said Henry waving his hand once. 'I must get round to cleanin' the chimney. You'll be 'ungry, no doubt. 'ave some vittles - the's watter in't barrel outside.'

Lewis went outside and splashed the surface of the water, wiping away dead leaves before cupping it to his face. He then noticed a dozen sheaves of corn woven into strips hanging around the door. He knew these were corn dollies – pagan symbols to encourage the Earth to provide good crops, probably put there by the old lady who was already up and about - she waved to him as she went into the hen house. Chickens squawked and flapped as she brought out two big brown eggs. Lewis went back inside and sat at the table, content with the black bread and cheese and to wash it down a wooden beaker of off-milk, but it was bitter and he was thankful when Mary came in and broke an egg into it. Good food or bad, it was too much to waste. He burped.

Lewis tried to think: this new day was the first day of the rest of his life but what was he going to do with it? Would this life unfold for him as he walked back to Evenfield or would he see a sign, a marker, a direction and think: '*That's* what I'll do!' Whose advice should he follow: his father's, Mr Wilson's, his own?

The previous day's events first hit him like a gigantic metal spade across the back of his head and then the sensation swung to the opposite extreme as a heavy sadness swamped him.

'My wife n' I've been thinkin',' said Henry, leaning forward. 'It's a lonely life 'ere an' well, if you ever wanted a new family you'd be welcome to stop with us.'

Henry finished his speech with a hint of a question. Lewis realised he was being asked to fill the shoes of their dead son. He'd lied to them he'd no family, but of course he did and his heart filled with sadness as he realised the emptiness in theirs. It would have been so easy to say yes and be 'adopted' into another family, retrieving lost security in one gesture. But it would never be the same, not really.

'I am grateful, but I cannot,' Lewis said apologetically.

Henry smiled weakly. Lewis brought out the folded one-pound note and put it on the table.

'But I'd like to pay you for my stay,' he said.

Henry's eyes widened considerably and he picked up the note with care and inspected it with his dirty fingers. 'I couldn't change a big note like that, son.'

He refolded the note and pushed it back across the table.

'You pay me back some other time.'

Defeated, Lewis put it between the pages of the book.

'Take some bread an' cheese for your journey an' a few apples,' said Mary, handing him a rag bundle, though her enthusiasm was muted.

'Thank you kindly. And I apologise for not 'avin' some coins to 'and,' said Lewis.

Henry produced a winding key, stuck it into the dial of the ticking clock on the mantle and turned it six times to the right.

'You should be in Shildon by nine,' he said.

Lewis sipped his tea quickly and stood and in that fraction of a moment became master of his own destiny. It sounded ridiculous. But here he was no longer in thrall to the duty of life in Evenfield, having to observe the ritual of others deciding what and where he could and couldn't go and did or didn't do. He was alone and the elation made him dizzy and just a little sick. If it all came down to one decision, then the decision had already been made and now everything that happened was simply about putting that decision into practice.

As they went outside, Mary produced a red scarf and a small stubbly root and before he could resist she wrapped it around his head, tucking the root under the brim against his left ear. He didn't know what to say or do and he felt a little silly.

'Crosswort that is, keep it against your head all day n' it'll keep the pains away,' Mary advised.

Despite standing with a tuber-bedecked bandana around his head like a greengrocer buccaneer, he thanked them, turned and walked away, picking up rhythm as he went out into the field, crossed it and rejoined the footpath running parallel with the iron road, where more mule-trains were at work ceaselessly trudging backwards and forwards on the far right side of the roads or the far left, clogging up the many arterial roads and lanes by which the towns and villages were kept functioning by their deliveries of coal.

He glanced back only once – they were still standing there, so he waved. Once out of view though he tore off the bandana and threw it to the ground. He didn't believe in old wives' remedies.

He walked up the worn, pitted road for almost an hour and passed a building of new bricks in the V of two branches of rails. Nearby, workmen were painting a long series of chaldrons with black paint. He walked on to Adamson's Inn and there it was again: the boiler painted green, the seams and frame yellow; the wheels and chimney remained unpainted. But it wasn't full of smoke or steam this time – men were loading it with coal and a little further away, a small knot of people were gathered around a tree upon which a printed sign was pinned.

'What does it say?' asked a woman.

Lewis stepped forward, studied the opening words and spoke slowly.

'The proprietors of the above hereby give notice – commencing at Witton Park Colliery, in the west of this county, and terminating – Stockton-upon-Tees – branches to Darlington, Yarm – 27 miles – formally opened for the general purposes of trade on Tuesday the 27th instant.'

'When's the 27th?' asked an older woman.

'That's next week!' said another voice.

'I'll bake some pies,' she said. 'Should be good business that day!'

'Better tell the gravedigger then, they'll be fallin' like flies after!'

'Where there's a crowd there's pickings to be 'ad an' I don't see many crowds comin' to this part of the county too often, tha's for sure!'

'Aye, she's right,' said another, among a general murmur of assent.

'Let the boy read on,' said another.

Lewis read aloud: 'It is the intention of the proprietors to meet below the tower at Brusselton near West Auckland, about 9 miles west of Darlington, at eight o'clock A.M. and after inspecting the inclined planes proceed at nine o'clock precisely to Stockton-upon-Tees, where they will arrive about one o'clock.'

'Four hours?' laughed one, 'Impossible!'

'We could buy fish n' be back to cook it for dinner!' shouted an entrepreneur.

'A superior locomotive', Lewis read on, 'will be employed, with a train of convenient carriages, for the conveyance of the proprietors and strangers.'

'I wonder if it's like bein' transported in a carriage pulled by an ass?'

'Why don't you bring your ol' man n' find out?'

Turning away smiling at jokes, Lewis set off to Evenfield and within two hours was standing once again on his village green. Though only away five days, they had been the longest of his life. He'd lost his father and his father's friends to injustice. He'd felt betrayed, but he'd also experienced kindness. He'd travelled on the Great North Road. He'd seen Durham Cathedral and Darlington. He'd witnessed a public execution and been ashamed. He'd lived in lodgings, eaten pies, drank rum, coffee and wine. He'd passed time at a prison. He'd glimpsed his poor father being carried away through the rain. He'd met and spoken with Edward Pease and three times he'd seen George Stephenson's steam engine and now here he was back at Evenfield. How could his world ever be the same?

He passed the gate to the pit. The colliery was still running – two pit ponies harnessed to chaldrons took them along 50 yards of rails to the weighing machine. Women nearby were washing the coal. Others broke it for loading onto carts or into saddle sacks for the mules, horses and ponies. Smoke billowed from the blacksmith's chimney as he hammered and battered and repaired picks and other metal tools for mining and sawed timbers for pit props. As Lewis approached, a figure looked over.

'Well, well, Lewis Lovatt. Come for a job?' asked Hackett.

He settled an eye on a tight-lipped Lewis.

'You know that gun wasn't my Dad's!' said Lewis.

'You wanna be careful what you say, boy!' Hackett retorted, his voice going cold. 'An' if you ain't workin' 'ow you gonna pay the rent?'

Lewis suddenly felt strong – he hadn't spoken to Hackett in the whining voice of a child that could never hope to hear fair judgement: he'd spoken in a slow voice and with a levelled statement of fact. He did not respond to Hackett's goad. Nonetheless, his face flushed as he passed the homes of Crosby, Dawson and Carr, not glancing in their direction but aware of faces crowding at windows to gawp. The vultures were just waiting for the nod.

He found the key under the back step, unlocked the door and stood in the parlour hearing only silence. He looked sadly at his smashed furniture and broken clock that now plunged the house into a deafening silence. Shuffling across to the stairs, he climbed them and lay on the bed struggling not to cry. Three times he stood and walked around stomping his feet in an effort to suppress anguish. He had such an appetency to sleep forever but something said: 'The boy has gone, like an unwanted friend walking out of the door. Now, you *must* follow the way o' the man!'

And so, moving like a ghost, he went downstairs and spent a short while clearing out the cold ashes and striking the flint. With some heat back in his body, he boiled up some tea. Clutching his father's best Sunday jacket to his face to recall the familiar odours, he passed the hours until sunset staring into space, his thoughts and memories tumbling over and over in his head.

Lewis slept until mid-morning and went to empty the chamber pot into the beck. As he was returning to the scullery he heard male voices approaching, so he ran in, locked the door and listened. There were three loud raps that made the hinges rattle.

'Rent's due!'

It was Hackett.

There was a pause and another three bangs, each harder than the first, that made the door shake.

'I know you're in there, young Lovatt! I know you can 'ear me!'

There was another pause and Lewis remained silent.

'We'll get the little bastard out!' Hackett said to his companions.

Holding his breath, Lewis heard receding footsteps, leaned against the door and slid to the floor. He had a terrible feeling of panic, but hot on its heels came a kind of relief too – he knew now how much longer he had.

Friday 23rd September

John Carr stepped out of his house and closed the door.

'What you want?' he gruffly threw at Lewis.

'To talk,' said Lewis.

'Nobody wants to talk to you!'

'What's happened to your brother?' Lewis asked.

'The Crosbys raised the fine as did we, sold everythin' we 'ad. Mrs Crosby's gone to Darlo today. I'm goin' tomorrow but Tom Dawson'll be breakin' rocks for six month.'

'What about Hackett?'

John Carr spat into the grass.

'Hackett'll get what's comin'!'

'How did they know which ones to arrest?' Lewis asked.

'Somebody told 'em,' said Carr.

'But who?'

'That's what we're all wonderin',' said Carr. Lewis blinked.

'Me? I wouldn't do that to me own Dad!'

'Why not? You'd get the house to yersel'!' said Carr and he turned and slammed the door. Lewis flushed red and angrily walked on to Tom Dawson's house but it was of course empty and would soon be let to another family while poor Tom broke rocks. At Mrs Crosby's house, her two snot-nosed twins came out shouting in unison: 'Our Mam says 'Bugger off!'' before going back inside.

'Come in, come in,' Leakey said, fussing as he opened the door to his youngest and brightest pupil. He made Lewis tea and gave him a crust of bread, butter and a slice of ham while Lewis told him all that had happened since Durham. At the end of the story, Leakey sat down, took off his spectacles and rubbed his eyes. Lewis had reluctantly told the story and with few trimmings as he felt its rendition would make no difference to the outcome. He'd had five days to prepare himself for the implications.

'What use education if we can't influence the hearts of men?' Leakey asked staring at the floor. 'What will you do?'

Lewis wanted to reply: 'I don't know! You're a man! Tell me what I must do!', but instead he said: 'I'd rather die than go down Crockatt Pit.'

'You *will* die if you go down Crockatt Pit,' said Leakey. 'It's only a question of time. Your poor father, my God, what sort of world have we made? Look Lewis, I've friends in Newcastle. I could write them a letter of introduction for you to find work.'

But Lewis wasn't listening.

'The Crosbys n' Carrs blame me for what 'appened. I have to leave, but where to go?' he asked.

'A solution will present itself,' counselled Leakey, looking down again.

The following day Lewis was in deep depression. He waited for the solution Leakey had predicted but none came. Lying awake listening to the moan of the wind, he slipped into a semi-daze and woke suddenly when he imagined he heard the door open downstairs but he realised it was a draught. Occasionally, he felt as if he was looking back at another life unconnected to his: his father's boots waiting for feet near the fire, Sunday suit hanging in the wardrobe awaiting a neat, bony frame, his scarf and cloth cap longing for a neck to cover and a head to protect. The kitchen and parlour held most memories. From every conceivable angle Lewis saw the outlined ghosts of his Mam and Dad and could almost hear their voices.

To change the air he wandered over the fields and moors around the village and ended up in the churchyard again alongside his mother's grave. He tried reading *Hamlet* and though he didn't understand all the words, he arrived at the scene when Hamlet was determined to discover the truth about his father's murder. Lewis thought of how Hamlet didn't feel compelled to avenge his father, nor to find out why, which made him dislike the young Danish prince, but he did feel as determined as Hamlet to survive and to find some way to right a wrong.

Sometime in the evening he was woken by the sound of breaking glass. Someone had thrown a rock through his upstairs window. Lewis ran outside but there was nobody to be seen. The rock had landed on his parents' empty bed. It made him angry, it felt like he'd been invaded, insulted, shamed. He cleaned up the broken glass. Downstairs he stoked the fire as in the coalhouse he was only able to scrape one bucket of mostly coal dust, so he sat around what may well be the last fire that house would ever see for an hour more and read: 'The serpent that did sting thy father's life now wears his crown.'

A short while after, the candle flickered and went out and he closed his eyes knowing the cock crow at dawn would stir him again. He slept fully dressed in his Dad's trousers, on his parents' bed, ready to run if needs be for he now did not know what surprises the night might bring.

* * *

Michael Longridge had bathed his face in cold water and glanced around at the Forth Street workshop. Despite Locomotion Number One being shipped down to Aycliffe the week before it didn't appear emptier, as 'Hope', the second steam engine entered into the ledger beneath 'Active', now occupied the attentions of his workforce and the third, whom they'd jokingly christened 'Black Diamond', as coal was sometimes known, was taking shape.

Hanging around the walls on hooks and from wooden beams were dozens of heavy iron tools, all a uniform rusty brown. Over 50 long-handled tongs were racked up alongside one another. A hand-operated, concertina-shaped bellows fed the furnace with oxygen. On the other side of the chimney stood a pile of coal the height of a man and in the middle of the floor was a huge iron anvil. On opposite walls hung more short-handled tongs, more hammers, dozens of iron wedge-heads used to nip off the ends of molten rods, wooden T-squares from large to small, three powerful vices clinging to the sides of a battered oak workbench and giant callipers like crab claws hung on nails.

Longridge was as familiar with a forge as Hackworth, but the shaping of iron to form moving parts was, at first, beyond him, so he'd simply watched the blacksmiths at work and asked questions, however ridiculous or insignificant. Then he'd tried it for himself.

'Why?' Hackworth had once asked.

'There's summat beautiful about 'em. It's like … I can't explain it,' he said with a hint of embarrassment, but then with more enthusiasm he said: 'To create summat so beautiful and so strong!'

A voice shouted his name, snapping him back to the present.

'Yes, John?'

'The carters 'ere, Mr Longridge,' said John Cree. John Cree had been with the company for a few months and was already showing initiative. Now, together, they rolled back the wooden gates to reveal a low dray with six horses and a group of workmen awaiting his orders.

'Get behind!' Longridge called, and they pushed 'it' into the open air to the foot of the ramp. The carters stared. From the outside, 'it' resembled nothing more than a wooden shed with glassless 'windows' on open-spoked iron wheels slightly bigger than a wagon's. One carter couldn't resist asking for a look inside. Longridge opened the door from ground level and pushed, showing the carpeted interior, cushioned seats around the walls and long wooden table down the middle.

'Hey, who're you expectin', the King of England?' the carter asked.

'Ah no,' said Longridge, 'If we were expectin' 'im, we'd 'ave built a throne!'

* * *

Bill was older than George, and sharper: he'd rustled horses, fought at Trafalgar in 1805 and lived a full life ever since, with periods of legal employment punctuated with periods of illegal employment. He retained a grim sense of humour that enabled him to get through his tough and uncertain world and, perhaps most importantly, he had a notion of how to keep ahead of the Peelers and their brand of rough justice. Before all the misfortune that had befallen him, George had to admit he'd been naive about the Peelers and justice in equal measures: he had once been sure they existed to protect innocent people from criminals but now his understanding had altered. Technically, he was now a criminal, but he at no point remembered doing or saying anything malicious, so it was very difficult for him to see himself as one.

The badly beaten Irishman who'd been loaded into the cart at Thirsk had died. It had been Bill who had noticed.

'That boy hasn't moved a muscle since they put him in!' he said.

Bill had seen death before. He touched the lad's wrist and put his hand on his chest and finally his ear close to the blue lips. He leaned back and said: 'He's dead.'

George's instinct was to attract the attention of the driver by knocking on the wooden walls, but Bill stopped him.

'Tha'll say nowt if thou knows what's good for thee. Let *them* find out 'e's dead!' he said, jerking his thumb to the front of the cart.

George slumped against the wall of the cart and looked with horror at the sight before him. They both cursed as the wagon lurched ceaselessly, throwing them backwards, forwards and side to side. To combat this they tried to lock themselves into the corners with arms and legs, wanting to look away from the man they never knew but it was hard on the muscles and bones and when they finally arrived at York Castle both felt as if they'd fallen down a thousand stone stairs. Finally the door opened and the soldier stuck his head in. He prodded the immobile Irishman a number of times.

'What's happened here?' he asked.

Bill said nothing. George was silent. The soldier pulled up the dead man's head by his hair, dropped it, then disappeared from view. He returned with a tall fat man in a once-tan-stained leather jacket and pants – the Turnkey.

'I think 'e's passed on,' said the soldier.

'What of, a broken-'eart?' said the Turnkey without laughing. 'Was 'e wealthy?'

'He was a Paddy, Hennessy was 'is name,' said the soldier. 'Gave us grief up at Northallerton.'

'Then 'e'll be poor. Tek 'im round back,' ordered the Turnkey. He looked at Bill and George with disgust. 'What've *they* done?'

'This n' stole a horse n' t'other threatened violence 'gain 'is master.'

The Turnkey was a big man and he enjoyed its implications.

'The'll be no vi'lence 'ere or yer'll be joinin' 'im round back! Either of you got money or friends with money?'

Both men shook their heads.

'I didn't think so,' said the Turnkey. 'You can get some work done then!'

George and Bill were ordered to carry the body of the man known as Hennessy to a large pit. Inside were a dozen corpses wrapped in grey bandages or brown cotton, laid in a row, sprinkled haphazardly with spades of quick-lime. The stench was putrid. The soldier put his fingers and thumb either side of his nose as they approached.

'Get down in there n' put 'im at the end!'

Together, Bill and George stumbled down the steep earth walls cut into the shallow pit, retching and gasping as they went. George noticed on one corpse a short woollen coat that had mostly escaped the lime. Humiliated and cold, as he was still in his nightshirt and trousers, he laid the body down among the others and wrenched at the coat on the other corpse, pulling and tugging. Only by putting his foot hard into the small of the corpse' back was he able to wrest it off the stiff arms, shake it free of the powder as thoroughly as he could, put it on and climb out, panting and gasping as a gravedigger, only his eyes visible above the scarf tied around his face, threw a spadeful of lime across. A priest arrived, mumbled a few words, made a sign of the cross and went away.

With seven other men from around the North of England, all bound for Australia, the two men were locked in a cell two-thirds underground. In the top third of the cell a small square glassless window about a foot wide – an iron bar down its middle - led out at ground level to the exercise yard, and beyond the yard's railings members of the public came to stare, paying a penny each to study criminals. There were no beds, just straw on the ground and in one corner a hole dropped to a channel flowing sluggishly underneath to the River Ouse and for cuisine the Gaoler passed half a loaf of hard bread through a hatch in the door. Their greatest dilemma was sharing out the water equally and trying to clean themselves with what pitiful amounts remained. George began to understand that not only was the loss of freedom counted as a punishment but also the loss of dignity.

The cellmates were from similar walks of life: two colliers, Christopher and Ebenezer from Wallsend, who'd run from their masters; Albert, a poacher on royal land; an Irish navvy called O'Rourke who'd stolen a chicken; and a Dutch whaler called Jack who spoke almost no English but had started a fight that ended up involving ten local men and caused destruction to property in Goole. There was also a gambler from Manchester called Kennedy who'd cheated at cards, and Arthur, a blacksmith who'd assaulted an army officer who had refused to pay after Arthur had shod four of his troop's horses. The job of distributing the drinking water fairly was left to Arthur: he was too big and strong to argue with. Luckily he was also kind.

'There's five ways out of here,' mused Arthur, pulling his chubby fingers back one by one, 'Not guilty, guilty, transportation or –' he held his fist above his head and imitated a hanged man. 'And the fifth?' asked George.

'Offerin' to give the Turnkey's wife a bone!' he laughed, and for the first time in days everybody laughed, but such bouts were rare. Laughter was almost dangerous as it sometimes turned to punishing bouts of coughing.

'Is there any other was out of this predicament?' George asked.

'Money,' said Bill and Arthur almost at the same time. 'Pay the Turnkey and he'll let you go,' added Arthur matter-of-factly.

'That's English justice!' sneered Bill.

The quicklime on the jacket he'd pulled from the dead body inflamed George's skin and blistered his hands, chest and back, so he laid it out on the grass outside the cell window to soak in the rain and mud. He wrang it out and laid it to dry when the sun shone. It took two days and despite the mud and stains, it was warm and wearable. The men complained they were not allowed to walk in the yard but their grumbling fell on deaf ears. Hunger was the worst source of discomfort. Bread and water were nowhere near enough for grown men; but griping was risky – it could prejudice the already limited generosity of the Gaolers.

At night, shuffling on their backs or sides or bellies on the hard flagstones, groaning and talking in their sleep, farting and coughing, some of the men sobbed. Sobbing was never ridiculed at night but discouraged in the daytime – the men each had their troubles but they also had a duty to behave as men, so they comforted themselves with memories of the good times: the women they'd loved, the children they'd fathered and alternatives they'd wished they'd taken just before being arrested. George thought about Lewis and wondered where he was and what he was doing and remembered that one occasion last year when he had specifically asked Leakey to take of Lewis 'if anything ever happened'.

The period in the cell came to an end when the door opened and the Turnkey said: 'Out, you dirty bastards! You gotta boat to Hull!'

He threw his apple core to the ground and snorted derisorily as some of them pounced on it, but not George. George wouldn't give the Turnkey the pleasure.

***

Mid-morning, the early shift came out of the Evenfield mine and Lewis stood at the window as figures trooped past his house, their hobnail boots and clogs clumping on the road, surreptitious looks in his direction, terrified even a glance would bring a warrant on their heads.

In the pantry Lewis found a stale crust of bread and cheese and washed it down with water, filling a small hole and blunting the sharp edge of his hunger. After a little while sitting in the kitchen, he stepped out of the house and across the field and went to the churchyard again. There, he plonked himself down cross-legged in the long dry grass.

'I have of late – but wherefore I know not – lost all my mirth,' he said, the words tumbling spontaneously from his lips just as they had tumbled from that part of his memory where was stored the vast empire of thus far accumulated words associated with *Hamlet*.

'Well, my big strong lad what will you do with yourself?'

There she was, a little distance away, dressed like a princess in her best lilac dress and fur-trimmed gloves, her beautiful chestnut tresses plaited.

'I don't know what to do.'

'You've already decided what to do and you've come to ask my permission but you don't need my permission - me and your Dad are here,' and at this she gracefully crossed her chest. 'We always will be. We are now. Life is like the shoes your Dad made: you just have to get the right fit and step into them and off you go. Wherever you are, find a quiet place alone somewhere and think about me and I'll be with you again.'

He spent almost all the following day in bed or indoors, hoping divine providence might filter into his life at some point and rescue him from his radical plan, but it did not and so after a short while, Lewis made the biggest decision of his life.

Sunday 25th September

The church bells of Darlington's St Cuthbert's struck ten times and began to peal. Altar boys opened the oak doors wide and the congregation emerged. On cue, beggars became fawning shadows, blending with the more solid shades of a multitude of Sunday suits, velvet coats and top hats. Amidst the swish of formal dresses, clicking heels and walking sticks, groups formed and peeled apart while at one side stood two figures at the church gates. Edward Pease, the Quaker, shook hands with George Stephenson, the Unitarian.

'I'm surprised to find thee here, Mr Stephenson?'

'Many important people are at church today and one likes to present one's public side now and then,' said George.

'We may teach you politics yet, Mr Stephenson,' said Pease.

'How is your son?' George asked.

'The end approaches but we are not afraid of death – our achievements in this world are how we remember each other,' said Pease, but he didn't sound convincing.

'I went through the same with my first wife, Frances,' said George. 'She too had the consumption. It's almost 20 years now but the memories are still fresh. Why some and not others, one wonders.'

The men stared at the ground for a few seconds.

'I'm not alone today,' said Stephenson, seeking to lighten the tone. 'Given the auspicious date, I thought it a good opportunity to bring together the family.'

A small group walked towards them. Each was uncertain, nervous, knowing that Pease's son was gravely ill.

'You know, of course, my wife, Elizabeth?' said Stephenson.

Stephenson introduced his second wife whom Pease had met three years before at Hetton and Pease lifted his hat and bowed his head as she curtsied. She offered her best hopes for his son.

'I retain fond memories of your wondrous cooking, Mrs Stephenson,' he said kindly.

'This is my big brother James,' George went on. James bowed formally.

'We met at Hetton a few years back, Mr Pease,' said James.

'Indeed we did,' replied Pease.

'Jimmy'll be riding with me up front on Tuesday,' said George.

Pease shook James Stephenson's hand.

'This is my wife, Jane,' said James.

Jane curtsied.

'And this is our youngest, John. He was a brakeman in Gateshead but we've got him with Longridge up at Forth Street.'

Pease and John shook hands but John remained silent.

'Shall we walk a little?' Pease suggested. 'My carriage is at Houndgate.'

Pease and Stephenson led; the others tagged along.

'I was sorry to hear about your adventures in London,' said Pease.

'I took it on the chin,' replied Stephenson.

'It sent a ripple of concern through the ranks,' said Pease with concern.

'Well, it's a relatively new science is railway surveying,' said George sensibly. 'You'll recall 'ow many surveys you did with Overton n' then mine, refinin' n' re-checkin.' And I put too much faith in William James – I'd no idea 'e'd cut so many corners, taken so many risks. But I'll be up at Parliament next spring and I'm confident. We just need to get Tuesday out the way.'

'I trust the proceedings'll go smoothly on Tuesday,' Pease said.

'The loco's been runnin' well since I brought it down,' said Stephenson. 'Hackworth's ridin' guard n' he'll be drillin' the brakemen tomorrow. We've devised a system, a sort of rudimentary semaphore, for stop an' start.'

'Good. Nobody must be hurt, Mr Stephenson,' warned Pease. 'The world will be looking to our little corner on Tuesday. Every person involved will be noted in a thousand letters, journals, newspapers, reports and conversations for years to come.'

'Do you really think our enterprise carries that much importance, Mr Pease?' asked George.

'We are the first, Mr Stephenson. Others could have done it before us – indeed other towns across the country will be linked up eventually, but we are the first. In the world.'

'You must be just a little proud,' Stephenson joked, 'religious principles aside?'

'There are moments I wonder I haven't allowed pride to get the better of me – 'tis considered a sin,' Pease smiled quite seriously.

George scrutinised the cobbles to hide his true thoughts. The word 'sin' amused him. In his past, he'd lazily followed religion and paid lip service to it, but over the years he'd questioned more and more its necessity at all. The principles of so many intelligent people were bound up in its fixed, unchanging roots, principles that fundamentally resisted change and veered from self-evident facts. Stephenson put his belief in science not spirituality and the only 'sin', it seemed to him, was to stubbornly stick to a belief simply because the Bible said so, despite reason and facts suggesting otherwise.

'But something deeper worries me' added Pease. 'Won't other towns want to emulate it and then other countries? And won't that allow generals to send armies to slaughter in great numbers?'

'The success may be only modest?' suggested Stephenson.

'Then if only modest, why have we convinced so many to pour such immodest sums into it?' asked Pease. 'And don't presume that just because we Quakers put up eighty thousand doesn't make the company a Quaker concern; thirty thousand was found from other sources whose motivation was less philanthropic.'

'Either way, it'll make for some marvellous memories when we're all old,' Stephenson smiled.

'Yes, I hope th'art right,' agreed Pease, calming a little. 'But whatever is gained in the short term is somehow or other paid for in some other way with some other penalty.'

'I don't follow,' said George.

'Bleaching linen is big business in this town,' said Pease. 'People like me make a lot of money from it. But when the bleaching's finished and the accountants are counting the profits, the residue is poured into the river and for a mile downstream dead fish litter the surface like autumn leaves. If the air is like a river, then where does all our smoke go? Will we see birds falling from the sky?'

He looked into the middle distance down to Feethams for an answer as a bemused George looked on. Just then a figure turned the corner and almost knocked into them.

'Mr Miles, good day to thee,' said Pease.

'Mr Pease, a pleasure to see you, sir!'

Pease and Miles raised their hats.

'This is Mr George Stephenson, Mr Miles.'

'The pleasure is mine, Mr Stephenson,' said Mr Miles. 'I wish circumstances could have been better for me. Nonetheless, I look forward to the opening on Tuesday.'

He turned to Pease.

'I'm sorry to hear about your son. My thoughts and prayers are with you.'

'That is appreciated. And my greetings also to thy wife,' said Pease.

'Well then, I shan't delay you,' said Miles apologetically. He passed on behind them.

'Mr Richard Miles,' Pease said quietly. 'To him more than most belongs the merit of bringing the iron road. Had he not fallen into financial difficulties and been obliged to dispose of his shares, it's probable he'd be with us today. Will history remember him, I wonder?'

They arrived at the Pease carriage. The coachman opened the door and pulled down two steps.

'All is well for the trial tomorrow? No hiccups?'

'No hiccups,' confirmed George.

As the carriage pulled away, Stephenson gazed after it until his brothers caught up with him and they retired to the King's Head for Sunday dinner.

Monday 26th September

Timothy Hackworth listened to the sound of the ticking clock until it chimed two. In his new office at Shildon the scent of new wood, fresh paint and tea filled his nostrils. Sipping cold tea from a chipped China cup, he wondered: 'Am I happy?'

He picked up a letter from his brother Tom who was working the forge in Wylam and another from Joseph Pease telling him about developments at Liverpool.

He listened again. It was dinnertime. The smiths, navvies and builders had gone to the inn, from where laughter and voices drifted. The men he'd selected had all handled free-moving wagons of coal with handbrakes and, as there were still a few minutes before they arrived to be given specific instructions for the opening, he cherished the pause.

'Am I happy?'

The problem with happiness, Hackworth concluded, was that it wasn't guaranteed, like winning a race or finishing a task – there was always another race and another task. He should have been happy and he was, up to a point: following an interview at the King's Head Inn in March with Edward Pease, he'd been appointed Locomotive Superintendent at Shildon at £150 a year plus a new house and all heating bills paid.

But he'd hesitated.

'The Stephensons are spoken of in the presence of the King, Tim, and in Parliament, but nobody knows thy name,' said his wife disdainfully. 'So you must hitch your name to theirs for a short while and then unhitch it again.'

The significance of the word 'hitch' seemed apt, as if Stephenson was driving the lead cart and he was hooked on behind. Hackworth wanted to design his own engines. By and large he'd stuck to Stephenson's ideas but he kept turning over one detail in his mind: once steam had been created, it was let out of the chimney with the coal smoke, but if he could redirect that steam back into the boiler it would make even more steam. The more steam produced, the faster the engine would turn. In effect, it was an engine that could 'eat' its own smoke. Given the deadline for delivery of the first loco in September 1825, he had no chance to try out this 'blast pipe' as he'd christened it but he decided to keep it in reserve for experiments on his own engines when his contract expired. There was no point in giving away all his aces to his employers – not that he gambled, of course, but the idiom suited.

So with George in Liverpool and Robert in South America, Hackworth decided not to ask for approval – he simply got on with it, sketching his own designs and having his men cast and shape the various pieces. He hadn't really wanted to take the job at all, nor the burden of the success or failure of an enterprise he felt was wholly the responsibility of the Stephensons but the wages and his wife had tempted him. And so there he was, wondering what the next few days would bring, especially the dawn of Tuesday the 27th.

The foreman, Jenkins, stuck his head in the office door.

'The lads's are ready, sir!'

Hackworth finished his tea and put on his top hat. He'd need to ensure he got the full attention of the 40 men – after an hour at the inn, they'd be like a gang of noisy children. He picked up a small wooden box of blue sashes that his wife had sewn, went out and mounted a small rise built to dump coal, looked down over their heads and waited for quiet.

'Now lads, tomorrow's our big day. You are to wear these round yer necks, over yer left shoulder n' under yer right arm to identify yer as brakeman of the Company. Is that clear?'

He gave the box to Jenkins, who handed them to the men, some confusing their left arm from their right. Hackworth produced two very large handkerchiefs, one red and one green.

'The locomotive has no brakes. The only brakes're the ones on each chaldron – that's each of you. The loco's moved forwards or backwards by the release of a valve n' a gear by one o' the two drivers: Mr Stephenson or 'is brother Jimmy up at the front. The locomotive can be additionally stopped by disconnectin' the steam pipe and by disconnectin' the gears. So, how then can they and me and all 40 of you communicate as one and at the same time? Don't answer that. You see 'ere two hankies: one red, one green. The red means 'brakes on' n' the green 'brakes off'. Red – on. Green – off. Repeat! Red on, green off! Red on, green off!'

One or two reluctant voices began to repeat the simple mantra and soon embarrassment was overcome and they all were shouting it, led with the deepest and most enthusiastic voice – that of Hackworth.

He called them to quiet again and asked: 'Is that clear?'

There were murmurs of comprehension, but that wasn't enough for Hackworth.

'Is – that – *clear?*' he asked a little louder.

A motley return of 'ayes' followed. Hackworth pointed at the vacant face of one of the workmen.

'You: I wave the red flag. What does it mean?'

'Er, top o' de mornin' to yer?' came the absent response.

There was general laughter and he was covered in friendly slaps. Hackworth smiled. Jenkins scolded: 'You dozy Irish bugger! Any more intelligent questions?'

'Yes, sir, what 'bout the shed on wheels?' came a call.

'She'll stay here tonight,' said Hackworth. 'Tomorra morn we'll push 'er up to the inn. So for the benefit of our learned friend, I'll explain again 'bout the red n' green hankies and then we'll climb on board the wagons and have a little dress rehearsal!'

* * *

On that Monday evening Lewis returned to Mr Leakey's house and asked if he could look at the map of the world. Leakey unrolled it and spread it out on his desk.

'What have you decided?' asked Leakey, having spent some time drawing up a list of merchants in Newcastle that might offer Lewis an apprenticeship.

'Where is Australia?' Lewis asked.

'As far as I know … *here*,' said Leakey, putting his finger on the southeastern tip of a large beige patch.

'How does a ship travel to Australia?' Lewis asked.

'Haven't we been over this already?' asked Leakey as he took off and polished his spectacles with a hanky, put them back on and peered closely at the map.

'Tell me again please, Mr Leakey.'

'The nearest port from us would be either Newcastle or Sunderland and would then go down the English east coast and across the Channel to the tip of Breton France, down the Bay of Biscay to the coast of Portugal.' He squinted. 'If going east, which they say is the shortest route, it passes down to the southern tip of Africa and across the Indian Ocean. I read last year that a Mr John Oxley founded a penal colony at a place called Moreton Bay in Australia, so there is some civilisation there at least.'

'An' if a man was to take a ship to Australia, would 'e 'ave to go from Hull?' asked Lewis.

'He could go from any port,' said Leakey. 'He may not find a ship that goes there directly, but they are connected to London and Portsmouth. From there one can sail all over the world, as Cook did.'

'How much would a fare be, do you think?' Lewis asked.

'A fare?' Leakey chuckled. 'I don't think people have given much thought to settling there as yet. Convicts probably outnumber citizens!'

Leakey turned his head and looked at Lewis. There was a certain air. These were the questions of a man, not the boy he knew.

'What are you thinking? To – to go to Australia?' Leakey asked, as if it was the last thing he was thinking.

'Why not?' Lewis said.

'But, but, but,' Leakey spluttered for words. 'It's the other side of the world! Your father has been sentenced to seven years' hard labour, even if he survives the journey!'

'There's no 'if',' Lewis was almost angry as he spoke. 'He *will* survive. I'll go n' find 'im. I'll find a job n' send 'im food so he doesn't starve an' when the seven years is finished, we'll stay in that new world, a world where there're no Sir Giles Crockatts! If I don't 'ave enough for the fare, I'll join a ship an' get to Australia even if takes me a year!'

'It probably will take you a year!' laughed Leakey. 'What about your home here in Evenfield?'

'It belongs to the mine, you know that, they all do,' said Lewis.

'Mine doesn't – I *am* the proprietor, a rare thing in this village. But you know, a house is bricks and mortar and a home is the place where the memories reside,' countered Leakey.

'Wherever I am in the world my memories are always with me!' countered Lewis.

'What about your belongings?'

'They can take everything against the rent!'

Leakey could stand it no longer – what he was hearing sounded fantastical! He went to the window and stared out. Part of him wanted to object again but another part of him kept thinking: 'why not?' The boy was probably safer anywhere but here!

'Don't be rash is my advice,' counselled Leakey. 'Put together important items: that way wherever you go you'll have something to remind you of home. And travel in your Sunday best – you'll feel important and others will treat you with respect. Should you regret your decision to leave or be unable to find a passage, you may think about returning.'

'And you think the best ports would be Newcastle and Sunderland?' asked Lewis.

'There's also Hartlepool and Whitby.'

'And Stockton,' Lewis suggested.

'Ah, yes, of course – Stockton. You can walk it in two days.'

Leakey felt sure that over the course of two days on the open road Lewis would have time to regret his haste and return to Evenfield to pursue a more sensible course.

'I *could* walk it I suppose,' said Lewis. 'Or I could go to Shildon tomorrow mornin' n' take the iron road. I've heard it say it would be possible in two hours.'

'Two hours to Stockton? I can scarce believe such a feat!' said Leakey, disappointed that two days of leisurely introspection was suddenly reduced to two hours.

Lewis looked at the battered desks and chairs that had furnished him with what he'd needed to learn about the world beyond Evenfield the previous few years, hoping that moment might mean something, communicate a vital clue about life, but if the schoolroom was saying anything it was simply: 'Good luck'.

'Think about it overnight, Lewis, I beg you,' implored Leakey. 'Make your final decision in the morning.'

'All right,' said Lewis, 'I will. But you see my Dad's all I've got. Don't you 'ave somebody like that in the world, Mr Leakey?'

'Oh, there was once a woman called Mary, a widow over at Wolsingham,' he mused wistfully and shook his head at a distant memory as he went to the bookcase, selected a book and handed it to Lewis. Lewis looked at the title: *The French Language*.

'It's very useful to communicate with men from other lands,' said Leakey. 'I wish I could think of something wiser with which to furnish you, but I'm all out of poetry at my age.'

'What is a paragon?' asked Lewis suddenly.

'A paragon is a thing of excellence,' said Leakey half-grandly.

Lewis smiled and nodded as if expecting such an answer. He said thank you, bade Leakey farewell with a strong handshake, turned and left. Mr Leakey stared at the back of the door for a full minute before sitting down alone at the same desk his star pupil had occupied for almost four years.

Lewis walked along the lane back to his house thinking about a paragon. For Mr Leakey's sake he would make his final decision in the morning but he was already pretty sure what it would be.

He suddenly heard an approaching coach and stepped back to let it pass but instead it slowed, the driver reining-in with skill. A man's head, the unusual style of his hat marking him as a foreigner, appeared at the window. Through a huge and drooping moustache he called to Lewis: 'Say kid, is this the right road to Shil-don?'

'Aye, three miles ahead, sir!' said Lewis.

'Thanks!'

The head disappeared back inside and the coach pulled away. The manner of the spoken English stuck in Lewis's head for the remainder of the walk home – he'd spoken the name Shildon like it was two words. Mr Leakey was right – it was a useful skill to communicate with men from other lands.

* * *

Sir Giles was in London and returning late Monday afternoon by coach. Silas had to be out no later that Monday at noon, so despite it being Sunday – a day before the deadline – and plus the fact that Hamish didn't want to find himself in an embarrassing stand-off with an unpredictable and disgruntled gamekeeper just as his Lordship was coming through the gates, Hamish had decided to try and get everything done when he thought Silas might least expect it. But he needed help – big, physical, burly help of the type often only available for hire on Sunday nights in a less salubrious Barnard Castle inn. He'd thought about asking some male members of the Hall's staff for help but was afraid of losing face more than he was afraid of Silas. Scroggins was right: he *had* been afraid to go to war but he didn't want to die pointlessly on some distant battlefield with his guts ripped open, crying for his mother, as had his brother. He worshipped his mother. She had had two boys and one had come to a sad end. He was the only one left – if anything happened to him she'd go to her grave knowing her life was wasted. He and his brother had been raised on a sheep drover's cottage on the treeless moors above the Penrith-Bowes road over the Pennines. The strong winds of spring and autumn, howling rain and snow of winter, the hard featureless earth and sun-baked stonewalls of high summer had carved a manliness into Jack and he'd thrived, but Hamish had suffered. He remembered the day they'd both climbed onto Gill Pike in a gale, a long fall below to jagged rocks. Jack had held out his arms and leaned into the wind so far that if it'd suddenly stopped, he'd have fallen to his death but instead he'd grabbed Hamish's wrist, laughing at his younger brother's fear as they danced on tiptoes on the rock's edge. A month later, Jack had joined the army. A year later he was at Waterloo and dead, another corpse in a yawning pit. How many breaths had Jack drawn since his birth? How many meals had he eaten? How many nights had he slept? How many thoughts had passed through his mind and how many words had fallen from his tongue? How many women had he loved? How many flagons of ale and loaves of bread? How many prayers and visits to church? How many miles had he walked in his short life? The answers didn't matter – they had all led to the same place: a shared pit of dead flesh blasted to bits by modern warfare in a foreign field. All that love his mother had sacrificed and the pain of childbirth was it to rob the enemy of one lead ball?

In Barnard Castle Hamish found three ex-miners for a shilling each, money he was happy to pay. He persuaded them onto the cart and ran over to Staindrop and up onto the estate and, with Hamish at the back, they barged into Silas's cottage just after dusk.

* * *

Up the lane in the tiny hamlet of Shildon, Stephenson had been given the room above Adamson's, furnished with a square table, two chairs and a small piano under a brown sheet.

He looked out of the window at the dark shadow of his engine silhouetted against orange fires and burning torches. A workman called Jenkins stood at the firebox warming his hands. Below the window the street was filled with the shadows of the many who'd travelled from the surrounding region, as well as navvies and miners, but as Shildon was unequipped for visitors, most slept in tents and hedgerows with fires to keep warm or blankets in which to curl up. A few soldiers hired by local magistrates stood around looking bored or drunk. The stagecoach from Darlington was led to the back of the building where horses were stabled with the four-dozen mares and geldings already there to pull wagons for the journey to Stockton. The constant sound of their whinnies and nickers filtered into the night.

Stephenson wandered over to the piano, lifted the cover and then the lid. The black and white keys gleamed in the candlelight. He pushed one randomly with one finger, the note echoing keenly in the room. There was a knock on the door. It opened.

'Mr Adamson, how art thou?'

'As well as can be expected, thank you, sir,' replied Adamson.

He carried in his arm a small baby and a young boy clung to his leg.

'It was to ask if I might find a place aboard your train to Stockton tomorrow Mr Stephenson?'

Stephenson studied Adamson for a second, then lowered the lid of the piano.

'Thinkin' of runnin' away to sea?' Stephenson joked.

'Not at all, sir,' laughed Adamson. 'I was just very struck by the idea, carryin' coals n' passengers to Darl'ton n' beyond. I know you're allowin' 'orse-drawns on the line n' I might be interested in applyin' wi' me own service as it were. It'd 'elp me mek up me mind if I could travel on your train tomorrow n' get a feel for it.'

'We leave about nine. Come n' find me n' we'll sort out a place,' Stephenson said to him.

'Thank you, sir. Oh, and there's a foreign gentlemen 'ere for you, sir, from Arm-erica.'

Adamson stepped aside and the doorway filled with a slim man with a long face and a drooping moustache, shiny brown leather riding boots, dark breeches, a striped silk waistcoat and cravat bulging from the vee. On his head he wore a hat Stephenson had been informed was called a 'stetson', quite flamboyant and unlike anything worn by Englishmen. He also carried a leather saddlebag over his shoulder as if he had a horse stationed nearby.

'Mr Stephenson?'

'Mr Strickland, I presume?'

The man spoke with an accent Stephenson knew pinpointed him as being American. He'd travelled by sailing ship across the Atlantic from Boston to Liverpool and then by coach to Manchester, Darlington and finally Shildon. He was an architect and engineer sent by the Pennsylvania Society for the Promotion of Internal Improvement and had made mountains of notes concerning canals. Pennsylvania had been named after one of its early founders, William Penn – a Quaker – and it was through the Family of Friends, as the transatlantic Quaker network referred to itself, that an interview had been arranged with Stephenson and others of the Company to learn about the men, should they wish to employ them, and the railway and engines, should they wish to purchase their skills, or their locomotives.

They shook hands and pulled up chairs either side of the table. Stephenson glanced at his pocket watch. It was already late but he'd decided to grant an audience - if Americans could be persuaded to adopt the system of the railway and locomotives to pull their trains, then it could be colonised quickly. This meant a lot of business for his Forth Street Works in Newcastle.

'I stopped in Darling-ton hoping to speak to Mr Pease but he was unable to see me due to the health of one of his sons, so I took the last coach and came here, hoping to catch you.'

'Yes, Isaac Pease's condition is most unfortunate. It's been an exhaustin' day preparin' for tomorrow: a day twice as exhaustin' to come, I imagine. How can I 'elp you, Mr Strickland?'

'Mr Stephenson –'

'Call me George,' said Stephenson, quickly interrupting. 'I'm not one to stand on Quaker ceremony.'

Strickland laughed and said: 'Well, George, I'm a Quaker but not one to stand on British ceremony so call me Bill. Perhaps you could tell me about your origins?'

'What do you mean?' George blinked, having never had anybody care very much about where he came from.

'Tell me about where you were born and when. Where did you live? What did you father do?'

Stephenson thought for a few moments.

'I was born second in a family of six, 9th of June 1781. My dad tended the winding machine for Wylam Colliery. We never had much money. I didn't know how to read or write until I was 18. What else can I tell you?'

'Tell me about your connection with steam engines.'

'It was steam engines themselves that were the catalyst to my getting an education.'

'Knowing how they worked, you mean?' said Strickland.

'The mechanism,' said Stephenson leaning forward, 'of a steam engine is called The Sun and the Moon Gear – the 'planet' gear moves around the 'sun' gear; that is it rotates but doesn't change position, see?'

Strickland cleared his throat nervously.

'No, forgive me, Bill,' said Stephenson, seeing the embarrassment of the American. 'It's double Dutch, I'm sure. Suffice to say, 25 years ago when I was a young man I said to my foreman: 'What, the earth moves around the sun?' The foreman 'ad a good laugh at that.' 'Dost tha' not know, lad?' 'e said. Well, feeling a bit of a gull, I determined to get an education. I thought about emigratin' to America at one point and indeed my sister Ann went wi' 'er husband but I couldn't afford it. Then there was the war of 1812, of course, with your very own America, and in the end we wisely signed a treaty: another war would've broken our backs. So it was school or oblivion!'

'It's never easy for people who speak the same language to hate for long,' said Strickland, who decided to move on to something more contentious but found himself looking closely at Stephenson's face and especially his mouth as he was having some difficulty deciphering Stephenson's strong dialect, a dialect of which his own ears had no previous experience.

'Much has been said about who invented the safety lamp?' Strickland said.

Stephenson laughed.

'There's a thorny one!'

He remembered well that first moment standing alone in the pit accompanied only by a hiss as the gas jetted through the fissure of and into the immediate path of the safety lamp he'd just had made. He was confident. But the Underviewer, Mr Moodie, wasn't quite so confident and he and others had stayed behind the makeshift wall of boards they'd erected to contain the gas. They'd given up remonstrating with the determined Geordie but feared for their own lives as well as Stephenson's. Stephenson had lit the wick and walked steadily into the pitch-black tunnel, the hissing getting more audible. Soon he could see the fissure and the current of gas seeping out. He held up the lamp so the top was caught in this current. For a few seconds the flame glowed brighter and then went out – without the gas in the tunnel around him exploding. It worked. The safety lamp was just that – a warning lamp to a miner that a dangerous build-up of gas was at hand and the miner would have any number of seconds to beat a retreat. The longer it burnt before going out, the better. It would save thousands of lives. He remembered the vain prayer that he had once made when buying himself out of militia in 1815 – why should he ever believe he could kill a man? Wasn't saving lives better?

'I formulated my theory, built my lamp n' conducted experiments *before* Sir Davy, but it was Sir Davy with 'is education proved 'ow it worked and the science involved. This I wasn't able to do. All I achieved, I achieved through observation, practice n' some risk. All he achieved, 'e achieved through education. I was an unknown workin'-class man from North East England. Sir Humphrey Davy was a peer of the realm n' a knight. Nonetheless,

I made a point of patentin' it. You'll 'ave heard of the tragic story of Crompton's mules, I take it?'

'I can't say I have, no,' said Strickland. 'Is it anything to do with horses?'

'Not literally, no. Mr Crompton worked in Bolton and invented a method for workin' spindles on looms called 'mules' – a brilliant invention. But the poor chap never patented it. By 1811 four and a half million spindles were bein' used and he never got a penny. So though arguments raged over who invented the safety lamp first, I was far from worried as I'd already patented my version and built somethin' more useful by then: a locomotive. Which brings us to today, does it not?'

Stephenson glanced at his pocket watch.

'George, I have one more question: how can you be sure this idea will be successful?'

'I take it you ride a horse, Bill?'

'Few Americans don't, George.'

'We say horses are our slaves Bill, an' yet we are in slavery to them. Tomorrow a new kind of horse will pull a hundred times its own weight over long distances in hours. I hope you will inform Americans that they'd be most wise to start drawin' up plans, for their future is in the iron horse.'

Stephenson shook the American's hand firmly and moved to the door.

'Find me out tomorrow n' I'll see to it you're given a place on the wagon,' he said, and closed the door behind him as they left. Strickland closed his notebook. Now all Strickland had to figure out was where he'd be sleeping but for Stephenson it was already decided – he descended the stairs, left by the back door and walked to his cart where a driver waited.

'Phoenix Pit, Etherley,' George said to the driver.

'Right you are, sir,' said the driver, and as soon as Stephenson was on board, he set the horse in the direction of Witton, which lay at least half an hour away by a twisting, pot-holed track.

* * *

Silas put down his empty tankard on the table of the packed Adamson inn and demanded the servant fill it again with warm, flat beer. He should have been hungry and a penny ha'penny could have bought him a meal but beer was only a penny and did more for problems than food.

Earlier that afternoon he'd spent hours walking from Crockatt Hall having left discreetly, arriving thirsty and hot just as the locomotive steamed into Shildon with some well-dressed types aboard. He was able to pick out the Geordie engineer, Stephenson, whom he hadn't seen for almost ten years. He doubted Stephenson would remember him – last time they'd met, circumstances had been very different. Nonetheless, he was discreet and slipped into the busy inn to drink and decide on his next move.

He'd come up that afternoon with his life crammed into a carpetbag, his letter of reference and the sum of £50 in cash that he'd recovered from his hiding place under the loose clay tile under the cupboard near his bed. He believed he still had £10 in a pouch buried in Darlington and, in comparison to those around him in Shildon he was, apart from perhaps Adamson and Stephenson, one of the wealthiest men there. But he had no idea what to do next, so like many Englishmen, he followed the adage: 'If you want your horse shod you go to a farrier, to clear your bowels you go to an apothecary and to get information you go to an inn'.

He knew the opening of the railway was at dawn and that it would carry coals to Darlington and Stockton so it seemed sensible to see if he couldn't find a free ride – Darlington and Stockton were big towns and there was work in the mills, tanneries and carpet factories.

After too much ale he ventured outside, feeling it sloshing inside him as he walked along the track, humming and seeking a convenient bush to sleep under. He stumbled and fumbled with his pants and urinated. The crowds had largely dispersed but here and there fires still burned so he finished pissing and through blurred vision spied a peculiar-looking coach. Struck by an impulse, he climbed up and through the door.

'Yer coach awaits, yer 'ighness,' he half-laughed as he crawled in.

The carpeted floor was as good as a bed.

'I think I'm in me cups!' he muttered, looking up to the ceiling. 'What did Silas Scroggins ever do wrong? What did Silas Scroggins ever do right?'

An apron of vomit tumbled down his front and a second after he was snoring like a hog.

Tuesday 27th September 1825

4 am

Lewis rose, lit the last stub of candle after blowing on embers in the fire and washed his hands and face. He ate the last crust of bread, using up the remaining butter, boiled some water and made a cup of tea using twice-stewed leaves and the last sugar grains. Dressed in his best breeches, stockings, shirt, waistcoat, jacket and hat, he packed cheese, two apples, his *Hamlet*, his French book with the £1 note folded and hidden between the pages and his mother's glove into a hessian bag he slipped over his shoulder. The £1 might come in useful for negotiating a sea passage. He wrote a short letter and put Leakey's name on the front. Then he let himself out and locked the door, carrying his worn-in shoes in his hand to avoid making a noise as he walked.

He hesitated. That moment, in front of his own house, with the key in his hand, was the point all this could stop – he could stay with Leakey and within a few days be smuggled out to Durham or Newcastle with a paid apprenticeship as clerk or office boy. But if he didn't do those things, if he did what he planned?

There was no contest. He walked noiselessly through the darkness. The many drovers who rode the carts and mule-trains to and from the stables in the pit grounds weren't yet roused, and nor was the blacksmith. He approached the pit entrance and froze: near the gate, in shadow, he saw a movement. It wasn't unusual to see people and carts moving around the pit at all hours but because work at the pit had been reduced there was hardly anyone about. Not wishing to be seen leaving, he crouched on the verge and heard a whispered: 'Come by.' He recognised the voice: it was Hackett, manoeuvring a cart. As long as he didn't move, there was a chance Lewis would be unseen. Indeed, Hackett would have passed by had it not been for the horse that sensed something in the darkness and faltered. Hackett urged but it refused again.

'Who's there?' growled the Foreman instinctively turning.

Lewis turned to run but running in the dark without shoes is fraught with difficulties, not least of which are in the mind: the body freezes, terrified of advancing into what it can't see, and in that second he felt his collar being wrenched round his neck and, as he twisted, found himself staring into the contorted face of Hackett lit by a shuttered lantern. Hackett was blindingly drunk.

'Runnin' away wi'out payin' yer rent, is it? Or 'ere to spy on me back-'ander?'

He laughed at his own words but Lewis's brain seemed to have seized. He'd no idea what Hackett meant. Hackett was sure the boy must know something or else why would he be here at such an hour?

'Now I've let the cat out the bag! Ah well, soon taken care of!'

He set off toward the pit shaft, dragging Lewis behind him.

'But we all know what to do wi' cats, don't we?'

Lewis tried to wrench himself free, tugging with his own hands in a vain effort to prise Hackett's fingers loose and digging in his heels.

'You should've seen your Da's face!' mocked Hackett.

They arrived at the shaft and holding Lewis's collar with his left hand, with his strong right Hackett tried a few times to pull on a rope to raise the platform above them, his intention being to push the boy between the gap and headlong to his doom, but with just one hand free it was impossible.

Momentarily, he let go of Lewis with the intention of a quick follow-up smack to the face but Lewis was quicker. Instinctively he ducked as Hackett swiped wildly with his right arm and the momentum carried him forward so he momentarily lost his balance and as he did, Lewis pushed hard with the force of both hands. Winded and flapping like a bird, Hackett fell backward with a gruff grunt into the black, without a scream, followed a second later by distant scrapes and, finally, silence.

Lewis listened, his heart thumping. He forced himself to breathe out and in and out and in again until his heart wasn't kicking his chest and he was on control of it. He staggered back to the gate on shaking legs, passing the horse patiently waiting in the road with its cartwheels muffled with rags. He picked up the shoes he'd discarded and went quietly across the village green. As he passed Leakey's, he pushed his envelope, now torn and creased, under the door and continued on until he was half a mile out of the village before putting on his shoes and setting off at a brisk pace for Shildon.

Today, Tuesday 27th September 1825 was *his* day and nothing was going to ruin it.

4.30 am

Upstairs in a back room of the house in Northgate, 17-year-old Isaac Pease, the most gentle of all the sons of Edward and Rachel had died in the early hours. A servant had been despatched and now stood on the steps wearing a black coat, armband and top hat with a black sash to induce respect from passers-by. Despite the early hour, interest in the railway opening meant the roads were already lined with ambling strangers.

Pease glanced at the clock on the chest – it would be another three hours before the sun appeared. He'd passed the night fitfully, neither retiring to his bedchamber nor changing out of his day clothes but the urge to sleep was weighing and his eyelids drooped. His wife Rachel had passed the previous evening at Isaac's bedside with the doctor and Isaac's three brothers, Henry, John and Joseph, who'd hoped their presence might lift the spirits of their mother, but the sight and sound of their youngest brother coughing up blood had been too much for them. The family was slightly better protected from the disease thanks to cotton masks soaked in camphor, an idea introduced by Pease's distant Quaker relative, Elizabeth Fry. Elizabeth Fry said that once the patient began coughing, healthy people should wear masks so they didn't breathe the same air but the male-dominated medical world didn't want to adopt her evidently sensible ideas: she was a mere woman. Much was dependent on the strength of the patient's constitution, they said, and as Isaac had often been ill as a child, the outcome was in God's hands. That usually meant death.

Unable to endure more, Pease had gone to his study and poured a large glass of brandy and, through tears, drank it while his wife and daughter had gone to Rachel's room to console one other and Dr Peacock had started cleaning the body, preparing for the arrival of the undertaker.

Pease knew that at that very moment ten miles to the northwest, Stephenson was preparing to begin the journey to Stockton and would pass Darlington at midday only half a mile up the road. And his son was dead upstairs.

The day before, Pease had taken the coach to Aycliffe Crossing with Edward, Henry and Joseph, along with Tom Richardson and Alf Kitching, where they'd mounted the shed on wheels. With two chaldrons of workmen tagged on behind, they had sat on the cushioned seats and looked out of the windows, enjoying the singular pleasure of mechanically enhanced motion as they were pulled to Shildon. Afraid to even let a smile pass his lips, Pease had suppressed an inner glow of pride as they moved, the repetitive creaking of the wheels, the rumbling of the un-sprung carriage, the chuffing of the steam and clanking of the pistons filling their ears. Occasional lumps of soot as big as snowflakes floated through the windows. There would have been none of that if the canal had been built, Pease reflected: hundreds of horses would have quietly and cleanly pulled a never-ending procession of barges backwards and forwards, but it was too late now of course. Yes, it had been a long, long story and this opening day of triumph should have been his just reward, but fate had played its part in the form of pestilence. Pease's money enabled him to afford a good doctor but the doctor might as well have been the undertaker, and often was. Nonetheless, Isaac was quarantined. Advice given to the rich was to send the victims overseas to places where the air was rare and sweet, like Switzerland. Advice given to the poor was: pray.

Pease's tired body could hold out no longer and he slumped, his eyes closing, head lolling. The empty brandy glass fell to the parquet floor but did not break. His hands dropped to his sides. His lips moved noiselessly as Dr Peacock entered, the cotton mask he had reluctantly adopted on Pease's insistence around his neck but his shirt and trousers spattered with blood. Peacock studied the sleeping man for a second and touched him on the shoulder. Pease started, adjusting his vision to the murk.

'I was – I had a – it's going to –! Doctor what news?'

'The Undertaker will be here around midday. There's nothing more I can do,' said Peacock, rubbing the bridge of his nose between fingers and thumb.

Pease thanked Peacock and the doctor advised him to get rest. As Peacock left, another figure entered: his second-born son Joseph. Edward gulped, coughed to rouse himself and stand and the two clasped for a short while in shared grief.

'Forgive me for saying what I am about to say, father, but I must,' said the son.

'Speak, my boy, don't be afraid,' said the father.

'We all know how much effort you've put into your railway project and how –'

'I shan't go,' his father blurted. 'Nothing thou sayeth will change my mind.'

'I felt you would say that, father, which is why I am asking if I could go in your place?'

'I cannot say yes and I cannot say no,' said the father. 'I must allow thee to decide for thyself. I ask only thou doth thy best to be discreet for I cannot say how others will view this.'

'Thank you, father,' said the son, relieved.

Joseph left the room immediately, lifted his riding jacket from a hook by the back door and walked through the long garden where the branches of apple, pear, plum and mulberry trees straining to the weight of unpicked fruit brushed against him. At the stables, he led out a fast horse and saddled her up. With luck and speed, he knew he'd be in Shildon within two hours. He'd manage no more than a walking pace in the dark but a decent gallop once the sun rose. With a last glance to the window where his brother lay dead, he gently heeled the horse's flanks. Getting along the busy North Road would be difficult, but his journey time would be reduced if he rode along the railway line. He had to be there, he just had to be.

5.00 am

Timothy Hackworth slept in one of two camp beds in his new workshop. In the other, James 'Jimmy' Stephenson had slept for a few hours, but had risen when his pocket watch had rung at five o'clock and had gone to inspect the locomotive, waking Hackworth on his way out by gently squeezing his shoulder. They'd been surrounded by the warm blacksmith's forge on one side and drawing desks on the other near the windows where in the daytime there was light by which to see. Hackworth roused himself, yawned, stretched and splashed his face with cold water from a bucket. He glanced at his prayer book set on the edge of his desk and thought of his wife, Jane, and his growing family up at Walbottle waiting for his invitation to come down to be installed in their new house.

Choosing a psalm from Wesley's Methodist prayer book, as he opened the Bible a slip of paper fell out. He picked it up. It was in his own handwriting: 'Arthur Woolf – The Woolf High-Pressure Compound Engine. Multiple cylinders produce less expansion in each cylinder so less heat is lost, increasing the efficiency of the engine.' His eyes flickered guiltily to the Psalm as he absently pushed the paper into his pocket.

'God is our refuge and our strength, a very present help in trouble.'

On another table was an open copy of Nicholas Wood's book *A Practical Treatise on Railroads*. He heard Wood's voice in his head: 'We shall see locomotives travelling at the rate of 12, 16, 18 or 20 miles an hour at most.' Hackworth knew it was simple to make locomotives progress because he'd worked it out. And one day he would prove it, but not today.

Finishing the psalm and crossing himself, he drank tea and pulled on a tight black jacket and a top hat. With the sun peeking over the horizon, he left the workshop and walked over to the workmen's tents. As he approached, a tethered job barked, rousing the sleepy men. From there he ensured that Jenkins, his able assistant, knew what to do when the train reached the foot of the incline this side of Brusselton and, satisfied, he set off walking up the incline to the engine house.

5.30 am

Sir Giles had decided to go hunting, refusing like a spoilt child, he felt guiltily, to acknowledge existence of this 'special' day.

He'd arrived late from London on an uncomfortable coach the previous evening and left instructions with Heathcote for his hunting clothes to be laid out, as well as his shotgun and ammunition. Woken at five, he'd taken a breakfast of bacon, eggs and Ceylonese tea alone in the Great Hall, surrounded by the shields, swords, suits of armour and moody paintings of his ancestors, all of whom seemed to be scolding him that day.

He lived to hunt, as had his father. For many years, hounds had been bred at Crockatt Manor and his family had hunted alongside those of Lord Darlington's on a vast stretch from East Riding to Northumbria. A hundred years before, his family's status had rivalled that of Raby, but then Sir Giles's great-grandfather had made spectacular losses investing in the doomed South Sea Bubble fiasco of 1720 and the family fortune dwindled until all that was left was the village, some tracts of timber forest, some mines and rented cottages. The Raby estate had bought up much of his family's land at a knockdown price but that had done little to affect the strong ties between the gentry.

This season, which had begun on Sunday 18th September, had brought out a small army of hunters, nearly all of whom talked about the railway. The chase that day had been exhausting – they'd killed five foxes, a stag and a dozen brace of grouse, pheasants and woodcocks before retiring to a banquet hosted by Lord Darlington and his wife.

But Sir Giles was fed up of hearing about the railway. Lord Darlington had fought hard against it for almost six years and Sir Giles had staunchly supported him, even though his good friend profited in the sale of land to the Railway Company and even Lord Darlington had had to reluctantly admit land values had risen considerably. Sir Giles had only been able to watch his neighbour's stature increase from the sidelines with depressing envy as he himself struggled with a fraction of the income. Still, he preferred land to gold. There was nothing quite as solid. Almost anybody could acquire or own gold if they knew how but land was deeply rooted in his family's history and roots. Land held the blood of ancestors. Without the land there was no Crockatt Hall and without that there was no title.

The problems had started because the original George Overton Route would have destroyed Raby's precious fox coverts, but even after the revised route missed the coverts all together, Lord Darlington had staked his ground and Sir Giles felt compelled to ally himself. Lords rarely listened to criticism in the locality and couldn't be seen to be listening to those below their class. No, they'd only been able to listen to criticism from other lords in the House and many had already been won over by the Stephenson camp. Of course, they weren't from the part of the world where the railway was being proposed and had been seduced by promises to ship large quantities of materials over long distances in short times.

That meant money and profit, something all lords not only enjoyed but also needed: running country estates was an expensive business.

It irked him they'd been unable to break the Backhouse Bank in 1819 – a public shaming never lived down but originally inspired by the Mathieson Affair back in '79. John Mathieson, a Scottish forger, had hand-drawn two Backhouse banknote replicas that he'd passed in Sunderland and Durham. He was hanged at Newgate Prison in July of that year but the spectre of fraud had hung around the Backhouse name longer and it was this ancient fear he and Lord Darlington had tried to tap once again but they'd failed only because the Quakers had closed ranks. Nonetheless, the lords had eventually voted *for* the railway, isolating him and Lord Darlington even more.

'It's not bloody fair!' he grunted, scaring a pheasant that he shot instantly.

It was, he felt, the fault of Napoleon, a rabid French dwarf who'd set the imagination of the uneducated of Europe on fire with dreams of Utopia. Luddites, rioters, assassination, Peterloo in '19 and Cato Street – that's what happened when you gave power to peasants: revolution and chaos.

The business of condemning the miners of Evenfield troubled him a little, yes, of course, like a small rain cloud that followed even on the brightest of days, but he'd covered his tracks well and Hackett was trustworthy. He'd decided to leave Hamish Jones out of it as the man was far too fawning for his own good but Scroggins was smart enough to sense a backstabbing when he saw one and have the good sense to call it a day.

'Bugger you, Stephenson!' he shouted, and another bird flew into his firing line.

Just then, he heard a cough. Instinctively raising both barrels, he swung around and found himself looking at Hamish Jones, his face bruised and red on the left side with a burst lip, holding up his hands not to shoot.

'What the hell happened to you?' Sir Giles demanded. 'I nearly shot you! Well,' said the lord cracking open the breech to fresh gunpowder smoke, 'I would have if I was loaded!'

'I fell, sir, in the woods – tripped over a tree root, smashed into a tree,' Hamish apologised.

The image of Hamish doing this and looking as he did, supposedly the master of his environment, amused Sir Giles.

'You look like you've been beaten up by a gang of navvies!'

Indeed, the gang of hired, out-of-work navvies that Hamish had hired at Barnard Castle had barged into Scroggins's cottage to find it empty, brushed from top to bottom, scrubbed and cleaned, even the bed made up spic and span as only an ex-military man like Silas knew. An envelope was propped up against a candlestick on the kitchen table with the words 'Hamish Jones' on it. In full view, a confused Hamish had opened the envelope and a white feather had fallen out. After the three men had beaten Hamish they'd taken his money pouch and everything in it, a cool six shillings in all – a shilling each for the job, they said, and an extra shilling for being a yellow belly, and they'd walked back to Barnard Castle across the fields, laughing as they went.

Sir Giles asked: 'And our little problem?'

''Tis done, sir,' said Hamish, rubbing his cheek as if to claim his bruise as a wound in the imagined fight with Scroggins.

'Good,' said Sir Giles, unimpressed. Hamish had known something was going on between Silas and his Lordship but he had no idea what. Unable to get an answer out of Silas, he thought he might carefully manipulate his words and see if his Lordship might reveal something.

'Your Lordship knows I've never been one to question, sir, n' for the most part I can't say I'm disappointed, but it'd put my heart at ease if you give me some idea why your Lordship took this decision? Although I were no great admirer, he was an able keeper, milord.'

Sir Giles lifted his head and said in a half-sinister voice:

'How's your mother? Is she well?'

'Very well, sir, thank you.'

'Good. Tell 'er I was asking after 'er. Now, where're the rabbits?'

Hamish knew that was the only answer he would get and he never mentioned the subject again.

6.00 am

'Oi've decided to go to America.'

'What?' Sean was half-asleep so was forced to repeat the question with more force: 'What??'

Seamus, who was fully awake, repeated the statement as calmly as he had the first time.

'Who?' asked Sean, surprised.

'In moi own land oi cannat own a clod because de Proddies stole it,' hissed Seamus. 'Here in England dey pay me to dig an' den call me worse dan dort but oi've heard dat in America a man can own a meadow de soize o' Donegal simply by stakin' his claim to it and oi've heard dat all religions are tolerated an' all men are treated equal. Now oi don't know about you, but dat sounds like heaven on earth to me, boy.'

'But dere's loads o' work ahead of us here, Seamus!' enthused Sean. 'Dis railway stuff's goin' to go on for years. Dey're already takin' on men in Manchester!'

'To hell wit Manchester! To hell wit all dese feckin' English! Diggin', boy, is for diggin' yersel a bit o' blunt to do sumpin' better wit!' Seamus smiled and almost laughed at how ahead of his brother he seemed to be.

'Oi've saved me a few pounds passage to New York from Liverpool an' a pony to ride dem Blue Ridge Mountains of Virginia an' get moiself a nice farm an' an 'undred cows.'

Leaving Sean fumbling for a response, Seamus walked towards the burning iron basket of staves outside the Witton pit entrance. He touched his tar-soaked brand to the flames, the other navvies from his gang following suit while Sean, thoughtful as ever, was last to light his. They'd worked, eaten and drank together since he'd arrived and they were close, but now he'd announced *he* was going to America. There'd been no mention of 'them', only him.

The 30 workmen, each carrying a burning torch, spread out on either side of the dozen coal wagons on the rails opposite the pithead shaft, two chaldrons separated by a blinkered horse. Only six of the wagons were loaded with coal; the remaining five were empty and fitted out with wooden planks to act as seats to accommodate the two dozen or so dignitaries and members of the S&D Company Committee who were, at that very moment, being shown the workings of the Etherley engine by Hackworth, as pre-arranged. They would then descend by foot the western side of the incline where they would wait to watch the wagons descend from the Etherley enginehouse. At this point, they would be picked up and taken up the 1,960 yards to the Brusselton enginehouse, also operated by Mr Hackworth, who by then would have run on ahead or by horse to ensure everything was going well. From there, the dozen laden wagons would travel 880 yards down to nearby Shildon.

George Stephenson, meanwhile, left the foreman's office and walked down the steps with William Stobart Junior and his father, Henry, the owner and William Chaytor, another owner, behind him. He looked at his pocket watch in the light of the flames and then up at the sky as the first tinge of purple blushed the horizon.

Faces looked at his expectantly, features ghostly and rugged. Over in their gardens, the female residents of the miners' cottages were wrapped in shawls.

The first of the horse-drawn chaldrons, 11 more behind, moved off along the track, followed by the second and third, fourth, fifth and sixth and so on, hemmed in by the low stone wall on either side, the jingling of the reins and crunching of boots the only sounds as they passed under the low bridge built to carry the Etherley road.

They trudged a little further for 15 minutes, Stephenson and Stobart at the helm, their boots scranching on gravel limestone ballast smashed into sizeable chunks by hundreds of convicts in local prisons. After a few hundred yards, Stephenson stopped and held up his hand. They'd reached the first incline where a length of rope lay between the rails. Standing close by was a pole of about 30 feet in height and on the top was a white disc fixed at its axle by a rope that led to two gears and a winding handle.

'But what am oi gonna do, Seamus, if you go to America?' hissed Sean, catching up with his brother.

'Yer a big lad, Sean, you'll tink o' sumpen'! Now get back into loine, boy, or I'll clatter ye!' said Seamus.

00.30 AM GMT - 7 hours – Columbia, South America.

For almost an hour, Robert Stephenson watched the ant struggle to get the berry over the twig. He thought about reaching out, taking the berry between finger and thumb, placing it on the other side and nudging the ant over. But he didn't. Instead, he watched.

He occasionally drew on his cigar and sipped the dark rum, gently rocking the hammock on the veranda of his bamboo house near the tiny hamlet of Santa Ana. *A Treatise of the Railroad* by Nicholas Wood had arrived the previous day by mule-train after its torturous journey with other supplies from La Guayra on the north coast of Venezuela. Robert picked up the book and, resting it against his face, breathed in the scent of the ink and paper and for a fleeting moment was breathing Northern England. The inside front cover bore a short message: 'To my dear friend, Robert, without whom this book could not have been written.'

Robert Stephenson had been in South America almost 14 months, sailing from Liverpool in June 1824 and arriving in Venezuela a month later, having accepted an offer to supervise mining operations entrusted by Thomas Richardson and enticed by £500 a year. On the voyage, he'd been staggered by the vastness of the ocean as he left terra firma. Other passengers had suffered seasickness, but he was spared, much to his surprise, and he'd discovered a new passion: sailing. On arrival, he'd rested in Caracas until October, and then set out for Bogotá, a distance of 1,200 miles through dense jungle undertaken entirely upon mules or on foot.

En route, he'd visited many of the districts reported to be rich in minerals, but met with few traces. It had taken him two months to reach Bogotá for an interview with Mr Illingworth, the commercial manager, and then he proceeded to Honda, crossing the Río Magdalena and shortly after reaching the site, arriving in January of 1825. Leases had been obtained from the Colombian government for the mines of Santa Ana and La Manta. The following month, October of 1825, operations would begin once a selected group of Cornish miners arrived.

The climate was hot in the jungle and near the coast but on the plains around Bogotá it was an eternal British spring and the variety and beauty of the indigenous flora and fauna and the appearance, manners and dress of the people with the mix of Spanish and the dying language of Chibcha, were beyond anything he'd experienced in his life. By day, the forest was infested with insects, moths with dazzling wings, hummingbirds, golden orioles, toucans and parrots, and in the evening, glorious sunsets seen from his cottage-porch astonished and delighted him. He began to understand why the ancient Peruvians had been renowned for their heathen worship of the sun.

His own dress was a hat of pleated grass, a crown nine inches in height with a brim of six inches, a white cotton suit and a poncho of blue and crimson. In this simple fashion he'd ascended the lower slopes of the breathtaking Andes, struck by the unfolding view of the forest that stretched to the distant horizon. There was an 18,000-ft volcano, Tolima, and the area was exposed to frequent tremors the first of which had terrified him (and amused the Indians who were used to it) but the Indians had been particularly impressed with how adept the white man was at making fire and tried in vain to trade their stick-method of making fire for his tougher, more resistant and more reliable quartz flints and iron spigots.

In front of the cottage was a wooded ravine extending almost to the base of the Andes and clothed in the vegetation of magnolias, palms, bamboos, tree ferns, acacias, cedars and almendrons with smooth silver stems bearing clusters of white blossoms.

Robert again studied the ant. It refused to give up. If only, he thought, a slight ledge was cut the ant could put its weight behind and push it over.

He thought again of the forceful, yet modest and unselfconscious, personality of his father. He never gave up either. It must have cost him almost a hundred pounds to pay for Robert's six months at Edinburgh University but what an investment! How it had widened his world and expanded his imagination! He'd attended lectures by Dr Hope on chemistry, Sir John Leslie's natural philosophy classes and natural history lessons from Professor Jameson, as well as some weekday evenings for more practical chemistry under Dr Murray, another inventor of a safety lamp.

Strange sounds emanated from the jungle and his servant, Juan, carried a burning torch to the edge and waved it, shouting warnings at the evil spirits. They had cleared a road in the red sand that led to the mountainside and begun to cut away the vegetation but the peons weren't accustomed to sustained physical work and contrived to desert when not watched. Money meant little to them. Such slow progress had been made that Robert had contacted his employers and requested Cornish miners be handpicked and paid to travel out to show the locals how mining was done. But he'd been full of doubt: Cornish miners had hard reputations, certainly reluctant to take commands from a Northerner. He'd have to gain their respect, but how? If his father had been here he'd have no problems with the Cornish who spoke their own language. But his father wasn't here and that was the point.

These reveries drew a sharp memory from his childhood in Northumberland: Straker. Straker bullied women and children or bragged about non-existent robbers he'd put to flight. So Robert and his friends hooded themselves one night, adapted an old pistol and waited for Straker. As he approached, they jumped out and shouted 'Stand and deliver!' and Straker dropped to his knees begging for mercy. It was the delight of that memory that armed him with the courage he felt he was going to need when the Cornishmen arrived.

The only other way to make progress in Santa Ana was to hold dinners and parties for the Spanish gentry happy to have European influence in that remote place. The parties helped relieve the boredom but they also had political uses. News of Robert's arrival meant that gold and silver were to be mined. That had stimulated the interest of other miners and since 'co-operation' with the local authorities was mandatory, speculators were trying to force him out. He learned that business wasn't conducted as in England with acts of Parliament, laws, magistrates and limited companies: in Colombia, everything was accomplished by what was tantamount to bribery or not at all. He opened a letter from Edward Pease.

'I assure thee the business at Newcastle, as well as thy father's engineering, have suffered very much from thy absence, and unless thou soon return, the former will be given up, as Longridge is not able to give it the attention it requires; what is done is not done with credit to the house.'

He'd signed on for a three-year contract in Colombia but the idea of losing the factory in Newcastle he'd worked hard to build pained him. He regretted his decision to leave England now, if only because he'd underestimated just how long it would take him to reach Colombia.

In his mind's eye he saw a flash of red brick and remembered their house at Killingworth and the sundial they'd built, the book *Ferguson's Astronomy*, the latitude of Killingworth and the Roman numerals MDCCCXVI. By that sundial, every passing stranger knew the accurate time of day – as long as the sun shone.

Robert gently reached out his finger and imperceptibly brushed against the twig. The ant hesitated, got its weight underneath and the berry rolled over, the ant clambering after it.

A native servant girl appeared in a doorway and told him in Spanish that dinner was served: a variety of fruits, tortilla and roasted chicken. Robert swung into a seated position, raised his glass to the dark of the jungle, cast his eyes to the cape of stars and whispered: 'Good luck, Dad.'

7.00 am

George Stephenson looked at the sky. Good weather was ahead. Far away, the moon was fading as the sun's rosy fingers appeared.

The horses were taken out of their traces and led to the side of the track as the workmen bunched up all 12 chaldrons – six of them piled with slabs of coal fresh from the Jane Pit – until they were hooked together.

'Get the rope hooked on!' Stephenson shouted.

Two men lifted the end of the rope, its strands coiled together to form a stump as thick as a young tree trunk and smoothed off by an iron cap from which hung a large iron hook.

'Now, yer know yer jobs,' Stephenson said. 'Follow on behind the last wagon, maintainin' a distance of 50 foot. If the rope snaps, that'll give yer enough time to throw these planks on the track. You fellows wi' hosses – bring 'em up the hill n' we'll meet yer there.'

Stephenson turned the winding handle on the vertical pole and the white disc on top began to spin like the sails of a windmill. This was the visible signal for the Engineman up at the winding house to engage the gears that operated the winding engine and reel in the rope.

Seamus, Sean, the other navvies and all the workmen clambered on the sides, in between and on the plank seats. They watched as the great length of rope lifted off the ground, taking on the enormous strain of the 12 chaldrons with groans, creaks, cracks and snaps. Slowly, the wagons began to move up the incline.

With the dozen real horses led up the hillside, the mechanical 30-horsepower winding-machine, built by Robert Stephenson and installed by Hackworth, did its job perfectly and John Grimshaw's strengthened hemp ropes pulled the dozen loaded wagons at a steady pace. Halfway up the sun rose above the horizon so Seamus tossed his burning torch to the ground and the workmen followed suit. Over 1,000 yards of straight and unwavering ascent to the crest 500 feet higher, they slowed as they approached the engine house and squat stone buildings where the Enginemen and their families lived.

The building that straddled the line drew them in under the gigantic horizontal winding drum set on a huge oak beam above their heads and as the flywheel turned, the gears slowed to a monitored crawl until eight of the 12 chaldrons were over the ridge and on the descent.

'Apply brakes!'

The rope was detached from the front and carried by two men, where it was reattached to the coupling hook at the back of the last wagon. The horses, meanwhile, were brought over the crest and led down the bank.

All the brakemen stepped back from their brakes as the Enginemen performed their well-rehearsed roles and for a few moments nothing happened. But then there was a jolt and gravity pulled the ninth, tenth, eleventh and final wagon over the ridge, the winding drum switching to reverse and the coil unwinding, watched with concern by a small crowd of families of the engine operators hoping their small but vital contribution went off smoothly. At the foot of the descent a fascinated crowd gathered, the colour of their cloth singling them out as men of distinction. A colourful public spectacle was unfolding.

7.30 am

'Hey you! Wake up!'

Silas adjusted his eyes to the harsh light of a shuttered lantern inches from his face, the brightness piercing his brain like a hot knife.

'What yer doin' 'ere, bonny lad?' asked the voice.

'Nae room at the inn?' Silas ventured as a joke, but the joke fell on unsympathetic ears.

'None 'ere neither, you'll 'ave to get out. Looks like y've cast up yer accounts.'

Silas got to his feet, aware of the bitter scent of alcohol-induced vomit about his person.

'Is this yer bag?' he was asked.

Silas picked up his carpetbag and went out of the door, the lantern-carrying man fixed with a face that seemed to be itching to punch Silas. He climbed down the two steps to the ground on shaky legs. The man with the lantern jumped down as another workman walked over.

'Do yer want us to call a constable, Mr Hackworth?'

'No, nae harm done. Fellow had no bed. I'm sure a few of us 'ere today knowns 'ow that feels!'

There was a ripple of laughter.

'On yer way. No stocks for thee today, fella.'

They released him and the man they called Hackworth shepherded the workmen away. Silas grunted a grudging thanks. All around people were coming and going or bumping into him. He managed to make his way across the road to a water pump and stuck his head under, operating the handle with one arm and doing his best to smudge away the stains down his front.

The previous night was a blur but sleep, however uncomfortable and temporary, had been a salvation from reality. Now it all came back: he was out of a job and in Shildon because there was nowhere else worth being. As workmen pushed the coach, he plodded alongside. Nipping across in front, he entered the inn, ordered ham and ale and sat in a discreet corner to eat, think and sober up.

8.00 am

With the rope detached from the last wagon at the foot of the 300-ft descent, the 12 were divided into groups of two and horses brought forward and re-tied by strong leather straps to the coupled chaldrons. Drivers mounted and took their reins and in this order they set off, the remaining six horses brought on behind as they moved towards the foot of Brusselton.

At the repaired Gaunless Bridge they halted and Stephenson ensured it was clear before he crossed in front of the first wagon, signalling for it to follow, and led the 12 across. The sun had made an appearance, bathing everything in that fresh light only a September morning can bring. Spread out on both sides down in the valley every champaign was taken up by onlookers. Sean remembered the day his brother had punched Hennessy near here and poor Hennessy had left to walk to Manchester to work on the canals and Seamus remembered too the day he and Stephenson had inspected the damaged bridge after the storms.

They stopped at a siding where a solitary wagon loaded with sacks of flour stood. At the bridge, built for its road access and where the carriages had stopped, Stephenson saw many faces: William Chaytor, Jonathon Backhouse, Christopher Blackett from Wylam Colliery, Thomas Richardson, Longridge and his faithful agent Birkinshaw, Messrs Otley, Barnard and Gilkes, secretaries to the S&D Company, good old Nick Wood, Jonathon Foster and the MP Mr Brandling alongside Mr John Lambton, MP for Yorkshire and Durham. There was also Francis Mewburn, George Sandars and John Kennedy from Liverpool, Dr Fenwick, Bill Cudworth, Jeremiah Cairns and the tall figure of William Strickland, plus a variety of wives. All wanted to congratulate him or offer words of encouragement, but there was so little time. He had a schedule to keep. Suddenly, time itself had a presence in his life, a great force pressing him towards an ending. Ladders were brought out and the members of the committee climbed up and took their places on the bench-lined interiors of the five empty wagons. After gathering a dozen men and pushing the flour wagon onto the line, a horse harnessed and a driver allocated, Stephenson shouted 'Forward!'

Led by the flour sack chaldron and under the strict attention-to-detail of Stephenson's tireless energy, the procession passed along the stretch towards the eastern foot of Brusselton Incline.

* * *

Lewis looked behind once again but there was nothing to see. All the way from Evenfield he'd been convinced a hundred devils were chasing him. He went over the events in his mind, wondering if there had been any point at which he could have done something differently. Should he seek a priest to confess his grave sin? But if he did, he'd surely be arrested? He would end up like those people hanged outside Durham Prison!

He – had – killed – Hackett. *Those words!* Was there a Heaven or a Hell?

Hackett had four children. Lewis put his hand to his chest at the place he thought his heart rested and said in a loud whisper: 'Oh my God! I've killed Hackett!' Or he'd robbed the children of a father! Or freed them from a tyrant but there had to be a reckoning for such a crime, there had to be! Even if he hadn't pushed Hackett, Hackett would have pushed *him* and that too would have been murder, an unsolved crime because Hackett would have lied to protect himself. Could Hackett have survived the fall?

Lewis sifted through the words Hackett had spoken: he'd planted a weapon in their house, falsely accused his father, and a gamekeeper had been involved. Flashback to John Carr outside Darlington Gaol a week before and he had The Impostor, the man who'd pretended to be William Wilson. What had John said his name was?

The stew of thoughts simmered and bubbled in his imagination. He wondered if a large sign with the word MURDERER was hanging above his head. Could people perceive such things? Out on the road alone he'd wanted to see others and blend in so he could feel normal, but he felt vulnerable, convinced they knew what he'd done. And what would Leakey do now that he had the house key? They'd ask questions. Leakey would say he went to bed that night and no key was on the floor under his door, but when he woke the following morning it was. Or would he? Might he protect Lewis? So whoever put it there, put it there during the night at the same time as they discovered a solitary cart, its wheels muffled with rags, laden with stolen coal. They'd find Hackett at the bottom of the pit shaft, but when? How much time did he have? The foreshift started at dawn so it could be that the body of Hackett had already been discovered. Would they think he'd killed Hackett? But why, what would his motive have been? Revenge? Lewis saw only one possible way out that morning as he approached Shildon, if only to ease his aching brain: get as far away as possible.

When he arrived at Shildon it was already crowded. He singled out two men slouching on horses, conspicuous red flags in their hands. Behind them stood the garishly painted locomotive, steam and smoke wafting from the tall chimney. A well-dressed young man on horseback worked slowly through the crowd, not easily done as the horse panted heavily, frothing at the bit and sweating heavily as if it had been ridden hard.

Lewis thought he had never seen so many people, not even in Durham or Darlington. He passed the open door to the Adamson Inn and smelled food and realised he was ravenous. Inside, a servant negotiated tables with a tray, so Lewis followed her to the counter where a serving man counted pennies into a box.

'A bacon 'n' egg's a shillin', young sir.'

Reluctant though he was to break into Wilson's £1 gift, it was either that or get very hungry. Still, breakfast wasn't expensive, so there'd be sufficient left to get leverage on a sea passage.

The man took the banknote, held it up to the light, studied it then counted out one red ten-shilling note and nine one-shilling coins into Lewis's open palm. Lewis counted every coin, grateful Leakey had taught him how.

He was handed a pewter plate. On it was a slice of crisp bacon, a spoonful of beaten egg and a hunk of bread. He had just sat on the edge of a bench and began shovelling the food into his mouth with his fingers when he felt a hand on his shoulder and jumped.

'I thought it was you!' sneered John Carr.

'You scared me!' said Lewis.

John must have come from Evenfield, so why hadn't he said anything about Hackett? Perhaps he hadn't heard about it? Perhaps they hadn't discovered the body yet?

'Scroggins got 'is marchin' orders from Crockatt Hall: friend of mine works down there,' said John Carr. 'God knows why, but there it is. Now, my guess is 'e's comin' through 'ere on his way to somewhere else – Durham or Darl'ton mebbes. 'e only left yestdee so couldn't've got far.'

Carr checked that nobody was watching and unsheathed half of the knife he kept on his belt.

'This has the bastard's name on it unless he comes clean to the Peelers.'

'I'm going to Stockton to find a ship an' follow me Dad to Australia,' said Lewis.

John guffawed in Lewis's face and Lewis realised how ridiculous it sounded, but added: 'I've been doin' a lot o' thinkin' these last days, John. Seems to me there must be a world where there's no Giles Crockatts.'

'There's no place in world like that!' sneered John Carr.

'You do as you want but I'm away to follow me father,' said Lewis.

Lewis offered his hand as he knew a handshake counted for something, but John ignored it, spat into a nearby spittoon and headed into the crowd without a word.

Lewis felt bad about what John had said. It confused him. John seemed more determined to get revenge on Silas Scroggins than he! Through his young life he'd never truly hit anybody with real violence. Of all the boys in the village, the boys who fought and beat other boys, he was the one who'd never swung his fist in anger. He'd rarely seen violence in the house, growing up. His father and mother had never fought. He'd never seen his father fight – apart from the punch he'd given the thug who'd pulled him out of his house a few weeks before. To George, courage and strength were only good when applied to work or supporting a family. This sudden realisation made Lewis feel vulnerable. He was anxious. He wanted to leave Shildon – now.

* * *

Seamus and Sean were impressed by the number of people lining the hill that led the mile and a half to the Brusselton enginehouse. As for many of the navvies there that day, the work they'd done gave them pride and the public's appreciation bolstered that pride.

'On de udder soide is Shildon. After dat de engine gets fixed on n' den de fun really starts!' Seamus said.

Pleasantly distracted as he was by the journey, Sean was in deep reflection. As with all big brothers, they had minds of their own. There was nobody to guide them. Everybody born younger looked up to them as if they had all the answers and whatever the eldest said or did, it influenced the younger ones.

Sean wouldn't have been in England at all if it hadn't been for Seamus. Now, it appeared, Seamus was going to exercise the same independent strength of mind and leave for the New World. If Seamus did that, he'd probably never see his brother again. In fact, he was more than his brother: he was his best friend. How many times had Seamus protected Sean in those first months on the gangs? But Sean knew being a man wasn't behaving as they did as snot-nosed kids running around Mammy's skirts in their slum beside the Shannon: it meant facing up to things. So he tried to imagine himself saying the thing he most dreaded: 'You go to America, Seamus, an' oi'm going down to Manchester to take me chances.' He rehearsed the words and tried to imagine his brother's response. Would it be: 'Aye Sean, you do dat son'? Or would it be: 'Why don't you come wid me?' The train of wagons began moving up the hill, jolting Sean back to reality.

'Will you look at dat fizgig down dere now, boy?' said Seamus nudging him and nodding at a pretty girl in a long blue dress and bonnet standing by the trackside.

Up ahead, George Stephenson was holding onto the side of the flour wagon with one hand when a young lad jumped on expecting Stephenson to tell him to get down, but he didn't. Nobody did. Passengers were exactly what were needed. So other boys and men took this as a signal and more leapt on to experience the novelty of being pulled up to the engine house.

The enormous drum wheel, operated by Tim Hackworth, pulled them over the ridge as the crowd behind mounted the hill on foot, swamped the engine house and moved down the other side, swelling the ranks that lined the track to Shildon. As the rope was attached to the rear coupling by a huge metal hook, gravity called and the train began to roll down in the direction of the smoke of the waiting locomotive. John Grimshaw, the rope maker, watched anxiously as his rope did an admirable job with the considerable weight. He knew the rope would hold as he'd tested it numerous times at his factory but accidents were possible and the worst time and place for such an accident would be here and now. Nonetheless, to be on the safe side, Stephenson had ordered one brakeman to be assigned to each wagon and to apply discretionary use of the hand-brakes. The wooden brake blocks against the iron wheels groaned intermittently like the whimpers of an animal under duress as the entire train descended the hill, passing three purpose-built bridges. First there was the Accommodation Bridge over a small farm road, then the Milk Road Bridge which had had to be built for a local farmer so he could herd his cows back and forth from farm to field, and finally the Dere Street Bridge, the underpass that carried the old Roman Road overhead and which had such little headroom that everybody sitting on the wagons was forced to duck to avoid injury.

8.30 am

Lewis saw the engine he'd gaped at three times in previous weeks, only this time it seemed fit to burst. It had been painted garish colours, in parts green and in others, yellow. Behind the coal tender was a big wooden barrel, as might be found holding a hundred gallons of beer where a line of workmen passed buckets of water from a well along a human chain to the top where it was poured in. Standing on one of the sidings was an empty chaldron and behind that a rough-looking stagecoach on wheels with the words Periculum Privatum Utilitas Publica painted on either side, and he remembered the day he visited Jonathon Backhouse in his office and saw those same words.

A shout went up and many heads turned to a quarter of a mile to the west where the train was descending, crowds on both sides fanning out. The descent was smooth and steady and within ten minutes the dozen wagons were on the straight to the inn. George Stephenson hopped off before it halted and strode along to join Hackworth.

'We're n' hour behind!' he said without ceremony. But there was no time for criticism – they had work to do.

The first seven wagons were uncoupled and horses brought forward pulling two chaldrons each. A driver pulled them along the track to the tender. The horses were removed and corralled in the field behind Adamson's, while all available hands pushed the wagons together until they were coupled with the flour wagon. The logistics were undertaken by Stephenson and Hackworth, who issued orders to gang leaders, and then the gang leaders put each man to individual tasks with urgent shouts.

Many sets of ladders, most longer – or taller once they had been lifted and placed against the sides of the wagons – than the wagons themselves, whose upper rims sat a good seven feet from the ground, were positioned against the sides and first men and then ladies helped by the men climbed up and into the wagons. On Number One, Jimmy Stephenson occupied the horizontal plank that stuck out from the left side of the locomotive, adjusting screws and taps and valves with either a spanner or pliers he kept tucked into his belt whilst manoeuvring precariously with his feet on the limited space. Stephenson and Joseph Pease shook hands, the former offering the latter his condolences, and after a brief conversation, Joseph Pease mounted the experimental coach and Stephenson continued on to the locomotive. Jimmy pulled a lever to test steam pressure and it screeched, sending alarm through the crowd.

'We've got to go!' Jimmy shouted.

Hackworth took an iron bar, pushed the points over, raised his arms and signalled with the green handkerchief. Slowly the train inched backwards until, with its impetus diminishing, the last wagon stopped with just enough space to connect the hooks. The train was now the locomotive and its tender, with one wagon of flour behind, then six wagons of coal and one empty wagon, then Experiment and then six more wagons for official passengers and 14 more wagons for workmen. Jimmy Stephenson opened the valves as George took a hammer and smashed chunks of coal, feeding them into the firebox and closing the damper with his boot.

'She's gonna blow if we don't get movin', George!' Jimmy snapped, this time more harshly at his risk-taking big brother.

'Take 'er, Jimmy!' said George.

The train of wagons and the coach shunted back onto the main line while Hackworth went down to the coal wagons where he ordered the Gallaghers to couple the chaldrons. The brothers did this quickly as the train was backing up towards them. Hackworth gauged the distance and held his red handkerchief high and for a second the train didn't stop but slowed and Hackworth gave the command to hook up the last 12.

Lewis had made his way along the long train of wagons, hoping to be able to find some space on board. Despite his Sunday best, workmen blocked access to all but the very well dressed and just before the wooden coach, he encountered a party of men complaining: 'But we are the surveyors!' without success to confused workmen. A cordon had been made around the ladder up to Experiment as VIPs were boarding but soon more people were arguing to be allowed onto the other wagons and the navvies cursed and grew rude in manner, despite passengers having been especially selected with lottery tickets they brandished above their heads like creditor's bills. Lewis noticed that many of the wagons were empty of coal but fitted with simple planks to act as seats but towards the back of the train the wagons were filled with large and jagged slabs of coal like mini black boulders. Above one wagon a banner had been erected on which were sewn letters that made up the words: *May the Stockton and Darlington Railway give public satisfaction and reward to its liberal promoters.*

'Excuse me, sir,' Lewis called. 'Is it true this procession will arrive at Stockton later today?'

'It's called a train, son, not a procession,' said Hackworth. 'An' the answer is yes, I most surely hope so!'

'Would it be possible for us to climb aboard as a passenger? I'd be 'appy to pay.'

Hackworth looked hard pressed. Ahead of him verbal disputes were arising between some of the workers and the people jumping on without permission but wanting to be passengers themselves, despite not all of them having tickets or invitations. He saw the face of one of the Gallagher brothers in the melee but could not hear exactly what was being said. Whatever it was, it seemed to have the desired effect and voices were lowered, tempers calmed and polite progress and co-operation was accomplished between all parties.

'Climb aboard!' Hackworth said absently.

Lewis tried to work out how to tackle the climb – the top was wider than the base so it took him all his strength to pull his bodyweight up the full seven foot and hook one then two legs over the rim. He found himself on the last wagon at a height some six feet above the crowd, perched uncomfortably on some slabs of coal that had been draped with coarse sacking. His own scaling of the wagon seemed to happen at about the same as others who were doing the same thing, which seemed to give a tacit signal to more and within minutes dozens of strangers were clambering aboard the wagons in a free-for-all. But there were no harsh or raised voices, everybody was very friendly and helpful and Lewis found himself sharing with two Irishmen.

'Climb aboard dere boy!' said Seamus as he strode quickly to the last wagon in the train, grabbing Sean, running alongside, by the arm and pulling him up.

Soon all the wagons down the line were topped with dozens of figures, so Hackworth held his green handkerchief high above his head. They felt a shudder followed by a bump. Lewis looked down. They were moving.

* * *

Silas glimpsed the face of the boy from Evenfield walk past the window of the Adamson Inn, distinct with his blond hair and Sunday best, cloth cap and sack around his neck.

He couldn't live with the chance he might bump into the kid or Hamish Jones again, but then, to confound the situation even more, the grouse beater John Carr arrived. Carr and Lovatt had talked, the conversation brief. Silas waited and watched but waiting only stretches time, so once they'd left, he paid and walked out of the door, turning away from the centre of the village and deciding not to wait for the train to start moving but using his own initiative by heading out to the Durham Road but had walked only a few yards when a strong arm slipped around his neck, pulling him bodily into a doorway. He felt a sharp prod in his left side. In the reflection of the window Silas recognised the face.

'John Carr I am, brother to Will. You lied in court! Why? Who put you up to it?'

'I divvent kna what yer talkin' about!' Silas protested.

'Ye knows right well! But first you's goin' t'turn out yer pockets n' spare some change to help us pay them fines. We're goin' to make you pay. Then we're all goin' t'the constable!'

The thought of turning over his money was something Silas could almost have agreed to, but the threat of the constable was too much and proved to be John Carr's undoing. If Silas had been in his place he'd have stuck in the knife, propped him against a wall and walked away as calmly as possible. But not John Carr. John Carr believed in justice. Silas wrenched forward and down. John's hand slipped from his neck and he stood for a moment blinking. Silas turned fast, put his right hand over his left fist, crooked his arm and rammed his elbow hard into John's face. The nose cartilage smashed. Silas turned and stepped quickly in the direction of Shildon, but the train had started to move and he found himself pushed along with the crowd. Hoping to be able to get to the other side of the train and put distance between them, he set off, glancing back and seeing a red-splattered face elbowing its way through behind him. Carr knew the rules of the game: no second chances. It wasn't easy to negotiate the uneven ground and people, children, dogs, riders and carts *and* keep an eye on the movements of his hunter, but Silas reached the front and slipped between it and the men on horses with their flags, jumping over to the other side.

'Watch out!'

He was over then and pushing back through the crowd on the other side that surged against him, suddenly full of rage, loathing their smiling, stupid faces. What right did they have to be happy? Noticing people leaping on the train with no objections from workmen, he found himself holding up his right hand to a brakeman and was suddenly free of the ground, the tracks jerking past beneath. The bulk of the chaldron concealed him from Carr, whom he saw stumbling past behind them, disorientated and blinded by blood, wiping his face with his sleeve.

With panic receding, Silas realised he was being pulled by the iron horse and two wagons in front was the wooden coach he'd slept in the previous night. He'd suffered for this invention of the locomotive. For years he'd been set against it because Sir Giles had. His superiors, with their educations, must know better than he so he'd copied them. But he'd seen the aristocracy's true colours since and the sensation of being carried along by a mechanical engine wasn't so bad after all, especially as it had saved him from serious trouble.

'Where we goin'?' he asked the man with whom he found himself sharing a tight standing space.

'Darl'ton first, then Stockton!' said the excited workman. So Silas decided to stop in Darlington and pick up the buried £10 if it was still there – perfect! He'd already seen a bit of the world and knew it offered enterprising men new opportunities. Then he'd see Stockton – a place where he knew nobody and nobody knew him.

10 am

For the first mile or so, though moving only slowly, Lewis noted how the animated passengers couldn't get over the novelty of being in this mechanised cavalcade pulled by a machine.

The sensation was so strange there was nothing with which he could compare it: at one moment it was like being on the tail of either a caterpillar-like dragon or a dragon-like caterpillar and then it was as if it was a long ship cutting through debris-filled water. In his childhood his father had made him a wooden trolley on wheels on which he was placed – Dad had pulled it and him along using a tethered piece of string – and he'd ridden in carts pulled by horses and in the many nights in his Box Bed with panels and no windows he had imagined portholes and then imagined worlds beyond as his horse-less carriage rolled by. But this was unlike those sensations and in this slow and certain state the great ramshackle, higgledy-piggledy length of connected wheeled wagons blindly bumbled on, the last wagon soon passing over the level crossing outside the inn like the runt of a single file litter of beasts as the bearded owner, in his apron, handed the baby in his arms to a nearby woman, paced rapidly over to the train and climbed aboard.

Further along, after 100 yards or so, Lewis made out a brick-built building with a large chimney and across to the left, he could see a smart new house being tiled. Men on the scaffolding stopped work as the train passed, more coming out of the workshop to clap and cheer. Set away further still but gradually sliding into their eye-line was a parallel line of about 20 chaldrons and horses full of workmen and navvies.

'Come on, come on!' Hackworth shouted impatiently at the leading driver of the convoy, waving his arm as he did so to encourage them to catch up behind.

Waiting for the last wagon of the mechanised train to pass, the leading wagon's horse was urged forward, the other 19 following suit one by one, meaning the entire train was now one half mechanised and the other half horse-powered, the total length approaching nearly a third of a mile and – or because – it was moving at barely more than a walking pace, the huge crowd either side easily followed, causing some commotion and confusion, the fields and stiles becoming clogged. Despite a large number having already officially taken their seats, more of the crowd leapt onto the sides, shouting at friends to join them. The engine far from slowed, though some wagons continued to jolt and shudder as the many small iron wheels rolled over the joints. Lewis looked down at the rails and saw how the sunken stone blocks seemed to dip in the earth as they passed and he was then suddenly aware of Hackworth standing up beside him, balancing precariously on the coal, staring ahead.

There was a violent wrench and everybody plunged forward as one, Hackworth almost toppling headlong between the wagons but for the quick thinking of Lewis who managed to grab the hem of his trouser leg, and then Seamus and Sean helped them. His pale face streaked with coal dust, Hackworth said: 'Good Lord, I think you saved us from a nasty accident there, lads!'

Behind, the drivers of the horse-drawns pulled up swiftly causing a chain-reaction of swearing navvies. Each of the chaldron brakemen was shouting too and asking what was happening and just then a workman ran back.

'The surveyors' wagon, sir: it's derailed!'

'Already? Damn it!' swore Hackworth uncharacteristically.

He moved quickly along the track with Seamus and Sean behind him and Lewis behind them. Well-dressed VIPs leant from the open windows of Experiment, some smoking cigars, others chattering as if there was no problem at all, while just beyond Experiment a larger crowd gathered, which included Stephenson. The derailed wagon had been emptied of its passengers. The surveyors stood around bemused as workmen pushed it back onto the rail with a unified 'Heave!'

The displaced passengers sought to take their places but Hackworth held them back.

'I pray yer patience, sirs!'

Hackworth stayed with the wagon, ensuring it was re-coupled correctly then George signalled to his brother and slowly the train moved forward again but after only a short distance again it shook violently and once more. Hackworth held up his hand and cried: 'Broken wheel!'

He looked up the line and saw the solution. He ordered Lewis: 'Go and tell Mr Stephenson to take the loco jus' beyond the next set o' points. We'll push it onto the sidin' n' then back up slowly n' re-couple 'er. Got that, boy?'

'Yes sir' said Lewis.

'Repeat it back to me,' said Hackworth.

Lewis repeated the message perfectly and Hackworth nodded his assent, so Lewis ran forward, pushing through the crowd with the important message and gave it to Stephenson via one of the workmen. Hackworth uncoupled the broken wagon at the back. The five wagons of coal and one of flour in front pulled away and stopped beyond the entrance to the siding half a mile ahead as everyone else walked alongside. A number of men uncoupled the broken wagon and put their shoulders to it and pushed it over, helped by enthusiastic sightseers and even Lewis himself, though it was hard as the broken wheel made traction difficult. Groups of bystanders shouted encouragement but an accident was inevitable. There was a cry. People went forward and found a man who'd been struck on the shoulder by the wagon and had stumbled under, though luckily none of his limbs had fallen across the track.

'What's yer name?' asked Hackworth.

'John – John Davison of Aycliffe Village,' moaned the man, his white face grimacing as he was pulled out and helped to the side.

'Are you alright, Mr Davison?'

'Yes, sir, I think so, sir.'

'Thank goodness!' said Hackworth with genuine relief. They stood aside as Stephenson backed up and Hackworth was able to re-couple Experiment; the surveyors were found seats elsewhere.

'We're thirty minutes behind,' Hackworth noted by his pocket watch.

Seamus, Sean, Lewis and Hackworth trotted back to the last wagon and climbed on. Hackworth raised his green hanky and let his arm drop and the train inched forward.

'I owe you me thanks, lads,' he said to Seamus and Sean and to Lewis: 'And well done for getting the message to Mr Stephenson.'

It should have been a proud moment for Lewis but Lewis was preoccupied with conflicting thoughts. At any moment he was afraid a constable or a rider was going to come running into town shouting: 'Murder at Evenfield! Arrest that boy!' He felt different emotions: defiance for having stood up to Hackett and bottomless fear if he were to be caught. Now he was part of this happy event and yet dared not allow his himself to enjoy the moment for his father was somewhere ahead and behind was an event that seemed unreal. The only luxury he could allow was the sun on his upturned face and his strong desire to keep feeling that every day for the rest of his life and luckily the weather was holding: his 'sun' making frequent appearances through the lattice of white clouds rolling in from the east but he knew it was customary in those parts for it to transform quickly from sun to rain.

Until that day, Hackworth reflected, all had been doubtful that carrying passengers on wagons would be mere fashion. After all, the idea was for the locomotive to carry coal to port and wagons pulled by horses would share the line, but the presence of people surprised him. He calculated. What if they could do five or six journeys a day and build more locomotives? The second locomotive, Hope, was already finished and would be working the same line from October. What if they had lines in both directions and five or six trains at the same time? A man could travel from Shildon to the sea, sell his wares and be home for tea. With the train he could do five times a week what he could only currently do once a week. That meant he could carry five times his produce, make five times the profit and pay his workers five times more! If all 30 wagons were filled with bread or cloth, it would turn the shopkeeper into a merchant, feed thousands and clothe nations. The bad winter of 1816 had begot famine in parts of Britain and thousands had died of hunger and cold but the railway system could put an end to such things.

Then, ahead, as the Aycliffe Road crossed the line – the same road Lewis and Wilson had crossed only a week before – the locomotive belched loudly, a cloud of steam and cinders shooting high into the air with a muffled bang. The train halted and a workman ran back to them from the front with more bad news – the pipe which directed heat from the firebox into the tubes that heated the water in the boiler had become clogged with the cinders of burnt oakum – unpicked and tarred rope that stopped up the tiny fissures between the wooden planking of the boiler and its iron framework.

It was then that Lewis suddenly realised he was looking across at the farm where he'd stayed the previous week with Henry and Mary. He saw the old lady come out of the front and look in his direction almost on cue. Now seemed a good a time as any, he reflected. He jumped down and ran across the field.

'You be young Lewis who stayed with us last week, aren't ye?' Mary asked with a growing smile as he approached.

'Yes, missus. Where's yer 'usband?' asked Lewis breathlessly.

'Up there,' she said, pointing to the roof.

Lewis stepped back and looked up. Henry was perched on the edge, his face black with soot.

'Young Lewis, isn't it?' Henry called down.

'I've come to repay you,' said Lewis and he opened the pouch where he stored his coins. He took out a shilling.

Despite his age, the old man clambered nimbly from the roof, wiped his hands on his black trousers and examined the silver coin in his dirty fingers.

'Fair exchange is no robbery. Now tell me,' he said, pocketing the coin then nodding at the train. 'What advantages does this contraption 'ave that a good old-fashioned 'orse an' cart don't?'

'It can pull all that weight n' all those wagons in one go,' said Lewis. 'That's almost a hundred horses n' carts!'

Henry took off his woollen bonnet and scratched his bald head.

'Well, I can't see the reason for it meself. An' who wants such big amounts?'

'People in London,' said Lewis. 'They can't get enough to 'eat their 'omes n' fire their chimneys n' fuel their factories.'

'London always sounded to me like a sort of Hades,' said Henry dubiously.

'I'm takin' passage down to Stockton. It is my intention to voyage to Australia,' said Lewis.

'*Australia*? Is that not a faraway land? Why you be wantin' to go there?'

'It's a long story, sir.'

'Indeed! Well, why 'as the steam 'orse stopped 'ere? Is it jus' to repay me me shillin'?'

'There's summat wrong wi' the engine. A blocked pipe,' said Lewis.

'A blocked pipe, you say?' said Henry, and then pointing at a big wooden rectangular box marked TOOLS he said: 'Might I be of some assistance, do you think?'

They hurried across the field to the front of the train where they found a small crowd of babbling workmen surrounding Hackworth and the two Stephensons peering into the open firebox in which blazed the coal. They were trying to reach in and chip away the thick soot using a rudimentary chisel not at all designed for the purpose but the heat kept them at bay as it wasn't long enough. Hackworth's face lit up he saw the old man with the wooden box marked TOOLS open the lid and bring out a pair of long-handled tongs and an equally long poker.

'Good thinking!' Hackworth said.

Using the long-handled tongs in the tool kit, they were able to reach into the firebox and lift out lumps of burning coals and drop them onto the side of the track where they were soon doused by buckets of water. With more room to manoeuvre inside the box and a less ferocious heat, the long poker was used to reach in and tap gently at the blockage of oakum at the back of the firebox that was reducing the heat emitted by the burning coal. The affair was over in ten minutes.

'Who've I to thank?'

All heads looked to Henry, his bemused face a few shades blacker than Stephenson's. Henry's tools were returned to him.

'I thank thee kindly, sir! Mr Hackworth, let's go!' shouted Stephenson.

'Every man to take his own convoy!' called Hackworth.

The workmen who had been idling by their wagons began ushering passengers back on board and the smoke billowed out with the steam once more as slowly the train slogged its way forward and, for the first time since Shildon, it moved faster. The cries and shouts of the 200 or so on board increased and then the last of the sightseeing riders tagging along either side ran out of navigable road. It was at last alone, unencumbered by horses, carriages and coaches and the journey was exhilarating but, with no suspension, every jolt was bone-rattling.

'How can you measure the speed of the train, sir?' Lewis shouted at Hackworth.

'Look, see that?' said Hackworth, pointing to a wooden post with the number 6 painted on it stuck into the ground by the side of the track.

'Each marker post represents one mile, so we measure the time it takes to go from one to the next and divide it into 60 minutes. We can do ten miles in 60 minutes so that should be...!'

'Six miles an hour,' said Lewis levelly. Hackworth stopped explaining: the boy was no fool.

'But I think without stoppages we should have mastered at least eight, maybe nine or ten!'

Lewis looked over to his right where, above the heads and carriages of sightseers, he saw the blacksmith's chimney at the Whessoe forge and as the grey smoke from its chimney passed over their heads from an easterly wind, it meshed with the black of the smoke from No. 1 to make swirling grey and silver dervishes in the sky. After five minutes, Hackworth, standing directly behind Lewis and gripping the lad's shoulders to stop from toppling, shouted: 'Darlington approaching! Jenkins - all brakemen to give me their attention n' await my signal. Pass it on!'

Jenkins repeated the message to the next brakeman and the message was relayed over the course of less than a minute until all 30 were glancing back. Hackworth was enormously glad he'd had them rehearse their roles the day before. The crowd thickened as the line curved round to the east and he hoped it would not pose a problem or accident.

He held the red hanky high as long as he could and then all the men, including him, put their bodyweight against the large wooden hand brakes, slowing the train to a halt in a din of creaks, squeals and groans as up ahead Jimmy Stephenson shut down the valves that allowed steam into the cylinders and then pushed the crude machinery into reverse. They'd arrived in Darlington.

12 - Midday

Hackworth pulled out his pocket watch.

'Time,' he said to the many faces that were expectantly turned to his, 'is the new commodity. Two hours to cover 12 miles, including total stoppage time, 65 minutes. Marvellous! Stand by yer wagons!'

The temptation for the brakemen to leave their posts and join in the celebrations at Darlington was strong: nearby, a fire burned and a huge spitted ox was roasting and the aroma wafted towards them making Lewis, Seamus, Sean, Hackworth, Jenkins and over 500 passengers salivate *en masse*. Seamus and Sean jumped down and made their way towards the food as the first of the horse-drawns caught up, also emptied out, and then swelled the crowd even more, almost all in search of food and ale.

Their late start from Shildon, a hamlet virtually cut off from the outside world with just one or two uneven tracks and a flimsy coach service, had welcomed a few hundred sightseers but now, at midday and in Darlington, the reception had swelled to an immense number. From Lewis's vantage point on top of the wagon, when he looked out on all sides all he could see were bobbing top hats and the noise was tremendous: a hubbub of chatter and laughter, the air ringing with 'Bravo!' and 'Well done!' and 'How long did it take?' and 'How does it work?' The locomotive and the Stephensons attracted the largest crowd of course. At the other end, Hackworth's black stovepipe hat wasn't alone: it was surrounded by dozens of others sported by manufacturers or engineers, along with white stovepipes atop the heads of politicians and journalists. Many men were pressing around the locomotive while women stood further away in small groups or carriages of various shapes and colours. A number of Sedan chairs were looking for fares and Lewis noticed one of the coachmen was a Negro – a rare sight. He'd never seen one. The poor man looked very uncomfortable as he was so often stared at by mocking strangers or jeering children. There were beggars too and skin-and-bone mothers pale with death, holding out their empty and filthy hands imploringly, oblivious to any 'special day' and focussed only on the life and death struggle between hunger and starvation; beyond this conflict, nothing else existed.

'Everybody down! Mr Jenkins!' Hackworth called above the noise.

'That includes you, son,' Jenkins said to Lewis. Lewis dropped down as they uncoupled the last six wagons from the main body of the train and moved the locomotive forward. Hackworth came to a point branch and pushed the rails over.

The last six wagons then began to descend by gravity towards the newly built drops around Westbrook, each brakeman shouting commands as they went, and then levers were pulled and the wagons' bottoms fell open, coal crashing in black clouds below where queues stood with empty baskets and carts to take what they could of the free gift.

Somewhere in the crowd a small brass band started to play *God Save the King* and everyone stood in silence until the anthem was over. Then, up ahead, the wooden coach discharged its dignitaries and joined top-hatted VIPs on a small raised grandstand to congratulate Stephenson who 'did the politics'. Jimmy meanwhile, took care of the 'technicals' and opened a hatch on the barrel: from it led a pipe of stretched leather, the end of which fell vertically 50 feet into the river Skerne where two workmen operated a Stephenson-designed hand-pump. A horse-drawn coal wagon pulled up close and workmen began shovelling replacement coal onboard.

Lewis made his way to the eating tables and soon held a tray with a bowl of vegetable soup, a small wedge of cheese, four hunks of coarse bread and two apples, all for a shilling. He thanked the serving women and made his way towards the back of the train, now six chaldrons shorter, and managed to get up. Within seconds, three or four urchins were underneath begging scraps. Lewis took an apple and tossed it down to the tallest boy who caught it and took a few bites before it was snatched from him by another ragamuffin.

'Thanks,' said the boy. 'My name's John Dobbin. What's yours?'

'Lewis Lovatt,' said Lewis.

'Thanks for the apple, Lewis Lovatt.'

'My pleasure, John Dobbin.'

Just then, John Dobbin pointed at a figure and warned: 'Catcher!' and he and the others melted into the crowd as a flat-faced man stole after them. Lewis froze. With his mother dead, his father transported and his home abandoned, he could be easily counted as an orphan and there were many due to war, disease and accidents: thousands of parentless, feral children. If the Child Catcher caught them, they'd be for the workhouse so doing his best to appear older by sitting upright and throwing his shoulders back, he wolfed the soup and licked the bowl clean as the man passed below obliviously. Lewis wrapped the two hunks of bread along with the cheese in a napkin that had accompanied the meal and slipped the parcel into his sack. Serving boys passed through the crowd gathering empty bowls and plates; Lewis leaned down and passed them his.

Hackworth appeared, chewing on a slice of pie and waiting for the signal to continue. Stephenson was struggling to supervise the addition of two extra wagons between Number One and Experiment, into which climbed men carrying musical instruments that glinted in the sunlight. The band was composed of trumpets and trombones, a big bass drum, a cymbal player and the conductor – a rotund man with a wiry moustache, beard and sideburns. Despite being crammed in, they managed to drink from a shared jug of beer, sipping, slurping, belching or simply refusing before passing it along.

* * *

Silas left the train at Darlington and, knowing the geography of the town, set off nimble-footed against the stream of people moving towards the turnpike.

The novelty of the journey hadn't been without its problems: repairs, the brakeman told him, but Silas had stayed where he was, half-afraid of losing his place and half-afraid John Carr might jump on. Then, when the train had broken down for the second time, he'd glimpsed the Lovatt boy who'd walked right past him unaware. Silas had kept his head down and, with keen eyes, he had watched every movement the boy made, both at the front and then at the back after he had returned there to take his seat on the last wagon.

Would he ever be free? For a short while since leaving Shildon he'd felt a liberating freedom. He'd felt it occasionally when he'd been in the army and again after leaving London. He'd tasted it often on the estate, especially in the mornings when he had set off across the moors at dawn, left to his own devices. The freedom of the open road was a different type of freedom. Nonetheless, he'd seen the Lovatt boy *again*. Why, oh why was that boy on the train?

Halfway along Northgate, as he strode with his bag flapping against his leg, he was distracted by the sight of a man dressed for a funeral on the steps of a large house, putting his index finger to his lips to noisy passers-by.

'Where's the railway goin'?' Silas quietly asked the man.

'What do you mean?' asked the man.

'I left it up there at the North Road Turnpike but supposing I want to catch it on the other side of town, where would I find it?'

'You'd need the Haughton Road: go down to the river, cross the bridge, follow the sign – you can't miss it.'

'Thanks, marra. Who's dead?'

'Isaac Pease, last night.'

'Ah.' said Silas, who had never heard the name and cared even less. 'My condolences.'

Five minutes later he was standing on the east bank of the Skerne where he remembered burying his leather pouch containing £10 over seven years before. But there was a problem: where the thorn bush had once grown, now stood a house. All of the land that had been deserted fields a few years ago was now built on or being excavated for foundations for new buildings. He'd hoped the distraction of the railway had meant the streets would be deserted and he'd have been able to dig up his money without arousing suspicion, but the house had him beaten. 'Bastard', he thought, 'You set yer sights on summat you've banked on for years, and when you finally get to it, it's completely changed or it's gone or it never was.' He looked around a few times and wondered if he hadn't made a miscalculation but he was pretty certain – either his £10 was still under there or some lucky builder had unearthed his trove. His spirits sank: £10 was a lot of money to lose. They said, he mused ironically, it was best to put one's money into bricks and mortar. Well, he had – literally but for no return.

Silas looked across the river and up Tubwell Row, cursing but also remembering: the last time he'd been to Darlington, he'd gone to the courtroom and condemned Lovatt and the others. Perhaps losing £10 was divine justice? But then another thought occurred: was the Lovatt boy following him? Not right then and there but on the train and, if so, why?

'Which way's Haughton?' he demanded of two Sedan-chair carriers passing by empty and in search of custom.

'It's an uphill march for nowt or I can tek you there in style for a bob, sir,' came the reply.

Silas impatiently opened the front door and climbed into the space, resting his bag on his knee as the two men lifted the chair and carried him towards Haughton Village. They began too slowly.

'Get a move on!' Silas shouted, suddenly afraid he'd miss the train passing further up the road or he'd lose track of the Lovatt boy. The panting men picked up speed. Perhaps John Carr and the boy were working together. What was it Carr had said? *We?* He'd said it three times. Was it part of a plan to exact revenge for what happened at Darlington? Within seconds he'd convinced himself this *must be* the case and that either murder or justice was on their minds. Why else would the kid be on the train? There were too many unknowns. What if a mishap were to befall the kid? Silas could make it seem like an unfortunate accident. The world was full of unfortunate accidents. With the uncertainty of the hours that lay ahead there would be opportunities. He'd hoped that by leaving John Carr at Shildon, the concern over his future would have been left behind too, but life wasn't so simple. Run or confront? The sight of Lewis in Darlington made him realise a harsher solution may be necessary.

12.30 pm

Wearing a solemn coat and solemn hat, the joiner, carpenter and coffin-maker William Ainsley walked solemnly towards Northgate, incongruous among crowds of happy, gaily dressed people making their way towards the railway crossing. He had planned to go himself, along with his wife and children, but a messenger arrived informing him of the death of Isaac Pease and his immediate attention was required so he sent his children and wife on ahead and returned to his coffin-stacked office, changed into his mourning coat, put on his black stovepipe, took up his bag and walked solemnly – for he thought of himself as a living advertisement for his profession – to Northgate. The corpse had been washed and dried and laid on its back on a leather sheet. Candelabras at the head and foot of the bed on the second floor lit the body. Beside the bed stood half a dozen buckets of bloodstained water and creased and stained towels over the backs of three chairs.

Ainsley put his bag on the sideboard, opened it and brought out a pivoted wooden yardstick. He unfolded and laid the homemade device alongside the corpse, measuring 5 feet, 11 inches and a smidgeon. He stood halfway down the centre of the body and leaned forward, holding the yardstick above until it was level. Two looped cords weighted with small lead balls measured the widest points: shoulders, elbows, hips, knees and ankles. He repeated the measurements to himself while writing them in his notebook. He crouched down to the same level as the table to ensure there were no obvious depth problems with the body and then leaned over to examine the face. Rigor mortis was setting in: he could ascertain this from the blue patches, but apart from a little wadding required in the cheeks, a mask of paint could be applied to give a healthy look. He let himself out after having informed a maid he would return the following day with a pine casket.

Walking along Northgate in the direction of the railway, and removing his collapsible top hat and black armband, he chuckled grimly at how the Catholics and Protestants loved their ostentatious ornamentation – vanity even beyond death. He could only dream of selling his 'The Majestic' package: 53 guineas, hearse-and-four, lead-lined oak coffin with brass handles and pageboy mourners recruited from the workhouse. But the Quakers had no need of ornamentation nor spent money on extravagant funerals – not even a headstone. A Quaker death was rarely profitable for a funeral director. Ainsley found his family and he cheered up swiftly, the dour thoughts of moments before blown away like ash in a breeze and they marvelled at the engine as it stood idling at the turnpike.

12.38 pm

Jimmy Stephenson sent a boy back to Hackworth to tell him they were ready and Hackworth waved his green handkerchief to acknowledge the message and shouted 'All aboard!' a number of times at the top of his lungs through cupped hands. The crowd began to disentangle itself, some surging back onto the wagons and the others, having travelled from Shildon, remaining. Few had a desire to go on as the return was a one-day foot slog, but there were just as many Darlingtonians willing to take up the vacant places and go on to Stockton.

Jimmy loosed a hot blast of steam from beneath the safety valve, lifting it with a hammer tucked in his belt, and Number One began pulling almost 100 tons, despite being about 50 feet shorter.

The Great North Road was jammed with carriages, horses and sightseers yards deep as the iron horse crawled over the turnpike towards the new sandstone bridge. Up ahead on the left stood a tubby man in a bright purple breast coat and a tall, slender stovepipe, flanked by others though none as dapper as he. The drivers and all the brakemen tipped their hat wear to him.

'Signore Bonomi!' Stephenson called out.

'Mister Stephenson, it is a wonderful day to travel!'

'And a wonderful day to travel on your bridge, Signor Bonomi!' replied Stephenson. Despite Bonomi having won the bridge-building contract and not Stephenson and despite the fact Mr Bonomi was English, unlike his father who was Italian, there were no hard feelings between the two and Bonomi accepted the affectionate use of his Italian title. Bonomi was a qualified architect whereas George was both an unqualified architect and an unqualified engineer, but they were still acquaintances.

Bonomi trotted forward flapping his arms and exhorting people to help so he could be pulled aboard the already overcrowded passenger coach.

''Tis that gentleman built Durham Prison!' Seamus said to nobody in particular.

Lewis had a flashing memory of the hanging he'd seen a week before outside that same prison, though so much had happened since it felt much longer, and again the hungry, empty reality of who he was, where he was going and why, soaked through him like an immersive baptism. The brass band near the front struck up a brisk marching tune to add to the unreality.

Once over the Bonomi Bridge, the train moved slowly east across the northern part of Darlington, along the embankment built by the hundreds of navvies who'd laboured day after day for over four years: a private army of spade-wielders hacking out the surrounding area like the jaws of a thousand beasts, re-arranging it to shore up the hundreds of tons of earth dragged from one place that had been turned into ballast to reshape the contours in another. Distantly, the grey spire of the Lady of the North changed her angle as they moved, and riders, men, women, children, carts, carriages and an empty Sedan chair with two tired drivers watched them pass. The harvest waited for no man and farmhands labouring through the fields of corn with scythes stopped only momentarily to watch.

For a little while they travelled through featureless countryside and then passed over the Sadberge to Dinsdale crossing where they were forced to slow down a little to avoid accidents by colliding with any of the many bodies that were moving around, emerging from more crowds gathered drinking around The Fighting Cocks Inn. Just then, a young man ran up and leapt on.

'Good day gents! Goin' down to Stockton is it?'

Without waiting for an invite, the pushy newcomer climbed in and Lewis and Sean made space. He had no shoes and only dirty and torn trousers and his legs and feet were filthy, as was the rest of him. It was hard to tell his age, certainly a little older than Lewis, but not much.

He looked down with wide-eyed wonder at the world moving slowly behind him.

'Jack Cook's the name,' said the young man to anybody who listened, which at that moment was only Lewis. 'I'm on me way to Stockton to seek a position. I'm from Great Ayton.'

'Great Ayton?' Hackworth chimed in. 'Cook country!'

'The same, sir!'

'You're related?' Hackworth asked.

'Cousins of mine, the Cooks, on me Ma's side,' said Jack.

'Well, well! It's not everyday you meets a relative of the man who discovered an entire continent!' laughed Hackworth.

Lewis stared blankly.

'*The* Captain James Cook, the local man who discovered Australia?' Hackworth said.

'Ah,' said Lewis, unable to show much enthusiasm for the man who'd discovered the place where his father had been sent.

'The priest in me village tol' me about this 'ere rail-way so 'ere I am!' said Jack.

'Where are yer parents?' asked Lewis.

'Puntin' on the River Tick – debtor's prison in York. If I could find a position, I could pay their debts n' get 'em out. Do you gentlemen know any places I might find work?'

'Can you read n' write?' asked Hackworth.

'I know me alphabet n' me name n' can count up to n' 'undred!' said Jack.

'What sort of jobs have you done?' asked Lewis.

'Domestic servant, mourner, carpenter's mate, woodchopper and porter.'

'Are they well-paid jobs?' Lewis asked, naïve to any world outside of Evenfield.

'Woodchopper: penny n' hour, plus spelks. Worked for a coachin' house in York, 'elped change horses for the Mail, cleaning n' loadin' the pistols. Ah met a man who worked Manchester to London. Got 20 quid a year! Is that true, sir? Can a coachman make that much?'

'Who taught you to read?' asked Hackworth.

Jack cast his eyes down.

'Work'ouse,' he said.

'What's it like, the work'ouse?' Lewis asked.

'No picnic,' Jack said, half-laughing. 'Up at seven, prayers n' breakfast, readin', 'rithmetic, supper at six, bed by eight, Sundays n' Christmas excepted.'

Hackworth's attention was caught and he suddenly found himself temporarily hooked up to a private conversation which was to have a surprising outcome. He was thinking about the Monitor System that had taught him all he knew and he was remembering himself some years before in a group of a dozen others his age and size and speech, all listening to the vicious Monitor Martin whose over-liberal use of the stick in favour of the carrot as an incentive to his younger wards remained embedded in his mind. He could hear Monitor Martin's voice droning out: 'Listen up you illegitimate oiks, you scum of the earth that nobody wants, you trash, take down this sum in your heads and add it up in pounds of weight and then write down your amount on your slate. Usual punishments apply for any fails.' 'Usual punishments' was the rod. Boys that were hopeless at sums or simply intimidated by fear were beaten repeatedly night after night and suffered terrible physical and mental horrors like nightmares and bed-wetting. He was thinking too of 'Sunday School' and endless catechisms which had seemed dull and useless then but at least gave him an edge for evaluating sense from nonsense in the world in which he was growing up. So he was thinking of many things when he suddenly said aloud to them: 'When we get to Stockton, I'll see what I can do for you,'

A smile flashed across Jack Cook's face. Hackworth knew he'd made a good choice – a kid who could sum up a situation in seconds? Hackworth knew a good thing when he saw it.

'Thanks kindly, sir!' exclaimed Jack, 'I may well follow you up on that, sir!'

'We've come down from Shildon an' stopped at Darl'ton,' said Lewis. 'I live in west Durham. Lived,' said Lewis, correcting himself. 'I've never been to the sea.'

'Never seen the sea?' asked Jack in such a way as to insinuate there was something wrong with Lewis.

'Have you ever seen the moors or Durham Gaol or down a coalmine?' asked Lewis defensively.

Jack Cook scrunched up his mouth and looked away and the two said nothing more for almost a mile.

At Oak Tree, Lewis opened his napkin. Jack Cook eyed the food hungrily, so Lewis gave him a hunk of cheese and Jack ate with very few manners and no shame, devouring it quickly.

'Yer not a bad sort, Lewis,' Jack winked at him.

After another mile or two, Lewis felt the train perceptively slowing down.

'We appear to be slowing for some reason! It's true our speed is nothing like it was approaching Darlington!' noted Hackworth.

Hackworth noticed a worker, visible by a sash given to him the previous day at Shildon, running back along the line towards them. When the man arrived, breathless, he jumped up onto the last waggon and gasped out: 'Mister ... Stephenson ... asks you to ... signal the brakemen ... to slow ... down and stop ... on his signal ... must stop ... at Goosepoool ... to take on more water ...because of extra weight of people ... Mister Stephenson's signal ... will be a red flag!'

'Understood!' said Hackworth. He had been wise to wait for the verbal message because if he'd given the brake command too soon they would have stopped where they were and not at Goosepool. He called on Jenkins on the wagon in front of them to pass a simple verbal message along the wagons: 'All eyes on Hackworth!'

Jenkins relayed the message to the other brakemen but it would have to get at least beyond the central wagon before Hackworth could give the signal so he hoped Stephenson would give him enough time: if only half applied their brakes they could wreck themselves trying to compensate for the half that didn't. Still the train slowed a little more and then Hackworth saw Stephenson waving his red flag up ahead of them. Hackworth had to wait until the majority of brakemen were looking in his direction and only then, finally satisfied, he waved his red hanky and applied his own brake and the brakemen did the same. By this clumsy method the train slowly came to rest until roughly the middle of the mechanically drawn section was level with the farmhouse at Goosepool.

From behind came loud expletives in an Irish brogue as the leading horse-drawn drew up only inches from the last wagon. The first driver jumped down and swore at the driver behind who had run into him setting off a chain-reaction all the way back. Alcohol-fuelled words were exchanged and suddenly the two drivers of the leading wagons were wrestling on the ground. Seamus jumped down from the wagon and grabbed both by the scruffs of their necks to hold them apart but both continued to tussle so Seamus tripped one into the dirt with a jab to the shin and the other received a knee between his legs.

'S'not my fault, sir!' protested one of the drivers rubbing his stinging shin. 'The speed keeps changin' n' I got 20 wagons behind!'

Stephenson had meanwhile run back to them and noticed the disturbance.

'Mr Hackworth, why didn't you respond sooner?'

'I couldn't give the signal until the message had at least passed the central wagon for the sake of the brakes, Mister Stephenson,' said Hackworth truthfully. 'And I do not recall an unscheduled stop here being mentioned.'

'What's 'appenin' 'ere?' said Stephenson, confused, looking at Seamus and the brawling men.

'The men're concerned the train's moving too slowly. It's no faster than a horse at the minute n' the horse-drawns're comin' clogged up.' Hackworth said.

'The problem is in advance of us,' said Stephenson, 'People don't understand this weight n' velocity cannat just pull up sharply as a horse.'

Stephenson lowered his voice and homed in on the navvies.

'I ask all men to keep their tempers today,' he warned quietly.

Among the crowd a well-dressed man in highly polished riding boots and an unusual black uniform that seemed to single him out as a cavalry officer, black and grey jacket fastened casually over one shoulder, approached the train. Certainly his presence and the smart phaeton carriage he'd been sitting in commanded respect. The crowd parted in silence to let him through.

'Herr Stephenson?' called the smartly dressed gentleman with a flat, almost mechanical accent, 'Doctor Hamel. Agent for His Most Esteemed Royal Highness, Emperor Alexander of Russia. I trust ve haff not inconvenienced you? Ve had problems getting ze coach from York last night unt came direct here.'

'Not at all, Doctor Hamel. We have a place for you up front in our private carriage. Please come this way.'

Stephenson motioned for the Russian to follow and started back along the track to Experiment.

The fighting Irishmen meanwhile shook hands.

'Shall we go an' see?' Jack asked.

The two lads jumped down and set off and, as no command had been given to the contrary, it was again a free-for-all as almost everyone descended. Lewis and Jack passed Experiment, back door open, glimpsing the packed crowd of well-dressed men chatting, drinking from tankards, smoking clay pipes or cigars or hanging from the windows drunkenly ogling a blushing, buxom lass being tricked into holding her tray high above her head. Lewis could see why Goosepool was so named: a young collie pup dripping and muddy, playfully chased dozens of the fat waddling birds flapping in the swampy marshland. Nearby stood a farmhouse and an inn: the gathering place for the geese herded there from all over the region destined for local markets. Stephenson was supervising a human chain of water-filled buckets set up between the large barrel, the ground and across the road into a field and then into a pond. Although not as efficient as a water pump, it was well organised and buckets were being poured at a regular rate.

'Watch out for reeds an' dead leaves – they'll clog the pipe!' Stephenson shouted.

'It's only to top it up, George. Not all stops are to be like this in future,' said Jimmy. 'And not all loads'll be so 'eavy!'

'I was thinkin' … maybe I should speak wi' *him* about a position,' Jack whispered to Lewis.

'Stephenson? Not now – he's busy,' said Lewis. 'Hackworth said he'd 'elp. Wait an' see.'

They watched a little longer and then George Stephenson peered into the water tank.

'Enough!'

The hatch was closed and the human chain ran back to take their places, piling up their buckets beside the line.

'Better get back!' said Lewis.

And then, as they passed Experiment, Lewis caught a glimpse of a face he recognised. He couldn't tear his eyes away and slowly but steadily Silas too turned his head. Instinct told Lewis to run, but what could he do in broad daylight? Images of John Carr boasting of vengeance, his father in the prison cart, Hackett falling down the pit shaft, burning torches and brandished weapons, broken windows and hurtful words – all collided at once. But the odder question: why the man had lied about being William Wilson – didn't arrive immediately.

'What are you doin' 'ere?' Lewis asked.

'Funny that,' laughed Silas nervously. 'I was gonna ask the same o' you!'

'Everythin' all right?' Jack asked Lewis.

'We're old mates, aren't we?' said Silas, raising his eyebrows, in a statement-of-fact way, rather than as a question, but only just.

'I'm fine,' said Lewis to Jack. 'You go on, I'll catch up.'

'Jump aboard,' Silas said, as Jack stepped away

'You sure, Lewis?' asked Jack doubtfully. He'd taught himself to sniff out suspicious-looking, ill-intentioned faces since birth – he had a feeling something wasn't right.

'Yes,' said Lewis, 'We already know each other!'

The train began to move so Jack trusted to a different instinct in the next breath and carried on as best felt right for him. He ran to the last wagon. Lewis was old enough to look after himself was Jack's conclusion and once Jack had disappeared out of sight Silas lent over, taking Lewis firmly by the wrist and lifting him up.

Silas thought Lewis knew him as Wilson, but Lewis, of course, now knew him as Silas Scroggins, the imposter, and he knew he had played a perjurous role in his father's wrongful sentence: it was because of this man that Lewis's life had been turned upside down. Perhaps it wasn't too late? But then what would he say about Hackett? It had been self-defence but whom would they believe? Both Lewis and Silas had secrets that needed to be hidden. But who knew what about whom?

'Did you 'ear what 'appened to my Dad?' asked Lewis.

Silas's eyelids flickered just a fraction and then he looked away.

'No, what?'

'Seven years in Australia,' said Lewis.

The words stuck in his throat as the urge to hurt this man welled up inside him. A quick shove such as he'd given Hackett and he could dislodge him, but though stunned, Scroggins wouldn't be incapacitated and he could leap back on and batter Lewis. Lewis suddenly felt the strength of Silas's grip on his arm and turned, the penny dropping in a split-second: it was Silas's intention to push *him* under! His feet slipped towards the gap. He closed his eyes. There was a moment of peace and freedom as he seemed to fly - but in fact he simply fell head first from the train into the grass verge, putting his arms out to soften his fall on the wet marshland and tumbling over on the ground. He heard: 'BRAKES!' shouted over and over by dozens of voices and he was able to sit up unhurt and watch as the train lurched to a halt, passengers leaping down and running back along the line. Where was Silas? Lewis got up and ran back, joining the crowd gathered around a figure on the ground. Unsettling groans pierced the chatter and Lewis found himself seeing not Silas on the ground as he expected but another man he didn't know. Stephenson arrived.

'What's 'appened 'ere?' he asked.

'The wheel o' the train crushed his foot!' said a brakeman.

As Lewis's eyes moved down to where the man's left foot once was, he felt nauseous. The fellow's boot hadn't protected it, squashing the ankle into an unrecognisable mush of black leather and red meat. Stephenson grimaced.

'What's the man's name?' he asked urgently.

'John Stevens,' came the reply, 'A navvy.'

'Well, 'e's not gonna be navvyin' for a while. Does anybody 'ave any brandy?' asked Stephenson.

A call went out and a hip flask found its way to John Stevens. The flask's contents were poured into his mouth several times to numb his immediate pain and several people carried him to a cart on the nearby road, which at Stephenson's insistence was dispatched to

Yarm to find a doctor. A veiled voice said: 'Looks like n' amputation to me!'

'Whose is this?' Jenkins asked, indicating the leather case cut in half by the wheels, alongside shirts and trousers and a shiny pair of tan riding boots scattered over the tracks. Nobody replied, and John Stevens was almost unconscious by this stage. Did the case belong to John Stevens or a third party?

As the crowd dispersed, so the sense of moral value shifted dramatically as the sense of urgency to continue the trip fanned their own self-interested eagerness again. Silas's clean and almost unworn shirts and boots disappeared forever, stolen as the crowd took its place on the train. Stephenson went back to get the steam engine moving again and Lewis, looking around for signs of Silas, jumped as he felt a hand on his shoulder.

'What 'appened?' said Jack Cook.

Lewis struggled with the truth: 'There's a man on the train who tried to kill me n' I don't know why.' How plausible did that sound? He replied: 'Nothing.'

'You look like yer've seen a ghost!' Jack said.

And it's the part where you should always say: 'Yes I have!' but you never do, thought Lewis, shaken, who walked back in silence and remounted the last wagon to find it had two new passengers on the sides and two more up on the coal and they were distinctly unhelpful, though words from Hackworth soon made them obliging.

Stephenson was worried: another accident could destroy the spirit of the day. His humiliation in Parliament in June had also made him nervous: safety was his responsibility. The accident was tragic for the victim and possibly his family, who may have lost its sole wage earner, but it hadn't, as far as could be seen, been the fault of the S&D. Passengers hadn't been encouraged to ride the train. But then neither had they been discouraged. Passengers were what Stephenson needed, but not clinging to the sides. How could such numbers be discouraged? He had made it clear in the wording of the act that he'd wanted passengers. But if he was going to have them, he would have to charge them and take care of their safety and comfort and control them with rules and regulations governing personal conduct on moving vehicles.

Meanwhile, the satisfying arrival of the train at Stockton obsessed him because he knew it would be the most striking signal of success that could be sent to those who doubted. Besides, what he was really looking forward to was the return trip the following day. The train would be almost empty of cargo and though much of the journey would be uphill, that was when its power would come into its own. The day after that, he'd be back on a coach and forced to endure the bumpy roads down to Manchester where a whole new world of problems awaited.

As they approached the inn at Early Nook, a farrier at the centre of a small crowd, stopped to watch, in front of him the flimsy picket near the Elton-Yarm Road cordoning off the freshly turned earth like an raw, orange wound. Within a month, there'd be a mile long single-track extension going down to a storage building and worker's home that so far was known only as the mysteriously titled Building D13 at Yarm where coal drops were being built.

'The's iron in them 'ills,' said Jimmy to his brother, nodding at the horizon. 'A wise man'd invest in a foundry.'

'A wise man will!' said his brother, laughing.

George took up a hammer, smashed a coal chunk into splinters, used the hammer to open the fire door, tossed shards in and closed it with his foot

'Whiteley Springs!' shouted Jimmy.

A well-dressed man on a conspicuously beautiful white horse watched them pass with a self-satisfied grin as his gaze first sought Stephenson's, then the gentlemen in Experiment and finally Hackworth at the back, making a great show taking off his hat.

'Richard Rowntree, former owner of the land we're passin' over,' said George sardonically. 'Demanded £700 – twice its value. The jury offered 'im a monkey. No wonder 'e's smilin'!'

'Yarm Junction!' called Jimmy

Stephenson stood on the water tank and steadied himself and then waved his red handkerchief in wide sweeping arcs to attract Hackworth's attention at the back and though he saw Hackworth respond with his, it took a further few minutes of sending mouth-to-ear messages from brakeman to brakeman from both ends of the train until the messages met somewhere in the middle and all brakemen applied their brakes. Thus, the procession came to a creaking, grinding, clanking, squeaking halt. Thomas Meynell, the Mayor of Yarm, greeted them first and shook hands warmly with George Stephenson, despite the latter's streaks of grime and soot of hands and arms, and everybody else watched or got involved as two more coal wagons were uncoupled from the end of the train and fixed to horses and pulled the mile down to the coal drops at Yarm Bank Top. The brakemen on the loco-drawn waggons and the horsedrawn waggonmen behind them all stayed in their places, supervised and scolded in equal measures by a patrolling Hackworth and Jimmy Stephenson. As the Yarm-bound wagons moved away, the crowd seemed hypnotised, desperate not to miss anything that might happen, by the movement and followed as if attached by invisible strings, ravelling over some half hour to get to the end and oversee the first 'drops' and then another half hour unravelling once again to where they'd started their detour, the locomotive and its slightly reduced train patiently waiting like a noble but very dirty animal with a suffocating, fiery, cinder-breath punctuated only by blasts of steam from the smoke-release valve as they kept her idling without overheating. This slight delay, lengthened by the leisurely stroling and chatting of many of the VIP's who seemed completely unpreoccupied with any record of time, consumed well over an hour of it. And yet throughout it all Lewis had stayed where he was, discreetly hidden between one of the wagons, hidden from wherever Silas may have been looking for him. He did not know it but Silas had done exactly the same thing except he was six waggons further down from Lewis and the two, in their discreet huddles, waited out the time. The crowd had returned again and within minutes hand signals had gone up and they were moving off again round the long, left-turn curve that took them across the Yarm-Stockton Turnpike.

Meanwhile, Lewis was wondering what would happen when they arrived in Stockton. He had no idea what it looked like. He'd never seen the sea; not even a ship. He had a little under a pound in money. Was it enough to buy a passage? He didn't know how to go about getting a ticket or if there were any passenger-carrying ships that went up and down the coast. Little by little, what had once seemed a good idea in another time and place began to lose its appeal as distance and time warped events.

Hackworth, meanwhile, was pre-occupied with signalling. His current system was inadequate. Something more visible and evident was needed: green and red flags instead of handkerchiefs, or a whistle or a megaphone perhaps. It was impractical to employ one guard per wagon for every journey up and down the line and it was poor planning that the locomotive didn't have a brake. Most vehicles with wheels had brakes. 'Hope' was under construction at Newcastle, to be delivered the following month. He would have free rein to look at brakes.

Wooden stalls had been set up selling fruit and vegetables, beer, coffee and bread. Over a hundred people milled around them and nearby a gang of road-laying workmen stopped their labour at a convoy of carts full of stones to watch.

'Looks like a MacAdam,' noted Sean Gallagher to Hackworth with self-assurance.

' 'tis that,' agreed Hackworth. 'Foundation raised for proper drainage, spread n' rolled to 15 inches: cheap, fast an' easy. We applied similar ballast under our rails.'

Trapped in the crowd was the York-Stockton mail coach and from its window a variety of heads strained to watch No. 1 and, as the last wagon of the mechanised train crawled over the crossing, they heard the loud cry: 'Rubbish!'

The voice's owner was the mail coach driver's mate, who cupped his hands and repeated: 'Rubbish!' – both a taunt and a challenge.

'Fear not!' said George to Jimmy,

Clear of the crossing and with a slight decline over the last mile and a half, the locomotive ticked steadily on as the coach and its team caught up to the back. The driver's left hand held long leather reins reaching down to harnesses. The horses jumped to a trot as 16 iron horseshoes clattered on the newly laid road. The driver stood, shouted and, raising the reins high, drew them down on some strange word known only to him and his horses and the trot upped to a gallop, the noise as tremendous as the sight was impressive, making the crowd part at a run as it moved swiftly level with the middle of the train. But Stephenson had seen it.

'Open 'er up, Jimmy. She can take it!'

Jimmy Stephenson tightened the safety valve a smidgeon and George opened a tap that let a tad more water into the boiler. The coupling rods stepped up their rhythmic jerking.

She might as well have been a horse: the Stephensons sensed her moods and knew how to coax her, but they both knew it wasn't simply a race against a coach, it was a race for progress. The coach represented the old way and the railway represented the new but speed wasn't important now. What was important was finishing the journey. It was the successful conclusion of a story that had started many years before, adapted and borrowed from Watt and Newcomen and Trevithick, before that the Frenchman Cugnot and before even that the genius of the Greek Archimedes. It was a magical moment. George felt as if a gigantic puzzle had just had the last piece slotted into it and he'd simply been a part of this long, unfolding journey. As much as the individual parts of the locomotive he was sitting on were as dependent on the others they were connected to, so he felt connected to the intelligence, unshakeable faith and invention of his predecessors.

As they rolled on, passengers began to cheer, as if Locomotion was a beast that could respond to encouragement.

Meanwhile, at the back, Hackworth's customary restraint made him less vocal as his employer up at the front, but upon his countenance was a quiet confidence. The long, straight stretch of line was irresistible to the locomotive and gradually those carts and horses that had tagged on since Eaglescliffe fell behind, giving the mail coach space. Number One puffed on but the coach horses had been on the road since Thirsk and had had to struggle up Yarm Bank heavily laden. Now, another lunge was being demanded and it was too much: almost as soon as he saw the train move effortlessly forward, the driver pulled back and Number One pushed ahead. But the race would have been over anyway, as

Stockton was coming closer view and blind speed could prove fatal to the crowd scattered in and around the knots of buildings, fields and fences encompassing Bowesfield that made up the southern region of the river port.

George and Jimmy, perched on either side of the boiler, shook their sooty and coal-encrusted hands across the top.

'We've done it! We've bloody well done it!'

The crossing of the Stockton-Stokesley Road came next and then the final 100 yards under the open sash windows of the houses fringing the line where figures crammed into the window frames reminiscent of crowded oil paintings. Yarm Band belted out tunes, the big bass drum drowning out the clickety-clack of the wagons. John Dixon pushed his horse slower and more carefully into the crowd until Number One was barely crawling. At the back, Hackworth stood aloft, hands comfortably on his hips.

The relief was unfathomable. A seemingly endless supply of patient crafting and chiselling all coming to the fore in that one crisp moment, for who would remember how many times hundreds of men had crawled from their beds every morning for four years to dedicate the few hours of daylight to realise something never done before?

Wide-windowed houses in Boathouse Lane and Moat Street were filled with happy faces cheering them as they neared the river where ships' masts, pennants and the flags of many nations fluttered in the breeze in the harbour, its shiny surface visible to the far bank where slipways cradled boats under construction or repair, the trading ships, colliers, brigs and schooners.

Lewis was wide-eyed at the gleaming polished timbers, masts wrapped in rigging, ropes and canvas. Dockers unloaded cargoes of tightly bound bales of wool, leather cow hides tied by the hundred, sacks of freshly ground corn and spars of timber planks. Cranes with pulleys and ropes balanced their loads over the gaping maws of boats and laid out nets cradling barrels of rum, coffee, sacks of sugar and open racks of tobacco.

Men of all shapes, sizes and colours worked on or lined the boats, but none of this industry was in operation as all the workers were massed around the train. For the first time, though the real ocean still lay a few miles downriver, Lewis had its salty scent in his nose and he saw many boats weren't floating on water but appeared to rest on a shiny surface of mud.

'I thought boats floated on water,' he said to Jack.

Jack chortled. 'Tide's out!'

'What do you mean?' asked Lewis.

'I mean sometimes the water's 'igh n' sometimes it's low. It's the moon,' said Jack.

'The moon?' asked Lewis.

'When it's close, she pulls all the water o' the sea toward her, n' when she's far away, it comes rushin' back again n' that makes an 'igh tide; summat like that!'

'*Brakes!*' shouted Hackworth at the top of his voice, waving his handkerchief as he did so.

All brakemen responded and up front, on a signal from George, Jimmy closed the valve completely. The train came to a halt.

3.45 pm

Hackworth pulled out his pocket watch.

'Three 'ours,' he said to himself, 'To do a journey that'd normally take two days with one tenth the load!'

Behind them, the first of the horse-drawns pulled up and the crowd swelled as workmen spilled out, crowding to watch the ceremonial despatch of the first coal from Shildon.

'Mr Jenkins, clear the wagons if you please!' he called.

Jenkins passed slowly from wagon to wagon persuasively clearing out those that were fitted with seats, but the crowds were so dense and each person so full of questions and curiosity that it was hard going as he passed the message to his men to encourage people to alight carefully. The plan then was to empty six wagons of coal by opening their forward trapdoors and manhandling or shovelling their loads off the edge of a sheer drop into a temporary storage depot before being broken up, weighed and transferred to the waiting ships' holds. But it would take a lot of organisation to detach the steam engine from the wagons and then manoeuvre each wagon to the coal-drop edge and unload it and Hackworth had just shouted: 'Stand clear below!' when he heard a more frantic voice cry out: 'Wait! *Wait*!'

It was the voice of Stephenson, breaking through the cordon with the Harbour Master having to shout due to the general hubbub.

'On account of the tide turning owing to your delayed arrival, we're asking you unload only one wagon,' said the Harbour Master. If the ships are fully laden, they'll get stuck on the mud bank!'

So the sole wagon was taken away to be loaded onto one lucky collier boat.

Meanwhile, Yarm Band cleared their wagons and worked through the crowd to a raised wooden grandstand cordoned off by a line of soldiers, where they took up their places organised by their conductor. Behind, an array of VIPs gathered round Mayor Wilkinson, proud in his tricorn and robe and carrying the ceremonial mace and Mr Foxton, the local businessman who had paid for the banquet. Experiment opened its doors and those inside climbed down, some the worse for wear. Lewis and Jack walked forward, Hackworth bringing up the rear. A sudden BANG sent a shock through the crowd as across on the other side of the river the first of seven large cannons fired the blank charge of a ceremonial salute. Six sharp reports followed, the whole sequence repeated twice in rapid succession.

'Waterloo cannons!' somebody shouted.

The reports thud-thudded off the walls of nearby buildings and, as the last of the 21 shots echoed away, a cheer rose and the band struck up *God Save the King*. When the anthem stopped, the booming voice of the town crier replaced it: 'Oh yea, pray silence for the Right Honourable John Wilkinson, Mayor of Stockton!'

Hundreds crammed around the grandstand and lowered their voices as the Mayor waited for a silence sufficiently quiet for him to be heard.

'My Lords, Ladies and Gentlemen, it is my great pleasure to welcome George Stephenson and members of the Stockton and Darlington Company, as well as all passengers. As of today, the price of coal has almost halved from eighteen shillings a ton to ten shillings a ton!'

This unexpected news produced unexpected cheers – a reduction in the price of coal by a massive eight shillings would change the lives of every person there. And there was more: 'And for those captains of the ships in our harbour, we say this: go and tell the world Stockton awaits you! Gentlemen, we may now retire to the town hall where a feast awaits and many toasts and speeches will be made. God save the King!'

Another chorused 'God Save the King!' went up and the tune played again and the audience joined in yet again, cries of 'Hear, hear!' and 'Bravo!' ringing out and hats tossed into the air at the end.

* * *

Silas had seized his chance, forcibly holding the boy and trying to push him through the four-foot gap between the two wagons linked by chains and hooks, so his neck or head or chest might get crushed, but the keelman called John Stevens had somehow pushed Lewis back or got in the way – it was unclear. Stevens had fallen onto the trackside just after Lewis, followed by Silas's case and one of his feet had been trapped under a wheel and mangled. On his horrible cries, chaos reigned as some brakemen hit their brakes, others waved frantically at Hackworth and others at Stephenson and only by shouts and screams over a hundred yards did the train begin to brake. Silas slipped down from the other side. Strewn along the track were his shirts, folded trousers and prized tan boots made in Barnard Castle and never worn. Cursing his luck, he found a discreet spot while a crowd gathered around John Stevens. Stevens had been brave or stupid but he had paid the price. It was unfortunate Silas had lost his carpetbag and spare clothes and unworn handmade tan boots but it wasn't the end of the world: his savings were in his inside pocket. As the train moved, he slipped back on between two wagons halfway down the train's length, and, as they stopped at Yarm he did not dare move for fear of discovery so stayed where he was between wagons, then finally they went through Eaglescliffe and the temporary 'race' with the coach had taken his mind off his problems. There was no 'race', he later concluded after hearing read to him exaggerated reports of one in a local newspaper. By coincidence the two modes of transport had met and shared some hundred yards of relatively un-peopled open space. That was all. How people loved to stretch the truth! But what he hadn't been able to fathom was why the Lewis boy, who obviously knew who he was, hadn't shopped him to anybody or shouted 'Arrest this man!' or whatever. Why had he stayed so quiet?

As they approached Stockton, malignant thoughts returned and, before the train stopped, Silas slipped down and mingled with the crowds, watching from a discreet distance the unloading of the coal from the nominated wagon along the quayside near Boathouse Lane.

George bloody Stephenson, he reflected, if it hadn't been for George bloody Stephenson he'd never have been wandering around Newcastle ten years ago starving to death and ready to do anything for money – even volunteering to be a soldier. True, Lord Darlington and Sir Giles had exploited him and sent him to Jericho as the saying went but exacting revenge on them seemed wrong, whereas exacting revenge on somebody who'd come from backgrounds as humble as his own seemed right. At Crockatt Hall, his life had had pattern and meaning, shape and reason. He'd done all that was demanded of him and his reward had been dismissal. Now he had nothing but his wits. For months, if not years, some perverted logic had seemed to suggest if only he could sink a killing knife into one of the causes of his unhappiness, like it were flesh and blood, the pain would stop, nights of sound sleep would return and time itself could be rewound and make him well. No, somebody had to pay. Silas had killed men legally in war, perhaps accidentally on the highway near London. Quickly a terrible idea threaded itself through his head.

Over to his right, the cannons boomed and made the crowds jump but because Silas had been under fire in battle, they had had no effect on him. As the salute added up, the noisy distraction should have been a perfect time to strike, stepping up behind Lovatt, sinking his blade into the boy's back up to the hilt, twisting it, pulling it out and slipping away again. But then the national anthem followed and even Silas had the good sense to stand still for that. When the crowd sang the words 'happy and glorious', Silas closed his eyes and was transported to that fateful day in June 1815, witnessing the suffering, bodies and screams of men beyond God's grace. There was nothing happy or glorious about war. God had abandoned him for what he'd done. Yes, there had been something decisive about that day at Waterloo, as if his senses had never been so alive. Killing, he chuckled at the morbid rhyme, was thrilling.

The crowd that had abandoned the grandstand and was now moving became denser as Castle Gate first narrowed and then expanded again as did the crowd, the throng entering the High Street. To one side, the defeated mail coach entered the town discreetly and made its way to the back of the Black Lion Inn. A soft black felt hat thrown into the air fell into Silas's path. He picked it up and pulled it low over his face. His hand slipped inside his jacket, fingering the worn handle of the gutting knife. The crowd cheered and the town crier announced a speech from the mayor.

Silas listened. Everyone listened. The Mayor's speech ended and then came the announcement of free food for all workmen, while the VIPs, Stephenson and his colleagues progressed up Stockton High Street to the Town Hall on foot, accompanied by the band. Silas watched, followed, stopped and waited. A nearby inn seemed to be calling his name. He hesitated.

5 pm

Despite the presence of one or two lords and Members of Parliament, there was no standing on ceremony: it was one large group walking to the Town Hall with the Mayor and George Stephenson at the head. The banners that had travelled with the train since Shildon were also carried along and the chatter and talk was cheery as the procession filed past the Shambles, temporary stalls open for business hawking food and drink. The head of the procession stopped outside the town hall, a large square structure with roads leading off lined with stores, stables, forges, workshops, houses, shops, printers and more inns. The workmen peeled away and gathered in or around the Black Lion, the King's Head, the Bay Horse the Vane Hotel and the Shoulder of Mutton. At the Town Hall, its distinctive clock chiming five, Lewis and Jack saw men checking names at the entrance.

'They'll not be lettin' the likes o' me in 'ere,' said Jack darkly and Lewis was about to say: 'Maybe this is where we say goodbye?', when his eyes fell on a hatted man staring at him intently across the square. Other figures crossed his line of vision and when the crowds parted momentarily, the hat and the man had disappeared. Or had he never been there? There were so many faces. Hackworth appeared and made a point of seeking out Jack.

'We're lookin' for secretaries up at Shildon. Interested?' Hackworth asked.

'Yes, sir!' spluttered Jack.

'Good. We can sort it out on the return journey tomorrow but they'll not let you into the Town Hall dressed like that. Meet us up at the staithes tomorrow at eight – we'll be settin' off back to Shildon then. Fair enough?'

'Fair enough, sir, thank you, thank you!' Jack gabbled, scarcely able to control his excitement.

As Hackworth left, Jack turned to Lewis elated.

'I can't believe it! I really did jump on the right wagon! But hey, what about you, you still determined to go to sea?'

Lewis nodded. 'I have to, to find my dad.'

'Well then,' said Jack, deflated, 'I suppose this is farewell. But it takes the wind out 'o me sails a bit.'

The two shook hands formally and awkwardly.

'That's really great news for you though. I hope it works out for your Mam and Dad,' said Lewis.

'Thanks, me too. Good luck, Master Lewis,' said Jack.

Lewis hid a smile and replied 'Good luck, Jack Cook!'

But he felt empty as his new friend left. He had enjoyed his company. It was with an equally restrained smile and final nod that Jack headed in the direction of the nearest inn. Hackworth and Lewis, meanwhile, had arrived at the front of the queue. Lewis was glad Leakey had insisted he wore his Sunday best: despite odd smudges, he looked the part.

Inside the town hall, the high ceilings were festooned with flags and bunting and around the walls were draped banners. Cigar and pipe smoke wreathed their heads. Large trestle tables took up the floor, each set with dinner services, silver knives and crystal goblets, and at each place was a high-backed chair. Cooks and servants poured liberally to all who asked. Lewis followed on the heels of Hackworth as they entered the melee, on one side drinkers five-deep at a bar, more cigar and pipe smoke stifling the air, and on the other side the steam and clatter of the busy kitchen with cooks and serving boys carrying trays aloft, a procession which they followed until finally they found themselves in front of an open door where the words 'The Long Room' were marked and this led to the most densely occupied space of all.

Hackworth tapped a broad-shouldered man on the back and was forced to shout above the din: 'Mr Stephenson?'

Stephenson had managed to make contact with water and a towel since he had arrived but there were still smudges on his face and arms and the pungent smell of burnt sulphur pervaded his clothes and hair.

'This is Master Lewis,' said Hackworth, still shouting, despite his mouth being close to Stephenson's ear. 'His friend at Aycliffe helped unblock the feed-pipe.'

'And you were there when the unfortunate Stevens fell under the wheels, were you not?' Stephenson shouted down to Lewis. 'I never forget a face!'

'I was, sir,' said Lewis, feeling vulnerable, as it put him back to that moment when he'd crossed paths with Silas.

'What 'appened?' Stephenson asked.

Lewis gulped for an answer.

'Too many people in too small a space, sir,' Hackworth replied for him.

'Yes, undoubtedly,' said Stephenson. 'I'm sorry for the man. I'll find out where 'e lives an' send compensation to pay for the doctor.'

Another tall figure joined them whom Lewis recognised.

'And you, Mr Strickland, what message will you take to your American friends?' Stephenson asked the man.

'I will take the message a new day is coming that will lay our great land open to conquest,' Strickland pronounced confidently. 'What I've seen today will tame the wilder parts of the West.'

'Excellent!' said Stephenson. 'Just don't forget to order your engines from Forth Street. And now gentlemen, you must excuse us, Mr Hackworth an' I have the dubious task o' sittin' at the Mayor's table.'

Stephenson took Hackworth's elbow and steered him away so Lewis was suddenly alone – despite being surrounded by people – and was unsure what to do when he heard a loud banging followed by an even louder voice as the Town Crier banged his ceremonial mace on the floor and espoused: 'My Lords, Ladies and Gentlemen, pray silence for the Right Honourable Thomas Meynell of Yarm!'

There was sudden silence followed by occasional comments, whispers, murmurs and laughter as Thomas Meynell stood to speak.

'Gentlemen, this has not been simply a journey of 26 miles but of *fifteen years* since – in this very room – Mr Raisbeck and Mr Flounders of the Tees Navigation Company mooted the idea of a canal or a railway. Before we eat, an act of which I am sure we are all in sore need, I ask you to exhaust yourselves once more in appreciation of their vision. I give you: Messrs Raisbeck and Flounders!'

Raisbeck and Flounders, with many more wrinkles, larger bellies and far less hair than they had had in 1810, stood and bowed to the applause like actors at the close of a great performance. Raisbeck proposed another toast to the King and the crowd stood to attention and in one voice raised their glasses.

'The King!'

After, a dinner bell rang and the room was largely cleared of lesser dignitaries and Lewis knew that meant him – he was lucky to have got this far. He watched hungrily as food and ale were served from trays taken up by an army of porters who dished out soups, hams, roasted chickens and tureens of potatoes. Guests helped themselves to the mutton, vegetables, bread, cheese and fruit, and the sugarcane rum delivered the day before by a Dutch trader who had made the long and perilous journey from Jamaica. Luckily, on some anonymous benefactor's instructions, serving boys passed among the crowd gathered downstairs with free bread rolls cut open and stuffed with wedges of cheese and Lewis gladly took one and wolfed down its contents with no ceremony. Upstairs he heard more toasts proposed and honoured: to the Stockton and Darlington Company, the Liverpool and Manchester, the Leeds and Hull, Liverpool and Birmingham, Bolton and Leigh, Newcastle and Carlisle and to that time in the future when the entire country would be linked to London and to Edinburgh by rail, though he had no idea what fool would propose such an incredible thing! Finally, one particular toast caught his ears: 'And I ask you all to raise your glasses to the man whose diligence and hard work has made this enterprise possible – Mister *George Stephenson!*'

This last name attracted the biggest roar, applause that seemed to catch like a fire in a haystack, spreading from the Long Room, down the stairs, igniting all those downstairs too and out into the street, for though many had struggled for years to bring about this event, it was universally accepted that it was down to a small handful, of whom the last was the leading contender.

Hackworth wondered if anybody would propose a toast for him but they didn't and, with just a tinge of bitterness, he recognised that moment in Stockton Town Hall might probably be the highest ranking his role in this story would achieve.

Lewis, meanwhile, was counting his luck. If he stayed in Stockton and Hackworth was to keep his promise of thanks, perhaps he could find a position in Durham or Newcastle? Because of his mother's stubborn insistence on attending school, he held keys to a better world: all he had to do was reach out and turn them. He'd set himself a singular quest: at that moment his father was suffering because of the treachery of at least three men: Sir Giles Crockatt was almost certainly one of them, Hackett his foreman was another and the third was Silas Scroggins. But Lewis was confused. It was traditional for men to covet the honour of their families or to give their lives to preserve that honour, yet here he was obsessed with getting to his father's side: he did not seek revenge on those that had sent his Dad away. It was this last thought that jolted him. He'd been dreaming, carried away, distracted by the atmosphere and the food and beer. He had to find passage on a ship to Hull, London or Australia.

9 pm

Night had recently fallen and caught many unaware as they fumbled through the darkness towards the light of the inns.

A dozen workmen and navvies sat around a fire not far from Number One, drinking from stone jugs, smoking and chattering. Nearby was a makeshift camp with horses corralled alongside long troughs of hay.

Lewis wandered through the campground, picking his way carefully around the front of Locomotion No. 1. The guard appointed to watch it was doing a half-hearted job, preferring the lively company of the Irishmen and the middle-aged Tabbies flaunting their bosoms like fruity wares while drinking and dancing in their dirty skirts. Lewis turned to the ships tied to the harbour side, stepped to the edge and peered at the black, shiny bed of mud. The ships' sterns, tied by thick ropes to sturdy bollards, consisted of banks of small glass squares allowing limited vision of the cramped inner quarters piled with maps and whale strange instruments. Sailors could be heard deeper within scraping, coughing and muttering. Planks of wood were the only access to the ship's deck, stretching high above the mudflats and dimly lit by oil lamps swaying from spars.

'There's six wagons of coal missin', man! Where are they?'

Lewis looked around. A familiar Geordie voice was scolding one of the navvies.

'Some sailors took 'em further up, sir. They made n' arrangement wi' Mr Raisbeck, sir, to ship it to London on tomorra's tide.'

'Ah, I see, fair enough. Well, go back to your revellin', lads!'

Stephenson turned into the light, looking with fondness at the locomotive. From the ground to the top of the boiler wasn't much more than a man's height, but he reached out and patted it like it was a horse and said: 'Well, hinny, you did it.'

Just then he spied Lewis.

'I've sneaked away, son,' said George. 'All this pomp doesn't suit me. Will you be travellin' back to Shildon tomorrow with us?'

'I want to find a ship to get to London or Australia, sir,' Lewis said.

'Australia indeed,' said Stephenson, his eyebrows arching. 'That's the other side o' the world. What makes thee so ambitious?'

'I've 'eard a man can buy a piece o' land for the price of an 'orse. I think I'd enjoy that, sir – to be king o' me own land.'

'A noble ambition,' Stephenson agreed. 'Do yer know any ship owners hereabouts?'

'No sir, I was just contemplatin' how to find a passage,' Lewis said.

'Well,' said Stephenson, casting an eye in both directions as if seeking something specific, 'I 'appen to know our company solicitor has a quay at the end of Finkle Street n' does business wi' a number of ships' captains. I'm sure if we were to 'ave a word we could sort summat out.'

'Thank you, sir,' said Lewis.

They turned and walked along the quay.

'How old are yer, lad?' Stephenson asked.

'Thirteen, sir,' said Lewis.

'Thirteen, eh? I worked up at Wylam when I was your age but I never liked going down the pit, never wanted to.'

'Me neither, sir,' said Lewis. 'Me Mam made me Dad promise never to send us down.'

'Is yer Dad a miner?' asked George.

'Yes sir,' said Lewis, choosing to say nothing of his father's current circumstances. 'But he wanted us to study. I prefer fresh air, sir, the animals, the birds.'

'So did I!' enthused George. 'I used to catch fledglings n' rear 'em n' tame 'em.'

'So did I!' said Lewis. 'Blackbirds mostly, they'd fly 'round our 'ouse n' drive me Mam mad!'

'Aye, mine too!' chuckled George.

The young man and the older one laughed over their point of common interest as they passed six empty wagons at the quayside. Stephenson stood on the closest gangplank, which led to the rail of a ship with thick spars, tied canvas sails and great lengths of netting fanning out in triangles to the sides of the ship.

'Ahoy there. Anyone aboard?'

A hirsute figure in a Breton jersey loomed from the shadows. He held a lantern.

'My name is Stephenson. Is your captain aboard?'

'Capitaine Stuyvers, him drinkin' in ze town. Back later. I am First Mate Rochefort. Vat are you vanting?'

'The festivities in town today are partly due to me. But I see you've already familiarised yourself with my cargo.'

He indicated the hold stocked with coal from the nominated wagon unloaded earlier when the tide had been out.

'I'm a friend of the quay's owner Mr Raisbeck. In the absence o' yer Captain, may I have a word aboard your vessel, sir?'

The sailor hesitated then nodded, knowing that name carried weight in this town. Stephenson and Lewis carefully crossed the plank. Lewis was relieved to step onto the deck but he was struck by the cramped conditions – there was barely room for the three of them. Crowded in as they were by gloomy cabins, rails and barrels drenched in the blackness of the night, Lewis shivered.

'This young lad is seeking passage an' desires to know if you can aid 'im?' Stephenson asked bluntly.

'Passage where?' asked First Mate Rochefort.

'Australia,' said Lewis.

Rochefort laughed lightly. Stephenson smiled too.

'Well, no wanting of respect, young sir, but zis is a cargo ship and Australia is a bit far for us. Best we can do is London. We don't be taking passengers but we 'ave important need of strong boys to shovel coal an' stack cargos in ze hold.'

''e can read, write n' add up,' said Stephenson in support.

''e 'as worked for you?'

'In a manner of speakin, aye!'

'Well, I s'ppose zat puts 'im on ze same deck with Cap'n now do it not, sir? Can 'e speak French?' asked Rochefort.

'No,' said Lewis. 'But I have a book.' He pulled back the cover of his bag and fished out Leakey's book. First Mate Rochefort looked at the cover and smiled before handing it back..

'Capitaine Stuyvers is a Dutchman but many of our crew is Frenchies like me. 'e is always lookin' for 'elp to write bills of sale n' letters of introduction at ports. But ze rest of ze time you work 'ard. We is keeping sober 'ours. It's ze hard life. You can share 'ammock space wiz uzzer sailors n' get tuppence a day wiz food n' rum.'

He stepped to the edge, hawked up phlegm and spat into the darkness, turning back before it hit the surface of the water with an audible splash.

'Tide she is comin' in fast n' if we time it 'appy, we can load another five ton for London tomorrow of zat coal you brought yesterday. Capitaine he reckon Dartford by Sat'day – double our money then back again. If ze train keep bringin' ze black stuff, we'll keep takin' it down to market - everybody happy.'

'I believe Mr Rochefort is offerin' you a job,' said Stephenson to Lewis.

'Will we go directly to London?' asked Lewis.

'First we'll stop at Hull to trade, but mark, iffen when we gets there all aboard is feeling you shall not be right for us, we ditch you zere, got it?' Rochefort did not mince his words but Lewis didn't want to spend his life sailing up and down the coast of England trading coal. He saw LONDON in big letters in his mind, but when Rochefort mentioned Hull, his heart almost leapt from his chest – Hull was where his father was headed. It might just be possible they'd cross paths!

'It's no pleasure cruise, yer know?' Stephenson warned Lewis.

'Come back tomorrow around eight, *mon gar*. We sail zen. *Salut*, gentlemen!' Rochefort called.

Stephenson and Lewis stepped back onto the gangplank as Rochefort retreated into the shadows. Lewis was elated, almost as elated as Jack Cook had been. Yes, today was a rather special day: thanks to Stephenson he'd found passage to Hull where his Dad was going, and he could get as far away from Evenfield as possible. What he'd do when he got to Hull was a problem for tomorrow.

'Fare ye well, lad. May thy God go with thee,' said Stephenson, shaking Lewis's hand.

'Goodbye Mr Stephenson an' thank you, sir, for everything,' he said.

Stephenson smiled with satisfaction and turned and walked into Finkle Street and the direction of the Town Hall. Lewis watched his broad back shrinking into the darkness and it was at that precise moment he saw a familiar figure slip out of the shadows and tag along behind.

* * *

In the smoky innards of the Blue Boar, Silas lost himself for an hour in three tankards of ale, two glasses of rum and a couple of pinches of Dutch tobacco. After, he was possessed of disorientating swills of anger and joviality as he tried to make sense of life.

Images and memories collided, some as far back as childhood and others as recently as the train journey that afternoon. None stayed: a face or some words would appear and morph into others. His memories, he felt, were like his life – unsettled. As many of the workmen and navvies sang and danced to a fiddle and squeezebox, Silas retreated further into imagination. A man with no teeth and sunken cheeks shared the other side of his table, looking on impassively while puffing on a clay pipe.

'Who's responsible for all this cobblers then?' said the old man.

'Some Geordie jackanapes,' muttered Silas.

The old man snorted up a mouthful of snot and spat it onto the spittoon.

'Wastrels n' whoresons the lot of 'em,' he said, staring into space with rheumy eyes, savouring the smoke that blossomed from his mouth.

In a fraction of moments, in the fuzz of alcoholic suggestion when sense and control are temporarily displaced by anger and hurt, Silas trawled up a myriad of memories so compacted, so squeezed and so suppressed by frustration he was filled with an urge to explode. When he wasn't drunk, he had found a way to live with regrets but when he was inebriated, he brooded and fantasised about standing those responsible for his unhappy state in his personal dock, in his personal courtroom, and imagined drawing pleasure watching them squirm as they suffered his own personal punishment. At that moment, George Stephenson stood in that dock, impassive, silent, full of dignity but forced to watch and listen to Silas through frightened eyes. But it wasn't George Stephenson he addressed – it was the old man with the sunken face and no teeth sitting opposite.

'I started me workin' life at ten in a lead mine on Plenmeller, y'kna?' said Silas to the stranger. 'But me Da died when the roof collapsed. Ten I was – two days wi' your Dad's corpse ain't right, not for a boy o' ten. So I followed the auld wall to Newcastle to a job at Killin'worth. Stephenson was Gaffer. 'e sent me down the pit the day they got the old pump workin'. It wa *me* shouted up: "I'm standin' on the bottom!" It was *me* took the risk goin' down. Me! An' *I* was sacked! Couldn't work it out – done me best, even had bruises. So I went to Newcastle starvin' to death and so joined up for the British Army not out of patriotism but sheer desperation.'

'We've all got our troubles,' said the old man, shaking his head impassively.

And then, through a window open to the mild evening air, he saw again a familiar profile flit past his line of vision.

* * *

Lewis leapt forward and they fell together, he and Silas, rolling over in the filthy gutter among the feet of men and horse manure, cursing, shouting and kicking as they tumbled. Stephenson walked on, oblivious. Disentangling himself, Lewis got to his feet and ran back rapidly along Finkle Street towards the harbour and Silas followed, both dodging people as they went. Lewis ran past the locomotive, attracting only momentary glances from the drunken, dancing Irish navvies and sailors until he stopped and looked back and saw in the flickering light of the fire the figure of Silas stumbling towards him.

Running out to the edge of the darkness, Lewis hesitated. Beyond was a black unknown. He had to hide. In the gap between the harbour wall and the side of a ship was a hanging knotted rope. He took it in his hands, pulled it firmly to test it was well secured and slipped over into the void, hands and feet locked round the knots as he descended. There he swung for a few moments as the rope and its centre of gravity settled and then he heard running steps approaching from above and the sound of forced breathing. Lewis listened intently, holding his breath for fear of giving his position away. For a moment he hoped his tormentor had gone, but a few breaths later the footsteps returned. Lewis looked up and staring down at him with a broad grin and fire in his eyes was Silas.

'*Ha*!'

Lewis closed his eyes. Whatever courage had brought him this far suddenly failed. Fear froze him to the rope. There was no way up; only down. It had been a bad idea to hide. He should have run. Now it was too late. He felt as he had felt the night his father had told him to pull the blankets over his head and imagine conditions down the coalmine. It was how he felt the same night Sir Giles's thugs had burst in and started this nightmare – terrified, frozen. Kneeling down on the harbour side, Silas unsheathed his knife and slashed at the shadows where Lewis hung. Lewis dropped down one more knot but his feet could feel there were no more knots and no more rope. Drowning in mud seemed like a hideous way to die. Was there a good way to die? He thought about Ben Hackett. The rope trembled. He looked up: Silas was sawing at it, giggling like a Bedlam inmate.

'Coverin' me tracks, boy, nowt personal!' Silas rambled, the stench of alcohol emanating from his maw even with a few feet between them, pushed out into the air with his breath. 'I got to think o' number one!'

One of the rope's strands detached and Lewis closed his eyes, resigned. His Dad's face came to his mind and he prepared to let go of the rope.

Suddenly, Silas got to his feet and seemed to be looking to find a better position to get at Lewis and just at that exact moment his central body jerked forward violently, his head banging with terrific force off the side of the ship and his body falling on top of Lewis, hands desperately clawing for something to hold on to – Lewis's arms and the sack that hung around his neck – but the flimsy strap snapped instantly and Silas and the sack tumbled into the mud. Jack Cook's strong arms appeared from above, grabbed Lewis's wrists and heaved him onto the safety of the harbour. The two boys collapsed onto one another gasping and then glanced at each other momentarily before scrabbling back round in the dirt and peering down into the darkness where, in the ray of moonbeams they saw vague shadows of the man and heard him flail in the stinking slime with pitiful cries of: 'Help me, I beg you, boys, please...*please!*'

After what seemed an eternity, but was in fact only a minute, the movements stopped and the voice reduced to a gurgle and then a final, deathly silence apart from the water lapping around the wooden jetty and the muted music.

The two young men continued to stare for a minute more.

'Mister?' Jack ventured. 'Mister, you there?'

But there was only the gentle sound of water and behind them the whistle of the flute, dance of the fiddle and sounds of laughter.

'I've killed 'im,' whispered Jack, terror in his voice. 'I'll swing!'

Lewis wanted to say: 'No, Jack, you won't 'cos he was already involved in stitchin' up me Dad in Darl'ton an' tryin' to push me under the train' but Lewis's life was becoming more complicated by the hour. Only that very morning Hackett, a man one third responsible for his father's plight, had possibly paid the price. Now the second had paid. The sole living party was Sir Giles – and perhaps John Allen – but they were virtually untouchable according to Mr Wilson. Besides, the only thing Lewis wanted to do was to put as much distance between himself and County Durham as possible but death seemed to be sticking to him wherever he went! The boat that sailed tomorrow morning was his ticket out of the nightmare.

'Followed me from town an' demanded I give 'im money. He had a knife.' Lewis lied.

'What'll we tell the constable?' Jack asked hoarsely.

'We don't tell the constable anything,' said Lewis quietly. 'Nobody needs to know.'

Jack Cook studied Lewis's face.

'Who's goin' to believe us, Jack?'

Jack looked for an instant more at Lewis and said: 'I 'ad you down as a real bacon-brained dudgeon, but you're sharper than a pirate's dagger.'

'Everythin' I had o' value was in that sack,' said Lewis flatly, thinking about his lost money and book and the last precious connection to his mother in the form of the glove. 'And now it's at the bottom of the River Tees. The only good news is I've found a place on a collier boat. I leave at high tide tomorrow.'

'Really? Crikey Moses! Seems like we both fell on our feet. Well, what do we do now?'

After another minute of watching and listening and making sure nobody around had seen or heard them, the two young men stood, brushed off the dirt and dried mud and walked back through the darkness, often glancing nervously around, past the fires and passing the locomotive as they returned to the busy town to find a place to sleep.

Wednesday 28th September

At around seven the next morning the sky was slate grey. Dawn didn't arrive as magnificently and splendidly as it had the day before. Nonetheless, a few dozen people had already gathered around the locomotive, many the worse for wear having been celebrating into the early hours.

Jimmy Stephenson emptied the engine's ashcan of its previous day's remains and then relit the fire using a glowing ember he plucked from the ashes of the Irishmen's brazier with tongs. More workmen arrived and began refilling the water barrel from the River Tees.

George Stephenson appeared, having spent the night in the house of Leonard Raisbeck on the far corner of the marketplace. His walk across town towards the quayside revealed almost every building stuffed to the rafters with people, all spare floor space let out to those who had no way of getting home and quite a few more snoozing in doorways.

Water was lapping just a few feet below the edge of the harbour, filling out the riverbanks opposite until almost touching the brickworks and shipyards. Fishing and rowing boats formerly stranded on the mud banks now floated, straining at their anchors against the turning tide like eager dogs on leashes. A number of ships had departed and a two-masted brig flying Swedish colours was moving lazily downriver under the power of a large sail, assisted by two boats laden with sailors pulling her with long ropes.

George Stephenson greeted his brother and glanced in the direction of Darlington where a number of wooden beams had been laid deliberately yet haphazardly across the tracks.

'Our enemies refuse to chuck in the towel,' George said irritably.

'But they can't stop progress.'

The Gallaghers arrived holding their heads and blinking in the daylight. They'd spent the night in a stable in Portrack Lane: stalks of straw lodged in their hair and clothes. Stephenson despatched orders to them to walk along the line and remove the obstacles and the two set to work as more people gathered around the locomotive. Hackworth arrived tired, having spent the night at The Ship Inn unable to sleep because of the raucous singing and dancing. This morning however, the conversations and voices were subdued.

By eight o'clock the engine had built up sufficient steam and both engine and tender, uncoupled from the wagons, were pushed forward onto a parallel siding. The 30 wagons were then pulled forward by horses – one horse for ever four wagons, until they were all just a few feet past the locomotive on the parallel track. Then the locomotive was shunted backwards onto the original track and hooked up with what had been the last wagon on the arriving train, the one on which Hackworth and Lewis and the Gallaghers had travelled the day before. It also meant that No. 1 was now facing the opposite direction for the homeward journey, with the tender being the first vehicle and Locomotion No. 1 with its chimney reversed, the second, followed by the empty wagons.

There wasn't enough money in the kitty to install sliding rails on which wagons could be turned, and nothing yet built that could take the weight of a locomotive for purposes of turning it. Turntables were in their infancy but once funds permitted, they'd build the means.

More workmen arrived and were organised into teams, each one dumping their loads of coal into a storage bunker where it would be later transferred to the many waiting collier boats keen to get to other east-coast ports as soon as they could to profit from their windfall. The contents of two of the wagons already taken by the Dutch collier brig, it took short work for the assembled hands to unload the other four wagons. With all the wagons finally emptied, Locomotion Number One was coupled to the leading wagon to begin the return journey.

Jeremiah Dixon arrived with his red handkerchiefs but minus the horses.

'Yer can ride up front wi' us, Jeremiah,' said Stephenson. 'Fasten yer flags to the front.'

Seamus and Sean lifted the first of half a dozen wooden beams off the tracks and manhandled it to the side.

'Have yer decided whatcha gonna do?' Sean asked.

'About what?' Seamus asked.

'Going to America,' said Sean.

'Oi've told ye: oi've saved ten pounds. Dat's enough for de passage,' said Seamus.

'And where does de boat go from?' Sean asked.

'Liverpool,' Seamus replied.

'Oi'm tinkin' o' going back to Oireland. If oi did, Liverpool'd be de place to catch a boat.'

Seamus dropped the end of his wooden beam and Sean cursed as he was forced to drop his end also.

'Now whoi would ye be wantin' to do dat, boy?' laughed Seamus. 'Dere's nottin' dere! Whoi don't you come to America wid me? We'd do famous well you n' me out dere, as we done here!'

'Is dat an invitation?' asked Sean.

''Course it is!' Seamus said, amazed his brother could be so stupid. Sean grinned with relief. They were friends again. They were going to America!

More workmen and brakemen, many of them missing their sashes, as well as a motley assortment of passengers who had travelled from Darlington the previous day with no real certainty of how they would get back other than via Shanks' Pony, also began arriving and Hackworth and Stephenson invited the crowd to board, posting one brakeman to each wagon.

'We can tek 'em back this time but there'll be no more free rides,' said Stephenson.

'We'll need tickets for the horse-drawns, Mr Stephenson,' said Hackworth. 'I could've raised five pounds just now in return fares!'

Across the patch of wasteland that stood between them and the outer edge of Stockton, a coach and horses approached, rolling out of Finkle Street towards them. It came to a halt and the coachman dropped down from his seat and opened the passenger door and out stepped Edward Pease dressed in mourning black. He walked over the grass towards them with the aid of his cane. He embraced his son Joseph who had arrived for the return trip to Darlington, most of the other dignitaries who had come down in the wooden coach having organised alternative return transport, and together they met the assembled members preparing for the return journey to Darlington.

'My condolences, Mr Pease,' said Stephenson soberly when he reached them.

'I trust thy journey yesterday was without serious setback,' said Pease, trying a smile.

'A couple of mishaps but we made it in one piece,' said Stephenson.

'Is there room aboard for the return journey?' Pease queried.

He was helped into Experiment.

Just then Jack and Lewis appeared at the edge of town walking to the harbour side and looking down guiltily at the scene of the drama the night before. Neither spoke. Jack looked across at the locomotive waiting to return to Shildon and Lewis noted his collier brig, under its prow *The Betsy*, unfurling her patchwork, grubby-with-a-thousand-dirty-hand-prints sails. Having shuffled off the damp cloak of night, she was in fact painted a bright black and white around the hull, decks, rails and masts and doing her best to maintain some dignity, despite the indignity of her current trading routes.

'Do you think 'e'll ever come back up?' asked Lewis.

''e might, but even if 'e does, we'll be long gone,' replied Jack. 'People will just say 'e got drunk an' fell in.'

'Look!'

Floating just below the surface they both saw a glove and a book. Lewis spotted wooden steps slippery with algae and carefully climbed down. Holding onto the rail with one hand, he leaned over and fished out the fur-lined glove and the book. The words *French Grammar* were just discernible on the cover and Lewis gently tried to open it but the pages fanned open, slipped out and disintegrated in his hands with no sign of the one-pound note, so he tossed it back. But the dripping silk fingers of the glove lay across his palm like a delicate fish and he felt relieved that he could retain a memory of his mother.

First Mate Rochefort leaned over the side of *The Betsy* and spotted the young boy from the previous evening.

'Vant you zat job or non? Get your arse on ze board – we're leavin'!' he shouted.

Lewis turned to Jack.

'When you get to Shildon you'll find a village about five miles to the southwest called Evenfield. There's an inn called The Cleveland Bay and three doors down the house of the schoolmaster, Mr Leakey. Will you tell 'im I found me ship? That's the message: 'I found me ship''

'I found me ship' - alright, I'll do it me first day off,' Jack promised.

They shook hands but it wasn't enough and they suddenly embraced, slapping the other's back.

'Good luck!' said Jack. 'And thanks!'

'It's you who deserves the thanks, Jack. You saved me last night.'

'Well then, let's just make sure what happened stays our little secret, right?'

Lewis, already in possession of an impressive pile of secrets, nodded solemnly and made sure his eyes and Jack's at least made a fleeting contract to underline the seriousness of their determination and intent in their mutually bound futures. He put a foot on one end of the gangplank. Despite the glove still being sodden, he tucked it into his trousers.

'Don't come over empty-'anded, boy, bring one o' zose sacks!' Rochefort shouted.

Lewis tried to lift one of the sacks of potatoes but it was almost beyond him and only with diligence and stubbornness and sheer brute force did he manage to drag it by the neck across the straining gangplank.

'The paragon of animals,' he said suddenly aloud, half-laughing and almost completely breathless.

There was a loud hiss of escaping steam and all the sailors turned to watch the locomotive moving in the direction of Darlington. Jack Cook sprinted towards it and climbed onto the back of the last waggon.